SHAMELESS DESIRE

His eyes roamed down to her shamelessly exposed legs stretched out in front of her. She twisted them beneath her bottom and under the protection of the shirt as best she could.

"There's no way I can get back the gold," he said. "But as for the romp—" he unfastened the top button of her shirt, and his fingers burned against her skin— "that's more easily seen to."

With a cry of rage, Sarah shoved against his chest and, catching him by surprise, sent him falling backward. Scrambling past him, she made for the door.

He grabbed the tail of her shirt, and she stumbled backward, falling hard against him, her hands pressing against his bare chest, the two of them sprawled across the rumpled blanket.

His powerful embrace locked them together so tightly that she could feel the full length of his body against hers.

His mouth savaged hers with a fierceness that was both frightening and compelling. She struggled to keep from surrendering to his demands, but a strong hand clamped hard across her lower back held her firmly in the place he wanted her.

And where she wanted to be. . . .

WANTON SLAVE

Evelyn Rogers

ZEBRA BOOKS
KENSINGTON PUBLISHING CORP.

Also by Evelyn Rogers:
  Midnight Sins
  Texas Kiss

ZEBRA BOOKS

are published by

Kensington Publishing Corp.
475 Park Avenue South
New York, NY 10016

First printing: June, 1990

Printed in the United States of America

To the great people at CSMS
You have offered support, encouragement,
and friendship
My debt to you can never be repaid.

Special thanks are offered to Marge Myers for her help in the historical research of Turkey. All names used in the book are fictitious, with the exception of the British ambassador Lord Stratford de Redcliffe, and the events are the creation of the writer. But the life of the sultans and their slaves was not too different from that shown herein, and the area of the Golden Horn, situated at the crossroads of Europe and Asia, remains one of the most beautiful and fascinating places in the world.

Chapter One

Sarah Whitlock knew better than to argue with her father when he cast his disapproval on her. She might as well converse with one of his precious Venetian porcelains.

The subject of her consideration stood across the parlor of the elegant London town house that served as their home. Body erect and leaning slightly toward a blazing fire, one boot propped against the hearth, his patrician head bent and eyes focused on the flames, he favored one of the figurines in his collection—the way some people resembled their pets.

Except for the slight movement of his morning coat across his chest, indicating a slow and steady breathing, he hardly seemed alive.

Sarah sat quietly on an overstuffed sofa, hands clenched in her lap, and debated whether to speak. After a late night for them both, he had summoned her to his presence at the uncivilized morning hour of ten, only to do no more than stare at various points of the room. Silence told her more than tirades would have that he was distressed. How she longed to shatter the composure with which he faced his problems.

Right now she was the problem. She pushed caution aside.

"About last night—" she began.

"In a moment, Sarah," he said without turning toward her. "I am gathering my thoughts."

He was *not*, she knew too well, deciding what questions to put to her. Papa wasn't interested in why she had planned and executed—rather grandly, she thought—her latest antic. His only concern would be for the priceless treasures he was certain she had endangered.

If he was as upset as she suspected, why didn't he shout at her, maybe even throw a valued object against the Persian rug? The idea was ludicrous. Alone or in company, Sir Edward would never do anything so common.

The minutes dragged by, marked by the Ormolu clock on the mantel. Sarah fought a growing impatience. She was twenty-five and proudly independent. She should have been able to express her opinions openly. It was unfortunate that Sir Edward Whitlock did not agree.

At last he straightened and shifted to face her.

Sarah was struck anew by what a handsome man he was, with silvered hair as thick as a young man's above an aristocratic face. Only his faded eyes had changed with the years, slowly losing the power to detect and judge with infinite skill. Papa worried about his eyes, fearing he would lose the sight that allowed him to gaze upon the art and antiques in which he traded.

He seemed to have no difficulty at the moment judging his only offspring.

A shiver of unease traveled down Sarah's slender frame. In all her life she had never managed to please her father, but neither had she quite so *dis*pleased him, either.

"Midnight gallops in the park," he began, "and that masquerade as an actress in Drury Lane. Even the night you dressed up as a young man and tried your luck in the gaming hells. I ignored them all."

"I wondered if you knew about those."

"I am not a fool. But you've gone too far this time, Sarah," he announced.

He might as well have been a magistrate and she a stranger in the dock.

"Something must be done," he added.

Off with your head.

Of course Sir Edward would never say anything so absurd. If only he had a sense of humor. . . .

Sarah shifted on the sofa and brushed at a tendril of blond hair that had strayed against her cheek. She caught herself, and the hand returned to her lap. She would *not* allow her father's somberly critical mood to unnerve her.

"Last night was a harmless prank," she said, holding his gaze.

Sir Edward's thick brows lifted. "Harmless?"

"Most certainly," she said.

"You call a six-piece orchestra smuggled into the British Museum harmless?" His shudder was all too visible. "And dancing amongst the displays. It is no wonder you are called the hellion of London."

Sarah had not realized her father knew of that particular appellation.

"There were a dozen other participants," she said. "We planned only one waltz, and that's exactly what took place."

"With you leading the way."

Sarah did not bother to deny the accusation. One of her swains had dared her to come up with a thoroughly outrageous site for a last dance of the evening. She could never resist a dare.

"The resonance was magnificent," she said. "Perhaps more music should be heard in those musty halls."

Her father's lips tightened.

"If you wish," she added, "I can write a letter of apology to the museum director. And to *The Times*."

"Just in case someone has not heard?" Sir Edward asked. "It is entirely in character for you to call as much attention to yourself as possible. It seems sometimes that is indeed all you are after."

Sarah's impatience broke through, and she stood.

"Then forget *The Times*. I have expressed my regrets already to the guards and to the police. And last night when you were summoned to escort me home, I tried to extend that apology to you, Papa, although I have no way of knowing that you heard, since until a moment ago you refused to utter a word on the matter. Tell me what you want."

Sir Edward's gaze was steady. "You have embarrassed me for the last time, Sarah. I want you to be the responsibility of someone else."

The words hurt, more than she would have expected.

"I am of age," she said, her chin tilted upward, her blue eyes flashing fire to match the flames at Sir Edward's back. "You need not concern yourself about me."

"There you are wrong. On your mother's deathbed I promised to see you cared for. Last night I was

10

somewhat belatedly forced to accept what a poor job I have done.''

For a moment Sarah was certain she read regret and sorrow in her father's eyes, and a longing to fling herself into his arms swept over her—to assure him with a daughter's gentle caress that he had done no such thing.

It was a silly, fleeting thought. Her reassurance would have been a lie. Sir Edward's idea of caring for her had been to hire tight-lipped nannies and, later, governesses whose primary interest had been in the exorbitant salary he paid. Many other women of her class had faced the same upbringing, but she had always wanted more.

Sarah took a deep breath, stilling the ache that rose in her breast. The parlor air held a musty odor not unlike Sir Edward's art gallery, as though the furnishings and carefully chosen accessories, a part of the room for years, still carried the odor of their packing. As though the occupants of the house did not really live there but were only passing through.

In the early years of her childhood, she had feared that one day while she was confined to the nursery Papa would move away and not tell her where he had gone. She had taught herself not to expect his presence when she needed him; she had even tried, with somewhat less success, to convince herself she did not care. Surrounded by luxury and blessed with ample food and clothes, she was far better off than many Londoners she could call by name.

And what about Papa? What did he really want and need? A wealthy man, he could afford the best. He had wanted the best in a daughter. His disappointment was all too clear, and now he wanted her gone.

She held herself erect. Pride had always been her dearest friend, pride and a spirit of independence. She would not let them desert her.

"I assume your thoughts are gathered. What have you decided?" she asked.

"You have perhaps forgotten that you are betrothed."

Forgotten the decade-old promise of a schoolgirl someday to link her fortunes to those of a man almost as old as Sir Edward? Of course she had not. Clinging to her youthful innocence, she had been trying to please her father and would have promised anything he asked.

But as the years slipped by, with only rare letters from her affianced, who was devoting himself in eastern climes to the development of his shipping empire, she had never seriously considered the marriage would take place.

"It is time you lived up to your word," Sir Edward said, "and I lived up to mine." He sounded resolute, impervious to whatever pleas she might throw at him, and she felt the beginnings of panic.

Since she reached the age of twenty-one, Papa had never curtailed her freedom. They led separate lives, sharing a roof and an occasional meal together, but little else. Except for the rare instances, like today, when he told her bluntly she had failed him, their communication was close to nonexistent. He had no idea of her interest in his business, nor of the skills she had been acquiring when he was not around. And he certainly had no hint of the charity work she kept secret from the world.

There had been times, increasingly rare, when she longed for him to make demands of her, or at least show that he knew she existed as a separate and unique human being with needs and longings of her own. But no demands had been issued, only disapproval. Until now. After four years of this oft' times strained co-existence, he had decided to give the one serious order he had ever given her. It was one so dreadful she could not accede.

"The betrothal was never made public," she said, no longer worried that her voice betrayed distress, "and you never particularly discouraged the men who came to call."

"I left discouragement up to you, Sarah, assuming you would honor the commitment made in your name."

"I do not love him, Papa," she said. "I barely remember him."

"Love? What has love got to do with anything?" *Didn't you love Mama?*

It was a question that had often occurred to Sarah, but it was one she could never ask. The long-deceased mother, known to her only through the portrait on her father's bedroom wall, was as much an enigma as he.

"Ralph Pettigrew," he continued, "is a highly respected gentleman."

"Who impressed you when he imported a pair of priceless Greek urns."

"His entire demeanor impressed me. He was quite taken by your spirit and by your beauty. When he asked for your hand, he vowed not to press the issue until you were ready for marriage."

"And is he now pressing the issue?"

"He has continued to express a wish that the union take place."

Sarah sighed in exasperation. "He's barely set foot on English shores in the past eight years. His

13

passions are no more employed in our relationship than are mine."

"Do not be vulgar, Sarah. Pettigrew's current home is in Turkey, but we have been in correspondence. You can be grateful he has not heard the news of your exploits and cried off."

Sarah felt far from reassured.

"It's 1851, Papa, not the Dark Ages. Women are not bound to seek the protection of marriage. It is I who will cry off. I plan to remain single."

"Then you will have to change your plans. You above all women need protection. And alteration. Ralph Pettigrew will make a well-behaved woman of you—if anyone can."

Sarah doubted the spiritless gentleman she remembered could move her to any real change. More likely, in a lifetime union with him, she would be bored into respectability, but she kept the thought to herself.

"Men do not particularly interest me," she said. "Despite my reputation."

Sir Edward nodded. "As far as I know, Sarah, you have never lied to me. Disappointed me, of course, quite often, but never lied, and I am certain you speak the truth now. For that, at least, I can be thankful. You inherited the fair beauty of your mother, but I have no doubt you will come to your marriage a virtuous if somewhat impulsive young woman."

Sarah, who placed no more special value on her virtue than she did on decorum, was not warmed by her father's faith, but neither did she relish losing her virginity in the bed of a dimly remembered fifty-year-old shipowner.

Sarah Elizabeth Whitlock *Pettigrew*.

The idea was unthinkable.

She began to pace the short distance allowed her in

14

the overly furnished room, her long legs carrying her past the ornate sofas and chairs, her mind racing. Papa remained by the fire, unmoving, unyielding. She knew he would not change his mind.

He thought of her as a gamester bent on disrupting his equanimity whenever she could. Her suitors called her courageous, and there were others who had more than once referred to her as a saint. Sarah had never decided quite what she was, or why a feeling of restlessness drove her to welcome outrageous challenges. She only knew she could share none of those views.

She came to a halt beside her father. "How do you plan to bring the wedding to reality? It might be some time before my betrothed can travel to London. There's no telling what mischief I can get into until he arrives." She flung the words as a challenge.

"If necessary, I will send you to him," Sir Edward responded. "I understand the sea journey from here to the Golden Horn can be most invigorating."

And confining, she thought, even as she brushed aside the certainty that her father truly did wish her far from the ordered quiet of his hearth and home.

Sir Edward turned from her and strode to his desk, where he proceeded to pull paper and pen from a drawer. "I will write Pettigrew today and see what arrangements he wishes. If he chooses Turkey as the site of your wedding, the dowry will be sent ahead."

Watching, Sarah knew her strongest supplications would do her no good, even as they took their toll on her pride.

The quill tip scratched against the paper, and at last he raised his eyes. "A word of caution, Sarah. I called you the hellion of London, and I am painfully aware the name is known in Bath and Brighton and Lord knows how many other towns."

Sarah stared at him without blinking. "I am quite certain that it is."

"Your foolish behavior of the past must and will cease," Sir Edward intoned solemnly, as though she had not spoken. "I have many friends in the embassy at Constantinople. Do not add the Turkish capital to your list."

Chapter Two

A month later, Sarah stood on the deck of the cargo frigate *Leviathan* as it plowed through the long, dark swells of the Aegean. Above the creak of the wind-swollen sails at her back and the whine of the straining ropes, her father's warning rang in her ears.

The hellion of Constantinople?

Impossible. The ancient capital, located at the juncture of Europe and Asia, drew merchants and adventurers from around the world. If only half of its reputation proved accurate, she would have to go far beyond anything she had ever done or thought of doing to earn such a title.

Hands clamped around a salt-crusted railing, her cloak whipping in the breeze, she stared at the distant coast and pondered her situation. She'd had weeks to accept her fate—and the same weeks to figure out an escape. Like a dutiful daughter, she was making the journey east while Papa set out on a journey of his own across the Atlantic to view the art galleries in the one-time colonies of New York and Virginia.

But sailing to Turkey as ordered and following through with the marriage were two different exercises. If her father had been listening carefully during their brief conversations—in truth more demands on his part and arguments on hers—he would have heard her promise no more than the voyage. For a change his inattention was her ally.

Once in Constantinople, Sarah was determined to convince Ralph Pettigrew that she would make a most unsuitable wife. For his good as well as hers. Surely she was clever enough. Throughout most of her adult years, with little effort on her part, men had seemed eager to do as she fancied—Sir Edward being the exception, of course.

With her arrival only a day or two away, she tried to concentrate on the particulars of her campaign. Impulse would not serve her now. But the breeze off the water insisted upon stirring strands of golden hair pulled loose from her bonnet, and the salt smell was sharp in her nostrils. The sensations were pleasant indeed, and she found it easy to abandon her serious thoughts.

Sarah's tall, slender body was rent with a deep sigh of appreciation. How could anyone be solemn or calculating on such a glorious summer's day? A Wedgwood-blue sky stretched overhead, its beauty unmarred by a distant dark band of clouds, and white-tipped azure waves rolled in front of the frigate's prow all the way to a ribbon of land on the horizon.

Could it be Turkey in the distance? Or perhaps it was another of the hundred emerald islands that dotted the water between Greece and her destination. She could not be sure. And she did not care. Whatever happened to her when she docked at the Golden Horn, she would enjoy today.

To her delight, a stork in full flight danced across the sky directly overhead, its contrasting plumage of white and black and its red bill and legs in relief

18

against the background blue. Storks, she reminded herself, were said to be a sign of good luck.

What must it be like to fly beyond the clouds where no one judged or made demands? Such an experience would be good luck, indeed.

Her gaze fell to the water, which she knew must be quite deep. She felt no fear of it, having learned to swim after an unfortunate experience aboard a skiff that had capsized in the Thames on her twenty-first birthday. Her escort, a gentleman who had turned out to be anything but, should not have tried for more than the one kiss she allowed him.

Sarah had learned two things from that afternoon: the importance of avoiding tussles in a small craft and the difficulty in getting herself to shore. She had not rested until she mastered the rudiments of water survival, using the private lake of a wealthy young lady who had been vastly amused by her chemise-clad friend's endeavors.

In time Sarah had come to enjoy the freedom that was a part of propelling herself from one side of the small lake to the other and back again. She even learned a little about sailing a boat. How unfortunate that not everyone shared her love of the deep. Etheleen Murphy came instantly to mind, and she spared a thought for the hapless companion that Sir Edward had hired to accompany her.

Murphy, as Sarah referred to her, was ensconced in their shared cabin below, locked in a losing battle with the seasickness that had overcome her shortly out of Liverpool. The half dozen other passengers sailing in the limited quarters of the cargo ship were sequestered with similar complaints. Only Sarah and the ship's crew seemed to have escaped.

"No respectable lady," Murphy was wont to say between bouts of upheaval, "goes unchaperoned on the deck of a ship. All those sailors and other unsavory sorts.''

Since when had Sarah ever been called respectable? Certainly not by someone as judgmental as the would-be caretaker.

Murphy could not believe her charge harbored no particular interest in the men.

Sarah glanced at one swarthy sailor balancing on a yardarm high overhead. He grinned down at her, and she could do nothing less than grin back as he returned to the task of lowering a sail. It had been Captain Reynolds's orders to trim the sails, convinced as he was a heavy wind awaited them by mid-afternoon.

The mate moved easily and gracefully about his perch high above the deck, as though he had been born in the sky, and he did not glance at her again. Sarah did not expect him to do so. The sailors were friendly enough, but that was all. Only the captain had ever spoken directly to her, and then with no more than polite concern for her well-being.

"Ahoy there!"

Her attention was caught by the sound of a man's voice that seemed to come from the depths of the sea. Her blue eyes sparkled with interest as she searched the waves.

At first the sea appeared inhabited by only the occasional fish that broke the surface. Then from out of a swell rose the white triangle of a lateen sail, followed by the prow of a low, narrow craft slipping across the top of the water in a parallel line to the *Leviathan*, its course in the opposite direction, away from the land. She recognized the vessel as an Arabian dhow.

Last, she caught sight of the man.

Her breath held.

Shirtless, he stood on the rear deck of the boat, legs spread wide to balance his body against the undulating movements beneath him, one bare arm waving in her direction.

One very muscular arm. Sarah could tell, even from a distance of thirty yards. The detail surprised as well as pleased her.

His trousers were dampened tightly against the outline of his body. She could make out almost every muscle, every contour. . . .

Sarah forced her eyes upward to the black hair ruffling in the wind and to the white grin splitting his face. Whoever the man was, he made a splendid sight, like a half-naked Neptune rising from the depths to claim another nymph.

Sarah pulled off her bonnet, letting the sea breeze release her golden hair until it whipped wild and free about her head and shoulders. She returned both the wave and the smile, and for a moment both vessels seemed to hang on the top of the waves, as if responding to Sarah's will.

"Hello!" she cried out brazenly. Her voice echoed across the water.

His answer was a beckoning gesture for her to join him. As if she would seriously consider diving into the watery depths and swimming about until he pulled her aboard. It was just possible, she thought with a start, that between the two of them the feat could be accomplished, and something deep inside her stirred.

For his benefit Sarah shrugged broadly as if in helplessness, but she could not still an inner urging to do as he bade. Abandoning ship in mid-ocean was a solution to her problem that she had not considered, and one at the moment far more appealing than journeying on to play an outrageous young miss.

Sarah and her mystical god-man stared at one another. A gust of wind caught in the dhow's sail, and just as quickly as Neptune had arisen, he was gone, the vessel dipping into another swell as it passed the stern of the frigate.

She stared at the spot where she had last seen the dhow, but it did not reappear. It was lost in the vastness of the Aegean, and Sarah was left with a feeling of abandonment. Or perhaps that the incident had been no more than a dream.

She chided herself for her foolishness, but at the same time she could not erase Neptune's image from her mind. He was not a god, she had to remind herself, just a man, and a brash one at that. She had no plans to avoid men, but neither did she want to thrust herself into the power of one. More than likely if he had fished her from the sea much as he would a day's catch, he would have ordered her to serve as his slave, cooking and caring for the sails . . . and other things.

It was those other things that entranced her mind. Just as the craft slipped from view, she had spied what appeared to be a cabin on the rear deck. His sleeping quarters, she figured. Why, if she were to spend the night—or nights—aboard with him, there would barely be room for both of them to seek shelter inside. And she doubted he would be content with sleeping on deck alone while she appropriated his bed.

He would be inside the cabin with her. They would be forced to touch.

Sarah's body warmed alarmingly.

He probably slept naked.

The warmth deepened.

He might even insist that she do the same, her breasts against his chest, her legs entwined with his, their hands resting on one another. All for lack of proper space, of course.

Eyes squeezed closed, Sarah fanned herself with her bonnet, unconcerned with the uselessness of her action in the face of a stiff breeze.

What on earth had come over her? Imagination was wreaking more havoc on her desires than the few bland kisses she had allowed her suitors. She had never before considered the particulars of sleeping with a man—at least not with any enthusiasm—and here she was picturing the encounter with great detail.

Sarah rationalized. What was the harm in imagining? Besides, if a woman *had* to lose her virginity, it might as well be to a godlike man who rose and disappeared with the sea. Especially one who looked like her Neptune.

She stood for a long time at the port rail, the shouts of sailors behind and above her amidst the rigging of the *Leviathan* easily ignored, as were the few fellow passengers who ventured briefly on deck. The thought occurred to her after an hour had slipped past that she must appear quite disreputable with her wind-loosened hair a mass of tangled curls and her cheeks blushed by the brisk air and by the images in her mind, but she could not stir from her post.

The minutes continued to pass.

"Is everything all right, Miss Whitlock? I couldn't help noticing you've been out here a long while."

She stirred from her reverie to face the short, broad man at her elbow.

"Why, Captain Reynolds," she said with a start as she stared into his weathered, solemn face. "Everything is fine. I hope I haven't taken you from more important tasks."

Sarah knew that such was likely, the *Leviathan* having been designed more for cargo than passengers. But it had been the first ship leaving for Turkey, and her father, despite a few halfhearted attempts to arrange a London wedding, had clearly been eager for her to be under way.

A letter from her betrothed had indicated he agreed with Sir Edward.

The captain tipped his hat. "There's nothing more important than seeing that the passengers are all right. Especially one that's given as little trouble as you."

Sarah grinned. "I am disgustingly healthy, am I not?"

"Nothing disgusting about getting your sea legs, Miss Whitlock." He swallowed. "Not that I should be mentioning legs to a lady."

"That's quite all right," she assured him. "We ladies do have them, you know."

Reynolds's narrowed eyes, long used to squinting across the glare of sun on water, turned to the waves rolling past them. Sarah suspected he was far more comfortable facing a storm than he was carrying on a conversation with a member of the opposite sex. And yet he had repeatedly made a concerted effort to see that she felt welcome. Sarah liked him.

"Are we making good time?" she asked.

Studying the afternoon sky, Reynolds appeared relieved to turn the conversation to matters with which he was familiar. "Bad weather for sure later today, but nothing the crew and me haven't faced a thousand times afore."

Sarah followed his gaze but could read nothing

24

particularly ominous in the distant line of clouds—nothing to give cause for alarm—although they had moved in closer since the last time she noticed them.

"Should be entering the Dardanelles afore nightfall," he continued. "The strait'll take us to the Sea of Marmara. We swing left up the Golden Horn, where we'll dock tomorrow night."

Sarah let him go on to describe the route, but she knew it well already, having long ago studied geography when she dreamed about some day seeing the world. Her governess at the time was positive that such knowledge would never do Sarah any good.

"Ladies need to know the social graces," she had sniffed more than once. "It's the gentlemen who study the world."

Ladies, Sarah could tell her from personal experience, needed to know everything they could. Otherwise a journey such as this to a foreign land, in the company of strangers, might prove frightening indeed.

Take the Golden Horn, for instance. Its name conjured up visions of vast wealth in the hands of pagans. In reality, it was a tideless, five-mile-long inlet that cut to the west away from the Sea of Marmara just as it narrowed to Bosporus Bay. The ancient city of Constantinople straddled both sides of the Horn, as well as the bay.

The bay in turn narrowed to a strait wending northeast from the Marmara and emptying into the Black Sea, whose shores touched on exotic lands—the Asian portion of Turkey to the south, Bulgaria and Moldavia on the west and north, and, circling on to the east, Russia.

A visit to such places no longer interested Sarah, not when the journey might be part of an extended honeymoon with Ralph Pettigrew.

"What is Constantinople like?" she asked the captain.

"A strange place," Reynolds said with a shake of his head, but she could see a gleam of appreciation in his eyes. "Can't decide if she's European or Asian. Mosques ornate with marble and tile right alongside wooden hovels. There's even a Christian church or two, fancy as you please. And what I hear about the serai . . . well, never mind. Such isn't fit for a maiden's ears."

"The home of the sultan, isn't it?" she asked.

"Some home. A palace is what it is—a walled city for him and his . . . wives."

"Does he really marry all the women in his harem? Aren't there hundreds of them?"

"He doesn't bother with such niceties. Against custom, I'm told. Just takes what he wants." Reynolds blushed at his audacity to mention such things, but he did not stop with his discourse. "Keeps 'em in a place called a seraglio. The Grand Seraglio, since it's right inside the palace. He's the only real man to go inside. The rest of 'em are—" He paused.

"Eunuchs," Sarah finished and could not resist adding, "He leads the life most men dream of."

"Now, Miss Whitlock."

"Captain!" The shout came from the rigging. "Ship approaching from starboard."

"What flag?" the captain called back.

"Can't tell. But she's coming on fast."

Sarah's interest was piqued. "Pirates, do you suppose?" She thought of swashbuckling, handsome men adorned with eye patches and wide grins as they jumped on board.

Reynolds shot her a patronizing look. "A while back it'd be a sure thing. Nary a one of 'em seen

26

around these islands for more than a year." He frowned. "Still and all, maybe you best go to your quarters."

An explosion sounded from starboard, and the *Leviathan* shook under the direct shot taken on her wooden hull.

"Gawd damn!" the captain yelled. "All hands on deck," he cried, deserting Sarah with a hasty "Get below" as he scurried in the direction of the prow.

The half dozen sailors who had been in the rigging dropped to the deck and began scurrying around her, most of them gripping pistols and knives. Other defenders spewed from below deck. The passengers other than Sarah had disappeared, and she found herself at the edge of a wild parade of hurrying men who seemed no more sure of what to do than she.

With an immediacy that robbed her of breath and resolution, the air erupted with shouts of fear and anger and with the roar of gunfire. Again and again shots landed with deadly accuracy against the frigate, so many that she could not imagine how the noble ship remained afloat. Trapped in the furor, she clung to the rail as though it could somehow protect her from harm.

A low mewing sound echoed in her ears, underscoring the cries and the explosions. She realized it came from her throat.

More shouts and gunfire and curses were thrown to the wind. Still she could not move. Fire broke out on the aft deck just as the attacking ship hove alongside, sending billows of smoke the length of the ship. It stung her eyes and burned her throat. Through the thick screen, she could make out the second vessel on the far side, a dark shadow that blocked out the world.

Choking, Sarah broke from her spell. For a brief,

frantic moment she considered her earlier option of jumping overboard and taking her chances with the sea. Even without Neptune to rescue her, the water seemed far safer now than did the ship.

She thrust the thought aside. Covering her mouth and nose with one arm, she forced her way toward the walkway leading below. As fearful as she was of being caught in the passenger quarters if the fire should spread, she could not leave Etheleen Murphy to a like fate. Better to drag her on deck and face the madmen threatening to come aboard.

She did not get far. A horde of dark-skinned men, swords unsheathed, scrambled over the starboard rail and onto the deck of the *Leviathan*, cutting off her line of retreat as they slashed their way amongst the outnumbered sailors who tried to bar their way. She stumbled backward, mindless of her destination, until her back came hard against the rail.

Dizzy with fear and a sense of absolute helplessness, she tried to take in the scene, but her mind would not let her. The smell of death was as heavy as the smoke, and the shrieks of the slayers froze her heart. These pirates with their hard, cruel faces and invincible swords were not the handsome men in her imagination. They must have sailed from hell.

They made short work of the frigate's crew. An ocean of blood stained the boards as the valiant men fell before the slashing curved blades. Their cries of agony obliterated reason, and Sarah watched in horror as the slaughter took its toll.

It all seemed to happen in an instant, this turning from a heavenly day to the hellish rain of death and destruction. The black clouds had moved in as quickly as the pirate ship, darkening the sky, and the once gentle sea, fed by an angry wind, grew tumultuous, buffeting the frigate about as though it were a toy. The air was heavy with the threat of a storm.

Gripping the rail, Sarah was dimly aware of the distant sound of thunder. It seemed that all the elements conspired against the luckless ship.

For one ghostly moment quiet descended. From out of the smoke obscuring the forward deck came the sound of gunfire. The captain emerged through the thick, gray air, a wild look on his face as he staggered forward, a blazing pistol in each hand. He stood, not twenty feet from her, and dared the villains to do their worst.

They made short work of him, cutting him down with answering gunfire, but not before he had felled two of them. He collapsed amidst the twisted, bloodied corpses strewn across the deck in the tangles of rope and fallen spars.

Sarah was certain she heard him moan. Without a thought for her own safety, she stumbled over the dead and dying to kneel beside him and cradle his head in her lap. The hem of her cloak trailed in the blood of his men.

Ignoring the dark, watchful eyes of the pirates hovering like vultures around her, she placed her fingers over his lips and felt a slight movement of air. He was alive.

His eyes fluttered open, then closed. "Miss Whitlock," he managed. "Thought I told you to go below."

"Hush," she admonished gently. "Save your strength."

He shuddered. "Don't do what you're told. . . ."

They were the last words he spoke.

Tears spilled down Sarah's cheeks as she rocked the captain in her arms. Gradually she became aware of stirring around her. A pair of scarred boots came to a halt beside her crimson-stained cloak. She stared up at the man.

Tall and thin to the point of emaciation, he stared back, his black eyes fired with triumph. Coarse, greasy hair hung long against his shoulders. His dark face was sunken, and a white, puckered scar ran from the corner of his mouth to the hairline at his temple. His sword clattered to the deck as he reached out with a bloodied hand to stroke her hair.

Fury overrode her fear. Slapping the hand aside, she stood and stumbled backward until her spine was pressed against the ship's rail. The man watched her movements, a sneer cracking his dirty, hollowed face, his thin lips pulled tightly against blackened teeth. He turned and shouted in a language unknown to her.

A trio of men responded, hurrying over to jerk her roughly away from the rail. Sarah did her best to resist them, slapping and kicking at what seemed a swarm of attackers and longing for one of their curved blades in her hand.

Nails clawing in desperation, she managed to bloody the face of one.

The answering blow against the base of her skull brought a quick end to her battle. She slipped into the darkness of unconsciousness.

Chapter Three

Jake Price stared across the wind-whipped Aegean at the storm clouds rolling in fast from the east.

"Looks like a bad one, Bandit," he said.

Jake's only companion aboard the dhow, a short, dark-skinned man in loose-fitting shirt and trousers, stood resolutely beside him on the narrow deck and nodded. His brown button eyes darted across the choppy waters. "You are correct, Bossman. A bad one."

The answer was expected. In the months Jake had known him, Bandit seldom disagreed with anything he said, but he often wondered what the man really thought.

"Got any suggestions?" Jake knew Bandit would have at least one.

"The island, Bossman. The waters will be kinder there."

"My thoughts exactly. We can—"

A gust of wind caught the rest of his words and flung them into the salt spray surrounding the low-lying craft. The forty-foot dhow, unnamed since he had bought her two weeks ago, slapped at the surface of the deepening waves, and her prow dipped and soared with the undulations, forcing Jake to tighten the muscles of his wide-spread legs to maintain his balance.

The wind chilled him, but he refused to grab for his shirt in the low-roofed sleeping quarters he had erected on the raised poop deck behind him. He liked the feel of the elements against his bare skin. His only concessions to civilization were trousers and boots and gloves, worn more for safety and comfort than for modesty's sake. Jake was not a modest man.

Nor was he a foolhardy one, despite his avowed quest for adventure and riches and good times, and he turned his concentration to saving the newly bought craft.

Bandit was right. The uninhabited island that had been serving as their temporary home was the logical destination for the prized boat. Its bay, hidden by a sweeping spit of land, would provide protection from the storm.

With a skill spawned from instinct as much as training—he'd been born in Boston thirty years ago, the last of a family of sailors, and had cast off to sea while still a boy—Jake threw himself into the task of altering the lateen sail of the vessel. The dhow's direction was into the wind, and he and Bandit moved as one to set a zigzag course through the turbulent water.

As he worked, he gave a thought to the frigate _Leviathan_ and to the fair-haired beauty who had waved to him from the deck earlier in the day when the sea had still been calm. The larger ship must be caught in this same storm, but her captain would surely possess a competence to see her safely into port. Jake found the thought reassuring.

The wind quickened, and the strain of muscle against rope invigorated him, driving all thought from his mind save that of the task at hand. Sure-footed, he moved with grace, bending and shifting as the sail swung about to take advantage of the swirling wind, powerful hands working the tackle, long and steady legs holding true. Beneath his ministrations the boat responded as he knew she would—like a woman aroused by his touch—and they skimmed the angry waters like a bird.

Jake's blood sang in his veins and he felt alive.

Eventually the clouds caught up with them, and the sky darkened, turning summer day to tumultuous night so completely that they could no longer tell where the ocean ended and the far horizon began. The rain held off. Thunder at their backs urged them on their way.

Without benefit of compass or astronomical assistance, Jake relied on dead reckoning to set their course. He could find the lone saloon in a dusty Arab town or a willing and experienced bed partner in a crowd of virgins. As well, he could find his home port, modest though it was, in the midst of an approaching storm.

His instinct did not fail him. With a slash of lightning marking their arrival, he and Bandit soon found themselves slipping into the protection of a sandy cove. The sky was lighter here and the breakers gently welcoming as they met the crescent of land, retreated, and surged forward once again in their timeless assault against the beach.

A dozen yards from the water's edge, Jake set about securing the sail.

"Let's spend the night off the boat," Jake said when he was satisfied his work was done. "I've a need for a still bed under me for once."

In short order the two men waded ashore, their footgear held overhead along with a couple of blankets, well protected from the lapping waves. The first fat splats of rain hitting the beach sent them running toward the crude shelter they had erected earlier in the week amidst the protection of the trees and undergrowth that grew in a semicircle around the far edges of the white sand.

Interlocking branches, heavy with fronds, were woven around the sturdy framework of the single room. A center post held the structure upright and, to Jake's way of thinking, was a marvel of engineering.

Dried mud extracted from the interior of the narrow island caulked the seams and together with the thick leaves made the structure watertight. A bottle buried in a burlap bag deep beneath the earthen floor—hidden in case uninvited guests should intrude during their absence—made the shelter inviting.

Jake lit the kerosene lamp and set it on the room's single piece of furniture, a crude table fashioned from driftwood. Stretching out on the blanket, he took a deep swallow of whiskey and felt content. He lay back and with one arm under his head began to relax.

A temporary home was all the shelter offered, but that was all he wanted while he spent his days sailing the dark blue waters of the Aegean, strengthening his mastery over the dhow. Spending so many years working as crewman and later mate aboard the large ships that plowed the world's oceans, he had forgotten the pleasure of controlling a smaller craft.

Building the hut was an impulse, but he felt unwilling to settle in any of the towns bordering the ocean. The acquisition of the dhow gave him a freedom to live where he chose, and for the time being he chose the island.

Sometime later when he had need of money or a

different kind of companionship than that offered by Bandit, he would seek civilization.

For now, he was satisfied listening to the howl of the wind and the patter of the rain as it landed on the sheltering palms.

"Are you sure you wouldn't like a drink?" he asked Bandit, who had settled on a blanket near the door. A waft of cool air brought in the smell of the storm.

Bandit turned his gaze away from the open portal and grinned, a white smile cutting across the brown of his face.

"My people do not partake of alcohol, Bossman."

Bandit spoke a curious kind of formal English in a singsong voice. Jake wondered if his accent was equally strange-sounding in the Egyptian, Turkish, Greek, and Persian that he also claimed to speak. He had no idea what Bandit's native language might be, since the quiet-spoken man rarely talked about himself.

"Just who are your people? Egyptians? That's where we met."

Bandit shrugged. "I have an uncle in Persia who says we are of the desert. Like the wind and the sand and the palms."

"So you're Persian." At last Jake thought he was getting somewhere. "What were you doing in Egypt?"

"I have another uncle in Cairo, Bossman. He claims we are of the sea."

Jake gave up. He could no more determine his companion's nationality than he could his age. Anywhere from twenty to forty would not surprise him. He knew from the unanswered questions he had already asked that he would get no straight replies. He hadn't even revealed his real name. In view of the circumstances of their meeting, Jake had dubbed him

Bandit. The name had stuck.

Their paths had crossed a month ago at the edge of a small village on the banks of the Nile. Jake had quit his job as mate on a clipper out of Boston and was traveling the river in search of pleasure and financial opportunity. He had rescued his newfound friend from a band of cutthroats—at a most inappropriate moment for him, although Bandit would certainly disagree.

Invited into the isolated tent of a nubile Egyptian dancer, Jake had been about to indulge in her freely offered favors. She was just the kind of woman he liked—dark and quiet and pliant, a welcome contrast to the tight-lipped ladies of his native Boston.

She had divested herself of all adornment save a smile just as he heard the cries of a person in distress. Jake wasn't out to rescue his fellow man, but with the sounds of human suffering and the crack of a whip filling the outside air, he found himself unable to enjoy the company of the dancer.

First things first, he had told himself, as he peered outside to assess the situation: one small man against six in a decidedly unfair fight, although from what Jake could make out the victim seemed to be giving a good account of himself. Action must be taken, and fast, or there would be little pleasure for him that night.

Roaring out of the tent, pistol blazing, he had surprised the half dozen villains, killed one, and sent the rest, along with their camels, scurrying into the dark. For his reward he had received not the physical release he was after—with trouble so close and so noisy, his dancer had decided retreat a wiser choice than *amour*—but rather the company of the energetic little man who in gratitude became his servant.

"Bossman," he had said as Jake scowled in the

direction of the departing morsel of delight, her dark robes fluttering behind her in the hot night wind, "I vow you will not regret what you have done."

Jake had nodded and listened to the mournful waters of the nearby Nile lapping at the land in the dark.

Bandit proved true to his word. The cutthroats, he reported, were grave robbers working the fertile valley. Certain the wily man they had captured and enslaved in Cairo was in turn stealing from their plunder, they were in the process of extracting a confession when Jake interfered.

The thieves had been right. Authorities from the village came upon them just as Bandit was revealing to Jake the thick bushes where he had stashed the appropriated property. Given no choice, he and Jake announced grandly the rescue of the treasures. A grateful Egyptian government had rewarded them well.

Jake immediately bought the dhow, a small but seaworthy craft, and set about making improvements on her, installing a galley below deck and sleeping quarters above. The costs soon depleted his funds by three fourths.

Bandit claimed to have taken his gold to the Cairo branch of his family. Jake wasn't convinced. In the short time the two spent in the Egyptian capital, he had been given ample evidence that Bandit could relieve a man of his monocle and disappear in the crowd unapprehended. Truth and honesty did not seem his primary traits.

But loyalty figured high in his character. He had vowed to stand by Jake as long as he was needed. He helped with the sailing and performed the cooking chores that were beyond Jake's ken. And he was someone to talk to on the occasions when Jake had need of conversation. Thus far the arrangement was working out well.

Shifting on his blanket bed, Jake accepted the crusty bread and white goat's cheese that Bandit had brought from the boat. The whiskey washed them down. With the wind and the rain providing an outside chorus, he stretched his long body and tried to draw forth an image of the dusky-skinned dancer as she had stood before him in her tent. Between rescuing Bandit and dealing with the authorities, he had been a long time without a woman. A little thinking was not in the least out of order.

A strange thing occurred. Instead of the Egyptian, he remembered once again the smiling beauty from the frigate's deck. He thought of her in detail, and a feeling of warmth settled inside him.

With Bandit toiling out of sight in the galley, he had brought the dhow out of a deep swell to see her leaning against the larger ship's rail, her face turned toward the wind, long strands of honeyed hair blowing freely from beneath the confines of a ridiculously inadequate hat.

Jake took a swallow of whiskey. Around him the walls of the hut swayed under the assault of the gale. The structure held, and he thought of the unknown beauty's well-being. Surely she, too, was somewhere safe. By damn, the captain better have been competent.

She had looked like an angel standing so bravely alone and in such obvious enjoyment of the wind and the salt spray. Most ladies of his acquaintance squealed at the least discomfort; Jake could not stand a female who squealed.

Her cloak had been pressed against her womanly body. He had been intrigued. For a moment he had thought she would accept his invitation to dive overboard and join him on the dhow.

How quiet and willing would she be? Would she strip off all but a smile, allowing him a long and leisurely look at the curves he was certain lay beneath her dampened cloak? Her skin would be silken and pale, and the hair at the juncture of her thighs as pale as the golden mane that had whipped in the wind.

Jake felt a tightening in his loins. The memory of her was bringing him little peace of mind.

He laughed sharply. What in the hell had come over him? Must be too much whiskey and too little rest. He wasn't given to brooding about women. Especially one like the elusive young lady who had answered his wave—an innocent, most likely, who had never known a man. He preferred his companions experienced and not cloyingly regretful when the night was done.

Outside the wind abated, and Jake felt his own aroused feelings settle down.

Most likely his angel was the spoiled daughter of an overly indulgent father, a lady from the silken strands atop her head down to her delicate little toes. He had met her kind often enough in the ports where his travels had taken him. Especially Boston. Whenever the ship he was on came into port, he had seen them eyeing him as he labored about the dock. Occasionally one or two of them spoke. They had liked his looks but not the size of his pocketbook.

They had teased, then run like rabbits when he suggested they do more than hint at invitations. He had grown weary of their games—and wary of the shotgun-wielding father he imagined would greet him if he ever taught one of them the lessons they craved. Jake was far from ready to settle down.

Angel would be the same as the rest, brave and bold until her protected world was threatened. Jake could figure why she had been standing on the deck alone. Ordered to her quarters below, she was letting the world know that no one could tell her what to do.

"Is something troubling you, Bossman? Your thoughts are heavy tonight."

Jake returned to the present with a start. "Nothing's wrong."

"Sometimes the Bossman's answers come too quickly. I fear you worry because much of your gold is gone. Or perhaps you are lonely for a visit into town."

"I get by," Jake said more impatiently than he intended. There were times Bandit was too perceptive for comfort.

Bandit watched him in silence, then spoke. "I can be of assistance, Bossman."

"You already have been. You are not my servant despite the role you have taken on."

"I cannot provide a woman—"

"I can get my own."

"—but I can provide the gold."

"You took your share and I took mine. We settled all that back in Cairo."

Bandit grinned. "Not exactly true."

Without another word he disappeared through the open doorway and into the lessening storm. A few minutes later he returned with a dark bundle clutched to his rain-soaked shirt. Jake sat upright on the blanket as Bandit knelt before him and with reverence placed the bundle at his feet.

Bandit made no move to unfold the dark, coarse cloth wrapped around the offering, and at last Jake did so, his movements slow and steady as seemed to befit the solemn occasion. He had no idea what the hell was going on.

The first clue was the exposed edge of the hard, irregularly shaped object. It glittered golden in the glow from the lamp. Jake's attention was captured by the sight. Slowly he removed the layers of covering. Lying against the black cloth and in contrast to its coarseness was a death mask, sculpted in gold, the sharp planes of cheeks and chin catching the full force of the flickering light. The eyes were almond-shaped, and the full, almost sensuous lips were caught in an eternal half smile.

Knowing little about Egyptian treasures, Jake supposed it was the likeness of some long-dead pharaoh. He reached out to stroke the surface. It was cold and hard, and yet, in its richness and depth of color, it seemed almost like a living thing.

"I was not truthful to the authorities in the village," Bandit said. "I did not reveal all that was hidden by the robbers."

Somehow Jake was not surprised.

"How did you manage to get it here?" he asked.

"In Cairo you gave your attention to the purchase of the boat."

"While you returned to the village where we met."

"It was simple to bring the mask aboard shortly before we set sail. It is heavy but not large. And you have respected my poor belongings and left them alone."

Jake studied the mask. "Your belongings are not so poor, my friend. There must have been many chances for you to bury it on the island."

"The Bossman has devoted many hours to his labors."

"And what are you proposing now?" Jake asked.

For once Bandit's dark eyes did not dart about in curiosity, but rather settled on Jake with surprising

41

seriousness. "On the banks of the Nile I was given the gift of life, Bossman. For such you have not been adequately repaid."

Jake glanced at the mask. "I cannot accept such a gift."

"I am not offering all. But you can help me reach a buyer, one wealthy and wise enough to compensate this poor owner for the mask's true worth. For such a service, I will share the proceeds equally."

"What do you have in mind? A bag of silver drachmas, perhaps?"

"Turkish lira may be more easily obtained. There are Greeks who can afford to meet the value of our treasure, but few have the privacy to display it without word drifting back to the jealous Egyptians."

"Turkish lira, you say." Jake's mind worked. "The sultan would have the resources."

"As no others would. The serai is hidden from the public eye by a high wall, although many are permitted inside. But in the private rooms beyond the Gate of Felicity—in the Grand Seraglio where the sultan often dwells—only the eunuchs and women of the harem are allowed."

"And you think I can arrange a meeting with him?"

"You can arrange to suggest the possible sale to His Excellency, the all-powerful Harun, a man who is famed for his worship of beautiful things. Americans are not immediately turned away. While I, a poor servant. . . ."

Bandit let his voice trail into the damp, still air.

Jake resumed his study of the mask. To return it now to the Egyptian authorities would only bring questions and the possibility of incarceration. To leave such a treasure buried on an uncharted island, unseen and unappreciated, would be an equal crime.

He nodded at Bandit, who more than ever seemed well named.

"I believe you have come upon the perfect solution to your problem."

"*Our* problem, Bossman. Harun awaits. On the morning tide I respectfully suggest we set sail for Constantinople."

Chapter Four

Sarah was drowning.

Her lungs screamed for air, and she waited for the water to rush in and end her misery. Her head pounded, her stomach threatened a violent upheaval, and her mouth was filled with enough cotton batting to stuff a chair.

Batting?

Sarah moaned. Rather a strange drowning, it seemed. Trust her to die in a manner beyond the ordinary.

Still, she could not breathe, could not move. With uncommon effort she shoved her heavy hands against the weight keeping her from floating upward to the precious, life-giving air. Her fingers brushed against a slippery coolness that in her troubled brain translated into silk. An even stranger ocean, it would seem.

She pushed. The weight seemed to evaporate, and inhaling deeply, she opened her eyes.

She closed them straightaway and tried to evaluate what that one painful second had revealed: shafts of blinding light slashing in from the right and illuminating swirls of color—red and gold and green and violet. She had awakened inside a rainbow.

She chanced a second look. This time her eyes adjusted more readily to the light, and she was able to make some sense of her surroundings. The rays of sunbeams came from a window high to her right; she kept her eyes cut left. A mound of pillows lay close by her head, the source, no doubt, of her suffocation. Not engulfing water or, as she had first thought, cotton batting, but silken pillows covering her head. She would have sighed in relief had she not been so miserable.

She was lying in some kind of bed, the likes of which she had never seen before. Additional pillows, soft and cool and numbering a dozen or more, caressed her and helped to soften the thin mattress which served as the underpinning for the place of rest. At her sides and head airy swaths of brilliant, transparent cloth were draped from ceiling to floor to form a sort of protective alcove, although protection against what she could not imagine. They could not hold out the cruel light.

Like the alcove, her body was wrapped in a shimmer of silk—an embroidered blue caftan of infinite beauty. The gentleness with which it lay against her bare skin seemed to lift the aching from her bones, and she found herself snuggling deeper into the comfort of her strange surroundings.

Had she died and gone to her reward? If this were heaven, it was far different from any celestial home she had ever envisioned.

Sarah's fanciful thoughts receded, and the past rushed in. If anything, she had been thrown into a curious kind of hell. How could she for one moment think of the pleasures of creature comfort? Anguish seized her, and she turned on her side to clutch one of the rejected cushions.

Memories flooded in; she relived them all: the attack at sea . . . the captain's bloodied body in her arms . . . the cadaverous villain who had ordered her capture. . . . And below deck Etheleen Murphy, trapped in a ship that must have become her coffin.

The sharp images faded, and she remembered being thrown into an endless void, surrounded by nothingness—for an eternity or a second, she knew not which—then came jagged periods of wakefulness, rude jostlings, as though she were being borne over rough terrain, and strange men's voices growling in a language she did not understand. Worst of all, as she remembered the carnage on the deck, she carried with her throughout it all a wretchedness that reached into her soul.

She had a dim memory of a liquid forced down her throat. Despite the dryness in her mouth, she could still taste its bitterness.

At last came consciousness, confusion, and despair. A low whimper escaped her throat.

Somewhere in the room a door opened and closed, and soft-soled slippers padded across the floor.

"Ah, the missy awakens."

It was a woman's voice, shouting in her ear.

Sarah struggled to sit up; but the insubstantial bed would allow her hands no purchase, and her legs became tangled in the folds of the caftan.

"The missy should remain still."

Sarah rebelled. As bad as she felt, she was taking no more orders.

After several attempts, she succeeded in sitting upright, her back supported by the cushions, the blue silk caftan smooth and comforting once again. Forcing her eyes open, she saw a robed woman kneeling close to her feet. Olive-skinned with brown eyes that seemed to fill half her slender, unlined face,

46

the woman peered at her in concern. There was intelligence in the stare, and sympathy. Sarah estimated her age not much beyond her own.

The woman lowered her eyes, seemingly concentrating on Sarah's bare toes emerging from a row of embroidery. "We have had much concern for the missy."

"We?" The word came out a croak, and Sarah cleared her throat. "Who are you?"

"Nadire," she said. "I am the missy's odalisque."

"Odalisque?" Sarah stared, puzzled.

"What the English call a slave. You are English, are you not? It is what we were told when you were brought in." The woman frowned. "Nadire displeases the missy. Another slave will be summoned. Perhaps a eunuch would more easily please."

Sarah's head reeled in wonder, and she reached out toward her companion. "No. You do not . . . displease me. It's just that I am very confused about what has happened." Her smile was tentative but not entirely insincere. "And I have never before owned an odalisque."

"I am told it is a good thing. If the slave does not require too much beating."

"I will not beat you. Only tell me where I am."

It was Nadire's turn to look surprised. "In the Grand Seraglio, missy. Beyond the Gate of Felicity. Nowhere else in Constantinople will the missy find such beauty."

"I'm in a harem?" Her voice broke, and she fell silent, horrified at the implications of what Nadire was saying.

A smile of pride graced the slave's face. "The *sultan's* harem. When the missy was brought in, the fools tried to take you to Mustafa."

The sultan's harem.

Another wave of dizziness washed over Sarah, and she closed her eyes to gain what little clearheadedness she could.

The sultan's harem. Surely this was some horrible farce planned for her arrival by a jokester gone mad, or better yet she was still trapped in a dream.

Opening her eyes to the worried face of Nadire and the touch of the slave's hand on her arm, she gave up hope that she was asleep. The memories that would not go away told her this was no farce.

She looked once again at the strips of colored silk that defined the area of her bed. "So I really am in a harem." She could hardly say the word.

"The Grand Seraglio," said Nadire.

"You say I was brought here. By whom?"

"I did not see them, but there is talk among the women—they were the scowling guards who protect Mustafa. It is said you were bought especially for him."

"Who is this Mustafa? You have mentioned him twice."

Nadire's smile turned into a frown. "Mustafa is the second son of the Sultan Harun. On the far side of the courtyard lies both his quarters and the *haremlik,* the rooms of his women. But the Kizlar Agasi saw the missy and knew such a one with her hair made of gold was meant for Harun."

Too many characters, too many complications. So she had been bought on some kind of slave market by the guards of a sultan's son but had been claimed for a higher purpose—the pleasure of the sultan himself. She did not know whether to be frightened or angry or puzzled, and she settled on all three, with anger threatening to take control.

"The missy should not worry so," Nadire went on. "The little lines form between her brows."

As if Sarah had nothing more serious to consider, like a remembered slaughter and for herself rape and perhaps death. Having no idea what sultans did with captured English women, she must go slowly, take one worry at a time, and in so doing bring a note of sanity to her insane world.

For now her only hope for freedom was the soft-eyed young woman beside her. "Nadire, please call me Sarah, not missy."

"If the missy wishes."

"The missy orders."

"So be it, Sarah." The slave dragged out the vowels from back in her throat and made the name a throaty whisper.

"And second, who is this Mister Agasi?"

Nadire giggled and seemed younger still, younger even than Sarah, who was beginning to feel far older than her twenty-five years. "Kizlar Agasi is his title, Missy Sarah. It means the keeper of the women. I do not know his real name."

Sarah gave up on changing her nomenclature.

"He is what the English call the chief eunuch," Nadire said, then expounded. "Black as the night and tall as the cypress trees, he is the emperor of eunuchs. As such, he is in charge of the sultan's harem. He is known as a kind man for all his power."

The keeper of women. The emperor of eunuchs. Neither explanation eased Sarah's fears. She tried to swallow but found her mouth still dry. She closed her eyes; by the time she opened them again, Nadire had scrambled to a shell-shaped fountain built into a wall by the door and had returned with a glass of water.

Sarah drank the cool liquid, extended the glass for a refill, and downed it as quickly as she had the first. When she was done, Nadire fluffed the pillows around her and insisted she lie down again. The pounding in her head gradually subsided, and she was relieved that her stomach did not reject the water her lips and tongue had so desperately needed.

Resting, a grateful Sarah once again took in the high-ceilinged room, the yards of color, and the brilliance of the loose, silken clothing covering her body. She wiggled her toes, relieved to find they responded immediately and gave her no pain. She brushed one hand against her hair, which was somehow brushed free of its tangles and rested long and loose against the pillows supporting her head. She inhaled a heavy and flowery scent, which she recognized as patchouli.

Someone had taken great care to see her pampered and perfumed. She could think of only one purpose.

"When," she asked, "am I to be raped?"

"Missy Sarah, do not worry about such things. You will not be harmed."

"Why else am I here if not to—" Sarah's voice broke. She could picture a wild-eyed, drooling fiend, hairy and naked, his breath fetid and his hands cruel, forcing himself upon her. Unlike the images of lovemaking she had summoned when thinking about Neptune and the dhow, she could not consider the particulars.

"It is a great honor to be in the Grand Seraglio," said Nadire. "To make love with a man is not necessarily a bad thing. Especially one as kind as Harun."

Sarah did not try to argue. A thought struck her. "You speak English."

"The sultan wills that all in the harem do so. He wishes to make friends with the English after so many years of trouble between the countries."

Sarah knew that diplomatic relations had recently been reopened under the greatly praised leadership of Stratford Canning, recently returned to Constantinople as Lord Stratford de Redcliffe. It would be just her misfortune to cause an international scandal and ruin what Lord Stratford had accomplished after years of work.

She remembered her father's warning about his friends in the embassy. He did not want to be embarrassed before them by her antics.

The *hellion of Constantinople* didn't seem so farfetched, after all. It was a name she would welcome as long as she could remain alive. Her practical English mind went to work. She had gotten out of scrapes before; the enormity of this particular one must not intimidate her.

Besides, Nadire had called the sultan kind. Perhaps he was not the monster she had pictured. Perhaps he did not actually drool.

She struggled once again to sit. "Surely word has gone out of my kidnapping and the slaughter aboard the *Leviathan*," she said, smoothing her twisted gown.

"I know only what the gossips in the harem say. The Missy Sarah's ship went down in a great storm. All were claimed by the sea."

"That is a lie."

Nadire shrugged.

"The world must learn the truth," Sarah said.

"The harem is your world now, Missy Sarah."

"Impossible!"

"You will be cared for."

"I take care of myself."

Nadire gifted Sarah with an indulgent smile. She obviously thought her new mistress demented to

51

wish such a foolish thing.

Sarah tried again. "The sultan is known as a wise and powerful leader of his people," she said, not knowing if she spoke the truth. She heard the desperation in her voice. "He will know only trouble can result from keeping me prisoner. Others will hear of my capture and demand I be set free."

"Others? No one outside the Gate of Felicity knows you are here. The Kizlar Agasi says so, and he is a man that knows all. But he fears you have been—how did the missy say it?—raped? By the men who would sell you into captivity."

"I haven't, at least not yet." She thought a minute. "At least I do not believe I have."

"The court physicians will examine you to make sure."

"They most certainly will not!"

"The Missy Sarah has much to learn."

Sarah could not disagree.

"Permit me to explain," Nadire continued. "You are my mistress, but also you are an odalisque. An exalted and lovely one. Different with your pale hair and eyes. But, like me, you must do what you are bid."

Little did Nadire know. Sarah's alarm settled into resolve. Moved by a spirit of conciliation, she had done as her father had bid, setting out for Constantinople and a meeting with an unwanted fiancé. And look where obedience had landed her.

She kept her thoughts to herself. Immediately she began to plan. Sultan Harun must be made to see that he could not keep her hidden forever. If he did not agree, somehow, sometime she would get away.

Once she escaped, she would cause a scandal of the grandest proportions. Of that she was fully capable.

In comparison, her midnight waltz at the British Museum would be as respectable as tea with the queen.

Papa thought she was after excitement and notoriety, did he? Surely he would hear of her endangerment and subsequent escape. He might even rush across the ocean to be by her side.

Or if not, she thought in a wave of sensibility, at least he would be grateful she was alive and well.

For the first time since awakening, she smiled. "Nadire, I see you have an answer for everything. I must depend upon you for many things, and right now I am famished. Do you think you could get me something to eat?"

Sarah had hoped to see the sultan soon. Instead, stripped of the caftan, she went through a dreadful examination by the imperial physicians, who announced that she was still a maiden. The humiliation of their indifferent hands and their dark, probing eyes remained with her through the long days and nights of her imprisonment. After such an ordeal, she truly believed that nothing worse could happen to her.

She was seldom let out of the small room in which she had first awakened; when she was, it was for short walks among the cypress trees and flowering shrubs of a central courtyard. As she strolled along paths lined with roses and carnations and hyacinths, she welcomed the summer sun and fresh air after the gloomy quarters in which she spent most of her hours. The blinding light of that first morning had seemed bright only because she had so long been in the darkness of her deep, unnatural sleep.

Used to the damp coldness of her native London, she could not deny the warm comfort in which the courtyard was bathed.

Because of the unusual manner of her arrival—sultans seldom had to depend upon kidnappings anymore, Nadire informed her—and because of her nationality, she was kept separate from the other women of the harem. Rarely did she see them strolling about the confines of the seraglio. More common were the black-skinned eunuchs in the passageways as she was escorted each day to the baths. Harun liked his women clean, and she must forever be kept ready in case he should summon her.

After the first day, she had given up asking when that might be. As the English poet Alexander Pope had penned, a little learning could very well be a dangerous thing.

On her walks to the *hammam*—the bath house—she searched in vain for possible exits that might lead to her freedom. Occasionally she saw pairs of deaf-mutes scurrying past, eyes downward. They seemed lost in their silent world. But no more lost than she.

Despite her growing frustration, which had taken the place of anger and fear, she enjoyed watching the passing of the page boys, cheeks painted, their plump little bodies clad in brightly hued silks. They seldom gave her more than a curious glance.

Two weeks went by, and all she learned was that the seraglio was a lovely and private place of courtyards and gardens, of cloistered quarters and dim passageways and high walls. Of the rest of the palace—the serai—she learned little except that the entire walled structure was built on one of the hills of Constantinople close to the waters of the Golden Horn and the Sea of Marmara and that it was like a little town complete unto itself.

For her it was no more than a prison. Strolling in the garden one afternoon, she grew tired of Nadire's extolling the virtues of her sultan. "What about Mustafa?" she asked.

Nadire avoided her eye. "He is different from his father. He is not kind."

"Has he hurt you in some way?" asked Sarah.

She shook her head. "I have heard tales of what he has done to others. Unhappiness seems to be his state, it is said, because he will never be sultan. That honor goes one day to his older brother, who lives away from Constantinople in Anatolia to the east."

"But are there not other rewards to being a sultan's son?"

"Harun has given Mustafa a great inheritance of gold and jewels and lets him abide in the serai."

"So Mustafa is wealthy."

"For him, I believe, this is not enough." Nadire would add nothing to support her opinion, and Sarah did not ask again.

And so the days passed in sameness, and the nightmares gradually eased. She could not complain of her treatment. The food was excellent, even to her English taste. Platters of exotic fruit—pears and pomegranates, grapes and figs—were brought to her each day, and she was offered an array of breads and cheeses and vegetables, although little meat was served. She even learned to like the thick sour puddinglike substance Nadire called yoghurt, especially if she mixed it with honey and fruit.

As the days turned into weeks, Sarah came to know that Nadire was as intelligent as she had first suspected. They had long talks about England and about Nadire's home in the Caucasus. She had been captured years ago during one of the many wars between the Turks and the Russians. She did not remember her family and could only estimate her age at somewhere over twenty. But she remembered the mountains and a journey once to the Black Sea.

"I had never seen so much water," she said on one such occasion as the long evening stretched toward another interminable night in the small room. "I thought it must extend to the edges of the world."

"You remember the sea and not your family? Perhaps you are a princess with an entire country mourning for your return."

Nadire shook her head, her eyes saddening. "I am no princess, Missy Sarah. In truth, I believe my family must not have been very kind. I have been treated well here. I do not complain."

Sarah's heart went out to the girl, and she felt ashamed that she had so often silently railed against the years of her own upbringing. At least she had been occasionally in the company of her father. If he did not hold her in deep affection, he had never been purposefully unkind. Equally comforting, she had possessed friends and, until a few weeks ago, the freedom to come and go as she chose.

"You have no wish to marry?" she asked softly. "To have a home of your own?"

"It is not my fate to please men."

Sarah studied the beautiful wide eyes of the slave and the graceful way she sat on the pillow, knees bent under her as she talked. "You are wrong, Nadire."

"Once the sultan called upon me. The visit was unsatisfactory. I did not arouse his desires. He did not call again. At the time he was much in love with the first of the *kadin*."

Sarah eyed her questioningly.

"*Kadin* is the name given to the women of the

56

harem who have borne him children," Nadire explained.

"He no longer loves her?"

"Alas, she was taken from him by a great illness. He has mourned her ever since. The son she bore, the first of Harun's many offspring, is the one who will become sultan."

Sarah studied Nadire. The slave was lovely with her dusky skin and huge dark eyes. Whatever task she faced, she moved into it with a grace that was close to a dance.

"If you did not please him," Sarah asked, "how can I?" She took hope from the thought. Perhaps he would send her in disgrace into the streets surrounding the serai.

"The Kizlar Agasi believes that you will do more than just please. He longs to bring a smile back to the face of Harun. It is why he did not let you be sold into the slavery of Mustafa's harem."

Sarah prayed the Kizlar Agasi was wrong. Unless Harun was pleased by a woman who would fight and scream and scratch against his advances.

With time passing slowly, Sarah had to fight a growing sense of hopelessness. Only her pitiful attempts at plotting an escape saved her sanity and her spirit. She noticed the paths taken by the eunuchs and the pages, the walks of the other women of the harem, the times of the meals and the times she was left alone.

And she asked questions, innocent ones of how the meals were prepared and where, the location of the sultan's quarters and of the stables, and exactly what lay beyond the Gate of Felicity. She learned there was another courtyard, larger than the one she knew, and to its left the meeting place for the divan, advisors to Harun. Beyond the meeting place, in the far corner of the palace grounds, were the stables, where Harun kept his mighty Arabian steeds.

Slowly a plan began to evolve. The women of the harem did not hide their faces. In the streets of the city, according to everything she had read, such was never the case. She could fashion a veil and robe from the material surrounding her bed. They would be rather colorful—Nadire told her that in Turkey it was the men who more often wore bright clothes—but she had no choice.

Thus garbed, in the night when Nadire was asleep in her bed of pillows in the corner, Sarah could slip into the courtyard and make her way past the tall cypress trees, past the room where the divan met, and on to the stables. If no horse was available, she would steal through the stable doors. The residents of the seraglio would not expect such boldness, having grown used to far more biddable females than Sarah. Veiled and robed, she could make her way to the English consulate. Lord Stratford would see she was taken in.

She chose a moonless night after Nadire had eaten a particularly large meal, pushed on her by her mistress to insure a night of deep sleep. Sarah had her escape clothes, snipped with a fruit knife during the predawn hours of the past week, carefully hidden underneath her own mounded pillows.

She watched Nadire's eyes grow heavy. Sarah's blood began to pound. Only a short while longer and then. . . .

Footsteps sounded in the corridor outside her quarters.

The door opened to reveal the tall, dark figure of the Kizlar Agasi.

Nadire scrambled to her feet.

He nodded once and then departed.

Fully awake, Nadire grinned.

Sarah's heart stopped. "What is wrong?"

"Nothing, Missy Sarah. Only it is time."

Sarah grew cold as she waited for the edict.

"A great honor has at last been given you, missy. You must be prepared to visit the sultan. You will stay in his quarters tonight."

Chapter Five

For the grand occasion, Sarah was scrubbed from head to foot three times as was the custom, a coarse bag wrapped around Nadire's hands for the task, and her hair washed in the yolks of a dozen eggs. Custom also dictated the removal of all body hair through the use of a quicklime depilatory and the razor-sharp edge of a mussel shell, but Sarah was spared this particular indignity.

"Harun has given orders," Nadire explained, "that if the English prefer their women hirsute, he can for one night accept the same."

"I must remember to thank him" was Sarah's only comment.

As the hour of midnight approached, Nadire bound her missy's hair atop her head, allowing a half dozen ringlets to rest against her neck. Her perfumed and oiled body was adorned in spangles, full red silk trousers nipped in at the ankles, and a matching bodice that barely covered the essential areas of her person, leaving abdomen, back and shoulders shockingly visible to all who might see her.

As far as Sarah was concerned, they were fighting clothes. Sometime during the second or third scrubbing, ignoring a heaviness of heart that would not go away, she had decided to be grateful for a chance to meet Harun. At last, she reasoned, she had a chance to talk to the man in authority.

Nadire set about painting her face—kohl and malachite for her eyes and a rose-colored salve for cheeks and lips. Absurd slippers with curved toes were placed on her feet, and as a last touch Nadire slipped over her head a golden, tissue-thin scarf that also draped across her face, leaving only her eyes uncovered.

"In some ways, even tonight with the English woman, Harun prefers the old ways," Nadire informed her as she secured the free end of the scarf behind Sarah's ear. "Do not look him directly in the eyes."

"Why ever not?" asked Sarah.

"Muslim women are not considered worthy enough to do so."

"Even in bed?"

"There," Nadire said, her eyes twinkling, "I believe the customs are sometimes overlooked." She fingered the veil. "The *yasmak* will be removed by the sultan when he wishes to see the missy. He will not be disappointed."

His disappointment, Sarah could have said, depended on his expectations.

She was escorted to the sultan's quarters by no less a personage than the Kizlar Agasi, his six-foot-tall body held erect, his dark eyes in his black face turned solemnly straight ahead. The two of them moved swiftly and wordlessly down the twisting passageways, Sarah's hands held stiffly across her exposed navel like a shield, her heart pounding beneath the sheer bodice. For all her silent boasting of how she would confront Harun, she had to admit

61

she was terrified.

The eunuch came to a halt beside a closed door, on either side of which stood a robed guard. Knocking once, he entered while Sarah waited in the passageway and wondered if there were a special ceremony involved with her introduction—something like the pagan rites used to sacrifice virgins to the gods.

"Come, Sarah Whitlock," the Kizlar Agasi said from the open portal.

With little time to consider how he could know more than the lone first name she had passed on to Nadire, she did as she was bid, seeing only a blur of candlelight after the dimness of the path. The eunuch salaamed his way from the room and closed the door after him.

Taking a deep breath, Sarah cast her eyes about. The first thing she noticed was the head of a man lying on a pillow of deep purple satin at the foot of a great gilded bed. She jumped, certain for a moment that somehow the sultan had been beheaded and she had been summoned as part of a cruel joke. The spangles at her abdomen and wrists jangled in the quiet.

She pulled herself together. The object was not a head at all, but the life-size replica of a man's face. She recognized it as a death mask. It was bathed in the pearly light from a hundred candles scattered about the room; its rich, pure lustre told her it could be made of nothing less than gold.

Entranced by the mask, she forgot where she was, forgot the terror that had accompanied her on the long walk behind the Kizlar Agasi. Despite the differences between her and Sir Edward Whitlock, dealer in fine antiques, she was still very much his daughter and could recognize a priceless work of art almost as easily as he. She knew right away the mask

62

was from Egypt and that it must be beyond price.

"The English woman approves," said a deep voice from her left.

For the second time since entering the quarters, Sarah jumped. She whirled, a small cry escaping her lips and blending with the noise of her jewelry.

The figure of a man emerged from the shadows. He was short and portly and garbed in a brocaded robe whose metallic threads were caught in the candlelight. His hair was thick and dark, in contrast to the gray eyebrows that bunched above his watchful eyes, and his face was deeply lined as though with sorrow or, Sarah thought, with the burdens of responsibility.

She pushed aside the kindly idea. More likely the lines were the legacy of decadence.

Sultan Harun, the imperial ruler of Turkey and the remainder of the diminishing Ottoman Empire, spiritual and governmental leader of millions, master of countless slaves and sole lover to a harem of three hundred beautiful women, nodded his greeting.

Sarah chose discretion and lowered her eyes. "You startled me."

"The English woman is needlessly troubled. Sarah Whitlock, you have nothing to fear."

From his point of view, perhaps she did not. He took slaves to bed all the time.

"But of course I am fearful," she blurted out. "Surely you know I am here against my will."

He did not respond, and she risked a quick glance at his face. To her surprise, he was giving his attention to the mask.

"Against my will," she repeated, more forcefully, but he paid her no mind. The mask had him completely in thrall.

It was clear the sultan was not concerned with her situation and, at least for the time being, not even interested in her.

"Beautiful, is it not?" he said.

Sarah murmured her agreement.

"I purchased it only this afternoon. From an American."

Sarah's eyes widened. "An American? I am surprised."

"That someone from such a young country could possess such a valuable object? He was himself a young man, and a bold one. I suspect he did not come by the mask legally."

"Which means you have bought stolen goods." Worse than foolish. Sarah could have bitten her tongue.

"Such is not my concern," he said with a wave of a bejeweled hand.

Of course it would not be, Sarah chastised herself. *She* was stolen goods, and the sultan had yet to indicate any regret over her predicament. Just because he hadn't thrown her upon the bed and ordered her to disrobe did not mean he was any less a despot than she had supposed—or that he would not attempt to do so before the night was done.

"I could not bear to have the mask out of my sight," he continued. "And I longed for someone to admire it with me."

"Surely one of the other women—"

He waved aside her words. "They think only of jewels and gossip. Such a golden treasure as this they would have me melt down and cast into necklaces to wear about their necks. I have hopes that the Englishwoman, having seen much of the world, will appreciate the mask for its beauty alone."

Sarah looked him directly in the eye. "You don't sound as though you like your women very much."

"They have their purposes," he said coldly. "And

64

they know their place."

And so should she. The order was implicit in his tone, and she felt a return of dread.

Sarah attempted to turn the conversation. "You speak excellent English, Your Highness," she said. "Where on earth did you learn?"

A proud smile softened the lines of the sultan's face. "My father was a great leader. He knew Turkey must take her place in the world, so he saw to it that I speak many languages. It is my own wish to learn all that I can about the English and their ways."

"They don't keep concubines," she said without thought.

"Then I must be careful to choose the customs that I wish to emulate. Please," he said, gesturing to the western-style bed, "take what comfort you are able. Remove the veil and allow yourself to relax. I have told you that you have nothing to fear, and a caliph does not lie."

Aside from the scattered candelabra, the bed was the only furniture in the room. The familiar pillows were scattered about the extensive width of its head, a thousand of them, it seemed, and Sarah thought how ironic it was that she had dreaded losing her virginity to the fifty-year-old Ralph Pettigrew. The loss was now to occur in a union with a man at least ten years older than he. And without the blessings of marriage.

If only she had jumped overboard from the *Leviathan* and taken her chances with the beckoning, dark-haired Neptune. To be locked in the arms of such a man, even in the cramped quarters of his small boat, was far more enticing than the situation presenting itself now.

"If it is my comfort you seek," she said, easing the golden silk from her head and face, "then I would much prefer the British embassy."

"Enough," he said, and for the first time the power of his position was evident in his voice. "I have summoned you so that together we might admire the mask and speak of art and other things. This we shall do."

"The English ways you wish to learn—" she began.

"Enough, I say. The English could well learn obedience from the Turks." With a swirl of the brocaded robe, he settled himself on the bed, a cushion of pillows behind him against the ornate headboard. He patted the satin covering at his side. "Come, Sarah Whitlock, and tell me about your galleries of art. Do they contain riches more beautiful than the mask?"

Sarah reviewed her options, giving consideration to the muscled guards at the door, and joined Harun on the wide bed. She made certain to leave between them all the space she could without having to worry about falling off the side.

Thus began one of the most remarkable nights in her twenty-five years. After covering the subject of London art works, Sarah went on to describe the roadways and carriages, the food, the concerts, the plays, the poverty of England's lower class, as well as the country's contrasting wealth.

Asking a few questions of her own, she discovered that his religion did not allow for the reproduction of the human form, hence the proliferation of mosaic tiles and rich tapestries around the palace instead of the paintings and sculptures that would be found in other such grand domains.

When food and drink were served, Sarah sipped at a glass of wine while the sultan took only the unfermented juice of the apple. As caliph to his Muslim people, he had forsworn alcohol, although he confessed that more than one of his ancestors had become addicted to the stronger beverage.

"And other drugs as well," he informed her. "Sometimes I regret that the poppy is grown in great abundance in my land. There are those who would trade in such a terrible harvest, but I have forbidden such a practice. It has caused some discussion among the viziers in the divan. Already there are dissenters who believe I move the country too close to the countries of the West."

She thought he spoke with remarkable candor, but of course he did not expect her to escape and tell of what she heard and saw in the Grand Seraglio. For all their shared interests and the growing regard in which she held him, she must remember that she was still his slave.

Sometime in the early morning hours, when the sultan at last paused, seemingly lost in his own private thoughts, Sarah attempted once again to bring up her own situation.

"About my kidnapping—" she began.

He turned his dark head to her. "The women of the English are proving quite stubborn. It is no wonder that the men so often become sailors and are gone for long periods of time."

"And sometimes those sailors die," she said angrily. In a rush of words she told of her experience aboard the *Leviathan*. For once, Harun did not interrupt.

Caught in her own description of the horror, she fell silent.

"I have heard of no such pirate ship," said Harun, thoughtful.

"Like the caliph," she said, "I do not lie."

"I will investigate."

"Good," Sarah said. "With your great powers you

can apprehend the murderers. And in your great wisdom you will set me free."

"Ah yes, my wisdom. I believe that perhaps the English woman does lie when it suits her purpose."

"Your Highness—"

Harun clapped his hands. "Enough talk for tonight. I grow weary. We will discuss the matter another time."

The door to the passageway opened to reveal a pair of waiting eunuchs, and she knew she was dismissed. With a sinking heart she realized he would listen to no more. She was swept by a sense of failure. She had let down Captain Reynolds and Etheleen Murphy. And herself.

Escorted to her room, she went to bed, her virginity still intact, and tried to draw comfort from the sultan's promise to verify her story.

At noon the next day, awakened by Nadire, she curled up in her nest of pillows and described to the wide-eyed girl how the evening had gone.

"He did not try to . . . do anything," she said. "Just talk."

"The missy must not be disappointed."

"About that you need not be worried."

Nadire shook her head sadly. "I pray to Allah that you do not long for a man, whether or not he be a sultan. Life is difficult for those women in the harem who do. They try to make the eunuchs show interest in them, but of course such things are impossible. Sometimes they even offer themselves to one another." She looked shyly at Sarah. "Do I shock the missy?"

While Sarah didn't completely understand what the girl was referring to, she hastened to assure her that her days in the seraglio were moving her beyond shock.

"And sometimes they try—" She came to a

complete halt.

Sarah's curiosity was completely aroused. "Go on," she urged.

"Things," she whispered.

Sarah, too, lowered her voice. "Things?"

"Cucumbers."

Sarah was lost. "Cucumbers?"

"Harun has ordered that they not be served to the women whole." Nadire looked at her knowingly. "They must be sliced."

Sarah watched with care the wide-eyed brightness of her slave and tried to figure out just what in the world she was talking about. Before she could ask, Nadire giggled.

"No need for the Missy Sarah to use such things. You can attract the great Harun, of that I am certain. I will teach you dances of the Turks. I do not know if they are different from your own country—"

"Undoubtedly they are."

A eunuch was summoned to strum upon a lyre, and Sarah spent the rest of the afternoon learning to undulate her hips in a manner that would astound even the most jaded of her countrymen, although she could never manage to kneel and lower her head backward until it touched the floor, all the while keeping to the rhythmic movements she had learned. When Nadire announced that her pupil had taken to the lessons with amazing speed, Sarah felt inordinately proud.

That evening the Sultan Harun summoned her for the second time, and she went to him dressed as she had been the night before, the filmy veil once again in place and her tall, slender body only half clothed. This time she was escorted by a pair of eunuchs she had not seen before. When she entered the sultan's room and heard the door close behind her, her heart pounding with hope, she saw the purple pillow and mask had been placed on a small marble-topped table beside the bed.

Sarah gave it no thought. She had done all the talking she planned to about art and beauty; freedom was uppermost on her mind. Harun must have learned the truth of her story. Understanding the horror of her situation, he would let her go. She could believe nothing less.

When he came into the room a moment later, he answered her hurried question with a shake of his head. "I have heard nothing of this ship you describe. The *Leviathan* was lost in a storm."

Sarah stared at him in disbelief. "Then you do not believe me. You do not plan to let me go."

"Women are excitable," he explained. "Creatures of feeling, not of thought. It is your great charm."

Sarah did not feel charming in the least, and she whirled from him, trying to decide what to do next.

"Did your father not beat you?" the sultan asked. "It would have done you much good."

"My father has never laid a hand on me," Sarah declared hotly.

"I believe, Sarah Whitlock, that was a serious mistake. You must be taught obedience, as all women must. Only in this way can men and women exist together in peace."

He spoke with finality. Sarah knew that arguing with him would be like talking to the tiles. In some ways, Harun and her father were alike.

"And I am to learn this obedience here."

"Do not entertain thoughts of leaving. Your fate has been sealed."

"But that's barbaric," she cried as she turned to face him once again. Wrapping her arms around her bare middle, she began to pace the room. "Such a thing as this could never happen in England.''

"I forgive you for your impatience, although I should order the whip for your back. My father and his father before him would have put you to death.''

Sarah did not want his forgiveness; she wanted his permission to leave—the room, the seraglio, and Constantinople—as fast as she could.

"What good is my presence to you?'' she said, trying a more conciliatory tone.

"What good, indeed?'' he said with a sigh. "You were to be sold into the harem of my son Mustafa. My old friend the Kizlar Agasi intervened, hoping you would stir the fire in my loins again.''

"But—''

"Not even the lovely Sarah with her pale hair and eyes the color of the sky can perform such a miracle. Such desires were buried alongside the woman I loved.''

Sarah remembered Nadire talking about his number one *kadin*.

"Was she always obedient?''

"Perhaps not all the time,'' Harun said fondly.

"Well, then—''

"Enough. Do not try to compare yourself with her. As much as I would like to grant your wish for freedom, you must surely see it is impossible. If your story were true and my people saved you by bringing you to me, then perhaps you could be returned to the embassy. But you have chosen to lie, and there is little doubt that you would relate terrible tales of the imagination to the exalted ambassador. Never would your countrymen believe that you have been treated so well. A scandal would result. And perhaps more, a rift between our peoples. This I cannot have. My women are proud to be in the seraglio. In time, you will share their view.''

Never, Sarah vowed. She must escape.

"That is all I wish of you tonight," said the sultan. "I am suddenly weary and wish to be alone."

Sarah was more than weary. She was eaten with fury. Bidding Harun good night, she slipped into the passageway outside his room, her scarf and veil once again covering her blond hair and English face. She knew that in the dark she would look very much like any of the other women in the harem, especially with her eyes made up with kohl, a little taller maybe—at five feet six inches she was as tall as many of the men—but not so grotesque that she would stand out in the middle of the night.

Allowed to walk back unescorted to her quarters at the hour of midnight, she understood that Harun was certain she would not escape. As much as he tried to understand the ways of the West, he did not understand how his will could be disobeyed, certainly not within the walls of his Grand Seraglio.

Harun was wrong.

Outside his door, instead of turning left down the dimly lit passageway that led to the rooms of the harem, she turned right and slipped into the courtyard, slipping off her jangling jewelry as she walked and dropping the golden pieces onto the grass. Twenty yards more and she was through the Gate of Felicity.

Luck was with her. The strolling guards, grown used to tranquil nights, were standing away from the open gateway and were deep in a discussion of their own.

In the larger courtyard beyond the gate, she hugged the walls, edging slowly toward the roofless passageway that ran alongside the divan. Her goal was as it had been when she first planned her escape—the imperial stables. She glanced up at the sky and was grateful for the cloud cover which hid both the moon and the stars.

A door to the meeting room opened, and light spilled onto the passageway. Sarah pressed herself against the wall. A man appeared, a tall, thin figure. Very thin. Much too thin. He turned, and she saw the scar on his face. Her heart stopped, and she bit her lip until it bled; but she did not make a sound.

He was speaking to someone unseen in the room in the language he had used aboard the *Leviathan*. She recognized it now as Turkish.

The few words she had learned from Nadire did her no good. Only one utterance stood out. A name. Harun. The malevolent look on the brute's face told her he did not speak of his sultan with affection.

He gestured with one forefinger across the base of his throat, then he laughed, an evil light shining in his eyes.

Sarah understood. Harun was to die, and by this man's hand. A throat cut in the middle of the night. If she had remained in the sultan's quarters, she would have shared his fate.

Her hand moved involuntarily to her throat, and she remembered a ship's deck, a tangle of bodies, the face of the kindly captain staring up at her. She had held him tightly, but no matter how much she prayed, she had been unable to keep the life within him.

Suddenly she forgot how Harun had been determined to keep her prisoner for the rest of her days, and only to save himself embarrassment before the English government. His life was in danger, and he must be warned. But definitely from outside the seraglio. The safest place for her right now was deep in the British embassy. Surely they would listen to her there.

It was in the sultan's interest, as well as her own, that she get away tonight.

First she must find out the identity of the unseen conspirator in the room, so she waited for Scarface to leave.

He shifted, and the light extended farther across the passageway and caught the curved toes of her slippers. Sarah edged backward. Her foot scraped against a rock, and the sound echoed in the night, capturing the attention of the one man in all the world she most wanted to avoid.

Scarface lunged for her. In a movement designed to take him by surprise, she ducked past him and ran for her life into the darkness, no longer trying to be quiet. She prayed for the guards to hear and thunder to her rescue, distracting her pursuer from his intents.

Yells came from behind her, and then an alarm was sounded; but Sarah did not slow her pace. The twisting passageway seemed endless. She glanced over her shoulder and made out the figures of men hurrying after her. At that moment the moon drifted from behind a cloud, and she saw to her dismay that they were waving the curved blades of wicked Turkish scimitars above their heads. She doubted she would have time for explanation before one in their number cut her down and claimed he was only defending his sultan.

Always fleet of foot, she hurtled onward, running blindly, punching at the passing doors in a desperate attempt to find one that was unlocked.

When she least expected it, one narrow, splintered door gave way, and she found herself in a pitch-black room. She slammed the door closed, stumbled over objects, heard a deep muttered curse and a woman's moan, and throwing herself forward, suddenly found herself through another doorway and into what appeared in the moonlight as a narrow alleyway. The wall of the serai loomed ten feet high to the right and left as far as she could see.

The sight of a wagon against the wall to the left directed her path of retreat. It took more agility than she had ever before used to jump into the bed, grip her hands on the rough stone of the wall's top, and haul herself up and over. She dropped to the ground, a shrub breaking her fall. Sarah ignored the scratches on her bare arms. She was outside the serai.

But she was not free of danger. The guards would be upon her in an instant. She took her bearings. The hill on which the palace rested sloped down to the water, and to the docks. She knew of no other place of refuge, only that she did not want to be trapped on some blocked street in the city.

If necessary she would throw herself into the Golden Horn and drown as the world thought she already had. Anything but fall victim to one of those slashing swords. Too well she knew what they could do.

Using the moonlight to guide her way, she began to run in the direction she prayed was right. Behind her came a lone, unintelligible shout. She paused to glance over her shoulder. A swarm of dark figures poured over the wall. The moonlight glinted on the blades of their swords; but a cloud drifted overhead, and all was once again in darkness.

But not before they had spied her standing stupidly a hundred yards away.

Sarah turned and moved like the wind, unable to breathe or think, instinct guiding her to what must be safety. She had no hope, only desperation. The filmy silk of her trousers rustled as she ran, her slippered feet barely touching the ground.

Behind her came a chorus of yells. In the squat dark buildings that she hurried past, lights flickered into life, and one or two doors opened; but no one came out into the street to offer help. She was not tempted to cry for rescue. No lone mortal could save her now.

She stumbled once onto the rough cobblestones, righted herself, and was grateful she had received only a few scrapes in the fall. The pain was negligible, as was the chill of the night air against her half-naked body.

The sound of hard, hurried footsteps behind her grew louder, but the shouts had stopped. The pursuers were intent on only one thing—her capture and, she feared, her execution. Odalisques could not be allowed to escape the Grand Seraglio, especially those who overheard conspiracies against Harun.

She would not let them win. The smell of water— real or imagined, she did not know which—came to her, and she set her course in its direction. Panic subsided, and with an extra burst of speed she hurtled down the hill and into the dark.

Chapter Six

Angel was dead.

Standing on an isolated section of wharf fronting the Horn, the night settling around him, Jake was surprised at how much the news shook him.

The only time he had seen the woman he dubbed Angel was on the deck of the frigate *Leviathan* answering his bold greeting, her hair blowing free and her smile beaming into the day. All golden like the sun itself, she had seemed to come from the heavens. She had radiated life.

And now the ship carrying her was on the bottom of the Aegean, victim of the storm that he, in his smaller and more vulnerable craft, had been able to outrace. According to a sailor down the way, all on board the frigate had been lost.

"'Twere a real tragedy," the sailor said. "Served under Captain Reynolds meself more'n once. Not a finer man to be found between here and Liverpool."

"Anyone witness how it happened?" Jake asked.

"Flotsam, is all. And it don't talk. None living left to tell tales."

"Any chance of survivors?" Jake persisted, remembering how he had decided she was a spoiled

77

brat and had thus dismissed her from his mind. He felt a curious need to apologize.

The sailor had looked at him with scorn, and there had been nothing left for Jake to do but continue making his way into the night toward the lonely stretch of wharf where he was moored.

Scratching at the beard he had sported for the past few weeks, Jake stared into the dark waters swirling around the dhow. All was quiet around him. The hour was long past midnight; clouds obscured the moon and stars, leaving only the lanterns from faraway boats to light the area. It was a fit setting for mourning the dead.

If that was what he was doing. He could not imagine what had come over him.

"Jake."

The sultry sound of a woman's voice drifted to him from out of the sleeping quarters on the dhow's aft deck. Overhead clouds shifted for a moment, and moonlight bathed the curved roof of the shelter he had constructed with such care. He thought of the woman inside, of her incredibly full breasts and narrow waist and the wonderfully wide hips that swayed when she walked. She claimed in her broken English to be a dancer. He hoped so. In his experience, dancers had marvelous muscle control.

"Jake," she called again, and he dropped all remembrances of the lost ship and of the fair-haired beauty who had, after all, been little more than a dream. He had a long-overdue celebration awaiting him. He was ready for a good time.

Arranging a meeting with the sultan had taken two weeks longer than he'd anticipated. Sultans and their viziers didn't believe every story of promised treasures that came their way. As it turned out, Bandit had known one of the palace guards—a distant cousin, he claimed. The guard had helped him convince someone of more exalted rank to listen and to make an appointment, but it had been up to Jake to make the presentation.

Yesterday he had been escorted into the serai by a member of the imperial court, who must have known any transaction concerning the mask would not be strictly legal. Witnesses to the meeting were limited to Jake's escort, who turned out to be a vizier from the divan, and a pair of guards, one of whom was Bandit's cousin.

Jake had gone in with confidence, sure of the beauty and value of the mask. Further, he thought his beard made him look rather distinguished, gave him the air of one to be reckoned with.

All had gone well. Jake's share of the gold, more than he had ever seen in his life, was stashed in the dhow's small galley until he could decide just what to do with it. Bandit had discreetly gone ashore with his portion of the money. Then Jake had, of course, found a woman, the buxom beauty who seemed as eager as he for a midnight tryst aboard the dhow. He could not for the life of him recall her name, but he remembered everything else about her that was important.

Determined to be uninterrupted, he had anchored away from the other boats. Already his body was responding to the thought of what awaited him. It had been a long time.

He cradled the bottle of Greek wine that he had gone ashore to purchase. The talk with the sailor had interrupted his quick return, but he pushed that delay from his mind. In a moment he would be cradling something far softer than a glass bottle.

He thought of those breasts.

He moved to step aboard.

The patter of running feet gave him pause.

He turned at the sound of deep, hurried gasps for breath. A woman's soft cry drifted out of the darkness, but before he could get a clear idea about what was happening, a body collapsed against him, knocking him off balance.

Fighting to remain upright, he loosened his hold on the bottle of wine, which fell through the narrow space between the boat and the dock and disappeared into the waters of the Horn.

He righted himself and the night creature who had landed against him with such force. They stood close to the pier's edge. He gripped warm, bare shoulders, his fingers meeting the resilience of soft skin.

"What—"

Deep, ugly shouts came from one of the dark alleyways leading onto the isolated wharf. Forgetting whatever he meant to say, he jerked his head toward the sound. Again the fickle moon drifted from behind a cloud, and he stared, stupefied, at the lone figure emerging from the shadows into the silver light, a sword brandished above his head. He came straight for Jake.

Before Jake could react, a horde of men, similarly armed, erupted from the alley and followed in the first man's path. From a distance of fifty yards, they appeared to be seven feet tall and bent on one aim: rending asunder whatever got in their way.

A muted cry sounded against his shirt; it was no louder than the mew of a frightened kitten. The woman in his arms looked up at him. Above her veil a pair of painted eyes were barely visible in the night, but in their depths he read stark fear.

Jake figured there was no time to ask for an explanation. The night creature pushed past him and jumped onto the deck of the craft just as a voluptuous naked figure emerged from the shelter, clutching her bundled clothes against her breast. The bodies of the two women brushed against one another in passing.

Jake watched helplessly as his erstwhile guest for the evening climbed awkwardly out of the boat and onto the wharf, her skin smooth and tawny in the ghostly light. Moving fast, she disappeared into the night.

Jake had no time to call her back, his attention being occupied by the slashing curved blade swooping down in an arch toward his throat. The first of the assassins had arrived.

Jake ducked, his elbow landing with precision against the solar plexus of the marauder and his fist coming down heavily on the man's wrist. The sword fell with a clang to the dock. Struggling for breath, the man dropped to his knees.

In one smooth motion Jake scooped the weapon into his hand and brought its sharp edge downward against the rope securing the rear of the dhow to the nearest post. He scrambled toward the prow of the boat, repeated the action, then jumped aboard just as the remainder of the horde pounded across the wharf and pulled to a halt at the water's edge.

With a mighty shove, Jake set the boat into the slowly moving waters of the Horn and grabbed for the pistol he kept on deck.

The closest man leaped toward him, and Jake fired. The marauder landed at the edge of the dhow, his feet seeking purchase, his arms waving as if in supplication to be allowed aboard. He teetered precariously, body arched and, with a rush of air and a groan, fell backward, blood darkening the front of his shirt. His head struck the dock, and like the bottle of wine before him, he sank below the surface of the

Horn and did not rise.

A second man jumped; he, too, landed in the murky inlet and splashed about in the dark, yelling curses whose precise nature Jake could easily imagine. The others dropped back.

Jake ignored the scantily clad figure huddled on the deck against the low waist of the dhow. He had other things to think about—a mild night wind and still waters holding priority for the moment. Ashore the men scattered. The dhow moved slowly twenty . . . thirty feet from the dock and, he prayed, away from immediate danger.

The uninvited passenger glanced up once toward the dock. Again came the kittenish cry of distress, and she shifted her body deeper into the shadows on the deck.

"You're safe enough now," Jake growled, more to himself than to her since he had no idea what language she spoke.

In truth, he was not at all certain of safety.

Skillfully he unfurled the sail and set it into the wind, wondering as he worked how long the bastards would take to find a ship of their own—a faster vessel that might easily trap them in the sluggish waters of the Horn. Used to the help of Bandit, he had to scramble about to take advantage of the scant night breeze. He had no intention of losing his boat or his life.

Grim-faced, he worked with cool efficiency, and the dhow slipped past the boats moored to the long line of wharfs, their masts and rigging rising beside him like leafless winter trees, their flickering lanterns adding light to the occasional moon. He heard men's laughter, and once or twice the high-pitched giggle of a woman, and thought of his lost celebration.

Then he remembered the scimitars. As best as he

could judge, there had been a half dozen men after him. Or more precisely, after the pitiful figure huddled on the deck. He could make out no details about her appearance and right then didn't give a damn. All he knew was that she had a great deal to explain.

He muttered a curse. She had better be damned pitiful when he gave her a chance to talk, or else she would find herself in the drink. He only hoped she spoke English. If not, he would somehow find Bandit to translate.

She stirred once, and he felt her gaze on him. Wide-set and thick-lashed above her veil, her eyes were all he could make out about her—except, of course, for the graceful curve of her body as she sat, knees bent under her, on the hard deck. He was rescuing a woman, all right. No doubt about that. Something about those eyes was familiar to him; he had no idea what it could be.

In the dim light, he knew she could make out little about him—except, of course, that he was a man and that he wasn't coming at her with a sword.

"Must be a better way for you to get a boat ride," he said. "This one's a little dramatic for my tastes."

She made no response, instead jerking her gaze away and staring across the aft deck and over the roof of the sleeping quarters, as if she were watching for pursuers.

She looked small and frightened, and Jake found it impossible to hold on to his anger. He had been more than a little scared himself, a fact that brought him no shame. He had a distinct dislike for unsheathed blades, especially those aimed in his direction.

Turning back to the sail, he tried to imagine what his new passenger had done to arouse such furor but could come up with nothing other than murder or theft. Not even sex offered and then denied could arouse such anger—unless she were very, very good. He would leave it to her to fill in the details.

At last they reached the juncture where the Horn flowed into the Sea of Marmara, and he navigated the dhow into the broad waters that flowed through the Dardanelles and emptied into the Aegean. Caught on the tide, the boat scooted across the calm surface, and Jake took a deep breath. For the first time he realized how tense he had been.

Securing the rigging of the lateen sail, he began to relax. "Looks like we've gotten away," he said, expecting no reply.

"Look again."

Jake stared at her for a moment. "You speak English."

She gestured impatiently, and Jake followed the path of her gaze. Looming behind them in the moonlight and moving fast was another ship, larger than the dhow, its trio of sails catching the night wind to full advantage.

"Damn!"

Nothing to do but escape. He had all that gold to spend—and, of course, an enticing fugitive to question.

A dark cloud moved across the moon, plunging the boat into darkness. Jake took it as a good sign. He couldn't watch the progress of the pursuers, but neither could they watch him.

"Think you can be of help?" he asked.

"Tell me what to do."

No hysterics. Good.

She seemed to know her way about boats, for which Jake was grateful—if he could feel gratitude toward anyone who was causing him so much trouble. They sailed through the night under the blessed cover of clouds, but Jake knew the pursuers were still somewhere behind them. He chose an evasive action, navigating the dhow across the wide body of water and close to one of the small islands that dotted the sea.

In a dark, shallow slip of water, he made preparations to anchor.

"What are you doing?" she asked, alarmed.

"What they don't expect. They think we're getting out of here as fast as we can, but there's too little traffic about, leaving us an open target. We'll wait 'til morning to move on."

"I suppose we're nowhere near the British embassy," she said as she stood at the far edge of the deck away from him, her arms wrapped around her bare middle. She had long ago removed her veil, but he had yet to get a good look at her face.

"You suppose right. Besides, it might not be a good idea to go there anytime soon. The men tonight didn't seem the kind to give up on their pursuit. They followed us by boat, remember? They're perfectly capable of lying in wait near the embassy."

The boat rocked in the undulating waves of the inlet.

"So it's just the two of us for a while," she said.

"Unless you've others that would like to come aboard. You seem very good at arranging my passenger list."

"There's no need to be sarcastic."

"A debatable point. I'll be pleasant enough once I'm sure we're safe. And once I know what the hell is going on."

He turned his attention toward securing the dhow. At last satisfied he had done what he could, he settled himself on the deck and leaned against the wall of the sleeping quarters, a scant three feet from his lone companion, who sat in the darkness opposite him.

A whiff of perfume mingled with the sea air, and Jake thought about her painted eyes and soft warm skin. He had to imagine the particulars of her features: high cheekbones, a small, straight nose, and full, sensuous lips with maybe the hint of a pout.

Jake's thoughts lingered on the lips. His blood was still pumping hard from the earlier anticipation of the dancer and from the arrival of the scimitars. A smile broke his solemn visage. Perhaps, for all its strange beginnings, the night wouldn't be a total waste after all.

"I rather think you owe me something," he said.

"An explanation?"

"We can start there."

"I don't know who you are."

"Jake Price."

"That's hardly enough."

"You didn't ask for even that a half hour ago. Sorry but I don't come with references."

She sighed. "It is I who should apologize. I'm rather shaken. This sort of thing doesn't happen to me all the time, Mr. Price."

"I don't imagine it does."

"Please accept my thanks for all that you have done. I'm afraid I've begun to see enemies where they do not exist. You couldn't possibly be involved in any of this." Her shudder was visible even in the dim light. "Those men . . . they were trying to capture me."

"So I gathered. Any particular reason why?"

"They were angry."

"An understatement, Miss—"

"Whitlock. Sarah Whitlock."

"So was I angry, Sarah, when you made your appearance. I suspect it's one of the emotions you arouse in men. But thus far I haven't come at you with a sword."

"You're American, aren't you?" She didn't wait for him to respond. "I've always heard Americans can be quite blunt spoken."

"I'll have to be careful. I wouldn't want to upset you."

"Don't be absurd."

Again she fell into silence.

Jake knew she was stalling. What kind of trouble could she possibly have fallen into? In this crossroads of Europe and Asia, it could be most anything.

"There's this man," she said at last.

Jake kept quiet during her pause.

"I found myself in a situation that I did not care for. I wanted to get away."

Perhaps his final guess had been right. She had teased someone with offered favors and then tried to back off. Sarah Whitlock would play hell teasing him.

"This man," Jake said. "He must have had other ideas. I take it the hounds chasing you tonight were sent by him."

"Rather loyal, aren't they? It's hard to find such devotion to duty back in London."

She sounded very much like a lady, despite the contrary evidence of her appearance. When she should have been in hysterics, she was calm. Caught by her charm, he had to fight the urge to pull her to him and find out just what there was about her that would push a man to send an army to track her down.

He barely managed to hold off. Even in these bizarre circumstances, she had an air of gentility about her that both enticed him and held him at bay, which didn't mean necessarily that she would protest his advances, when and if he decided to make them.

Jake had the strong feeling there were hours of leisurely exploration ahead for them both.

"You make me forget how frightened I was," she said.

"Good."

"Almost."

Jake caught the quiver in her voice. Sarah Whitlock, whoever she was, was not in control of herself as much as she had first appeared.

"The men . . . the swords—" A sob stopped her.

So she wasn't far from hysterics, after all.

Jake was struck by an uncharacteristic feeling of charity, although he told himself it was only a dislike for a crying woman. "Perhaps you shouldn't try to talk more until morning," he offered.

"Perhaps not." She drew a few deep breaths before adding, "There's really nothing else to tell. At least nothing you need to know."

Liar. Jake kept the opinion to himself. He was beginning to like the air of mystery surrounding her, but it was one that needed clearing up. After almost losing his life in her behalf, she owed him the truth. Going right back to the city might easily prove dangerous. He hadn't been joking about the thugs probably lying in wait.

"It will be daylight soon," he said.

"I don't know if that's good or bad," she said.

"Any morning you wake up alive and well should be considered good."

"You have a point."

He could sense her smile in the dark.

Jake insisted she crawl into the sleeping quarters and try to sleep. He thought about crawling in after her and offering whatever comfort seemed appropriate but decided to wait. He wanted Miss Sarah Whitlock rested and as ready as he.

88

"We'll set sail before long," he said. "Don't worry, Sarah. You'll be taken care of."

She didn't ask him what he had in mind.

Using a blanket as a pillow, Jake stretched out and tried to assess just what kind of situation he was in. An English woman—correction, a *beautiful, half-naked* English woman—had crashed into him in the night, chased by a half dozen armed men. She had not exhibited hysterics, had evaded explaining her situation, and except for a halfhearted attempt or two to cover her exposed middle, had seemed at ease with her state of undress.

She was an adventuress of some kind; he would bet money on it. Maybe a female equivalent of himself. He was especially glad that the two of them spoke the same language. When he whispered to a woman, he liked her to understand.

Jake stared at the dim outline of the Asian shore a dozen yards away and thought about the isolated strip of land he was temporarily calling home. And about the hut. Thanks to Bandit's thoughtfulness, the boat carried enough provisions for at least a week.

He and Miss Sarah Whitlock were strangers in a strange land. Anything could happen, especially after the bizarre happenings of tonight. Now that they were both safe—or at least they were for the time being—he found himself able to shrug. The two of them could have a cozy little tryst to make up for the one he had missed. And it need not last for only one day or one night.

"Yes, my pretty one," he whispered into the pink light of early dawn, "I'll see that you're taken care of very well indeed."

Chapter Seven

By the time the sun was sitting full and golden above the eastern horizon, traffic on the waterway was heavy. At Jake's insistence, his passenger remained out of sight in the aft deck quarters.

"There's lots of boats like mine, and back in the Horn no one got a good look at me. It was far too dark. But if you hang about, I might as well put a sign up that reads *Here she is.* If," he added, "you think they'll still be after you."

"They will" came the muffled response.

She looked out only once—when he was handing her a breakfast of bread and cheese. All he caught was a glimpse of tangled blond curls and a paint-streaked face.

"I must look a fright," she said, keeping head bent and eyes averted.

"Not in the least," Jake said and meant it. "Get much rest?"

"No. I kept imagining. . . ." Her voice trailed off.

"You're safe now," he assured her. "Try again to sleep. I'll call you if I need help."

"You're being very kind," she said after a moment.

Jake didn't feel kind, just curious about the kind of

90

woman he had on board. The adventuress he had decided last night? Or the victim of some strange circumstances. They would have to be pretty damned strange to explain away her silken trousers and painted face—not to mention the scimitars.

He waited for her to say more, something provocative, something to give him a clue. When she didn't, he shrugged off his disappointment. Delicacy of approach must be her English way.

He concentrated on getting them to the island fast. At first all the passing craft looked suspicious; after a while, he was able to ignore them. Without incident the dhow skimmed across the wide, smooth sea, along the length of the narrow Dardanelles, and into the broad, deep waters of the Aegean. Checking on Sarah, Jake found her deep in sleep and made no attempt to disturb her.

Throughout the day the wind held steady, and by afternoon he brought the craft into the protected waters of the island's crescent cove.

It was only after he had dropped anchor that she stirred and made her first real appearance of the day. And what an appearance it was—filmy red trousers wrinkled and pressed to her slender hips and long legs, her bodice cupping her breasts with enticing efficiency, her hair that glorious mass of golden tangles. She continued to keep her face turned from him, insisting still that she "looked a fright."

Jake disagreed. Since its abrupt beginning, this whole incident had taken on the air of an Arabian fantasy: a beautiful damsel in distress . . . a hero—a wealthy hero—to her rescue . . . an uncharted island awaiting their arrival.

He scratched at his beard, which had grown thick and fast. He wondered if she would like it rubbed against her soft face.

91

She scanned the island. "It looks uninhabited."

"It is. But I've built a shelter at the edge of the beach."

"Oh, there it is. Looks rather flimsy, doesn't it?"

"It serves its purpose."

"I'd like a bath if that's possible." Slender fingers brushed against her trousers. "I don't suppose you have anything more suitable I could put on."

"I can come up with something."

She hesitated. "I'm rather embarrassed, you see."

Jake was surprised at her touch of shyness. Or maybe she was just playing coy. Once they were ashore and knew each other better, he would have to ask her which.

"Trust me," he said.

She sighed. "I've trusted you up until now. Surely you won't disappoint me."

Behind her, Jake grinned. He liked the implications of her words.

"I'll make an effort not to. You'll find a pond of fresh water close to the hut. Rain water catches there, and an underground spring feeds it, too. Should do all right for a wash-up."

Jake tossed a rope ladder over the side of the dhow, but before he could help her overboard, she scrambled unaided into the waist-high water and, with slippers held overhead, made for shore. Slowly she emerged onto the beach, crimson trousers rendered transparent by the sea. She might as well have been naked. He watched the view in silent appreciation and decided he could grow rather fond of the styles of the East. Especially when they covered—or more accurately, revealed—such a delectable Western body.

Gathering a bundle of clean clothing and grooming supplies, along with a couple of blankets, he followed.

She skipped across the surface of the sand. "It's hot," she shouted over her shoulder.

"Put on your shoes," he called.

She laughed. The sound was silvery. "Don't want to. It feels so good to be alive."

Watching her run across the beach, Jake had the strange feeling that he had known her forever and at the same time that he didn't know her at all. Could he possibly be wrong about the kind of woman she was? He hoped not as he felt a familiar urge begin to stir.

He tried to reconcile the memory of last night's nearly hysterical woman and today's laughing temptress and was left more intrigued than ever.

She disappeared into the brush behind the hut. He listened to a thrashing about and a brief cry of "Hello." She sounded like a child at play. Or a coquette. "I've found the pond."

He removed a clean shirt from his bundle, deciding it would cover her as much as the exotic clothing she had worn last night. His long legs took him quickly along the path she had not seen. Through the low-hanging branch of a tree, he could make out her still-clad figure in the clearing, one foot dipping into the water.

He draped the shirt on the end of the branch. "Here," he said. "This ought to do. There's a comb and a bit of soap in the pocket."

She sheltered herself behind a thick bush. "You think of everything," she said.

"I'll scrub your back if you would like," he suggested.

A long silence. "No, thanks. I'll be all right by myself. As I said, you *do* think of everything."

Jake grinned. "My mind's been working"—and a few other parts, he could have added—"ever since you crashed into me last night. When you're finished, I'll be waiting in the hut."

First a quick swim, however, and he hurried back to the inlet near where the dhow was anchored, stripped the damp shirt and pants from his body, and tossed them into the sand near the water's edge. The shallows felt warm against his legs as he waded away from the shore, then colder as the ocean floor fell sharply away.

Diving beneath the surface, his powerful arms pulling him through the water, he felt a strange elation sweep through him. By all rights he should be exhausted, but he felt better than he had in a long time. Exhilarated, in fact. Damned strange, considering the near disaster of last night.

Ah, but he was to have his reward.

And there was all that gold.

The gold. He had thought of it only briefly since the delightfully mysterious Sarah had jumped aboard. Funny how she managed to occupy his mind. The water supporting him wasn't cool enough to drive the gathering heat from his body.

He would pull out the cache of coins later, just to remind himself of the good fortune that had befallen him. And it had all started with rescues, first of Bandit and later Sarah. He might turn into an honorable man after all.

He continued to swim for a quarter of an hour, giving Sarah time to finish her ablutions. Ashore he pulled on a clean pair of trousers and headed for the hut. He would unearth the bottle of whiskey, stretch out on the blanket, and wait.

First he ought to shave. Considering her delicate English skin and all, she might not like a bearded man. He himself wasn't all that fond of the itchy thing and had brought razor and soap ashore for himself. Yep. A shave and a drink and then, the way he figured it, Sarah.

Grinning in anticipation, he headed for the hut.

Sarah took her time in the pond, using Jake's bar of soap to scrub the last scent of patchouli from her skin and to shampoo her hair. At its deepest point, the water came up to her waist, and she had to lean back to rinse the last of the suds from her gradually untangling curls.

She did not mind the inconvenience. How pleasant it was to bathe herself once again and to dispense with the smelly eggs that Nadire insisted would leave her hair shiny and thick.

Kneeling on the soft bottom of the pond, she rested her head on the surface of the water, strands of hair floating around her like radiating light, and stared up at the blue sky. Patches of white clouds passed overhead, and the sun filtered down through the trees. Somewhere a gull cried, reminding her of how close she was to the sea.

She let her mind wander. How truly glorious it was to be alive, and how miraculous. Twice she had brushed against death, on the *Leviathan* and on the mad chase through the city. She had no idea why she had survived the former, unless it was because the pirates wanted her for the slave market; the latter was entirely because of Jake Price.

She must be the luckiest woman on earth. Jake could have done terrible things to her—thrown her into the Horn or assaulted her in the sleeping quarters last night—but he was a gentleman through and through. And so brave.

She was struck by guilt that she should have been spared when the crew and passengers aboard the *Leviathan* had not. And then there was the Sultan

Harun. Away from the seraglio, she charitably forgot his intention of keeping her imprisoned. To his way of thinking, he was behaving in a perfectly understandable manner. Of course he was wrong, but he didn't deserve the fate that Scarface had planned. She definitely would have to do something about him. She would need to come up with some sort of a plan.

Not for long could she hold off speculations about Jake. He was the most wonderful man she had ever met, and it was not only because he was so brave. Her heart pounded every time she heard his deep American voice. It seemed to caress her. Silly thought, but she could not push it from her mind.

And, oh, it wasn't only her heart that reacted to him. Ever since their talk in the predawn hours, she had felt a funny tingling deep within her each time she glanced his way.

How absurd it all was. She never reacted in such an irrational fashion toward men. Not independent-minded Sarah, who wanted only to live a life of her choosing, beholden to no one, especially a man.

She wondered what he looked like beneath that scruffy beard. If the rest of him went along with those dark, probing eyes, he was quite handsome.

Not that she was moved by an attractive face or form.

Sarah pulled herself up short. Of course she was. Jake Price was tall and broad-shouldered and dark-haired. And he had wonderfully long, strong legs. She had gotten a glimpse of those when he walked out of the water; his damp trousers had left little for her to imagine—but a great deal about which she might speculate. She was shameless, indeed, as Papa would be quick to tell her.

Who could resist such a hero? Last night, seized by terror as she ran through the ink-black streets of the city, she had known no mortal man could save her. Then Jake had presented himself. Thus far he had proven himself extraordinary in rescuing her from harm. She fully expected him to continue in the same vein.

She felt a warmth steal through her that had nothing to do with the sun. She eased beneath the surface of the cool pond and came up slowly, water streaming from her hair. Pulling herself to a grassy bank, she squeezed as much moisture as she could from the mass of wet curls and set to work with the comb. Jake's comb. Jake's pond.

With an insight that took her breath away, Sarah understood what was behind her thoughts. Whether it was the lushness of her surroundings, or the pleasure of being free after so long in the seraglio, or the magnetism of the man awaiting her, she could not say, but for the first time in her life she wanted to make love.

The realization sent a shiver down her spine. How unreal and inevitable it all seemed: a handsome man . . . a small island . . . and Sarah. Jake stirred her as no one ever had, and she was certain she stirred him. He was a gentleman, all right—at least an American version—keeping his hands off her despite the burning look she had spotted in his eyes.

A gentleman through and through.

He did not have to continue in that role.

If she read those eyes right and she didn't prove faint-hearted, just for a while she would let herself be Jake's woman. Or rather, she would let him be her man.

Her resolution was firm. Everyone had decided who would be the first to bed her. Her father had said it would be Ralph Pettigrew. The slave Nadire had been convinced no less than the Sultan Harun would do, and she had had a seraglio full of eunuchs and guards to back up her belief.

As long as she was destined for someone's arms, she most certainly preferred that someone be Jake Price. Sensing her innocence, he would be gentle. Valuing the gift she gave him, he would show her respect. Sarah's breath caught. Losing her virginity was going to prove very enjoyable indeed.

And once that was out of the way, she would tell him the truth about her troubles in the Grand Seraglio. Last night—or rather early this morning—she had been hesitant, worried that somehow he might use the information for profit. And she had remembered the vow to reveal all only within the walls of the embassy. It had seemed right to keep the details of her recent past to herself.

What a cynic she was turning into! She considered herself a good judge of character. Jake was an honest and honorable man.

When she was satisfied her hair was free of tangles, she stood and let the shimmering sun bathe her in its drying warmth. Nadire would be pleased that she was enjoying such simple sensations. Nadire taught that pleasure was everything; it was the way in the seraglio.

Sarah remembered the seductive dance that Nadire had shown her; slowly her feet began to move in time to the remembered rhythm, and her hips to undulate the way she had been taught. She couldn't quite bring herself to look down at her naked body to see if she was doing everything right, but she had a feeling that she was. Still, she could not manage to kneel and bend her head backward to the ground, but she figured that any man watching would not mind too much.

What would Jake think if he could see her now?

She smiled. Once he got over the shock of her exhibition, he would probably approve. He might be a hero, but he certainly wasn't a saint. Had he not offered to scrub her back?

Maybe, just maybe, after the completion of the "act," as a friend had called it upon returning from her honeymoon—somewhat disappointed, Sarah had thought—she would dance for him. He might even give her a pointer or two.

Swept with a sudden impatience, she reached for the shirt Jake had so thoughtfully left her. Its tail hit her just above the knees. She liked the feel of the soft cloth next to her skin, and most of all she liked its scent. It reminded her of its owner. Jake Price radiated masculinity in a way no other man ever had. She hoped she did not disappoint him.

She hurried along the narrow path that led to the hut, peered into the open door, and saw Jake, his back to her, lying on a blanket on the far side of the center pole and greeting her with the sonorous sound of his snores. They weren't too loud, she thought, not at all like her dignified papa's, who could take the paint from the walls when he was in his deepest sleep.

She decided to let him have his rest. She stood and glanced toward the boat, where surely there was food aboard. He would be hungry when he awoke. She was ravenous now.

She gave a quick thought to her clean, dry shirt and decided to leave it on the beach. Naked, she waded to the boat, scrambled aboard by way of the rope ladder, and found what she was looking for—bread and cheese and fruit—in a larder below deck.

Fish might be appetizing. Sarah could taste its fried goodness right now. Only she didn't know how to catch one, and she couldn't clean and cook it if she did. Her education had been amazingly unhelpful for survival on a deserted isle.

Somehow she managed to get the foodstuffs back to the hut. Dressed once again in Jake's shirt, she settled herself outside and waited for him to stir. When her head began to nod, she did not try to fight sleep.

The cool breeze coming off the water awakened her, and she sat up with a start. The sun was resting on the far horizon, its pink light reflecting off the expanse of wine-colored sea.

She peered inside the hut. In the dark interior she could barely make out Jake shifting about on the blanket; she smiled in anticipation. Pushing aside an unexpected niggling doubt, she entered, lit the lamp resting on the room's lone table, and stood waiting for him to turn to her.

At last he did, sitting and turning so that the full illumination from the light fell on his face. Noticing that he had shaved, she boldly knelt beside him, and for the first time since meeting they got an unobstructed, close-up view of one another.

Sarah stared open-mouthed. "It cannot be," she said.

Jake returned the stare. "I don't believe it," he said.

"Neptune?" she whispered.

"Angel?" he whispered at the same time.

She studied him, even as he studied her. Her eyes drifted over the clean-shaven planes of his face, lingered for a minute at the shock of black hair that had fallen across his forehead, then drifted downward.

He was bare chested, just as he had been the first time she saw him, only close as she was, she could make out the fine dusting of chest hair that started just below his throat and narrowed like an arrow at the waist of his trousers.

There was no mistake. He was her Neptune.

She closed her eyes. What had he called her? Angel. She rather liked the sound.

Once again she looked at him.

"You were on the *Leviathan*," he said, his eyes dark and puzzled.

"And you were on the small boat."

"You're supposed to be dead."

Sarah was not sure those were the words she wanted to hear.

"Obviously I am not," she said, trying to be glad he had at least remembered her from that quick passing weeks ago.

"I don't understand," he said.

The painful memories swept into her mind. "I was rescued," she said, unable to put her thoughts into more exact words. The time was wrong to describe the horror she carried in the back of her mind. She would tell him everything later.

Lifting his hand to her face, he caught a stray curl between his fingers. She imagined she could feel his touch. Around Jake, even her hair tingled with anticipation.

"You're a lucky woman, Sarah, to have survived. And I'm a lucky man."

She smiled. Until today, she had not felt very lucky. The events of her life, which in these sultry summer months had taken on all the aspects of a nightmare, were turning into a wonderful and evocative dream.

"I've got us dinner from the boat," she said, shyness stealing over her.

"Good. I'll get the drinks for a toast."

While she brought in the food, Jake went to a corner of the hut and proceeded to dig into the dirt.

101

He came up with a burlap bag; from it he extracted the bottle of whiskey, which he held up with pride.

"Cheers," he said as he passed her the bottle. Sarah tried to be a good sport, but she could get down no more than a trickle and proceeded to embarrass herself by coughing. Some hellion she was turning out to be.

Worse, she had trouble swallowing her food. Jake kept studying her in the oddest manner, as if he could not quite decide what to make of her. She got the feeling she was disappointing him in some way.

When he declared he could not eat another bite, she set the food aside and, very businesslike brushed the crumbs from the blanket, moving carefully around the center pole since Jake had informed her that it was the primary support for the roof.

All the time she worked, she knew he was watching her, his back propped against the framework of a side wall of the small enclosure. She found her breathing becoming decidedly irregular, and the tingling returned to the base of her spine. Under his steady gaze, she felt her breasts swell and harden, but that was impossible.

"Come here," he ordered.

Her heart caught in her throat. Even while she thought about a cowardly escape through the open door, she found herself kneeling beside him. His fingers stroked her free-falling hair.

"Who are you, Sarah Whitlock?" he asked. Again, his voice was a caress. "You have me confused."

"A woman." She bit at her lower lip. "Nothing more."

"A woman is all I want."

Sarah could not breathe.

"My mystery woman," he said huskily. "Maybe it's time I found out a little something about you."

He brushed his lips against hers.

The feeling was electric. Sarah trembled.

"I'd like you to do that again," she said.

He complied, only this time the kiss was more lingering and the touch of his lips more sure. Sarah wanted to touch him, but in his half-naked state, she did not know where to put her hands. At last she rested tentative fingers against the tight sinews of his chest. She felt the stricture of his muscles, and within her own body there grew an aching need she had never known before.

He pulled her full into his embrace, shifting around until she was sitting on his lap, and she let her hands steal upward around his neck, her fingers coiling in the thick hair at his nape. She curled her body into his and delighted in the way the two of them seemed to fit so well against one another.

His lips moved against hers and parted, and she was startled by the touch of his tongue seeking entrance to her mouth. Before she could decide how to respond, she felt the rough tip of his tongue brush against hers. She tasted the saltiness of the sea and an indefinable sensation she could only describe as the taste of a man.

Strong hands stroked her back as his kiss deepened. One hand stole to her side, brushed against her breast, then cupped her fullness.

Sarah started. She had never been touched so intimately before. But she had no inclination to push him away.

He broke the kiss, his lips moving to the corners of her mouth, across her cheek, and down her angled neck to press against her pounding pulse.

She bit at her lower lip. "Tell me what to do, Jake," she whispered in a trembling voice.

He stopped. "What did you say?" he whispered to

her throat.

"I don't want to do the wrong thing," she said, suddenly certain that she had done just that.

He did not move.

Sarah stirred nervously. "You know, when we do the act."

Easing his embrace, he lifted his head, and Sarah rested her forehead against his, her arms still around his neck, only not quite so tightly as before. She listened as his breathing gradually slowed.

At last she said, "I shouldn't have talked, should I? Women aren't supposed to talk."

In response, he moved her off his lap, and she sat beside him on the blanket.

"Give me a minute," he said, his knees bent, his bare arms wrapped around them. Corded sinews lined the tight, brown skin.

She pulled her gaze away from the fascinating sight and was shaken by the dark look in his midnight-blue eyes.

"You're a virgin, aren't you?"

He made it sound like a crime.

"What has that got to do with anything? I know what we're going to do."

His lips flattened.

"In a way," she said.

"Then you know more than I."

Sarah felt the ground sink beneath her. "Then I really did something wrong, didn't I?"

"Not you. Me." His voice was filled with disgust.

He raked his fingers through his uncombed hair. "Damn! I should have known my luck wouldn't hold out."

"I don't have the vaguest idea what you're talking about. You haven't forced me into anything."

"Angel, I don't seduce virgins. It's about the only thing in the world I haven't tried, and I'm not about to start now."

"Even those who want to be seduced?"

"Especially the overeager ones. I figure they'll cause the most trouble later."

Stung, she said, "Why? Because they're disappointed?"

Jake merely looked at her. He shifted away and reached for the bottle of whiskey resting on the table.

Sarah was swept with a feeling of failure. Pride came to her rescue. "I was merely testing you. To see if you were the gentleman you have been until now. I am pleased to see that you are."

"Ha!"

Sarah's temper flared. "Not completely a gentleman, of course, but close enough." She stood and stared down at him. "Now if you will please show me where I am to sleep, I would be most grateful. The loan of a blanket would be appreciated. I've always wanted to sleep under the stars."

Jake stood beside her. "Don't bother, Angel. You can have the hut. I'll take the boat. And for God's sake pull down that shirt as far as you can. If I stand here much longer, I'm liable to lose the only scruple I have."

He paused in the doorway. "Besides, I don't want any angry father coming after me with a shotgun. The men last night were enough. In the morning you can tell me what the hell is going on with you."

Sarah stared in disbelief as he made his departure. In the suddenly quiet hut, she tried to organize her jumbled thoughts and feelings. The man had actually turned her down! The first man she had ever offered herself to, the man she had thought such

105

tender thoughts about only a short while before.

The man to whom she had planned to give her virginity! He hadn't wanted it! The thought was lowering indeed.

Collapsing onto the blanket, she set about deciding just how she could ever face him again.

Chapter Eight

Sarah dreamed that one of the Aegean's fabled sea monsters had come out of the deep to devour her as she slept upon a sandy beach. The shapeless mass of his scaly body hung with seaweed, his red eyes boring into her like beacons of fire, he rose out of the water with a roar and bore down upon her naked helplessness.

She screamed and sat up, only to find herself lost in a dark void.

"Having a nightmare, Angel? Something troubling your conscience?"

Heart pounding, Sarah fought against panic as she peered into the dark. She had been dreaming, nothing more. There was no beach and there was no monster, only a lonely, roughly made hut with a hard dirt floor—and someone speaking to her from the open door.

Again she screamed.

"It's only me, Sarah."

Only Jake Price? Sarah took several long, slow breaths. As she struggled to wakefulness, last night's humiliation came back in a rush. She had sooner face the sea monster than Jake.

She ran her fingers through her hair and blinked twice, trying to sort her thoughts. "What time is it?"

"It will be light soon. Long past time for us to have a talk."

He stood so still, and there was something in his voice, an edge of steel, that alarmed her more than the dream.

"Where is it?" he asked.

She squinted but could not make out anything about him except the dim outline of his tall, lean frame. She did not have to see more to realize he was furious.

Sarah wrapped her arms around her body and wished she were wearing more than just a man's shirt. A brace of pistols might do for a start. "Where is what?" she asked.

"Still the innocent, Angel? Except that this morning I'm not buying it."

"I don't know what you're talking about. Have you been drinking?"

"There wasn't enough in the bottle to do me much good. Couldn't sleep. A short while ago I started searching the ship for another, thinking Bandit might have hidden one away for an emergency. That's when I found it was gone."

"*What* was gone? You don't explain yourself very well."

"That makes two of us."

He strode into the hut, and as she scuttled backward, stopping solidly against the side wall, he skirted around the center post and lit the lamp, which he held aloft. Blinded by the light, she covered her eyes.

"Can't you turn that thing down?" she asked.

He returned the lamp to the table. "Not until I have the truth from you. For once."

"I don't know—"

Suddenly he was beside her on the blanket, his hands gripping her shoulders painfully, his angry face inches from hers. She realized with a start that in addition to not wearing a shirt, he was also without trousers. She was in the grip of a crazed and unclothed man.

"The gold, damn it! You took it yesterday when you got the food."

Sarah could think of nothing but his nakedness. "I don't know—"

He shook her, hard. "Stop it, Sarah."

Sarah would burn in hell before she let him know how much he was hurting her. "Get your hands off me," she hissed.

"Not until you tell me what I want to know."

His hold lessened slightly, enough to ease the sharp edge of pain but not enough to allow her to escape. Jake had truly gone mad. She doubted he was crazed by unsatisfied lust for her. He wanted gold.

"I assume you had some money hidden on the boat."

His eyes burned down on her like the monster of her dream. Much as she would have liked to look elsewhere, she could not decide on a place that would not unsettle her more.

"You damned well know I did," he said.

"I damned well did not know any such thing until you came in here like a lunatic. Is there a full moon outside? Perhaps that would explain your behavior."

She caught a look of hesitation on his face and hurried on.

"You either dreamed it up in the first place—a possibility I can by no means overlook—or you've misplaced it. Unless another of your women, one of your whores, took it. Have you actually seen it since I came on board? If you have, I'll eat your hat for breakfast.''

It was an ill-chosen boast, considering his state of undress; but at least he was giving her his undivided attention, and she hurried on. "The woman who was on your boat two nights ago. She could have been carrying something when she left.''

She could see his mind working, remembering the broad-rumped figure that had scrambled onto the dock just after Sarah arrived.

"It would appear you have been fooled by a woman, all right, only I'm not the right one. You need to think with your brains, not your . . . your nether parts.''

She knew right away she had gone too far.

"And you, Angel, need to think before you speak.'' His eyes roamed down to her shamelessly exposed legs stretched out in front of her. She twisted them beneath her bottom and under the protection of the shirt as best she could.

"You're undoubtedly right, of course,'' he continued. "I left the boat for a quarter hour to get a bottle of wine. She used the time well. It would seem I'm out the treasure as well as the romp.''

Sarah swallowed. The fire of anger had completely gone from his eyes, replaced by a dark speculation that unnerved her even more. "We all make mistakes,'' she said.

"And a thinking man tries to rectify what he can. You told me to think, Angel.'' His voice softened to the intimidating caress of yesterday, and his hands stroked her shoulders. "Would you like to know what I'm thinking now?''

Trapped between the wall of branches and his crouched body, she tried to hold on to what dignity she could. "It makes little difference to me.''

110

"I'm thinking that there's no way I can get back the gold, at least not without a great deal of effort. But as for the romp—" he unfastened the top button of her shirt, and his fingers burned against her skin— "that's more easily seen to."

Unable to tolerate his dark stare a moment longer, she directed her eyes to his throat—and immediately realized that was a mistake. He had such a strong neck, and of course there were those dark curls of black hair that marked his body so unlike that of a woman's.

"I'm a virgin," she said feebly. "Remember?"

"Somehow that doesn't seem to matter as much as it once did. Besides, you didn't care last night. Why should I? For all my troubles, I should get something out of this fiasco. You wanted me to tell you what to do only a few hours ago. I wasn't ready then." His fingers moved to the valley between her breasts. "I am now."

And to think she had believed he would treasure the gift of her innocence. In truth, he had reduced it to payment for other, more tangible losses. With a cry of rage, Sarah shoved against his chest and, catching him by surprise, sent him falling backward. Scrambling past him, she made for the door.

He grabbed the tail of her shirt, and she stumbled backward, falling hard across him, her hands pressing against his bare chest, the two of them sprawled across the rumpled blanket.

She managed to rise, but he pulled her back down beside him, his arms holding her tight, their bare legs in a tangle. "Ah, a woman with spirit. I just might like that, especially if the resistance doesn't go on too long. I wouldn't put it beyond you, Angel, to be playing games. Are you really a virgin? Let's find out."

111

The fight was enjoined, Sarah struggling to free his hold on her, twisting her head away from the lips that were moving inexorably toward hers. Only she knew she was fighting more than just him; she was fighting the hot feelings washing over her in waves. His powerful embrace locked them together so tightly that she could feel the full length of his body against hers. He was all hard angular planes and seemed to fit into the soft valleys of her own body in ways she could never have imagined.

Most distressing was the feeling of his manhood pressing against her. Only the thin cotton of the shirt kept her from feeling the most intimate part of his body flesh to flesh. Each struggle she made against him only increased the pressure of his touch, and she found herself responding in the most peculiar way, her body moistening and throbbing and aching for something that was fast becoming impossible to deny.

She was shocked at the firmness of him and her own wanton reaction. He was her enemy, not her lover, she screamed to herself, but it was a certainty that she could not hold in her mind.

His mouth savaged hers with a fierceness that was both frightening and compelling. She shifted her hips away from him, desperate to keep from surrendering to his demands, but a strong hand clamped hard across her buttocks held her firmly in the place he wanted her—and where she wanted to be.

This time when his tongue invaded her mouth, she knew how to respond, parting her lips wider and brushing her own tongue against him. A moan escaped from deep in his throat, an animal sound, and set the blood pounding in her veins ever harder.

She rubbed the palms of her hands over his chest,

rejoicing in the strength of his powerful muscles. He was everything she was not—hard-muscled and knowing—and she felt her will surrendering to Jake's stronger demands. Locked in his embrace, their heat and desires mingling, she threw her arms about him and thrust her breasts against his chest.

He responded by breaking the kiss and trailing his lips down to her throat and to the deep opening of the shirt. As large as the garment was, he was able to move it aside with a sure movement of his head and expose the hard peak of one breast. He startled her by running his tongue over the tip; the result was another new sensation, one that threw her deeper into abandonment. The low moan that she heard this time came from her throat, not his.

He lifted his head, and their eyes locked.

"Sarah," he whispered. "Angel."

She bit at her lower lip.

He kissed her breast again, then looked at her swollen mouth. "Talk," he whispered huskily. "Tell me how much I please you."

But Sarah could not put into words the desires raging through her. She did not know how.

With one hand still firmly in place across her buttocks, he moved the other to the remaining buttons of the shirt. One by one, he unfastened them and slowly folded the last thin barrier between them aside. His eyes followed the unveiling, stopping low on her abdomen, just above the triangle of pale hair between her thighs. His fingers left the open shirt and traced a burning path around her navel and into the wiry curls.

Even in the throes of abandonment, this was too much for Sarah.

"No," she said, moving one hand to grip his wrist and hold it still. "I can't."

He glanced up at her, surprised. "Still playing games? We both know you're no innocent," he said, his voice as unyielding as his body.

Desire deserted Sarah as quickly as it had taken control.

"I said no."

"Move your hand, Sarah," he ordered. "You've gone too far to stop now. You're a woman of passion to equal mine."

Jake didn't know her very well. She moved her hand, all right, but only to slap his face. His astonishment gave her just the opening she needed, and she jerked her body away from him. "I said no, and I meant it."

Clutching the shirt across her bosom, she rose quickly to her feet and jumped across his supine body.

Jake wasn't quite finished with her.

"My turn to say no," he said, grabbing her by the legs and pulling her back down. Thrown off balance, she pitched forward and reached out for anything that might support her. Unfortunately, the first thing her hands came in contact with was the center post. When she fell beside Jake, the post came with her, followed by a cascade of leaves and branches that had once been a roof.

Jake moved quickly to cover her body with his and took the brunt of the collapsing debris. Terrified, she huddled against him, her head buried against his chest as the carefully woven structure came apart. It was over in no more than a few seconds, and all sounds ceased, except for the cry of a gull overhead and, incredibly, the crash of the surf on the shore.

Her breath came in gasps.

"Are you all right?" he asked.

She nodded her head.

"Let me hear you say it."

"I'm all right," she whispered against his bare skin, dust catching in her throat. "What about you?"

"Ah," he breathed. "Such sweet concern. Aren't you a little late?"

Suddenly everything was too much, especially Jake's sarcasm, and she burst into tears. Beneath a jumble of tree limbs, he cradled her gently until she was able to get control of herself. "I never cry," she sniffled at last, enormously embarrassed by her display of weakness.

Shifting, she managed to move her head and look over his shoulder at the first pink rays of day. She glanced around her. All was desolation.

"When the roof went," Jake explained, "there was nothing to hold the rest of it. At least most everything fell outward. I'm not sure I could have supported it all."

With the lamp buried deep under the mess around them, she could barely make out his face in the dim morning light. "We need to find out if you really are all right. Move or something."

As if jumping to her command, he shifted his back suddenly and shrugged off the weight that had been holding him down. He jerked her to her feet and pulled her roughly across the wreckage to the cool, clear sand away from the hut.

Sarah rubbed at the ankle that had come in contact with an unyielding board. "Was all that haste necessary?"

He gestured toward a ribbon of smoke curling up from the pile they had just deserted.

"The lamp!" she cried.

They got to work dumping sand onto the smoke,

Sarah assiduously avoiding staring at Jake's bare bottom when he stood in front of her. She never so much as glanced at his front. As far as she could tell, he had suffered no more than a few scratches in the collapse of the hut. All in all, he looked in fine condition.

It was only when they were both certain that all danger of fire was past that he swam out to the boat and returned with a bundle of clothing over his head. As it turned out, he had brought two pairs of trousers, one for each of them, and she pulled on the oversized clothing, tucking in the now-buttoned shirt, and bound the two garments together at her waist with a piece of rope.

"You look like Bandit," he said, studying her from tousled head to bare feet. "Sort of."

"I told you I didn't take your gold!"

"I didn't say *a* bandit. Bandit is the name of a friend. Says he is more my slave."

"I've got one of those," Sarah said. "In the seraglio. Nadire is her name."

Jake's eyebrows rose. "The Grand Seraglio?"

Sarah nodded.

"You'll have to tell me more about Nadire," said Jake.

How curious it seemed that they should be standing here on a deserted beach beside the ruins of Jake's shelter, remembrances of thwarted passion just below the surface of their minds, and discussing their servant friends. But Sarah wasn't about to complain.

"I'm sorry about the hut," she said.

He shrugged. "It wasn't built to last forever."

She thought that was rather noble of him, for she knew how proud he had been of the thing.

Sarah caught herself. She must not think too kindly of him, or else she would find herself truly compromised. She remembered those moments just before the crash—the demands of his lips and hands and the eagerness of her own body to respond. And yet she had pulled back. Despite all her proud and personal boasts, she was not ready for lovemaking.

Obviously Jake disagreed. Once aroused, he could be a very determined, and persuasive, man.

"How about some breakfast?" he asked. "You can talk after we eat."

Sarah knew there was no postponing the inevitable. As much as Jake kept her on edge, he was at the same time comforting, although she doubted he would like to hear her say so. She was soon settled down on the beach with a cup of boiled coffee. It tasted wonderful, accompanied as it was by the fresh air blowing off the sea and the steady pounding of the waves.

Sitting beside him on the dry sand, she found herself telling him all—the unfortunate plans her father had for her, the slaughter on shipboard, and at last, the highlights of her experiences in the harem. About the only thing she did not tell in detail was a lesson or two Nadire had taught her.

She could not leave the subject of the sultan. "Someone wants to murder him. He might—" her voice broke and she took a moment to gain control— "already be dead. They might have—"

"No," said Jake firmly. "Don't think like that. With all the commotion you described in the harem, I doubt if anyone suspicious could have gotten near the sultan."

"But that's the point," she said, unable to accept his argument. "The man that Scarface was talking to

117

is very likely someone whom the sultan trusts."

"Then you'll have to trust in Harun's ability to protect himself. He comes from a long line of survivors, Sarah. He isn't the first of his rank to be threatened."

Sarah sighed in acquiescence. "You're right, of course. Harun has more guards in the serai than are in Windsor and Buckingham combined. If only I could warn him about the man with the scar." She shuddered. "He was there on the dock, you know."

"I remember him. Unfortunately, he wasn't one of the ones who fell into the Horn." Jake studied her thoughtfully. "I'm surprised you are so worried about Harun. After all, he wanted to keep you prisoner, didn't he?"

"I cannot just leave him to die, no matter what his intentions were. Besides, he reminds me of my father."

Jake choked on the coffee.

"I don't mean in any physical way," Sarah said. "My father is a dealer in antiques and art. Harun, too, likes beautiful things."

And both, she did not add, liked to have her under their control when they were not ignoring her entirely.

She went on to describe Harun's latest acquisition, a marvelous death mask from Egypt.

"Made of gold, was it?" Jake asked. "Eyes slanted, lips full and smiling?"

Sarah's eyes widened. "You're the American who sold it to him. I should have known. No wonder you knew about all of the guards around Harun. And the gold coins—"

"Were my share of the sale. Bandit, who actually found the mask, took the rest."

Sarah didn't ask exactly where this servant/slave had found the priceless treasure. She doubted it was in a bazaar.

"You were about to celebrate—"

"There had been a few plans made."

"—and I came along."

He glanced over her shoulder toward the mound that had once been his hut. "You have a rather dramatic way of interrupting my plans."

Again Sarah remembered those last few moments before the roof caved in.

We both know you're no innocent.

Jake thought he had her figured out. The camaraderie she had begun to feel with him faded. She meant nothing to him except the means to an end. He was what was called a lusty man, and he was certain she matched his lust. She needed to set him straight.

"About what almost happened—" she began. She felt his dark gaze on her.

"What about it?"

"It's not to happen ever. I do not want it."

He laughed sharply.

"I mean what I say, Jake."

"Then you don't know yourself very well. You're a passionate woman. Under the proper circumstances, you would change your mind readily enough."

Their eyes locked for a moment, but before she could respond, he stood and studied the water, as though all had been discussed on that subject. "We better get under way. The tide will be leaving soon."

What he said made sense. They must return as soon as possible, but she was struck with an irrational dismay that Jake thought so, too. For some reason she preferred staying for a while and arguing about her lust.

119

She stood beside him. "Whatever you say, Captain."

He grinned at her. "It's about time you realized my status. I've got some gold to find," he explained. "And you to take care of."

"Unnecessary. You can leave me on the dock where you found me, if you don't mind. I'll find my way to the embassy."

"Oh, but I do mind. You're much too valuable to abandon."

"Valuable as what? A . . . love object?"

"It's an idea worth considering. But perhaps I used the wrong word. Vulnerable, maybe." He glanced back at the mound of branches at the far edge of the beach. "I'm not sure that's the right word, either."

"I've apologized already, Jake, for the hut, but I do not regret ending what should never have begun."

"I wonder if you know what you really want."

"I want to be back in England. In the life I never should have left."

"Untouched. That's what you mean."

Cold and lonely and unloved. Sarah knew that was what he implied. "Untouched by you is what I really mean," she said. How easily he was dismissing everything she believed about herself.

"Don't worry about losing out on your *romp*, as you so indelicately put it," she added. "I'll see that you get paid for your troubles. I just might be able to match what you lost."

He stared solemnly down at her, an unreadable darkness deep in his eyes. "Thanks anyway, Angel, but I can take care of myself. It just occurred to me that after I've placed you in the loving arms of your fiancé, he will see fit to give me a reward."

Sarah stared at him open-mouthed. "You're going to sell me to him?"

"A rather harsh judgment. You were on your way to meet him when the pirates hit. I'm simply seeing your plans carried through."

"My *plans* were to break our engagement."

"You will be free to do so."

"Then the British embassy—"

"Is not safe, as I have tried to explain. Not without an armed guard escorting you there, and I don't have one at my disposal. Maybe your fiancé can come up with one. He may need it from time to time."

"You are a bastard," Sarah hissed.

"Could be. But not now. Face the facts, Sarah. You're going to end up with Pettigrew sooner or later. You need a man to take care of you. For your own good if not for his."

With that, he bent to gather the remains of their morning repast and the coffeepot and cups, bundled the whole thing up in the blankets, and waded toward the boat.

Sarah resolved then and there not to do as Jake bade. She would return as much of the lost gold as she could—as soon as she communicated with her father that she was still alive, he surely would send her what she wished—but she would not be sold! The decision as to how she would live her life must remain in her hands.

In a rising flush of anger, she stared at Jake's back. "I'm not going to let you turn me over to someone as you would chattel," she called after him.

He ignored her. She knew what he was thinking— that in her heart she would rather remain with him. A passionate woman, was she? She would show him.

"And I'd rather make love to an octopus than to an uncouth man like you," she yelled.

He kept treading through the water.

"And furthermore, you were right about my father. He adores me." She screamed out the lie as Jake made his way up the rope ladder. "Only he wouldn't have come after you with a shotgun. Whips are more his style. He would have flailed the hide from your bones."

Chapter Nine

Sarah felt a mixture of embarrassment and outrage as she followed Jake to the boat. She hardly knew herself anymore. At the beginning of summer she had been a sophisticated and self-assured Londoner with a dozen courtly gentlemen begging her favor. Restless, maybe, and occasionally foolhardy, but nothing worse. Since traveling east—and falling into the company of Jake Price—she had turned into a fishwife.

"Better hurry up, Sarah, and climb aboard," he called as she neared the boat.

Another order.

Jake's high-handed attitude was the problem here. Like her father, he thought he knew what was best for her. Sarah was not completely sure herself how to approach her growing problems, but he had yet to come up with a plan for her that she could accept.

She would always be grateful for his bravery before the slashing scimitars—and forever regretful that in his embrace, or simply in the contemplation of it, she had behaved like a fool.

She forced herself to climb the rope ladder hanging from the dhow. The weight of her wet clothes—

Jake's borrowed shirt and trousers—pulled her back toward the surf.

"Here," Jake said, extending his hand.

Without looking up, and without speaking, she placed her hand in his and let him pull her on board. He turned away.

Wringing water from her baggy trousers, she readjusted the rope serving as her belt and did what little she could to help as he prepared to set sail. Very businesslike he was, and she decided it was an attitude she could adopt, too. At least he was not lecturing her or ordering her about. And for once he was fully clothed.

After they were well under way, she could be quiet no longer. Standing beside the waist of the dhow, she watched him lean against the mast of the lateen sail and stare across the expanse of water. A stiff breeze ruffled his hair, and she noted the thick stubble darkening his cheeks. It wouldn't take long for him to grow another beard. Jake was a very hairy man, and she had to brush aside a memory of his naked body kneeling beside her in the hut only a few hours ago. How difficult it was to remain angry with a man who made her feel hollow inside.

She cleared her throat. "What exactly do you plan to do when we arrive?"

His answer was brief. "I'll find a place for you to stay, out of sight, of course, and find this Pettigrew. The rest is pretty much up to him."

"I'll have to tell him I've been with you for a few days. What if he decides he doesn't want me?"

Jake's dark blue eyes drifted slowly over her hair blowing in the wind, paused where the damp shirt rested against her breasts, and moved down her trouser-clad legs to stop at her bare feet. "He'll want you, all right. If he's any kind of a man." Jake looked

124

away. "And if he can keep you settled down."

This told Sarah exactly what Jake thought men wanted in a woman. Sex and obedience. Since she was ill disposed to deliver either, she began to make plans of her own.

She didn't question Jake again until they were settled for the night in a cove off the Dardanelles and dining on fried bonito that he had caught. She was making every effort to be at least civil and had even managed to clean the scaly fish, a difficult task with Jake making unwanted suggestions as to how she should proceed.

Sitting cross-legged on the moonlit deck, Jake across from her, Sarah licked her fingers and studied the pile of bones on the plate in front of her. "You would think I was starving."

"You've had a busy few days," he said. "And a very busy night, although perhaps not the way either of us might have chosen."

Sarah was startled to feel a return of the stirring that had made her behave with such abandon.

"A gentleman would not say such things."

"No, he probably wouldn't."

Sarah concentrated on straightening the rolled-back cuffs of her shirt. "You may have trouble locating my fiancé since I don't remember the address on his letters. He was supposed to meet the ship."

"Probably Pera, on the northern side of the Bosporus, past the settlement of Galata. Used to be the site of the brothels, or so I'm told. The British colony is there now."

"Not Constantinople?"

"Pera's part of the city. The area you've been calling Constantinople is more accurately named Stamboul, at least by the Turks. Sometimes Istanbul. It's supposed to be built on seven hills. Like Rome."

Sarah stared into the dark and tried to imagine what the city must be like. "I've been there more than two weeks and couldn't describe so much as one street to you."

Jake's eyes were steady on her. "Perhaps Ralph will show you around."

"You have a one-track mind, don't you?" she asked, forsaking civility.

"The sooner you're where you should be, the better for us both."

"The sooner you'll get some money, you mean."

"That's right."

Sarah directed her fury to cleaning away the remains of dinner, pitching the fish bones far out into the water. Her thoughts were directed to what she would do when they returned. Any woman who could invade the British Museum with a small orchestra, who could race a spirited gelding in a race against men and take second place, and who could get away with posing as an actress on the stage—any woman capable of all those things, foolish though they may have been—could get herself to the British embassy without help from a man.

From there she would decide how to pass on the information about the proposed assassination of Harun. Perhaps she could arrange to talk to the sultan in person. This time he would have to listen and believe in the gravity of her situation—and of his. Sarah had no doubt of Scarface's evil intent. She prayed she was not too late.

When all was cleared away, there was nothing left to do but go to bed. At Jake's insistence, she took the covered sleeping quarters and he took the deck. She lay still in the gently rocking boat and listened to Jake move restlessly about the deck. She tried in vain to concentrate on her escape, much as she had thought about escaping from the seraglio.

Pride and the remains of humiliation told her that once they were docked in the Horn, she never wanted to see Jake again. And yet she did not know how she would react if sometime during the night he crawled into the narrow quarters beside her and pulled her into his arms. She doubted she would push him away.

Frailty, thy name is woman. Shakespeare had a point.

At last she fell into a restless sleep. Early the next morning they were en route once again, passing quickly through the traffic on the Sea of Marmara; they neared their destination by late afternoon.

As they sailed through the bay of the Bosporus and shifted direction to port into the Golden Horn, she caught a whiff of the malodorous tanneries lining the mile-wide strait on its course toward the Black Sea. The odor drowned the clean salt scent of the water.

Somewhere in the hills to her right, amongst the tile-roofed structures away from the northern bank of the Horn, awaited the apartment occupied by Ralph Pettigrew, an apartment he perhaps planned as her new home. More important, the British embassy was there. If only Nadire had taught her more Turkish than a few parts of the body, she might be able to ask directions. As it was, she was poorly prepared to exist on her own.

She directed her attention to the high hills of the city on her left. The part of Contantinople known as Stamboul rose majestically above the water, its peaks crowned by the domes and minarets of mosques and palaces and by the green, graceful tips of the city's cypress forests. Somewhere in the midst of all that beauty lay the Grand Seraglio, itself a work of art

with its carefully laid-out courtyards, arched passageways, and marble walls.

Sarah forgot the minarets and the marble walls.
Behind all the grandeur of the city lay an ugliness
that she could not put from her mind.

"Get out of sight, Sarah."

Startled from her reverie, she realized they were
coming close to a row of ships moored to a crowded
section of the dock.

"We'll stop here," Jake said. "No need to advertise
your presence until I've had a chance to look
around."

"Of course," she answered brusquely.

As much as she agreed with him, Sarah still took
offense at his tone. Just once she would like him to
ask her to do something. She wondered how many
requests she would grant if he ever learned to say
please.

Jake watched Sarah disappear into the low-roofed
quarters on the aft deck. At least she hadn't argued
with him. When he had docked here a few nights ago,
he was wealthy and ready for a good time and, as far
as he knew, safe from any threats. He was returning
penniless, frustrated, and minus even the humble hut
on his Aegean isle. And there was a possibility that
whoever was after Sarah was also after him.

He ought to be filled with a disgust of her. He
ought to be glad he was close to getting her off his
hands. But Jake seldom went by the rules of common
sense or ordinary behavior, and now was no
exception.

He pushed aside the image of Sarah scooting out of
sight and concentrated on the business at hand. In
short order he had the forty-foot dhow nestled

between an American frigate and a clipper ship out of Bombay.

"Throw me the rope, Bossman," he heard someone call from the dock.

Jake grinned at the short, olive-skinned man standing at the edge of the pier. "Thought you might be here," he called back to Bandit.

Working together, they secured the dhow, and Jake jumped onto the wooden dock. He studied the assortment of humanity moving about the waterfront—sailors and dock workers, most of them, intent on their own business. For a while his attention was caught by the noisy unloading of crated cargo from the frigate twenty yards behind the dhow. No seraglio guards with waving scimitars came at him. No one gave him or his small craft a second look.

"I have been awaiting your return," Bandit said. "I knew it would not be long in coming."

"I didn't leave by choice."

Bandit's ever-moving eyes darted about the deck of the boat and stopped at the dark opening to the sleeping quarters. A pair of eyes stared back at him, and a soft woman's voice hissed, "Ask him about Harun."

"How is the sultan?" asked Jake. "There is someone aboard with a special interest in his welfare."

"The someone should know that Harun was seen only this morning in the streets of the city, surrounded by the entourage that accompanies him each time he leaves the serai."

"That's good to hear," said Jake.

"A strange story passes among the sailors," Bandit said. "A superstitious and fanciful lot they are, as you will no doubt agree."

"Try me."

"They speak of a beautiful young woman pursued through the night by a host of madmen who wish to do her great harm. And of another man who stills the slashing swords and carries the beauty to safety. It is a tale more like a legend than a recounting of the recent past."

"Any details about who the young woman might be?" asked Jake. Like Bandit, he kept his eyes averted from the sleeping quarters.

"She is shrouded in mystery, Bossman. Although it is said one of the madmen bore a scar across his face from long ago. Such a man has been seen watching the small boats as they sail into the harbor. Perhaps the tale is not without truth."

"It might also have been said that the scarred man threatened to do harm to Harun, and the woman heard more than was good for her."

"Such would cause great danger."

Jake nodded in agreement. "Any details about the man who saved her?"

"Only that he is tall as the sky and bearded and possessed of a mystical strength."

"Now that part seems possible."

"Such is the story as I have heard it. About the boat little is known. It does not bear a name."

"I confess to knowing a little something more of this legend," Jake said, scratching at his bristled face. "The man of strength lost mightily on the night of the rescue, even though his life was spared."

"How is this?"

"Once he owned a sack of gold coins, but no more."

"This part of the legend I had not heard," said Bandit.

"There was another woman already aboard the

nameless boat. She left hurriedly while the man was employing all that mystical strength. She did not leave poor."

"Another woman. We must find her."

"My thoughts exactly. Unfortunately her name is unknown."

"A curious oversight," observed Bandit.

"The friendship was to have been for no more than one night. Tell me something," said Jake. "About the first woman you mentioned, the one being pursued—if she needed shelter for a short while, would there be a safe place in all of Constantinople for her to hide?"

"Such a place is known to me." Bandit grinned. "I took the liberty of securing a small room close to the Grand Bazaar."

"You're a man among men, Bandit."

"I once had a wife who said much the same thing."

Jake looked at him in surprise. "And I thought you had only uncles and cousins. Are you married still?"

"No, Bossman. It would seem I was not the only man among men. I hope one day to have another wife. Perhaps someday fortune will smile on me again."

Jake wasn't sure marriage and good fortune went hand in hand but kept his opinion to himself. Together they worked out the details about how to get Sarah to the apartment without detection. Best done after dark, Bandit said, and Jake agreed.

"In the dark she might pass for a young boy. She's wearing my clothes right now."

Bandit made no comment.

"Some sort of cap to cover her head, maybe," Jake continued. "She has the damnedest golden hair. In this city it's sure to capture attention."

Still, Bandit remained quiet.

"I've kept her safe up until now. She'll be off my hands as soon as I can arrange for someone else to be responsible for her."

"I heard that" came a muffled voice from the boat. "I can be responsible for myself."

Bandit looked from Jake to the boat. "The beautiful young woman presents difficulties."

"You might say that," said Jake. Without looking in her direction, he added, "If you don't keep quiet in there, I'll strap you to the mast and take the first offer I get."

"It is perhaps to be wished that night comes quickly," Bandit said. "I will find the covering for the young boy's head, as you have suggested, Bossman, and will return with fresh fruit and some very old and ripe cheese. And I would humbly suggest that in the meantime a razor be applied to your face. It would be most unfortunate if someone bearing a scar were to confuse you with the bearded man from the tale."

"Most unfortunate," Jake agreed.

True to his word, Bandit returned with the promised goods. He was greeted by a clean-shaven Jake.

"I took the precaution, Bossman, of bringing a disguise for you, too." He held out a bundle containing a plain brown robe and a wine-red fez.

"Do you really think these are necessary? Most Turks have gone to Western wear."

"But not all. We should take every precaution that we can."

Jake reluctantly agreed. Food was set inside for Sarah, and the two men sat on the dock, backs against a pair of posts, and ate. Slowly the sun slipped behind the hills to the west while Jake gave an expurgated version of the past days and nights.

"The lady is in much trouble," Bandit said.

"The lady sure is. She needs someone to take care of her and get her out of here. This fiancé ought to be just the one."

Bandit stared thoughtfully at him. "There is something in the Bossman's voice that says perhaps he is not sure."

"Oh, I'm sure all right. The unluckiest moment of my life was when Sarah Whitlock came running at me out of the dark. We've both been running ever since. She's just too expensive for my blood. Let someone else take care of her."

"Is Miss Whitlock beautiful?"

Jake paused. "If you like long blond hair and blue eyes and long legs and. . . . Yes, I suppose you could say she's beautiful. But then so is a jungle cat. If it's to live around a man, it should be kept in a cage."

"It has been a difficult time for you," Bandit said. "And perhaps for the lady."

Jake didn't respond. Despite its beginning, the time had come close to being perfect. When he had held that vibrant, silken body in his arms—when she had trembled against him and returned his kisses with a passion matching his own—the missing gold had been no more important to him than the blowing of the wind.

Then she had fought him and shown him more than words ever could that her passions included not only lust but rage. She did not like submitting her will to a man, but by God someday she would have to do just that. He pitied the poor man who would have to tame her. Ralph Pettigrew had a fight on his hands.

But it was Pettigrew's fight and not his.

A pair of drunken sailors, singing a bawdy French song, strolled by. Jake eyed them suspiciously.

They paused beside him.

"*Bonsoir, messieurs,*" one said with an exaggerated bow. He stumbled and righted himself and brushed at his blue-black sailor's coat.

"*Bonsoir,*" Jake returned.

The other held a bottle high. "*A votre sante,*" he toasted.

"*Merci.*" Jake watched as the sailor downed half the contents and passed the bottle to his comrade, who finished it off. They proceeded to argue over who should buy another as they continued their drunken stroll into the twilight.

A quarter hour passed before Jake spoke. In the boat's sleeping quarters all was quiet. "It looks dark enough. I need to get this over with."

"Should I summon the lady?" Bandit asked.

"Might as well."

Jake stood as Bandit climbed aboard the boat and knocked against the wooden structure hiding Sarah from the world. He kneeled, peered inside, then stood and turned toward the dock.

"I have bad news, Bossman."

Jake jumped on board the boat beside Bandit and stared into the dark shelter. The dark and empty shelter. Sarah was gone.

"We've got to find her," he said between gritted teeth, then added, "Damn!"

"Such are my sentiments," said Bandit.

The two men spent the next half hour searching along the wharf and neighboring streets for signs of her. The few men they accosted appeared not to understand any of the languages Bandit tried, or else swore they had seen no one answering the vague description he gave.

When they returned to the boat, Jake stared long and hard into the dark, oily water and called himself a fool for believing she would stay where he had put her. He spoke the words out loud, but true as they were, they brought him little comfort.

While sitting on the dock and waiting for night to fall, he had done a lot of thinking—about Sarah and her maddening ability to destroy his peace of mind and body. She affected him more than any woman ever had, in good ways and bad. He hadn't had a restful sleep, much less an untroubled thought, since she first threw herself into his arms.

To make matters worse, there were the calamities that had befallen her since she first set sail for Turkey. Not all the facts fit as he had heard them. Either she wasn't telling him everything—a definite possibility—or there were goings-on concerning her that she didn't realize. Whichever the case, she was caught in a far more complicated predicament than she realized. Jake felt it in his bones.

He could think of only one positive aspect of her disappearance. She had taken the cap. He held out a dim hope that she would not be recognized before reaching safety.

Chapter Ten

On the deck of the American frigate anchored twenty yards behind the dhow, Sarah listened to Jake castigate himself. She could not make out more than his tall, dark figure on the cloudy night, but each of his words carried easily across the night air up to her perch. She agreed with every one.

Crouched beside the coils of rope on the frigate's aft deck, she forced herself to an admission. Jake might have acted like a fool, but then so had she. What on earth had possessed her to climb down the rope ladder into the polluted water by the dock? So he had wanted to get rid of her, had wanted her to be the responsibility of someone else; the knowledge had come as no surprise.

But his words had echoed too closely the sentiments of her father. And here she was, soaked and soiled with unimaginable filth, hiding on a strange vessel, unable to ask for assistance from anyone lest he turn out to be an enemy, and not knowing in the least where she might find the British embassy. Or the French or the Prussian. She would take the first one she came upon.

What she ought to do is steal back down the

gangplank and tell Jake she would go with him and Bandit to the hideaway. Jake's man seemed a sympathetic sort. She rather thought they would get along.

She would do that if she had any sense, but Sarah could not forget Jake's casual dismissal of her, nor his determination to hand her over to another man as if she were some sort of chattel. She had not pleased him.

Give old Ralph Pettigrew a chance at her seemed to be his attitude. Blast Jake Price!

Sarah was caught in a quandary. Should she hate him? Should she seek his help? Peering over the side of the frigate, she watched Jake and Bandit walk away fast in the opposite direction. She opened her mouth to call out to them, but at the same moment a trio of sailors began making their way onto the ship. Ducking behind the high coil of rope once again, she turned her anger onto herself.

Earlier in the evening, while waiting for permission to depart the dhow, she had peered through a crack in the roof of her hiding place and watched as the Americans finished their unloading and, in small groups, wandered ashore. She had thought they would not return for hours. And the watch could not be everywhere at once. The ship, looming dark and close behind the dhow, had seemed a fine place to hide for a while.

So much for her clever plans.

"I'll get the money," one of them was saying as they reached the deck. "It's stashed below."

"Shouldn't have left it in the first place, mate. There's women and whiskey out there waiting for us. No time to be lost."

"Be quick about it," the third one growled.

Chancing a quick look at the sailors, Sarah

watched in fear as they walked in her direction. She shifted farther behind the rope. Something fat and furry brushed against her hand, and she squealed, then bit her tongue.

"What was that?" one of the men said.

"A rat more'n likely."

Sarah didn't find the words encouraging.

"Didn't sound like no rat to me."

She listened to the footsteps draw nearer and tried to burrow under the ropes. The footsteps halted, and a broad hand gripped her by the shoulder and lifted her to her feet. She held her cap firmly in place and kept her eyes down, hoping she looked like a boy. She felt like a fish on a hook.

"What have we here?" he asked. "A stowaway?"

The man rested her on her feet and shook her. "Out with it, lad. Is it mischief you're after? You'd not want to be sailing on this tub."

"I'll get a light," another said.

Sarah tried to squirm away from her captor, but she was no match for his strength. His grip on her shoulders held firm.

The light from the lantern spilled onto her damp, clinging shirt.

"Lookee here, mates," the captor whistled. "This is no lad. Or if it is, 'tis the strangest shaped one I've ever seen."

"Let me go," she cried, slapping at his arm.

"And an even stranger voice."

He removed her cap, setting her long hair free.

"Fortune smiles on us," he said to the others. "No need to go looking for a woman tonight. This one speaks English, too."

"I ain't one for sharing, Bingo" was one response.

"Then go find your own. I've found mine. Allus did say these foreign ports were the places to go.

Nothing like this 'un stowin' away back in Virginie.''

"Wait a minute," protested the third man. "Don't she match the description of the woman the Turks was asking about on shore today? In some kind of trouble with the authorities is what they said."

Squinting, the man called Bingo moved his face close to hers. She tried to smile despite his sour breath.

"Don't look like no criminal to me," he said.

Sarah summoned her courage. "I'm not," she said hurriedly. "Take me to the British embassy and you'll find out soon enough that I speak the truth. The men who are after me are the real criminals."

"There was a reward offered for her," another said.

"I'll match it," Sarah bluffed.

Bingo's small, hard eyes studied her, then he turned to his friends. "Don't look like she could come up with more'n a dollar or two. Not that she don't have somethin' to offer. I been at sea a long, lonely time."

"Get your brains out of your arse, Bingo," one of the men said. "Rough 'er up and the Turks might decide she ain't so valuable to 'em."

Bingo's stare took on a calculating look. "Maybe so."

The sailor hurried on. "Seems to me we ought to bundle 'er up and find those Turks. Demand they up the money some, seein' as how they claim she's broken the law."

Bandit nodded at his companion, then shifted a gap-toothed grin back to his captive. "We'd be doin' our civic duty."

Sarah gave up reason and decided to scream. She got out little more than the beginnings of a screech before Bingo's hand clamped across her mouth.

"Keep 'er hushed up, Bingo. Watch is comin'."

She twisted and kicked; but her damp slippers landed ineffectually against Bingo's shins, and she was the one in pain. A soiled rag was used to gag her, and a burlap bag was dropped over her head. Thrown over the shoulder of one of the men, she continued to squirm; for her efforts she got a blow on the head.

This time when she awoke, something about the scent and feel of her prison told her she was once again in the Grand Seraglio. Only it wasn't the same fresh-smelling room with sunlight streaming in and with yards of rainbow colors draped around her pillowed bed.

These quarters were musty, windowless and dark, with only one candle sitting on a tiled table to provide light, and the uncurtained cushions not half so billowed as before. Nor was Nadire close by to assure her that all would be well. She was completely alone.

The room made her previously hated quarters in the harem seem like the serai's grand salon.

Maybe she was wrong about being in the seraglio, she thought. Perhaps this was an ordinary Turkish prison. But when a middle-aged woman slipped into the room to bathe and dress her, she knew her initial guess had been right. Sarah tried to communicate in both English and French, but the woman looked blankly at her, then indicated with her hands and a shake of her head that she was mute. When the slave set about her work, Sarah knew it would be useless to resist. She hoped she was being prepared for Harun. For all his stubbornness when she begged for her freedom, he had not abused her.

The harem costume, covering even less of her body than the one she had worn before, was the color of the Egyptian death mask—a rich, deep gold. She was thoroughly sprayed with perfume, and her hair was brushed and allowed to hang free.

She tried to keep her spirits up. Harun was her friend, or as close to one besides Nadire as she was likely to find in the serai. He might even have learned the truth of the *Leviathan*'s loss. She would tell him of her discovery concerning the assassination attempt, describing Scarface in greater detail than she had done before; in his gratitude he would release her.

And she could return to England and take up her life once again.

In her heart she knew such a happy ending was not to be. Since she had tried to argue with her father about her betrothal, her luck had been consistently bad. Even when fortune seemed to favor her, as it had the night her footsteps were guided to Jake's boat, she ended up losing something. Pride, freedom—in her mind they were the same.

Somehow Jake's determination to get rid of her was the bitterest blow of all, although she could not imagine why.

A knock at the door brought her musings to an end. The slave walked slowly around her, casting critical eyes over her person, then gestured for Sarah to answer the summons.

Guided between two six-foot-tall, black eunuchs down an arched cloister she did not recognize, she was brought to a high, gilded double door. It was far more ornate than the simple portal leading to the bedroom of Harun.

One of her guards pushed open the doors and, when she was inside, closed them behind her without making a sound or an announcement of her arrival. She took a half dozen tentative steps, her slippered feet striking noiselessly against the Persian rug. The incense was heavy and the light dim, but she was able to make out in the center of the huge room at least one person lying atop a mound of pillows behind a curtain of yellow gauze.

From the Oriental bed came a woman's cry of pain, then a deep growl, and Sarah knew the sequestered bodies numbered at least two. The cry came again, a pleading sound that carried with it a hint of pleasure, as though whatever discomforts were delivered to the woman were not entirely unwelcome.

But that was absurd, Sarah thought.

Behind the gauze the pillows shifted violently, and she saw a shadow rise like a monster serpent over the second figure. Eyes adjusted, she was able to see the hunched, dark form thrust against the supine body. Again and again.

Sarah whirled in embarrassment, but the door at her back was locked. A woman's scream broke the quiet, and then came a slap. A man's deep voice spoke but in such a low tone that she could not tell the language he used.

A rustling sound from behind the curtains drew Sarah back to the half-hidden scene. The gauze parted, and out stepped a naked woman, dark-haired and dusky-skinned. Her hips and thighs were ample, and her breasts pendulous; except for the pouting expression on her broad face, she looked like a nude study in a Renaissance painting. Not knowing where to look, Sarah concentrated on her thick, wild hair and on the red, angry mark a hand had left on her face.

She glanced sullenly at Sarah as she shuffled to the far corner of the room. Unashamed, she stood facing her rival.

At least that was what Sarah assumed was her own role in this Turkish *ménage à trois*. When the curtain

142

parted once again, she kept her eyes trained on the carpeted floor, certain that a naked man would emerge. She was equally certain it would not be Harun.

Sarah was surprised to see a pair of wine-colored slippers beneath the hem of a gold and scarlet brocaded robe. Her eyes moved slowly up the rich folds of cloth, stopped for a moment at the powerful-looking hands that were fastening the heavily embroidered closures of the robe, then continued on to the narrow chin and firm, unsmiling lips, past the sharp nose and highly defined cheekbones, until at last she was looking in his eyes.

Black and burning at the same time, like smoldering coals, they stared back at her. When she considered the eyes together with his lean, olive face and thick black hair, Sarah decided he was one of the handsomest men she had ever seen—almost as handsome as Jake—but in a dark and forbidding way that was unknown in London. Tall and motionless, he seemed more carved from ebony than created from flesh and blood.

Except for the look in his eyes. No artist could capture that fire in mere wood.

"Welcome, Miss Whitlock."

Sarah jumped at the suddenness of his rich, low-pitched voice.

With some effort, she got control of herself. "How do you know my name? I do not know yours."

"You are a woman to whom I should not give advantage. Your escape from the harem of my father has caused much distress."

Sarah's stomach tightened. "Then you are Mustafa, Harun's son."

"His second son, to be exact." Mustafa's dark eyes narrowed momentarily. "My exalted brother toils in the hinterlands of Anatolia, learning to rule in preparation for the day our father is called before Allah."

Nadire had told her much the same thing and had hinted of darker truths about the man standing before her—of cruelty born from ambition and greed. Looking at the hate that glittered in the depths of his eyes, Sarah could believe them all.

She glanced at the naked figure now slouched in the corner. "And how do you toil?"

"As best I can, Miss Whitlock." His gaze moved slowly down her half-clad body. "As best I can."

Sarah could not control a shiver.

"Does the English woman fear me?" asked Mustafa. "Good. I have been put to much inconvenience in looking for that which was purchased for me and me alone."

Without looking at the naked woman, he snapped his fingers, and she moved in silence to his side. His gaze pinned to Sarah, he began to knead the woman's buttocks. He slapped at them once, twice. The woman closed her eyes, but not before Sarah saw a mixture of fear and arousal in their depths.

Sarah's heart pounded as she wondered what crude assaults lay in store for her. She longed to pound at the locked door behind her and cry for someone to let her out, but she knew her pleas would go unanswered.

"Take note, English woman, of how the slave Tezer obeys me," said Mustafa. He reached over the woman's shoulder and squeezed her breast.

Sarah winced in sympathetic pain, but the slave did not move.

"You must do the same," added Mustafa.

Sarah forced her eyes to remain on Mustafa's lecherous face. "I will not be so complaisant as Tezer."

144

"Such is my wish. Your struggles will not go unrewarded."

The cruel twist of Mustafa's mouth robbed his face of the handsomeness Sarah had observed, and she realized with a start that he was deriving great pleasure from inflicting pain.

Disgust took the edge off her fear. "Where is Harun?" she asked. "We are friends. I demand to see him."

Mustafa shoved Tezer away. Stumbling, she caught herself before falling and once again retreated mutely to the corner, but not before Sarah caught sight of the bruises on her buttocks and thighs.

"You are not meant for my father. It was I who bought you before, but that fool Kizlar Agasi intervened and had you taken to the wrong harem. You are now exactly where you belong."

"On that point we most certainly disagree." She considered for a moment telling Mustafa of the overheard plot against his father but rejected the idea. For all she knew, Mustafa was behind the proposed assassination. It was a terrible thought but one she could not wholly push from her mind.

"Enough!" Mustafa snapped his fingers. "I did not send for you because I longed to argue. You are dismissed."

Sarah started. "Dismissed?"

"Please do not suffer too much disappointment, Miss Whitlock. It is matched by my own. Much as I would like to teach you what you must endure, tonight I have been called elsewhere. I wanted only to see for myself that you were indeed in my power." He stepped close, his strong hand gripping her upper arm until she wanted to cry out. "Make no mistake about your situation, woman of the West. You *are* in my power."

145

He turned and uttered a few sharp words in Turkish to Tezer, then said to Sarah, "You will spend your days with the other women of my harem. It is separate from my father's and run somewhat differently, as you will learn."

"Harun kept me away from the other women."

"Perhaps," Mustafa said with a twisted smile, "my father is smarter than I have supposed. At any rate, my women have little freedom. They live only for me. I have ordered Tezer to see that you do not try to communicate with anyone, however. You will find that they speak only Turkish—when they choose to speak, which is rarely. When I have taken care of my business, I will return and show you the ways of Eastern men."

With brocaded robe whirling behind him, he headed for a side door, then paused. "Do not, Miss Whitlock, think you can escape again. I am much more thorough than my weak-minded father and take unkindly to disobedience."

The moment he exited the room, she heard the double door behind her open, as if a system of signals existed that she could not hear, and she was escorted back to her quarters by the same pair of giant eunuchs who had brought her to Mustafa.

Alone, the door to the passageway securely bolted on the outside, she fought a rising panic. Mustafa was a formidable foe—and, she admitted in her heart, a frightening one. It did not seem an exaggeration to view him as the embodiment of evil.

Snuffing the candle, she lay on her bed of pillows and tried in vain to figure out how she could possibly get away.

As Mustafa had ordered, the next morning she was

taken to the room where the other women of his harem spent the day. The space provided them was as large as an English ballroom and well lit with midsummer sunlight spilling in through a dozen high windows. The tiled floor was terraced, rising in wide tiers until the highest level which lay ten feet above the door, but still, Sarah noted with regret, too far below the windows to allow escape.

The bottom tier measured twenty yards across and thirty deep; its central feature was a shallow oval pool partially lined with potted palms, giving it the atmosphere of an oasis.

Lying in various positions of repose about the room and around the pond were Mustafa's odalisques, most of them bare-breasted and wearing nothing more than harem pants. Sarah counted close to fifty women resting singly or in small groups against the ubiquitous rainbow-hued pillows scattered along the tiers and beside the pool. Except for a half dozen who appeared to be little more than children, they were like the woman Mustafa had been with last night—dark-haired, olive-skinned, and well endowed.

She thought she recognized Tezer, but she could not be certain, as they all carried with them a sultry, sullen air. At the moment they were staring indolently at her.

Grateful for the red silk robe her mute slave had brought her, Sarah hugged the garment to her naked body. Mustafa had said they were not to communicate with her, and Sarah had no wish to defy his orders, at least not right away—not until she decided who might be able to understand her and, more importantly, be willing to listen to what she had to say.

She had been kidnapped against her will, and she had knowledge that could save the sultan's life.

147

Surely someone would find at least the latter information of interest. If only she could spot someone to trust.

One by one the women returned to the activities that her entry had interrupted—munching at figs and grapes, allowing one of the eunuch slaves to anoint their bodies with perfumed oil, or simply staring vacantly into space. The young girls whispered softly among themselves.

Sarah slipped quietly into the room and found an isolated spot on a tier halfway to the top. A white-skinned eunuch set a bowl of pomegranates beside her and promptly moved backward down to the pool, where he began to wave an ostrich-plumed fan over the body of a slave lying beneath one of the palms.

Unable to resist the ripe fruit, Sarah ate, then snuggling against a nest of pillows, fell into a fitful sleep.

She awoke later to find that nothing much had changed, except that several of the women had shifted their positions either closer to or farther from the pond. A few left the room but returned within the hour, and Sarah suspected they had taken strolls in what must be an outside courtyard.

Once she made a move to follow a pair of odalisques, but by the time she reached the door, the massive body of one of the black eunuchs was blocking her way. She retreated to her perch.

By the time she returned to her quarters in the gathering of night, Sarah felt more alone than she had ever felt and, worse, dangerously without hope.

Day followed day with little diversion, and Sarah found herself slipping deeper into despondency. At the end of the week, she tried to break the monotony, as well as her frightening sense of helplessness, by communicating with several of the women through words and gestures, but without exception they shook their heads angrily and turned away.

She noticed, however, that the eunuchs did nothing to stop her attempts, and she determined to find one among the harem who might be sympathetic.

The next day she found such a person, a new slave who was seated on the top tier. Sarah noticed her as soon as she came into the room. It was Nadire.

Sarah forced herself to move slowly up the terraces. She rested against a pillow in the high corner and closed her eyes. An hour later Nadire moved to her side.

"Missy Sarah," the slave whispered in her ear.

With seeming nonchalance, Sarah studied the room. No one seemed to be watching.

"How did you find I was here?" she asked.

"In Harun's harem there is always gossip. I heard of a fair-haired slave given to Mustafa. I feared the truth."

"But how did you manage to change harems? Mustafa indicated the two were separate."

"And so they are. But in his absence from the serai, it is a simple matter to slip from one courtyard to another. If one possesses the determination."

"I have the determination to leave," Sarah said with all her heart. "Please get me out of here."

"Harun was saddened when the missy ran away."

"I've got to talk to him. I found out—"

One of the women lying beside the pool turned her head in Sarah's direction, and she broke off, turning her attention instead to the women moving into and out of the room.

"We must be careful, Missy Sarah," Nadire hissed and slowly made her way down the tiers until she, too, was supine beside the water. The two did not talk for the rest of the day.

By the time morning came, Sarah fairly ran toward the room which she had learned to hate, her eunuch guards close behind. Robe belted tightly, she shoved open the door and stepped inside.

By now the women had grown used to her entry, and no one paid her any mind, even Nadire, who was once again resting on the top tier. Sarah perused the room for some place she might have missed where the two could talk without interruption. The dozens of women, familiar and distinctive now, were engaged in their useless occupations, and there was a smaller than usual complement of white and black eunuchs, some of them robed and others in the more typical Western attire of shirt and trousers.

Glancing toward the pond, she caught sight of one of the latter crouched beside the water, his back to her. Something about him held her attention. White-skinned, he wore a full-sleeved shirt and straight trousers, bound at the waist by a wide black sash. Thick black hair rested against his collar, and she could see the muscles bunch and stretch beneath the cloth pulled tightly across his back as he oiled the naked body of one of the odalisques.

Sarah tried not to stare, but she could not help herself. At last she understood what the something was—masculinity. He radiated it from across the wide room. She looked at the women again. Like her, they were watching him. They, too, had caught the difference.

If the eunuchs were aware of his presence, they did not show it. Perhaps, Sarah decided, it was because a few of the women kept them busy with demands. A conspiracy was afoot. There was a man in the room, a real man, and they had no intention of letting him get away.

The woman lying before him shifted onto her back, and he reached for the vessel of oil. His broad hands moved slowly across her throat and between her ample breasts. Suddenly Sarah could feel those hands caressing her, and she stood in shock, unable to move, unable to breathe.

Just then he looked over his shoulder and his eyes caught hers.

Sarah had been right.

The man was Jake.

Chapter Eleven

Sarah sought refuge beside Nadire at the top of the room. It was either scurry up there or hurtle through the air in the direction of the pool. More than anything else in the world, she wanted to give Jake a gigantic kiss of welcome. She had never been so glad to see anyone in her entire life.

For the time being, kissing was out as an option. With four dozen half-naked women and a squadron of eunuchs holding guard, she would only give away Jake's plan for her rescue. If he had a plan. And if that was why he was there.

Of course it was, she told herself as she hurried up the tiers. So what if he was after no more than a reward from Ralph Pettigrew? The thought was decidedly disturbing, and she asked herself if that could really be motivation enough for him to risk his life.

Against all reason and against the knowledge that she was ill deserving, she had another scenario in mind. Virile, strong-willed Jake was braving death so that the woman he cared for could live.

Settling against a pillow close to Nadire, she found herself unable to look in any other direction save the pool. Whatever Jake had in mind, it apparently included a thorough inspection of the harem wenches. Jake had good, strong hands, and he knew how to use them.

Sarah's nipples hardened against the soft red silk of her robe as she remembered the night in the hut—a night she had thrown away, and all because she had been frightened by the power of desire. Once she and Jake were far from the seraglio, she vowed to conquer that fear.

But they would never get out if he continued to provide such coveted services as he was doing now. After five minutes of agitated observation, Sarah was ready to stand up and shout, "Enough!"

"Missy Sarah has noticed the new eunuch," Nadire whispered.

Sarah started. "You mean the one by the pool?" she asked, waving a hand nonchalantly in the air.

Forgetting Mustafa's warning against conversation, she hadn't bothered to lower her voice much below its normal tone, but no one turned around to glare. For the time being, as long as Jake lubricated the beauty stretched out at his feet, the harem was a room of spellbound onlookers.

One of the women who had been curled in languorous leisure on the tiled rim of the pool behind Jake unfolded her body and sauntered over to him, her wide hips shifting rhythmically with each barefooted step. Her low voice did not carry to Sarah and Nadire, but the sharp Turkish retort of the odalisque currently benefiting from Jake's expertise came up loud and distinct.

"They argue over who is to be served," Nadire said.

Eventually the second woman took the place of the first, and Sarah's eyes wandered around the large sun-filled room. "Do you think he means to get to

153

them all? What if Mustafa enters, or the guards notice what is going on?"

"There is nothing wrong with oiling the bodies of the women," Nadire said, "although I believe Mustafa would not like this particular eunuch putting his hands on the women. There is something different about him."

The slave sounded as entranced by Jake's presence as the other spectators.

Sarah could have told her exactly what that difference was. She tried to convince herself that the building anger and frustration in her breast could not possibly be jealousy—since their abortive love-making, she and Jake had done little but argue—but she could think of nothing else it could be. All the women looked so ripe and ready, and from her vantage point she could see he was not trying to discourage them.

If she and Jake did eventually make love, she would be only one in a series of conquests for him. Granted, it was one for which he had been forced to exert himself out of the ordinary, but one nevertheless in a long line.

Jake liked women. A eunuch! What a farce.

And how shallow she was being. Here he was risking his life to get her out—for her safety or his profit was beside the point right now—and she was worrying about the methods he was choosing. Instead of thinking how she wanted to stop him, she ought to consider how she could help.

She stood and stepped down a tier.

"Missy Sarah," Nadire hissed. "What are you doing?"

"I must demand my place in line."

She hurried down before Nadire could say more. The women glanced at her as she passed, and several began to whisper; but she concentrated on her goal.

Nearing the pool, she paused beside one of the palms. Her thumb played with the tip of a frond as she studied Jake's bent figure huddled beside the dusky-skinned odalisque. From the corner of her eye, she saw one of the genuine eunuchs draw to attention. She smiled at him and shrugged, as if to say she only wanted a closer look.

Temporarily satisfied, he returned to his conversation with another of the guards, and Sarah returned to her task. Jake was no more than six feet away, his side to her, the object of his ministrations sitting as he oiled her back. Sarah sensed more than saw the awareness that came over him as she edged near.

The odalisque glanced up, and Sarah realized with a start it was Tezer, the woman who had been with Mustafa.

"Cekilir misiniz," the woman hissed.

Sarah knew just enough Turkish to realize she was being ordered to go away. Tezer had seemed to welcome and loathe Mustafa's cruel hands, but there was nothing ambivalent about the look in her eyes right now. The slave definitely preferred Jake's touch.

"Mustafa would not like what you are doing," Sarah threw back at her, knowing the slave would not understand what she said, but also knowing she would recognize the name of her master.

"Mustafa," she repeated, "wants you for his own." She waved disparagingly at Jake, at the same time keeping her eyes away from his hands as they lay against the woman's bare shoulders. "Mustafa"—she stressed the name—"may be here any day. He should not find you with such a man, even if he is a eunuch and worthless to women."

"No," the woman whispered, then added in a

heavily accented voice, "no, leave."

"You understand me," Sarah said in amazement.

"Biraz Ingilizce." Tezer stared up at her in defiance. "I speak the English."

"Good. Then you understand that I want the eunuch. Now," Sarah ordered. "Otherwise I will tell Mustafa that you have talked with me each day and have told me bad things about him."

"Hayir!"

"Yes! I need only a little while with the eunuch. My back is pained, and I have need of a massage."

Sarah caught the quirk of Jake's lips as the woman reluctantly eased her body from beneath his oiled hands. A parting spate of Turkish accompanied her exit, but Sarah had no idea what she said.

Unfastening the robe, she lowered it to expose her shoulders as she took Tezer's place.

Jake leaned close, his lips inches from her ear, and pressed his fingers into her skin. Sarah winced.

"Where do you hurt, Sarah?" He kneaded her taut muscles as though she were a mound of dough. "Or is it just your conscience that bothers you?"

She opened her mouth to argue just as one of the tall black eunuchs strolled slowly behind the row of potted trees, his eyes on Sarah, and she swallowed her retort. Jake's hands gentled, working lower over her shoulders and down to the rise of her breasts. He yawned loudly. The eunuch shrugged and moved away.

Jake's fingers neared her beaded nipples, and Sarah fought to concentrate; but all she could think of were the sparse dark curls of hair on his forearm. She could count those curls if she had enough time.

The backs of his hands, free of hair, were sunburnished; her skin looked milk white beneath them.

She trembled.

"Uncomfortable, Sarah?" he whispered. "Good."

His thumbs teased the hard tips of her breasts.

"You—" her voice caught—"must stop. I can't concentrate."

"That's no way to stop me, Angel. You're dangerous when you think."

His hands were warm and knowing as they caressed her aching fullness, and Sarah was powerless to stop him. Her back arched, and her breasts were thrust more firmly into the cradle of his touch. Surely he could feel the pounding of her heart.

Suddenly the pressure eased. "Sorry," he whispered in a none-too-steady voice as his hands returned with slippery ease to her oil-moistened shoulders. "Afraid I got carried away with the role."

Sarah took pleasure from the knowledge that he had been as shaken as she. The element of danger had aroused them both.

He continued with a more circumspect massage in momentary silence, then whispered, "Tell me your routine."

Forcing herself to match his control, she did so as briefly as she could, including the approximate location of her windowless room.

"Catch your robe in the door tonight if you can," he said, "near the floor. I'll be looking for a spot of red."

He moved his hands from her, and she knew it was time for someone else to take her place.

The rest of the morning passed slowly, with eunuchs and odalisques alike passing in and out of the room; all but Sarah were free to roam within the confines of Mustafa's harem, which Nadire informed her included a courtyard and a communal bath.

Shortly after noon trays of fruit, garnished with vegetables and cheese, were brought in by the

157

eunuchs who worked in the kitchen. Sarah was used to such service and paid it no special attention until she noticed one of the servers.

"Bandit," she whispered under her breath. With Nadire sitting next to her and Jake still busy beside the pool—would his hands never tire?—she decided the room was getting rather crowded. If she had more compatriots in Constantinople, they might be able to outnumber the regular guards.

She glanced sideways at Nadire. The slave was staring at Bandit as he shifted about the room distributing the midday meal, her huge eyes taking in every gesture he made. He was dressed in the plain loose robe of the kitchen help, and his dark head was bent toward the women that he served. There was grace of movement about him, as well as a sense of confidence, that communicated itself to the top tier.

Nadire seemed entranced.

"I see you have noticed another new eunuch," Sarah said.

The hint of a smile stole onto Nadire's face. "This is a strange day indeed, Missy Sarah."

Without seeming to have any purpose other than his assigned task, Bandit gradually worked his way to the top tier. He paused before Sarah, glanced sideways at Nadire, then glanced at her full on.

"It's all right to talk," Sarah whispered.

Nadire's smile broadened.

Bandit bowed over the tray of food. "I will be in the courtyard with Bossman."

His eyes caught Sarah's for only a second before straying once again to Nadire. At last he moved away, leaving Sarah with a decision. Nadire had proven her loyalty by entering the harem of Mustafa, a man she did not like, in order to make sure her Missy Sarah was all right. But she also was loyal to Harun and had stated her disapproval of Sarah's earlier escape.

Sarah bit into a slice of cucumber. "Nadire," she said, "what would you think if I tried to escape again?"

Nadire's eyes widened in alarm. "No! It is too dangerous. Mustafa is not a man to cross. He is not presently in the serai, but one cannot be sure how long he will be gone."

"But what if I made it out safely? Would you think it wrong?"

Nadire thought a moment, her eyes wandering over the room. "A life of such indolence is not for Missy Sarah. This I know. It would not be long before trouble would visit you here."

"Trouble brought on by me, is that what you mean?"

"The possibility exists."

Sarah paused only a moment. "I need your help."

"Oh, please do not ask."

"You don't have to drug the guards or anything like that." Sarah paused. Something in the slave's eyes prompted her to add, "That is, unless you have access to something potent. *Do* you?"

Nadire repeated, "Please do not ask."

Sarah took her response as affirmative.

"Then my request is for something that you might not find unwelcome. A private talk with the eunuch who served us our food."

Nadire looked decidedly interested.

"He is called Bandit. He will be in the courtyard shortly, along with another whom you can trust."

Nadire nodded toward the pool, where Jake was continuing his indefatigable labors.

"Right," Sarah said.

"The English women are very resourceful, are they not?"

"Sometimes we have to be. In this case, however," she said, staring at Jake, "I would give all the credit for resourcefulness to an American man."

"And perhaps to the man you call Bandit?" asked Nadire.

Sarah gave her a quick, questioning glance. Nadire's eyes blinked back innocently.

"Bandit, too," said Sarah.

Nadire did not ask for details, gaining Sarah's gratitude, especially since she could not supply the slave with any facts. Jake had come to get her out, and Bandit was helping him. Nothing else mattered.

The longest hour of Sarah's life came during the afternoon, when Jake, Bandit, and Nadire were simultaneously absent from the room. Nadire was the only one of the three who returned, and she indicated that she would talk later with Sarah.

Bandit was not present at the serving of the evening repast, and the conspiratorial talk with Nadire that Sarah had been awaiting with growing agitation consisted of one order. Her red robe was to be used to mark the bolted door of her quarters.

"As Aga Jake has requested," the slave said.

"Aga Jake?"

"It is a title of respect. He did not seem to mind that I chose it."

Aga Jake. Sarah let the name play in her mind.

When the time came, she did as she was told, letting the robe fall from her body as she entered the private and dimly lit room where each night she tried to sleep. The only other garment she had to put on was the golden harem costume she had worn before Mustafa. Dressing hurriedly, she pulled up a pillow and settled in for what she hoped was a short wait.

Later, she jerked awake and was immediately at full attention. What had brought her from the sleep that she had been certain would not come? A noise in the passageway outside her quarters. Heart pounding, she padded barefoot across the room and pressed her lips close to the narrow crack between frame and door.

"Jake?" she asked in a nervous whisper, rubbing sweaty palms against her harem trousers.

The only answer was the sound of a bolt slipping from its moorings. A moment later, the door eased open.

"Jake," she sighed in relief.

His dark eyes studied her from the shadowy passageway.

"Let's get out of here," he said at last.

She grabbed for the red silk robe lying at her feet.

"No," he said. "Wear this."

He thrust into her hands a plain brown robe. "And for God's sake, put on the headpiece and veil."

Sarah hurriedly did as she was ordered, adding only her leather slippers.

"Wait," she whispered, aware of his impatience. Grabbing up the red robe, she stuffed it with pillows and arranged it carefully on the bed. Someone checking on her and not bothering with too close an inspection might be fooled into thinking she was deeply asleep.

Jake nodded his approval. Outside he slipped the bolt carefully back in place and began to move stealthily down the dark passageway, Sarah close on his heels. Needing the security of his touch, she gripped his hand. It was smoother than she remembered—the result of all that ointment from his earlier activities.

As far as she could tell, he was dressed in the same shirt and trousers he'd worn during the day. The same black sash was tied around his waist, its long

161

tail brushing against his thigh as he walked.

The only addition was the fez sitting firmly on his head. She thought he looked rather debonair and exotic.

Occasional lanterns lit the cloister; these they hurried past. Jake guided her into the courtyard, where they crept around the perimeter to the opposite side.

"Mustafa's quarters," Jake said, gesturing toward the direction from which they had come. "Harun's harem is over here."

"You're taking me to Harun?"

"Think again, Sarah. We're getting the hell out of this place as fast as we can."

"Where are Mustafa's guards?"

"Sleeping peacefully, I hope. Along with a few of Harun's."

"Drugged?"

"Your friend Nadire proved most helpful."

In the dark, Sarah smiled. At least she had been able to contribute something to her own rescue, if only the help of someone else. She doubted Jake would demonstrate much gratitude.

Perhaps she could help in a more direct way, she decided as she turned from him. This side of the courtyard looked familiar. "I believe the meeting room of the divan is down here. We can get out farther along through the stables."

"With an armed escort close on our heels? Isn't that how you tried to get away?"

Sarah ignored him and took the lead. Concentrating on her route, she was surprised when he grabbed her by the wrist and pulled her into the shadows against the wall.

"Wha—"

She got no further as his lips covered hers. His

body pressed her hard against the rough surface, but she did not try to fight him. When she heard the unmistakable sounds of footsteps, she felt her heart in her throat.

She squeezed her eyes closed. The footsteps drew nearer, nearer, seemed to hesitate directly behind Jake, and at last passed on into the night. Still, Jake did not move. With danger moving steadily away, she realized the force of his mouth covering hers had eased and what had been an action to quiet her was moving rapidly into a kiss.

As the pressure of his body against hers also eased, her hands stole upward and rested against his chest. She could feel his heart pounding; her own heart answered with a pounding of its own. The peril of their situation only heightened the sexual pull of his touch.

Her fingers crept upward, and she stroked his smooth-shaven cheeks. His lips were sweet upon hers; the familiar taste of him made her feel at once safe and in far greater danger than any offered by a wandering guard.

Jake broke the kiss. "Don't speak," he whispered into her mouth, "or I'll have to silence you again."

Sarah did not necessarily take that as a threat.

"But the stable—"

Jake brushed his lips against hers. She shut up.

"I know where it is. Before Bandit got me in here, we studied the serai from the outside. Put your hand in mine and trust me. I'll have you out of here in a flash. And then," he said, his voice thick with meaning, "we'll go to a special place I have in mind. A place where we can be alone."

Chapter Twelve

Just as he had promised, Jake soon had her out of the seraglio and into the quiet streets. Slipping through the stables past a sleeping guard ("Nadire again?" Sarah had whispered, and Jake had nodded once, sharply), the only danger that presented itself came when one of the Arabian steeds snorted loudly enough to waken even the drugged guard.

Jake let go of her hand long enough to soothe the animal.

Outside, Sarah paused to breathe deeply, but Jake jerked her into a fast walk through the deserted, twisting streets.

"Keep your eyes down and your face covered," he ordered as he hurried through the dark.

Sarah stumbled on a cobble and righted herself. "Where are we going?" she asked.

"I told you. A place we can be alone."

"Not to Ralph," she said.

"No," he answered brusquely. "We're going to my room. Unless there is another destination you would prefer."

"And if I have such a destination in mind?"

"It will have to wait."

Despite all that common sense and pride had taught her, Sarah felt a shiver of anticipation. Jake's kiss was still on her lips. She hoped the journey would be short.

It seemed to her they wandered for miles, past open doorways from which came the laughter and arguing that signaled human habitation. Twice they ducked into the shadows and listened to the strike of a night watchman's boots against the cobbled streets as he strode past.

They passed a large domed building, and Jake slowed the pace.

"The Grand Bazaar," he said. "We're almost there."

They came to a halt before a low, long building. Three doors faced the street. Jake went to the one on the far left and, working at an ornate lock securing the apartment, quickly opened the door and pulled her into the black interior.

She waited in silence, listening to the sounds of Jake walking about in the dark and lighting the lamp. She pictured the economy of movement with which he did everything, the masterful way he took charge, and her heart quickened.

He raised the wick, and a flickering illumination spread across the small, white-walled room.

Removing her head covering and veil, she shook her hair free and looked around, keeping her eyes turned from him. She did not want him to read too soon what surely must be the message in her eyes.

A western-style bed took up one corner, and a table and pair of chairs another. Beside her to the right was another table holding a porcelain bowl and pitcher. Two high windows to the left were outlined in blue and white tile, and the floor was covered by a fine Persian rug and a scattering of colored pillows.

"It's lovely," she said.

"Bandit's work," Jake said with a shrug.

Sarah thought he sounded a little curt. "Do you know if he's all right?"

Jake nodded once. "You didn't hear him, but he was close behind us. I don't imagine he'll show up again until tomorrow."

"You said earlier that he was the one who got you into the seraglio. How?"

"A cousin is one of the sultan's guards. Bandit has a store of relatives around the world. As my life grows more complicated, I'm finding them very useful."

Sarah felt his dark eyes on her. Accusing eyes. She *was* a complication, but she had never planned to be.

Moving past him to the table, she studied the teapot that rested in its center. Her fingers stroked its cool, curved surface. "This is very valuable," she said.

"Bandit bought it at the bazaar."

"He really is amazing," she said, then glanced at Jake. He looked lean and bristled and wonderful. A shade tense, perhaps, bordering on grim, but then she ought to be used to him that way.

"But he isn't the only one who is amazing," she added softly. "So are you."

Jake removed the fez and tossed it aside. It rolled across the rug and came to a stop against a fat golden pillow.

"Not amazing. Just stupid." He shook his head in disgust. "I didn't realize you would leave the dhow."

Sarah had misread him. He was far more than tense or grim. He was furious.

"I'm sorry—"

"Not good enough," he snapped. "Are you so spoiled and bent on having your own way that you don't care what havoc you cause?"

His words stung. "That's unfair," she shot back at him.

"You've been nothing but bad news ever since we met."

"Then why did you bother to come after me? It is obvious that whatever is to be my fate, in your eyes it's no more than what I deserve."

"Why, you ask? Good question. I thought maybe I had pushed you into running away, that maybe you had a point about not wanting to go to your fiancé, although he'd have to be damned bad to be worse than Mustafa, according to what I've heard."

"In other words, you were salving your conscience."

"Sounds dumb, doesn't it? Or maybe I just felt responsible for you—the way the Chinese do when they save someone's life. Although I believe that in China, one salvation is usually enough."

Sarah welcomed the rage that swept over her. It was far less dangerous than the warm, hungry feelings that had been stealing into her heart and mind.

"You're right about one thing, Jake. You did force me into running away. It was probably one of the dumbest things I've ever done"—she ignored the skeptical look on his face—"but I didn't much care for your plans to sell me to Ralph."

"A reward for your safe return is hardly a sale."

"A fine distinction at best, Jake. To me, they amount to the same thing. I regret very much that you lost your gold."

"I've never blamed you for that."

"Somehow I got the idea that you had. At the least you expected some sort of compensation for your loss."

Taking off the hot heavy robe, she tossed it aside.

The coolness of the room brushed across her skin, but she was too heated by anger to draw comfort from it. Clad in the golden bodice and trousers of the harem, she stood before him, hands on hips, and glared. "I will forever be grateful for what you did today, but I will not do everything that you order. I will not be your slave."

Sarah felt she could touch the tension between them. It weighed heavily against her.

Jake's dark eyes raked slowly down her half-clad figure. He let out a long, slow breath of air. "Why not mine? I imagine you've been somebody's. Did you enjoy losing your innocence to the son of a sultan?"

"No more than you did fondling every breast you could get your hands on all day."

Jake edged nearer. "All in the performance of duty," he said softly. His gaze stopped at the thin bodice that barely covered her. "Would you like to know how yours compared?"

"Quite favorably, I am sure."

"Perhaps I need another sampling." Jake's eyes were trained on her nipples that hardened and betrayed the coiled arousal she so wanted to hide.

"After all, Angel, there were so many others."

"Oh!" she cried out, lifting a hand to slap him, but he caught her wrist, his fingers burning into her skin. He pulled her hard against him, her arms twisted behind her back, her wrists captured in the powerful grip of one hand. His breath was hot on her cheek, and she realized that the pounding of her heart was not caused by fear alone. Around Jake she had no pride.

Caught in the consuming flames of anger and hurt and longing, she tried to pull free.

"Not yet," he said huskily. "I rather liked the shape of your breasts. High and firm and nicely

168

resilient. The others were much too soft."

Sarah fought for air. "Too bad you feel that way," she managed. "I prefer you in the role of eunuch."

"Why, Sarah? Did you really like what Mustafa did to you? I hear he hurts women. Roams the city in the dead of night and inflicts his particular kinds of gratification on the peasant women and whores. In the harem I suppose he is more circumspect."

His fingers squeezed hard against her wrists, and his free hand stroked her neck and shoulders with an unyielding determination that at once frightened and thrilled her.

She shoved one shoulder against his chest, fighting herself as well as Jake, but he gave no ground.

"Do you like to be hurt?" he demanded. His hand cupped her face. "Do you?"

He gave her no chance to respond. When his lips covered hers, Sarah tried to squirm out of his grasp, to twist her head away, but every movement seemed to drive him onward to his mastery of her. His ardor burned into her skin, caught in her veins. Liquid desire spread through her. She was caught in the power of him, as she had been the night on the island. Her own determination strengthened, not to pull free of his embrace as she had done then, but to meld her own needs with his. They wanted the same thing, and she could not deny herself any more than she could deny him.

With her arms pinned behind her, she could do no more than arch herself against him, her body softening under his warmth, like newly gathered honey. She felt the change in him, the tightening sinews, the infinitesimal shift of his shoulders and hips that brought the hard planes of his body in contact with her gentler curves.

He lifted his head.

"Free my hands," she said, her breath ragged.

Brushing his lips against hers, Jake did as she demanded, and she wound her arms around his neck.

His eyes, dark as the Turkish night sky under which they had sailed, locked with hers. "Make no mistake, Sarah. There will be no hut tumbling down tonight."

Frissons of fear and longing worked their way along her spine. She had wanted to find out whether or not she would still be afraid at the time of joining; now she would know. She dropped her gaze to his parted lips. Time stood still. Nothing in all the world seemed half so important as that sight.

All fears dropped away, leaving only the longing. She yearned to taste Jake, to touch Jake, to feel his skin rubbing against hers. She wanted to know anything and everything about his body. Willingly she would let him learn the same about hers.

Loosening one hand from his neck, she touched his lower lip with her forefinger, ran the tip along the inside of his mouth, against his teeth, against the rough edge of his tongue, then brought the finger to her own mouth. She could taste his desire.

"Sarah," he whispered. The hands that had been holding her stroked across her shoulders and back, then slipped to the curve of her waist and the swelling of her buttocks. He held her tightly, and she felt the hardness of him pressing against the parting of her thighs.

She thought to tell him that she was still virginal, but his kiss stopped her before she could utter a word. When his tongue brushed roughly against hers, she forgot her innocence. She was a woman, not a child, and it was as a woman that she would welcome all that was about to happen.

His demands made her worldly wise, and she

opened her mouth wide in welcome to his invasion. Her body writhed against his, her hips undulating as they had in the harem dance, only this time the dance was not subtly provocative but direct and insistent and demanding.

He broke the kiss and burned his lips down her throat, pressing against the throbbing pulse before trailing downward. Her head dropped back as she exposed the fullness of her breasts to his gaze and, far better, to his lips and tongue. As he kissed her through the filmy bodice, her nipples tightened, and she felt her breasts swell under his assault.

His teeth closed gently over one beaded tip. She wondered for a fleeting moment if he truly planned to hurt her, assuming that was what she wanted since she had not denied it, but instead of pain he brought her only pleasure. One hand cupped her other breast, then with an impatience that she shared, pulled the cloth away and stroked the naked, rising fullness.

Her body would not be still. She rubbed against him, moving her breasts and her hips until she heard a low growl deep in his throat. Her fingers pulled at the fastenings of his shirt and stole inside. She felt his muscles constrict each place that she touched, and she realized that the low growl she heard a second time came from her, not from him.

His lips grazed her bare abdomen, and his tongue dipped inside the concave navel that was exposed by her low-cut trousers. Sarah felt her legs weaken under her, as though she had no bones inside. She was all flesh and pounding blood and nerves that threatened to explode. As she felt herself falling, he swept her into his arms, holding her close, one strong arm under her knees and the other around her back. His hand fondled her breast, and his lips returned once again to her waiting mouth.

171

Around her the room whirled at a dizzying pace.

He broke the kiss and laid her on the bed. Bereft of his warmth, she wanted to reach up to him, to cling to him, to hold him tightly against her forever.

But Jake had other plans. Swiftly he tore the clothes from his body. He was without modesty, just as he had been that night in the hut. This time Sarah did not wonder where she should look. She looked everywhere . . . from his hard-chiseled face, down the strong column of his neck, across the expanse of chest that she had stroked only seconds ago, to the lean hips and thighs and powerful calves dusted darkly with body hair, and at last back to the tumescence that proved without words how much he wanted her.

Made bold by her own wants, she stared at him. Could her chaste body hold and satisfy him? Could the pain of which he spoke be the invasion of a man inside a woman? Did it happen every time?

Even as the edges of fear returned, she felt the warmth that had melted throughout her body burst into flames. Her body burned for him, and the heat centered in the valley between her thighs. She felt a strange moistness that she did not question. When Jake dropped beside her on the bed and began to undress her, she welcomed him with open arms.

He removed the scant bodice and trousers with a skill that said it was not the first time he had removed such clothes from a woman. His hands lingered over her breasts, brushed down her abdomen, stroked her thighs and calves. His fingers drifted softly across the instep of each tightly arched foot. Her already tingling nerves tightened everywhere he touched until her entire being was a network of throbbing desire.

His hands began their inexorable journey upward, his thumbs circling across her taut skin as he slowly

172

progressed. When he lingered at the juncture of her thighs, playing in the pale, wiry pubic hair, she had to bite her tongue to keep from crying out. He rubbed his fingers across the coal-hot center of her passion. She writhed under his touch.

He shifted his body upward until his lips captured hers once again, but his fingers did not stray from between her legs. Sarah moaned with satisfaction. She felt the heat rise. Strange pounding sensations took hold of her. She brushed her tongue wildly against his and groaned into his mouth.

"Touch me," he commanded, and she knew what he meant. Made brazen by rapture, she slid her hand down his chest, the flatness of his abdomen, the wiry bristles of hair that thickened above his thighs, and at last held him within her fingers. She did not know how hard to enfold him, was not sure whether a man could be hurt. Perhaps men liked pain.

Her strokes were gentle at first. She felt Jake's breath grow more uneven, and she quickened the movement of her hand. Remembering how he had teased her breasts and her own intimate self, she rubbed her thumb back and forth over the tip of his shaft until she felt a few drops of moisture.

"Sarah," he growled, lifting his head. "Angel. You go too fast." His lips pressed against the hollow of her shoulder, then burned upward until he reached her ear. He ran his tongue around the lobe.

"You have learned your lessons too well," he whispered. "I cannot wait."

Before Sarah could take in exactly what he meant, she felt him part her thighs and press the hardness of his body against her.

His hands cupped her buttocks and lifted her beneath him until her knees bent and she felt her hips rising off the bed to meet his.

"Jake—"

He plunged inside, and she cried out.

His pause was only momentary. Sarah buried her face against his neck and, unable to do anything else, not wanting to do anything else, wrapped her arms tightly around him, accepting the rhythmic thrusts of his body and, after a moment, welcoming their increasing power as the passionate throbbings returned.

He had indeed hurt her, but the pain subsided, in its place a burgeoning sweet intensity so strong that she was incapable of thought. She embraced him and matched his thrusts until their bodies became one. She was his equal in ecstasy, giving and taking what her body demanded, and what his demanded in return. As waves of rapture washed over her, she knew not which was his flesh and which was hers.

Spasms shook his body, more violent than her own, almost frightening in their vigor, and still she clung to him. The spasms slowed, then at last ceased, but Sarah could not let go of him. No longer ignorant of the power that came with passion, she clung to the last trailing fragments of rapture.

At last the beating of her heart slowed, and she was able to draw a deep breath. She was swept by a feeling of immense satisfaction. Gone was the aching that had burrowed deep inside her the first time she saw him riding his boat like a god. In its place was contentment. Not a restful kind—after all, Jake still cradled her in his arms—but a feeling of happiness more wonderful than she had ever imagined.

Jake held her for a long time, nestling her against his body, their sweat mingling, their hearts thrumming with the same erratic beat. She felt her body grow languorous from the sheer serenity that had invaded her. Making love was a glorious experience—fiery and demanding and then after its peak, when she felt her whole being explode, a gradual winding down and an inner peace. With that peace came a lessening of the loneliness that had been a part of her life as long as she could remember.

Snuggled against him, she was close to sleep when he eased her arms from around his neck.

His eyes were darkly concerned. "You were so still. Are you all right?" he asked.

She looked up at him in confusion. "Of course I'm all right. Am I not supposed to be?"

"I assumed at the seraglio—well, hell, you know what I assumed."

Sarah's mind cleared. Shifting free of his embrace, she pushed the matted, damp hair away from her face. "Of course I know. You assumed that Mustafa had taken me to his bed."

"Had *forced* you into his bed. It damned near drove me crazy."

Sarah remembered the island and Jake's declaration that he did not deflower virgins. He had seemed proud of the fact. His one scruple, he had called it. She felt the beginnings of a chill.

"And you wanted to find out if he had. In a way that would offer irrefutable proof."

Jake laughed sharply and without humor. "Do you really think that's why you ended the night in my bed, Sarah?"

She sighed and looked away, unable to respond until she had an answer to a question of her own.

"Do you have any regrets?" she asked.

"Do you?"

The echo of his voice hung in the air. She felt the sweat from their bodies across her breasts and

175

stomach. Worse, she felt the moisture from his body thick between her thighs.

How was she supposed to answer? That his lovemaking was the most glorious thing that had ever happened to her? That she wanted him again and again because she did not believe she could ever get enough of the thrills he aroused? That he had touched something deep within she had never known existed?

He would be embarrassed by such a declaration, and a little part of her would die.

If only she did not still feel the brush of his skin against hers, did not still carry the scent of him in her very pores, she might find it easier to be nonchalant, easier to lie.

"I didn't break," she said. "As a matter of fact, I found the whole thing rather nice."

The words sounded silly—shallow, even—but wasn't that how he already thought of her?

Jake held still for a moment. She could not meet his eye.

"Rather nice, was it? That's the first time I've heard it described as that. From your reaction," he said, a hard edge to his voice, "I thought that you liked it. For what it's worth, Angel, you were good. Damned good. One of the best."

He moved from the bed and began to pull his trousers over his long legs—legs that had so recently been between hers. She shook off the image.

Finding her breath coming hard, she sat up. "I had reason not to tell you I'd not slept with Mustafa," she said.

He reached for his shirt. "I'd almost rather not know. Did you believe I would stop the way I did on the island? I think not."

"How clever of you, Jake."

176

Sarah welcomed the return of her old self-reliance. Jake was passing her on to Ralph Pettigrew, just as her father had done. Except for one minor exception, her personal condition hadn't changed since she left Liverpool.

"I have already promised to repay what I can of your missing gold," she said coolly. "I do not want you to collect from my fiancé." She flicked back the tangled hair from her shoulders and forced herself to look at Jake.

"Ralph—" She paused. "Strange, isn't it, that I've never called him that to his face? He's expecting an untarnished bride. My father told me as much, and it certainly is Ralph's right. In my present state, I doubt he would be willing to pay very much. You're better off depending on me for your reward."

Jake stared down at her, his eyes glittering with mockery. "All this to decrease your value? I don't believe it."

"You should." She shifted as if to rise, desperate to cover her cold, damp body but determined not to show a sign of weakness. "Is there some way I could bathe? This process is rather messy."

Again Jake laughed. She did not like the sound.

"Messy but nice," he said. He gestured to the bowl and pitcher in the corner. "Help yourself." Tightening the sash at his waist, he headed toward the door.

"Where are you going?" she asked. Against all reason, she did not want to be alone.

"I'll spend the night on the boat. It's what I usually do when you take over my quarters. Tomorrow I'll visit your awaiting bridegroom. I'll let him decide whether he wants you or not. He can determine what value you have."

"Then you're going to tell him about us."

"I'll leave that little chore to you, Angel. If you've

got the nerve. I said you were good, and you were, but as far as I'm concerned, you're more trouble than you're worth."

The door slammed behind him just as she heaved a pillow at his departing back. Aga Jake indeed, she thought just as she burst into tears.

Chapter Thirteen

Well, buddy, you certainly handled that little scene with grace. Like a bear in heat.

Jake ignored the curious stares of the few late-night carousers as he made his long journey on foot to the dhow. He didn't often talk to himself. Tonight it seemed appropriate.

He couldn't get Sarah out of his mind. He could still feel her under him, responding. . . . He'd never been so aroused. From the moment he kissed her in the seraglio, with a guard strolling three feet away and Jake not caring, he had known he would take her to bed.

Sarah was an impetuous woman. Her nature got her into one predicament after another during the day; she was far better suited for nights. For loving. He'd been a bear, all right, with the way he had grabbed her and fondled her and made her his, but golden-haired Sarah with her flashing blue eyes and ready passions had been a tigress in his arms.

He shook off the specific images that crowded in— her seeking, bruised lips and curious hands, her silken skin and long legs. He and Sarah no more belonged together mating than did those two species

179

of animals. Except for a mutual and energetic enthusiasm in bed, they did not fit.

Jake was a rover, a sailor of the seven seas. He had a few ideas about his future, but nothing he wanted to act on right away. Nothing that included settling down.

Sarah was the kind of woman who cast out tentacles. She might not realize it, but she did. For all her foolish impetuosity, she was an English lady; he was an American bum. For her, he was no more than a side adventure on the way to the rest of her life, whether she would admit it or not, and that's all she could be for him.

She had been lying when she said why they had made love. To despoil her for her fiancé? Hell, no. She hadn't been thinking of Ralph when she rubbed herself against him, when she brushed her tongue against his, when she parted her legs and. . . .

Damn! There he went again.

By the time he climbed aboard the dhow, he was wound tight as a spring.

"Bossman," said Bandit as he scrambled from the sleeping quarters, "I did not expect you tonight."

"Yeah, well, here I am."

Jake grabbed for a blanket inside the shelter.

"Is Miss Whitlock safe and well?" asked Bandit.

"She's safe enough."

Jake spread the blanket on the deck.

"The Bossman was very brave tonight in the seraglio."

"No more than you."

"Not so. I did not have the woman in my protection. If I had been seen departing at that unlikely hour, I could have claimed to be about my cousin's business. I had no reason to worry for my safety. You were the one unafraid."

180

"Don't fool yourself, friend. I was worried, all right. Those eunuchs may have been without some body parts you and I consider essential, but they had swords to make up for the loss. And we were a little outnumbered."

"What you say is true. We owe much to the slave Nadire," said Bandit. "Without her help we would not have been able to administer the narcotic to so many of the guards. I wish strongly that she is not found out."

Something in his voice pulled Jake's attention away from his own frustrations.

"Maybe you should have asked her to come with us."

"It was discussed only briefly in the courtyard. For most of her years she has been in the seraglio. She would not leave."

"People get used to a way of life," Jake growled, turning back on himself once again. "Don't want to change."

"We speak of Nadire, of course."

Jake did not answer.

"The Bossman should take the shelter. I will sleep on the deck."

Jake shook his head. "Crawl back inside," he said, "and I'll stay out here. Since meeting Angel, I've grown used to bedding down under the stars."

Sleep was a long time coming, and when it did Jake dreamed he was lying naked beside an oasis, a vast desert surrounding him and a merciless sun beating down with the heat of a million fires. Try as he might, he couldn't drag himself into the shade of the palm trees beside the shallow water. His skin blistered and broke, his lips cracked, but he was helpless to move.

A drum roll sounded. From behind a nearby dune,

which glistened stark white in the cloudless sky, marched a pair of breasts, scimitars suspended under them as legs. More breasts followed, and more, in endless progression. As each pair moved past him, a blade slashed toward his broken skin. Summoning all his strength, he scurried backward like a crab to protect himself from harm. With each scurry, he drew farther away from the shady comfort of the oasis and deeper into the desert heat.

He jerked awake. The blinding sun of his dream was replaced by its real counterpart, an orange disk which sat above the eastern horizon and spread its warmth across the land and water.

Lying still on the hard wood deck, he waited for his deranged mind to settle into its usual channels. The images from his sleep still seemed real to him, more real than the sun and the sky and the rocking motion of the dhow. He wasn't given to fanciful visions, awake or asleep, and he didn't quite know what to make of this one.

He licked his lips, and his hands lifted unconsciously to his face. His skin was warm but undamaged, and he began to shake off the dream. He heard shouts from the wharf and the frigate anchored close by, and the slap of sails being unfurled. The day was well under way.

Rolling to his side, he glanced inside the sleeping quarters, but Bandit was no longer there.

Jake sat and stretched. The muscles of his back and shoulders protested. He'd worked long and hard yesterday at his tasks.

If anyone had told him he would grow weary of touching women's breasts, he would have laughed. He wasn't laughing now. He never wanted to see another. . . .

Hold on. What if Sarah were here now?

But she wasn't. There was no reason for her ever again to be aboard the dhow.

By now Jake was fully awake. He had business to take care of today—Sarah Whitlock business—and he decided a Turkish bath might steam a little of the weariness out of him and prepare him for dear old Ralph.

Bandit arrived just as he was leaving. He brought a container of the sweet, thick Turkish coffee that Jake was learning to like. Jake drank it down, announced his various destinations, and headed out toward the center of the city, a change of clothing under his arm.

An hour later he strolled out of the bath, clean-shaven and feeling five pounds lighter after the session in the steam-filled room. The only part he'd taken no notice of—a departure from his normal behavior—was the dark-eyed woman rubbing him down with the thick towel that was as much a part of Turkey as was the coffee.

He'd had his hair trimmed until it came to the edge of his shirt collar. All he lacked were a coat and cravat to present himself as an American business-man. But not in Constantinople in the late summer. Ralph Pettigrew would have to take him as he was.

Walking briskly toward the ancient viaduct that crossed the Golden Horn, he kept as much as he could in the shade. The British sector, located in the northern portion of Constantinople known as Pera, was cleaner and quieter than Jake had grown used to in this part of the world, primarily because it lacked the vendors that crowded the city's streets. Most anything could be bought from the vendors, from coffee to textiles to women. Jake decided the British preferred their purchases to be more circumspect.

And there were all those brothels located only blocks away. He harbored little doubt the English gentlemen were familiar customers behind their doors.

He asked for directions to Pettigrew's home, a neat, whitewashed structure of modest size with a shaded garden on either side. An elderly housekeeper in cotton apron and dress met him at the door. She eyed him suspiciously as he asked for her employer.

"Don't hold with peddlers," she said, starting to close the door.

"But I'm not selling anything," Jake protested, thinking that Sarah would disagree. "I've come with news about Mr. Pettigrew's fiancée."

"Leave the poor man alone. He's had enough bad news."

"Not this time." He briefly explained his mission.

The woman responded with a skeptical glare, a look of disbelief, and at last a broad smile. She directed him to the Englishman's place of business, the headquarters of his shipping company Eastern Ports of Call. Pettigrew's private office was in an old warehouse a block off the northern bank of the Horn.

Jake was surprised to find the one-story building looking a little shabby on the outside. The interior was no more impressive—dimly lit, a worn carpet on the floor, a musty smell in the air, and without, as far as Jake could tell, a sign of any decorative art. Sarah would soon fix that.

A clerk sat in the small outer room, an array of papers in front of him on a plain, massive desk; behind him was a partially opened door. He glanced up as Jake entered. His hair and skin were both pale, and Jake wondered how he managed to keep such a complexion living under the Turkish sun. A limp black suit hung on his slight frame, and he wore a loose black tie.

"Could I help you?" he said in a voice right out of

184

London, cordial enough, but his eyes studied Jake as though he'd come to rob the place.

So much for Jake's attempts at respectability. He got the feeling Eastern Ports of Call didn't get much off-the-street business.

"Is Mr. Pettigrew in?"

The clerk frowned. "If this is in connection with the payments—"

"It isn't," said Jake, cutting him off and wondering at the same time if that was smart. "Tell him that Jake Price would like to see him. It's a private matter."

"I don't know—"

"What is it, Samuel?" came another distinctly British voice from the room behind the clerk. This one was deeper and more authoritative.

"A Mr. Price," the clerk began, but Jake was already circling around him.

"Don't bother, Sam," said Jake. "I'll introduce myself."

The second room was larger than the first but just as plain. The primary differences were in the large bare desk and the thickset man behind it.

The Englishman came to his feet.

"See here," he said huffily.

Jake moved closer to get a better look.

Tall as Jake and thirty pounds heavier, Ralph Pettigrew sported a full head of gray hair and pale, nervous eyes beneath matching gray brows. His lips were thin and tight and his face ruddy, as though years at sea had left him permanently marked. He had a weak chin, Jake thought, to go with the weak mouth. About fifty, Jake estimated, fifty-one at the most.

So here was the man Sir Edward Whitlock had chosen to marry his only daughter. On first sight,

Jake didn't like him; he had a feeling he wouldn't much care for Sir Edward, either.

But it wasn't up to him to like the two men. That was Sarah's chore.

"Mr. Pettigrew." He extended his hand, which was ignored.

Jake could play the same game. He dropped his hand to his side and got to his business. "I've come about your fiancée, Sarah Whitlock."

Pettigrew's face darkened. "Please, Mr. Price, if this is some kind of jest. . . ." He paused and brushed a broad hand across his eyes.

Jake felt a twinge of sympathy for him and hurried on.

"Miss Whitlock is alive."

"Wha—" Pettigrew stopped, his face and voice hardening. "If this really *is* some kind of jest, I'll have you horsewhipped!"

"That much of a bastard, I'm not," said Jake. "Believe me, she's alive. And she's well."

"But that's impossible! The reports said all on board were lost."

"All but one. She was rescued by a passing boat."

Which was true enough, as far as it went. Jake wasn't about to spin out the complete story. Let Sarah do that. He got a clear picture of how her tale of misadventure would be received. Even leaving out a few details about last night—and he was certain that with the light of day she would decide to do just that—the events of the recent past would seem far more like fabrication than fact.

She had no proof she'd ever been inside the Grand Seraglio, other than a flimsy bit of clothing she'd worn on her dash to freedom. And she could have bought such wear at any bazaar.

Even Jake had his doubts about one or two of the

early parts. He damned sure knew the story wasn't complete.

"I . . . I hardly know what to say," stumbled Pettigrew. He sat heavily back in his chair and stared up at Jake. "Where is she?" His voice quickened. "Is she outside?"

This question Jake was prepared for, and he went on with his tale of half truths. "She's in a private home recuperating. Not," he hastened to add, "from any injuries. But she was unconscious for a while and is in general exhausted. I believe she didn't know who she was at first. That's why the delay in getting the news to you."

"Take me to her," Pettigrew said, once again officious as he leaned across his desk toward Jake.

"Not a good idea."

Pettigrew eyed him narrowly, his pale eyes staring warily at Jake. "Is this some kind of ransom attempt, Price? Do you have any proof that you're telling me the truth?"

Jake started to speak and found that he couldn't follow the course he had charted days ago.

"No ransom," he said. The words were as much a surprise to him as they were to Pettigrew. "I'm not after a reward. Whether you believe me or not about the rescue, is up to you. But I can tell you that you haven't seen Miss Whitlock in years. Correspondence by letters, I believe, has been your method of courtship, and most of those to Sir Edward."

"It's not an unusual circumstance. You could have guessed. Or picked it up from embassy gossip."

"True enough. But I didn't. Miss Whitlock is fair-haired with blue eyes and a tendency to get into trouble. She's quick-witted and like her father has a good eye for fine porcelains. At least I suppose she has, from the things I have heard her say."

"You know all this?"

"When she finally had her wits about her, Sarah—Miss Whitlock, that is—was most talkative."

Jake could read the doubt in Pettigrew's eyes soften with the beginnings of belief. The Englishman came close to smiling before the suspicion returned.

"So how are you involved? And just who is this family she's staying with? Turkish? English? I would hope they are respectable. After all, a lady of Miss Whitlock's sensibilities should not be exposed to the cruder elements that abound in this country."

Jake was tempted to tell him about her stay in the seraglio. The Englishman could decide for himself if the sultan was respectable or not, and if he could be called crude.

"The family is American," he said instead. "The residence is in Stamboul. I volunteered to let you know about her rescue. She was afraid you would suffer physically if she suddenly appeared on your doorstep. The shock and all."

Considering your age. Jake's meaning was obvious.

Which Pettigrew understood.

"I see," he said. "So she really is alive," the last said softly as if to himself. He seemed lost in thought.

"Is it possible for you to get word to her father that she's all right?"

Pettigrew stirred from his reverie. "Sir Edward is, I believe, traveling about the American colonies."

Whatever pleasure he took from the acceptance of Jake's news didn't keep him from being all business now.

"The United States, you mean," said Jake.

"Of course. The United States. A message will be dispatched right away. I sent word of the sinking of the *Leviathan*, but I'm not certain he ever received it, considering the uncivilized nature of the country in which he was traveling."

Jake let the insult go.

So Sir Edward Whitlock might or might not know that the daughter he'd shipped off for an arranged marriage was presumed drowned. Jake wondered if he might or might not care.

Pettigrew stood and walked around the desk. "Enough of this delay. You must take me to her right away."

"I said it's not a good idea, and I meant it."

The Englishman came to a halt beside Jake and eyed him suspiciously. "See here, Price, I am, after all, her fiancé."

Jake had done a little improvising up to now, but he had already decided how he would answer Pettigrew's expected demand.

"She would rather travel to you. She'll get there, all right. Take my word for it, Ralph, she's in good health."

Damned good health, he added to himself and was struck with regret that he'd volunteered to arrange for her reunion with her betrothed. The things he was doing in her behalf—voluntarily or not—had him thinking he didn't know himself anymore.

"You seem to know rather a great deal about her condition," said Pettigrew.

Jake could have added a few more details that Ralph might not appreciate, but he contented himself with a shrug.

"I am not convinced you are not seeking some sort of reward," said Pettigrew, worry in his pale eyes. "I am prepared to offer a small one, rest assured."

Now Jake had a second chance at a little money. In Sarah's behalf, he resented the "small one."

"I said that was not what I was after."

"So what am I expected to do?" asked Pettigrew.

"Prepare a place for her to live until the wedding. Wherever you planned for her to stay before."

"Actually, it was a room in the embassy. It's there for short-term guests. The ceremony was not to be postponed for long."

"Someone will bring her to the embassy."

"You?"

The hostility was unmistakable.

"Someone."

Jake took a hard look at Ralph Pettigrew and thought of last night with Sarah. An image of her lying beneath the portly body of her betrothed flashed across his mind. What difference was it to him, he tried to ask himself, if she chose to lie beneath the entire British fleet? It was a question without a clear answer.

Fool that he was, he could not turn her over to this pompous man right away. It was best for her—even Bandit would agree—but he found himself hard to convince. And there was the fact that Sarah most definitely did not want the wedding to take place. More and more he doubted the wisdom and affection of a father who would put his daughter in such a situation.

Sarah had never once expressed worry about what her father was suffering, had not asked that he be informed of her surviving the disaster aboard the *Leviathan*.

Perhaps she knew her father was not lost in grief.

"Miss Whitlock will let you know when she feels strong enough for a carriage ride to the embassy," said Jake.

"But you said she was all right."

"She is. I know the circumstances are unusual, but you will have to honor her wishes. It would, I am led

190

to believe, get the marriage off to a much happier start."

"Tomorrow, do you think?" asked Pettigrew.

"She will let you know."

With a brief good-bye, Jake left.

Ralph dropped heavily into his chair. He ought to send someone to follow this Jake Price and find out exactly where his beloved Sarah was, but he couldn't think straight, couldn't act fast enough. Already, Price was probably lost in the labyrinth that was Constantinople.

Ralph sighed. Sarah alive. He could hardly believe it.

What if this Price were up to some kind of cruel joke? What if—

He could not extend the thought. The American had described the beautiful young woman he had wanted for so long. The story, preposterous as it seemed, had the ring of truth about it—perhaps because it *was* so preposterous. And Price had declined a reward.

Ralph decided to question no further. Sarah was alive.

He knew he had sounded pompous in front of the American, but by damn, he hadn't liked the man from the start, even with his good news. So sure of himself, bursting in the way he had.

A small reward. God, what a failure I am.

Ralph wanted to offer the earth in return for the blessed report. Only he didn't own the earth. He had barely managed to hold on to Eastern Ports of Call, thanks in part to the receipt of her dowry.

Removing a bottle of brandy and two glasses from a bottom drawer, he called to his clerk to come share

191

his celebration.

"She's alive, Samuel," he said, lifting his drink.

"I couldn't help overhearing, sir," Samuel said with a suitable note of apology.

Ralph let the warm liquor ease down the back of his throat. He wanted to savor every sip, every bit of warmth and light-headedness that it could offer.

"Still find it hard to believe," he said. "It's a miracle."

"It only wants one or two more of a more monetary nature to be a complete salvation," Samuel said, swallowing his portion in one gulp.

"Don't be greedy. We will take one miracle at a time. Besides, I've told you everything would be all right."

"But three ships lost, Mr. Pettigrew, and all in the last few months. I'd been certain this job would be gone. And you've treated me decently, too."

"It's true enough about the storms and the pirates. We have had a string of bad fortune. Lost too much valuable cargo. I've never tried to deny it. But Sarah's alive. That's sure to be a good sign."

After another drink, Samuel returned to his desk to complete the correspondence for the day. Ralph returned to the brandy.

A third drink, and he found himself turning maudlin. All his life he had loved the sea, built up Eastern from nothing until it was at one time the largest foreign shipping firm sailing out of the Horn.

Unlike most men, he had never longed after women. He had cared for his mother, right enough, had kept her in comfortable circumstances for years in Bath while he sought and found his fortunes in the world; but he had never lived under the same roof with her, not after reaching his majority, and when she died two years ago, he had not been able to return

192

for the funeral.

Still, he had been a loving enough son. It was care of her that had helped influence Edward Whitlock in his petition for Sarah.

He saw the young beauty for the first time when Sir Edward had asked him to dine. She was only seventeen, but she had served as her widower father's hostess without flaw. She had been all golden and pink and fresh, and he had fallen in love for the first and last time in his life. What a fool an old man could be.

Not that he had been old—barely into his forties—but old as far as she was concerned.

He could still hear her silvery laugh. Even then, she had a bit of a reputation as a scapegrace. He had heard tales through the years, with all the gossip at the embassy, and little of it kind. There were too many people going back and forth to London and telling everything they heard.

But he could forgive that. After all, she was dreadfully young. Give her a few years as his wife and she would mature into a fine companion. Even some of the conservative element in the embassy and their sharp-tongued wives would see what a charming representative she was of young British womanhood. For his part, he would show her the world.

If he had enough money. To insure that, he had sacrificed his honor. He had not lied to Samuel about the security of his position; everything should turn out all right with the company. He was close to having enough capital to replace the lost ships and cargo. Close. If only he didn't have to fulfill certain promises.

No purpose served in doubts now. None at all since Sarah was all right. He had feared her reported death was somehow mixed up in the dealings he had made.

But there was no death. He had been wrong.

Again, he thought about Jake Price, the bringer of the marvelous news. He was struck by jealousy, the curse of the middle-aged man in love with a younger woman. It beat hard within his chest.

Price was a handsome man, in a lean, hard-edged sort of way. There were hints of danger in the way he carried himself, in the insolence of his steady gaze. Some women liked the sort. The Sarah that he remembered would.

But she was a woman of honor. She would not go back on her or her father's word. Ralph was under no delusion that theirs was a love match, at least not on her side. He would never expect it. But if things worked out as he planned, she would grow to respect him. He would shower on her the riches of the world, the finest art and antiques, the objects he knew she treasured.

Respect would grow in her heart.

And he wasn't too old to father a child or two.

Maybe tomorrow he would see her.

He put away the glasses and bottle and bade Samuel good night.

"Got to make preparations," he said, his step as jaunty as that of a man half his age. "Notify the embassy. Locate her father. A million things to do."

As he left the office, he did something he had not done in years. He hummed a tune.

Chapter Fourteen

Jake returned to the apartment to find Sarah and Bandit sharing a pot of tea. They sat across from one another at the small table, Sarah in the golden harem costume she had worn from the seraglio and Bandit in his usual coarse shirt and trousers and rope belt.

"Very cozy," said Jake as he closed the door behind him. The scene shouldn't have bothered him, but it did.

Sarah, her honeyed hair lying thick and shining against her bare shoulders and back, flicked him a look of disdain and returned to her cup of tea.

Bandit stood and executed a brief half bow. "Good morning, Bossman. I feared Miss Whitlock would grow hungry." He gestured to a bowl of fruit and a half-eaten loaf of bread resting beside the teapot. "She has been most gracious with her thanks."

"Oh?" asked Jake.

Sarah rolled her eyes. "Bandit is a charming companion. He not only kept me from being bored in my imprisonment; he has been most entertaining."

"Did he tell you about his various uncles and cousins?"

Sarah smiled at Bandit. "We both talked about

195

our families."

Jake's irritation grew. "I would like to hear about yours sometime, Sarah. You've not told me very much."

Sarah's smile died. "Unlike Bandit, you have shown little interest, which, of course, is only to be expected. My family is no concern of yours."

Bandit headed toward the door. "I will return within the half hour."

"No need—" Jake stopped. Bandit was gone.

Sarah turned a cool gaze on him, her hands resting in her lap. They seemed stiffly held, unnatural, as though if left unattended they might behave in a wayward fashion.

Jake could easily make out the shape of her breasts beneath the thin bodice, and through the film of golden cloth that served as trousers, he could see the shape of her slender hips and graceful thighs. Despite the reserve with which she faced him, she made an enchanting picture.

Beneath the table a slipper tapped impatiently. "Did you see my betrothed?" she asked.

Jake shook himself from his perusal. "I did. A very proper gentleman, he is, and greatly relieved at the good news of your survival."

"You got your reward, I imagine. Or did he want to see visible proof that I am indeed alive?"

"He believed me. When I mentioned that you had a tendency to get into scrapes, he knew right away that we'd met."

"Then I'm certain you were suitably paid for your troubles," she said, giving one hand the freedom to wave in the air. "Ralph Pettigrew is a very wealthy man."

Jake knew he could be maddeningly superior, but this morning Sarah was outdoing him.

"What troubles are you talking about?" he asked. "The ravaged hut? The seraglio?" Some devilment inside him prompted one additional suggeston. "Or maybe you were referring to last night."

Sarah flinched as though he had struck her. "How dare you."

She flung back the chair, sending it crashing to the floor, and strode angrily toward him. "It's certainly a good thing that Ralph is a gentleman. It's been so long since I've been around one, that I am sure to find him a marvelous change. Bandit excepted, of course."

Jake felt a wave of regret wash over him. He had never intended to mention their lovemaking, certainly not in such a clumsy way. Against better judgment, he couldn't keep from staring at the way the blue of her eyes so easily held the fire of her emotions. His gaze trailed down to her parted lips. Could they still be bruised from his kisses? No, he decided, they were always this full and inviting. He studied the slender grace of her throat, the rise of her breasts above the bodice, and moved quickly back to her eyes.

"How different we were last night," he said, as much to himself as to her. "For a little while."

She closed her eyes briefly, thick lashes dark against the blush of her cheeks. When she opened them again, the fire of anger was gone, in its place a wide and wounded look. "I never want to think or speak of what happened between us again." Her voice strengthened. "You were unkind to bring it up."

Jake stepped away and ran his fingers through his hair. "My apologies, Sarah. You make me say the damnedest things. But don't be completely hypocritical. You did claim that losing your virtue would be useful in the breaking of your engagement."

Sarah nodded once and looked away. "So I did." Her fingers played in the folds of her harem trousers.

"What did you tell Ralph?"

"Nothing that would ruin your reputation. As promised, I'm leaving that up to you. He got the impression you were staying with a respectable American family and would travel to the embassy when you felt strong enough. I took the liberty of saying you were rescued from the storm by a passing ship."

"How clever of you."

"I wasn't sure he would believe your story about the slaughter aboard ship, or about the seraglio. Certainly not coming from a stranger."

She returned a sharp gaze to him. "You sound as if you don't believe it, either."

"I'm the one who fought off the swords, remember? That's not something I do every day. It seemed pretty strong proof you had indeed gotten yourself into some kind of catastrophe."

"So all I need to get Ralph to believe me is to find Scarface again and—"

Her voice broke, and her eyes darkened with remembered fear. Jake was struck with a longing to embrace her and say she would never be endangered again.

But that was not his purpose, and it sure as hell was not his way. Sarah had to make up her own mind about what to do.

"Ralph will believe you without the dramatics," he said, keeping his distance. "I got the feeling he's been quite upset."

"My loss must have been a great inconvenience. He has waited a long while for us to be wed."

"Not just an inconvenience, Sarah," said Jake. "His feelings go deeper than that. I assured him that a temporary loss of memory kept you from letting him know of your whereabouts."

Sarah turned from him and walked to the edge of the bed. Lifting a pillow, she cradled it against her chest and abdomen and turned to face him. The top edge of the pillow rested just below her chin.

"I don't understand, Jake. I thought you would be dragging me to him right away. Either that or bringing him back here."

"Both options occurred to me."

"And now you say it's up to me to decide when to leave."

He shrugged.

"Why?"

Jake did not know how to answer her. It certainly wasn't any of his business whom she married. But Ralph Pettigrew wasn't the one, no matter how much he cared.

"Sarah—"

A knock at the door stopped him.

Sarah started. "Could you have been followed?"

"It's me, Bossman," they heard from the street.

Jake let Bandit in.

"I have been to the Grand Bazaar," the servant announced proudly. "There are many treasures there, but also Miss Whitlock can find—" he coughed softly—"more suitable attire. The clothes that she wears must remind her of unpleasant memories."

"You are very wise," Sarah said with a smile.

Jake pulled a small bundle of coins from his pocket. "I'm not completely without funds." He tossed the money to Bandit. "Buy what you think appropriate."

"Can't I be allowed to shop for myself?" Sarah addressed the question to Bandit.

"There are many women on the street and in the bazaar," Bandit said.

"Of course there are," agreed Sarah. "All robed and keeping their eyes cast to the ground, right?"

"What you say is true," agreed Bandit.

She turned to Jake. "I've got a robe. You brought it to me, remember? And whether or not you believe it, I can be suitably humble."

Jake glanced back at his servant, whose eyes were pinned to the carpet and whose hands were pressed together as if in prayer. He turned back to Sarah. She stared boldly at him, and Jake realized he was outnumbered. Sarah had made a friend and supporter of Bandit. He was not surprised.

"Just be sure," he warned, "that you speak little, if at all, and never look at anyone directly. Not even me, especially when someone else might be watching. Those blue eyes of yours are too distinctive. They're impossible for a man to forget."

"Why, Jake," said Sarah, flashing him a provocative smile, "if I did not know better, I might think the man you're referring to could very well be yourself."

When Sarah exited the small room and stood in the early afternoon sun, she felt as though she had been let out of prison. Inside, Jake's presence had been as much a threat to her sense of independence as the four walls and the locked door. Outside, she could tell herself she was free.

She leaned against the stone wall of the building; like anyone newly freed, she felt disoriented. So many people swirled around her on the crowded street, and rumbling carriages and single horses wended their way around the pedestrians. Dust and heat and noise hung on the summer air and made thinking difficult.

She had so many things to remember: keep her head and face covered, her eyes to the ground, and her

200

mouth closed. No one must hear her speak and realize she was other than she appeared—a veiled and hooded Turkish woman wearing the expected heavy, dull robe and following meekly wherever her lord and master led.

The wool scratched against her skin, the harem costume offering little protection, and she wished for the layers of clothes that the other women wore underneath their own robes—except that all those garments would be dreadfully hot beneath the Turkish sun.

She fell in between Jake and Bandit, shuffling along slightly to the rear to show she knew her subordinate lot in life. Jake was wearing the red fez and, like her, kept his head low. His skin was darkened by the sun, and his hair was as dark as the night. Except for his height, he looked little different from the Turks past whom he strode. It seemed unlikely anyone from the seraglio would recognize him as the eunuch who had so diligently anointed the harem women yesterday. Other than the women and guards and the kitchen help, few had seen him. Bandit's cousin was to spread the word the new eunuch had taken suddenly ill and was in the hospital reserved for the slaves.

Sarah stole a look at Jake, caught his frown, and looked quickly to the ground, trying as she walked to sort her thoughts. She had spent the first hours after his abrupt departure telling herself she hated him. As well she should. He had left in the middle of the night—after sharing with her what had to be the most intimate of experiences between a man and a woman—and vowed to get rid of her as fast as he could. As much as his presence was hurting her, she had been crushed by his absence.

Eventually she had cried herself to sleep.

By morning she was convinced he was right to send her on her way. He was an unfeeling brute, and their time together had been nothing special to him. She would adopt the same attitude and gladly leave. After Bandit had appeared with food and a friendly smile, the world seemed a habitable place.

And then Jake had returned. One look at him and her heart had turned over. How proud she had been of her calmness on the outside; on the inside had been nothing but turmoil. Questions had crowded her mind. What if he pitched her onto the street right away? What if he said Pettigrew was waiting outside to carry her to the embassy? Either was possible—even probable—and she had been proud of the cool smile she had directed his way.

But nothing about Jake was predictable. He had completely confused her by saying she could determine when they would part.

And men claimed that women were hard to figure out.

She tried to concentrate on their route. The Grand Bazaar was only a short walk from the apartment through the cobbled, crowded streets. Before leaving the apartment, Jake had told her a little of what to expect.

"Everything's for sale," he had claimed as he unlocked the door. "Even people if you know where to ask."

"Women, you mean," she said.

"Men, too. Young boys."

"And cucumbers, I imagine," Sarah said. "Whole, I mean."

Standing close behind her in the room, Bandit coughed.

Jake looked at her, a puzzled expression on his face, but Sarah gazed back at him without expression.

202

She had figured out why the vegetable was never served unsliced to the lonely women. The idea had been difficult to accept, the execution even more so, but she was certain she was right. However, that did not mean she could reveal her newfound knowledge to Jake.

At last he went on. "If you've a different kind of perversion, there's opium. Lots of poppy fields in the eastern areas of the country. Constantinople is a primary market."

Sarah remembered Mustafa's rough hands on the slave Tezer. "After the harem, no amount of decadence would surprise me."

"You have to give the sultan credit," said Jake. "He's discouraged both the growing and the selling of the drug. But his reforms have a long way to go."

"He could start with a few personal habits," said Sarah. "Three hundred women kept in virtual imprisonment should seem rather excessive even to you."

Jake's answer had been a grin. Her heart had taken to skipping a beat whenever he smiled that way. Sort of crooked and quick. She wished he would stop.

The memory of that smile stayed with her as they walked along the street. One open doorway caught her eye. Inside the small room were crowded a dozen men in the tattered clothes of beggars. They stood in line before a black cauldron from which a more carefully dressed man was ladling soup.

Bandit pressed close to her side. "The Turks do not let their people go hungry. Free soup is provided for those who cannot pay."

Sarah nodded once and thought what a country of contrasts this was.

At last they came to the open gates of the Grand Bazaar. She thought she knew what to expect inside,

203

but she was wrong. Shuffling silently through the wide entrance, she entered a universe of wonder. Wide corridors stretched in three directions away from the entry. Each corridor was arched, the highest point of the ceiling a soaring fifty feet above the crowded floor. Imbedded in the arches were bands of intricate tile at five-foot intervals; between the bands were stretches of masonry darkened by smoke and age. Elaborate scrollwork decorated the walls.

From each of these corridors wound a hundred other passageways, the total of them forming a labyrinth that was as complex as the one from the myth of the Greeks. The Grand Bazaar was like a giant walled and roofed city in the heart of Stamboul. Along the sides of the winding routes a thousand peddlers had spread their wares, leaving only a narrow path down the center for the patrons to make their way.

Sounds and smells assailed her. Chattering voices in a scattering of languages, all of them unintelligible to Sarah, rose around her and echoed along the high, arched way. She caught the insistent bargaining of the peddlers, the sharp laughter and harsh retort when a price was scorned. From somewhere in the mass of people and goods came the faint but distinct bleat of a sheep.

She breathed deeply, distinguishing the separate aromas of coffee and spices and musty wool, of ripe fruit and unwashed bodies, and the mingled scents of a hundred Oriental perfumes.

The Turkish bazaar was as different from Harrod's as chaos was from order. She could have stayed there forever.

Bandit guided her and Jake to a corridor branching off to the left, and they made their way slowly through the crowds. Keeping her eyes to the ground,

Sarah was still able to take note of the noisy transactions that they passed—more arguing than buying, to her mind.

At last Bandit paused before a stall of brightly colored clothing piled high on tables and spilling onto the ground like jeweled water. A small, dark man arose from the midst of his wares and smiled. His teeth were a mottled brown, and his eyes were sharp. Sarah was glad she would not have to negotiate a sale.

Edging away from him, she fingered the rough texture of a nearby caftan. No one stopped her, and she began to search through the disorder. The clothing was not exactly to her taste, crudely sewn robes and trousers in wool and linen and unwashed silk. Nothing fine that would last a long while. But then she was not buying a trousseau, just something to wear until she made up her mind to leave Jake's room.

Which, of course, she would do right away. There was no reason to hang around any longer than necessary, certainly not since she was to be allowed to go to the embassy and not the home of her betrothed. Jake had gotten his money from her fiancé. If she could find out how much, she would ask her father to repay the amount.

Turning her attention to the business at hand, she selected one complete outfit—a pair of full trousers, a gauze smock, heavier waistcoat, and a close-fitting caftan that came to her ankles. For her feet she selected a pair of leather socks and overshoes, the latter to be worn out of doors. Bandit bargained for what seemed an eternity, an amount was at last settled upon, and they left, Jake carrying the bundled purchases.

Sarah continued to observe what she could, to

breathe in the exotic scents of cardamom and incense and musk, to listen to the multitude of sounds as they journeyed back through the corridor. She spied a long table of porcelains and could not resist stopping. Jake's warning glare was easy to ignore. The porcelains were Chinese and were lovely, and after all, there were other women studying the goods for sale. It seemed more curious for her to walk along and show no interest in the wares than to stop on occasion for a brief perusal.

She picked up one of the porcelains, fingering the smoothly glazed surface and marveling at the lines and colors the unknown artist had used to recreate the flower vine that wound around the gracefully curved bowl. She couldn't remember seeing anything quite so delicately wrought.

She caught Bandit's eye, and he nodded his approval. He really did know fine work, and she wondered about his history. He had talked about uncles and cousins, but he never revealed much about himself.

She looked at Jake to see if he had a similar appreciation of the art work. His attention was directed away from her to another woman arguing with a vendor of jewelry twenty feet away.

The woman kept her eyes down, but Sarah could see they were outlined in kohl. The veil she wore was of a finer, thinner cloth than her own, and the shape of her profile was faintly distinguishable. She waved a graceful hand in the air to punctuate her remarks. Jake seemed entranced.

Was it only Sarah's imagination or could she really see the hint of a voluptuous body beneath the woman's flowing robe?

She felt a stab of jealousy. Impossible. She was

206

simply irritated that he would be so brazen when they were trying not to call attention to themselves.

She glanced at Bandit. He, too, was watching the woman.

"Bossman," he said under his breath.

"Take Sarah back to the room," Jake returned.

"Is this the woman from the tale of mystical powers?" Bandit asked.

Jake shot him a knowing look. "Get Sarah away. I'll be back as soon as I can."

Sarah opened her mouth to speak, but Bandit's tug on the sleeve of her robe kept her silent.

She looked sideways at him. He winked.

She looked back at Jake, who was still watching the argument over the jewelry.

"Do not worry, Miss Whitlock," Bandit whispered, urging her away. "I will explain."

Short of causing a scene, there was little Sarah could do except follow Bandit's lead into the open air and through the streets. Repeated glances over her shoulder failed to locate Jake, and she waited until they were safely inside his room before speaking. Whirling on Bandit, she threw back her hood and lowered her veil. "Mystical powers? What is going on?"

"It is an old story and of no concern now, Miss Whitlock. The truth is that Bossman has lost something very valuable to him."

There was only one thing Sarah could think of that Jake valued. "The gold from the sale of the mask," she said.

"Ah, I should have known you were told."

"Jake was furious when he discovered the woman had taken it all. He claims not to blame me, but I do not believe him."

"Do you think the Bossman would lie?"

"It is not beyond possibility."

Bandit's voice softened. "Do you not like my master? I thought that perhaps you did."

Sarah stirred restlessly. "It doesn't matter how I feel. After I leave here, I'll never see him again."

Bandit shrugged. "This is too bad. I had hopes the two of you . . . but then it is none of my concern."

Sarah thought he looked almost sad. "You're a romantic, aren't you, Bandit?"

His dark eyes twinkled. "I see things as they are, sometimes, and sometimes as I wish them to be."

"And how do you see me?" she asked, surprising herself with the question.

"As a woman who wishes to be respected. As a woman who longs to be loved."

Sarah blinked back her astonishment. "I expected you to call me an adventuress—someone foolhardy and perhaps a little brave. You make me sound lonely."

"And you are not?" asked Bandit.

"How could I be?" she asked, coming quickly to her own defense. "I have the affection of many friends. And the respect, I might add. They are constantly daring me to difficult feats, confident I can accomplish them."

"Perhaps I am wrong in my humble perceptions."

"You most certainly are," she said. "And of course," she added hastily, "there is my father. You can't forget him. Now what about this woman at the bazaar? She's obviously the one Jake brought on board that night. Do you think he can force her to return his money? She's probably spent it long ago."

"It was a great sum, and there has been no talk on the streets of a woman with sudden wealth. I suspect she has it well hidden." His dark face was lightened by a smile. "She is the dancer Fatima, admired in all of Constantinople for her grace and beauty. Until today in the bazaar, I did not know that she was the one chosen for the Bossman's celebration."

Again Sarah felt the uncomfortable prickles of jealousy. The beautiful Fatima had been naked and waiting for Jake when Sarah had intruded that dreadful night on the wharf. Without the scimitars, it was reason enough for Jake to be furious. She had truly interrupted his life.

"He couldn't remember her name," she said.

"I must talk with the Bossman, sometime, about his ways with women. But on to Fatima. I know where she performs. Others dance there as well, but she is the reason most men frequent the place. As for myself, I do not care for the coffee."

"Does Jake know where this place is?"

"It would seem he does not. I believe he wishes to follow her."

For the gold, Sarah told herself. *For the gold*. "She might see him and run away."

"Such is possible."

If the dancer got away again, she would surely be smart enough to hide where Jake could not find her, and the gold would be out of his reach. If that happened, Sarah would forever be in his debt. An idea seized her. "Can you take me to this place?"

"It is a coffee house where women seldom go."

"But sometimes they do."

"Sometimes they do."

"I can wear my robe. No one will know. She might run from Jake, but she did not get a good look at me that night on the dock. She will think me harmless." Sarah grinned. "I can run pretty fast if I have to. I've

209

had a little practice lately."

"The Bossman will be very angry."

"Everything I do makes him angry," Sarah said with great feeling. "He's rather like my father in that respect."

"The comparison surprises me."

"As it does me." Sarah grew solemn. "Jake thinks I am a burden. It was the last thing he told me last night."

"This, too, surprises me," said Bandit. His warm brown eyes rested on her face. "The Bossman is not always wise."

She seized Bandit's hand. "It is very important for me to make up for all the trouble I have caused. Let me help him catch her, Bandit. I promise to return here if you say I must. No arguments."

Bandit frowned.

"Jake risked his life for me," she said in a rush. "If I can repay him tonight, then tomorrow I can leave." Her voice caught. "It is very important that I leave with honor and pride."

Bandit looked at her for a long while. Through the edge of the door she could hear the noise from the street.

"You have a great need for this, do you not?"

"A very great need."

"Then of course we will go to the coffee house. But long after the fall of night. Fatima does not perform until late. If Bossman has not returned by ten o'clock, we will go to him." A hint of mischief flashed in his eyes. "In truth, I wish almost that he is not here."

He left to purchase food and drink for their supper, and Sarah paced the length and width of the room. She started to put on the myriad of clothes purchased in the bazaar but chose instead to keep on the harem costume. The softly draping head covering and veil she tied around her waist. Donning the robe, she paid little attention to the scratch of wool against her skin. By some chance if she were caught, in the filmy gold bodice and trousers she could claim to be one of the dancers.

Sarah was learning to plan ahead.

Before Bandit returned, she slipped the robe over her costume. They ate in silence and, after a long and tense wait, exited into the starry night. The streets of the city were still crowded, and carriages rumbled noisily by; but the heat of the day had mercifully eased. She knew that before long the streets would be close to deserted. Turks did not travel about late in the dark.

She and Bandit kept to the sideways and alleys and soon came to their destination. The coffee house was on the corner of a busy intersection; they walked into a small, smoke-filled room of crowded tables and an open area where Sarah assumed Fatima would perform.

She was relieved to see two other robed women amongst all the men. Jake sat alone at a table and studied the room. She stayed in the shadows, Bandit close by her side. Jake did not look their way.

Leaning close to Bandit, she whispered, "If I could get to the back where the dancers prepare themselves, I could cut off her escape—in case she spots Jake. You could wait by the door."

"I do not like this, Miss Whitlock. We should not go our separate ways."

"Take me to the dressing room. If you do not approve of my being there, I will not remain."

Bandit hesitated but at last agreed.

"There is a back door," he said, guiding her

211

toward the entrance.

They were soon easing inside the coffee house by way of the alley. They entered a long, dark hallway, at the end of which was a lighted room, its door half open. At the other end was a closed door; the noise coming through it told them it led to the wooden dance floor and to the customers.

The smoke from the main room was less oppressive here, but the heavy scent of patchouli kept the act of breathing from being any easier. They inched toward the lighted room and heard the harsh sounds of an argument between a man and woman.

Bandit listened quietly. "Fatima refuses to appear tonight," he translated.

"But why?"

"She has seen someone in the audience—"

"I knew it!"

"And the other dancers have already departed. The owner claims he will be ruined if she does not perform."

The door flew open, and Fatima came running out. She was clothed in the same robe she had worn in the bazaar, but her face, unveiled, was not nearly so calm. Sarah could recognize panic when she saw it, having felt it herself several times in the past few weeks.

Directly behind Fatima was a wildly gesticulating Turk. The dancer turned and spat out something in Turkish that surely would have stopped a marauding army, but the owner kept coming. Just as she reached Sarah, he grabbed one sleeve of the robe. Trying to help him, Sarah grabbed the other.

Like a snake shedding its skin, Fatima slipped free of the robe and slithered between Sarah and the Turk. The dancer was wearing harem pants but had not quite gotten around to putting on her bodice.

Bandit stared at the naked chest in surprise as if he couldn't decide quite where to grab. Sarah glanced at the barely concealed behind and was reminded of the broad rump that had brushed past her on the boat. The woman had been Fatima, all right.

The dancer shoved Bandit aside and scurried out the alley door. Sarah started to follow; at the same time the owner made the same decision. A collision resulted, and when Sarah tripped over the abandoned robe, she fell in an awkward heap, bringing down with her the owner and Bandit.

The owner came up yelling, threw himself out the door, and came back within a minute as angry as anyone Sarah had ever seen, which meant he was indeed furious.

He stared down at her and shouted a portion of the furious diatribe he had been throwing at his star performer.

Bandit, still sitting beside her in the hallway, nudged her side. "Your hood and veil have fallen. Perhaps we should leave."

The door to the main room opened, and the dark, towering figure of a man entered. He soared seven feet tall, and his face was twisted into a brutish frown. A pistol was strapped to one thigh, and to the other was a sheathed but still evil-looking knife.

"The guard," Bandit said unnecessarily. "There is seldom trouble at the coffee house because of him."

The two Turks had the routes to both alley and coffee house effectively blocked. The only path open to them was the one to the dancers' room. Sarah stood and began inching backward. The owner barked something, and she came to a halt.

He quit talking, instead sidling close to her side,

213

his eyes studying Sarah much as she had studied the porcelain bowl in the bazaar. He stroked her hair. Sarah cringed.

"I have a small pistol in my shirt," said Bandit.

"No," Sarah hissed, fearing for Bandit's safety. She could not imagine anything short of a cannon stopping the guard.

The owner spoke a few words to her.

"He wants to know if you can dance," Bandit translated.

She looked wide-eyed at Bandit. "For heaven's sake, why?"

"I believe the answer is obvious."

She looked back at the irate Turk. "Nadire taught me," she said. "I was told that I learned my lesson well." She blinked twice, her mind working hard to keep up with her racing pulse. "Do the men bother Fatima when she dances?"

"The owner, whose name, by the way, is Faruk, will not allow it. They may whistle and shout and say things that perhaps Miss Whitlock has not before heard, but they do not touch."

And they would be shouting in a language she could not understand. She took what comfort she could from the thought and swallowed her fear. "Tell Mr. Faruk I will do as he asks."

Through the wall at her back she could hear the strains of an off-key stringed instrument and a lute in the main room. The noise of the crowd eased. It was a crowd that included Jake, who had hoped to retrieve his gold. Sarah had hoped to help him. On this unfortunate night neither hope would be met.

"I do not like this," said Bandit.

His was a feeling Sarah shared. "Tell Faruk I need a moment to prepare," she said as she headed toward the lighted room. Her heart continued to pound. This was surely the wildest thing she had ever done.

She turned to find Bandit in deep conversation with Faruk, the guard hovering behind them with a puzzled look on his face.

"Please assure him," she said, "that it will not be necessary to harm either one of us. All will go well."

Chapter Fifteen

Alone in the small room where the dancers prepared for their performances, Sarah stilled the battling butterflies in her stomach.

She could handle this latest challenge. All she had to do was take it one moment at a time.

Tossing her robe aside, she studied the swaths of gold she wore underneath. The clothing had been good enough for Mustafa's harem, and it was good enough for Faruk's coffee house. Cut low across breasts and abdomen, it was far too revealing, of course, but there was nothing she could do about that.

Removing the veil she had hidden beneath her robe, she stroked a kohl-laden brush close to her lashes and studied the result in the mottled looking glass. Satisfied, she donned the jangling brass belt she'd found on the table beside the face paint. Loops of cold metal tickled her stomach each time she inhaled.

When she draped the diaphanous scarf over her head and just below the bridge of her nose, carefully hiding all her pale hair and most of her features, she was confident no one could recognize her.

And that included Jake, sitting out there waiting for a dancer who was long gone from the premises. She must remember not to look at him directly. He had made much of her eyes.

It was to her benefit that the room was dimly lit and smoky, and the men were expecting to be entertained by a Turkish dancer. All she had to do was avoid tripping or otherwise making a fool of herself, which she simply would not do. Nadire had taught her well. She almost wished the girl could be present to observe.

Oh, yes, she assured herself as she fastened the clasp on an ankle bracelet, she could manage this feat and get back to Jake's apartment long before he did. Chances were when he realized tonight's performer was not Fatima, he would rush into the night to find her again and miss most of the performance. She held on to the comforting notion like a cloak covering her vulnerable state.

She took one last glance in the looking glass. The painted eyes of a dancer stared back. Beneath the veil, she smiled.

Padding barefoot down the long hallway, she passed Faruk, who stared at her in admiration.

Farther along, Bandit did the same, although his encouraging nod was tinged with a shade of concern. She winked at him, and the worry faded.

The seven-foot-tall guard opened the door leading to the main room, the music of strings and lute quickened and she followed its sound. The moment she slipped into the coffee house, all talking ceased. Unfortunately, so did her breathing, the beat of her heart, and all helpful functions of her brain.

The only part of her operating normally was the left foot that moved instinctively backward toward the door. The right foot followed its example, bringing her against the frame of the portal that offered escape. She felt the firm hand of the guard against her spine; the hand shoved her back into the smoke and quiet.

She caught her balance halfway across the six-foot-wide wooden floor, which backed up to a narrow platform where a musician strummed impatiently on his stringed instrument. It seemed to Sarah that his fingers were caught in a repeating chord. It was the first coherent thought her brain delivered.

The lute joined in repetitious musical protest of the delay. A low murmur drifted from the semi-dark. She caught the name Fatima more than once. Perspiration beaded on her brow. She was hemmed in on three sides by men who had waited a long while to be entertained; Turkish men did not have the reputation of patience, especially where women were concerned. Stark fear over how that impatience might erupt forced her to shift her feet, to sway her hips, to jangle the jewelry that hung low on her hips. The brass that had tickled her skin when she first wrapped it about her person now felt hard and threatening, like the flat edge of a knife.

She felt awkward and out of step with the music; worse, she sensed the men shared her view.

Her mind skittered desperately backward in time to the Grand Seraglio and the lessons of Nadire, but all she could think of were watching eyes, especially Jake's. He would not have gone so soon, not with the way her luck was running. She remembered how she had once danced naked under the trees beside an island pond. She had dreamed about dancing for him one day.

But not like this; never like this.

She concentrated on the pond, imagining the smell of salt air, the cry of gulls, the damp sand beneath her feet. Dancing had seemed natural then. She let the feelings she had experienced come back to her. The rhythms of the wind in the trees took over, and her heart beat in time with the music only she could hear. At last her breathing grew regular. Lowering her eyes, she imagined she was standing on a sandy bank, alone and awaiting what she had thought would be her first time with a man.

Her hips began to sway and her shoulders to undulate, not awkwardly as they had moved before, but with a grace and naturalness that pleased her. She cared not whether her movements pleased anyone else.

She was once again the provocative nymph she had been. She thought about Jake awaiting her in the hut. She thought of his naked body next to hers, of slick skin pulled tight over bunching muscles, of powerful, hungry hands that would not be denied.

The tempo of her dance quickened. She was barely aware of the hush that had settled over the room or of the pulsing beat of the responding guitar and lute.

She eased slowly around the floor, her bare feet arching and lowering, twisting and turning, her entire body functioning as one fluid entity without separate parts, without even bones. Each movement of hands and breasts and hips took on the true meaning of the dance. Sarah was a woman offering herself to the man of her choice. The man of her dreams. She would please him with the softness of her skin, with the fullness of her breasts, with the supple motions of her hips and thighs.

He would respond with the special power that was his—hard muscle and knowing hands and firm, demanding lips.

Sarah's thoughts drifted to the night in Jake's room. Once again she lay under him. Without willing herself to do so, she knelt on the wooden floor, her hips and shoulders swaying in time to the music's primal rhythms, her back arched, the jewelry jangling in harmony with the lute.

Lower and lower her head dropped backward until it rested for a moment on the floor. With sylphlike ease she pulled her body upright and slowly stood. A moment of shakiness passed, and she gave herself completely to the spiraling beat of the dance. She whirled, her arms open wide to welcome Jake into her embrace. She was lost in love and the demands of the flesh.

Desire for him pulsed within; her skin burned for his touch, and she felt the heady wine of passion course through her veins. Round and round she whirled. She grew dizzy with need as she danced for him and only him. Her eyes squeezed closed, and the image in her mind was of his dark face looming before her, his long, lean body bending close. When she could stand the image no longer, she collapsed in a heap on the floor, his name a soft whisper on her lips.

The quiet around her was deafening. The reality of time and place came back with a rush. All the rapture had been only in her mind.

Cheers erupted, loud and coarse and insistent. Sarah cringed from them. A short, simple dance had been her intention, but she had delivered far more— her deepest longings, her private desires. She felt naked and vulnerable, stripped of all decency and pride. She had made a fool of herself, and she wondered how she would ever get out of that cursed place and into some dark corner where, like a hurt animal, she could lick her wounds.

A hand clamped onto her wrist and removed all choice.

"We're getting the hell out of here," a voice rasped in her ear.

Jake.

She was too weak to protest.

A robe was thrown over her, and he lifted her to her feet. Her knees buckled, and she collapsed against him.

"Walk," he demanded.

The cheers turned ugly. She could hear the hard protests of the men crowded into the room. They wanted more . . . more. She did not feel proud.

Suddenly Bandit and the coffee house guard were there. They were an incongruous pair with their disparate heights, but working together they cleared a path toward the door leading to the street. Behind them, Sarah hurried alongside Jake.

Outside, she tried to pause and catch her breath and let her mind settle into some kind of patterned thought, but Jake did not give her the opportunity. Showing no mercy, he dragged her through the shadowed streets that led to his room. Her bare feet felt bruised and cold as she half-ran, half-walked beside him.

Occasionally she seemed to catch a glimpse of Bandit somewhere ahead, but she could never be sure. And Jake certainly gave her no chance to ask.

In the sky directly above them rode a quarter moon, a silver sliver of light that sat amongst the stars like the curved blade of a scimitar. The streets were almost deserted. She and Jake hurried past an occasional pedestrian or lone horseman hurrying, like them, through the half dark. Once she heard from an open doorway the sound of laughter and amiable argument—human sounds. Jake did not seem human at all.

By the time they arrived at the room, Bandit was

nowhere in sight. Jake pulled her inside, locked the door, and lit the lamp, each action completed with firm determination. When he turned a thunderous stare on her, she pulled the robe tightly around her and waited for the storm.

He seemed to be fighting for control. At last he said, "Did you enjoy this evening?"

His voice was surprisingly low, but she was not put off by the pitch. A knife could be delivered with only a whisper of sound.

"Did you like entertaining the Turks? Was it a special lark to inflame a roomful of men?" he asked. "Or were you there to torment only me?"

He stepped close and dragged the robe from her shoulders. It fell to the ground at her feet, and he kicked it aside. Removing the gossamer silk covering her head and lower face, he tossed it beside the robe. Slowly he walked around her. She felt his eyes raking her half-clothed body.

"Quite a little performer, aren't you?" He stood directly behind her and spoke close to her ear.

Startled, she tried to turn. His hands gripped her shoulders and held her in place. His body was near to hers, but only his hands touched. His hands and his hard, ugly words—both bit mercilessly into her and hurt.

"Jake—"

"Tell me," he said, interrupting, "do you plan these little tortures? Do you go out of your way to lay traps for me and leave me without a moment's peace? Is that why you followed me tonight?"

Sarah's temper flared. "I see you have figured me out," she said bitterly.

"And how is that?"

Sarah shivered under the warmth of his breath on

her neck. "Ever since I jumped onto your boat, I have thought of nothing else but making your life a living hell. Surely you have not enjoyed my company. I never intended for you to do so for very long."

His hands massaged her shoulders, and he drew her back against him.

"Don't undervalue yourself, Angel. You've had your moments. Like tonight. I found myself quite wrapped up in your dance. If that's what it was called. More like a blatant offering of sex." His hips rubbed against her buttocks. Sarah tried in vain to pull away.

"Once I got over the shock of seeing you," he said, "I was even getting aroused. Is that what you planned, Sarah?" Again his hips shifted suggestively against hers. "Is it?"

Sarah had to fight against leaning back into his strength. He was being Jake, misjudging and condemning, judge and jury in his own tightly run court, and she was found guilty without so much as a word in her defense.

The ugliness of his condemnation gave her strength. She would not try to explain the purpose behind her presence, nor the unfortunate circumstances that had led to the dance. He was partially at fault, having somehow let Fatima know of his presence in the audience, but he was not likely to accept his share of the blame.

"Just when did you recognize me?" she asked coolly. "I thought I was well disguised."

His body eased its pressure, but his fingers began to stroke her shoulders. "I knew who you were the moment you stumbled into the room. How could you think I wouldn't? I know your body very well . . . the curve of your hips . . . the shape of your breasts."

223

Sarah could take no more. She jerked free of his grasp and whirled to face him. "Stop. You don't know what's in my heart and mind," she hissed, "despite all your cleverness. I never intended for such a thing to happen. I was trapped into it."

Jake's eyes were filled with scorn. "Bandit tried to tell me something like that when he came to my table. He brought the robe, thought it might come in handy. The dance had already begun, and I wasn't listening; but I got the impression that you had fooled him the way you've fooled me. Twice. When you left the dhow, you got yourself kidnapped again and thrown into the seraglio, where who knows what atrocities might have been committed against you."

"Nothing—"

Jake hurried on. "If I hadn't gotten you out of the coffee house tonight, you might have gotten yourself raped."

"I didn't encourage anyone on purpose."

"Cut it out, Sarah. You didn't exactly hide your charms, either. Besides, you have an effect on men just by walking into a room."

"Is that supposed to be a compliment?"

"A statement of fact."

She saw her performance through Jake's eyes, and she suddenly felt tawdry and obvious. Utter hopelessness took hold of her. She had gone to the coffee house to settle accounts with Jake, to help him get back his money, to make it possible to part from him with pride, but she had harbored another reason, one she did not understand any more than she could deny. Buried in the recesses of her mind was a stinging question: Would Jake retrieve the gold and leave the beautiful Fatima, or would he demand interest, the lovemaking that had been denied him

MORE PASSION AND ADVENTURE AWAIT... YOUR TRIP TO A BIG ADVENTUROUS WORLD BEGINS WHEN YOU ACCEPT YOUR FIRST 4 NOVELS ABSOLUTELY *FREE* (AN $18.00 VALUE)

Accept your Free gift and start to experience more of the passion and adventure you like in a historical romance novel. Each Zebra novel is filled with proud men, spirited women and tempestuous love that you'll remember long after you turn the last page.

Zebra Historical Romances are the finest novels of their kind. They are written by authors who really know how to weave tales of romance and adventure in the historical settings you love. You'll feel like you've actually gone back in time with the thrilling stories that each Zebra novel offers.

GET YOUR FREE GIFT WITH THE START OF YOUR HOME SUBSCRIPTION

Our readers tell us that these books sell out very fast in book stores and often they miss the newest titles. So Zebra has made arrangements for you to receive the four newest novels published each month.

You'll be guaranteed that you'll never miss a title, and home delivery is so convenient. And to show you just how easy it is to get Zebra Historical Romances, we'll send you your first 4 books absolutely FREE! Our gift to you just for trying our home subscription service.

BIG SAVINGS AND FREE HOME DELIVERY

Each month, you'll receive the four newest titles as soon as they are published. You'll probably receive them even before the bookstores do. What's more, you may preview these exciting novels free for 10 days. If you like them as much as we think you will, just pay the low preferred subscriber's price of just $3.75 each. *You'll save $3.00 each month off the publisher's price.* AND, your savings are even greater because there are never any shipping, handling or other hidden charges—FREE Home Delivery. Of course you can return any shipment within 10 days for full credit, no questions asked. There is no minimum number of books you must buy.

4 FREE BOOKS

TO GET YOUR 4 FREE BOOKS WORTH $18.00 —MAIL IN THE FREE BOOK CERTIFICATE T O D A Y

Fill in the Free Book Certificate below, and we'll send your FREE BOOKS to you as soon as we receive it.

If the certificate is missing below, write to: Zebra Home Subscription Service, Inc., P.O. Box 5214, 120 Brighton Road, Clifton, New Jersey 07015-5214.

FREE BOOK CERTIFICATE

4 FREE BOOKS
ZEBRA HOME SUBSCRIPTION SERVICE, INC.

YES! Please start my subscription to Zebra Historical Romances and send me my first 4 books absolutely FREE. I understand that each month I may preview four new Zebra Historical Romances free for 10 days. If I'm not satisfied with them, I may return the four books within 10 days and owe nothing. Otherwise, I will pay the low preferred subscriber's price of just $3.75 each; a total of $15.00, *a savings off the publisher's price of $3.00.* I may return any shipment and I may cancel this subscription at any time. There is no obligation to buy any shipment and there are no shipping, handling or other hidden charges. Regardless of what I decide, the four free books are mine to keep.

NAME _____

ADDRESS _____ APT _____

CITY _____ STATE _____ ZIP _____

TELEPHONE (____) _____

SIGNATURE _____ (if under 18, parent or guardian must sign)

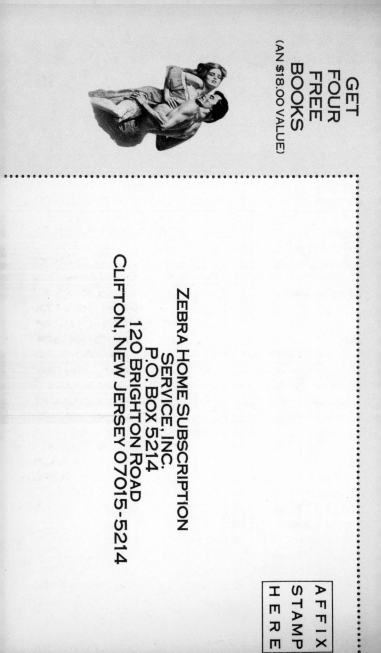

GET
FOUR
FREE
BOOKS
(AN $18.00 VALUE)

ZEBRA HOME SUBSCRIPTION
SERVICE, INC.
P.O. Box 5214
120 BRIGHTON ROAD
CLIFTON, NEW JERSEY 07015-5214

AFFIX
STAMP
HERE

the night Sarah had jumped aboard the dhow?

For all her high-sounding purposes of paying her debts and leaving with pride, what Sarah had really wanted was for Jake to get his treasure and come back to her. Whatever happened between them then simply would have been out of her control.

But he thought she had been after a cheap thrill in the coffee house. How little he thought of her.

She fought against the tears building in the back of her eyes. "Bandit understands me," she said. "Better than you ever will."

His look of scorn held steady, and she darted for the door.

Jake grabbed her arm. "Not so fast. You offered quite a lot tonight. To a roomful of men. I know you like to tease, but don't you think it's time to deliver?"

He stood close, her shoulder almost brushing against his chest, his breath coming hard and fast, his eyes dark as the night and lit with a fire that glowed brighter than any star. His face was lean and sharp, and his lips curved into a humorless smile. "I'm only one man, Sarah, but I'll do my best to compensate."

"I was not offering myself to you," she lied, unable to pull her gaze from his smile. It mocked and taunted her at the same time.

He could never know that she had danced only for him . . . that she had wanted him beyond all reason . . . that she had forgotten the room and the music and the crowd. She had been transported back to the deserted isle and, toward the end of the dance, back to his room and his bed.

The devastating thing was she wanted him again. Her eyes drifted up to his, and she saw the fire of his desire blaze higher. He knew exactly how she felt.

When he drew her into his arms, she fought

225

against herself as well as him, pounding her fists against his chest, twisting her face away from the lips that were far too near, far too demanding. But all she did was rub her body against his, inflaming them both. Desire swept through her in an instant, and she found herself at the edge of losing control, of giving herself and her pride and her heart to a man who craved only her body. And she did not care. *She did not care.*

Jake's arms were steel bands around her. "Don't you want me, Angel?" he growled. "Isn't your body hot and hungry like mine?"

A desperate surge of denial gave her the strength to shove free of him. She backed toward the door, not knowing where to seek relief from her own traitorous will. He caught her and pinned her against the wall. The rough surface scratched against her bare skin, but far more dangerous was the hard body pressed against hers.

Damn you, Jake Price, damn you, screamed her mind. She parted her lips to speak, but all that issued forth was one whispered word.

Jake.

He took it for yes.

As his lips brushed against hers, her hands spread in feeble protest against his chest.

"Tell me to stop," he said huskily.

Sarah could look at nothing other than his lips—lips that she knew too well could ravage her and drive her wild. There was no denying the power of her need for him. She studied the hollow of his throat and the tanned skin visible in the opening of his shirt. She closed her eyes to keep from pressing her tongue against that skin. Already she could taste him.

She felt his hands burn their way across her shoulders and the fullness of her breasts. His palms worked against the tips. Even leaning against the wall, she had to hold on to his arms for support. Her head dropped to one side, and she was caught in the mood of the erotic dance that had never quite left her, just as it had never quite left him.

His fingers worked at the fastening of the bodice, and he removed it from her body, throwing it aside as he bent his head to her throat. His lips pressed against the throbbing pulse he found there, then drifted downward across each breast, lingering at the hardening nubs while his hands stroked their fullness. The tip of his tongue was rough and relentless as it teased the tight buds. Beneath his assault, her body swelled in aching need.

Sarah gripped his arms and felt the taut muscles constrict beneath her grasp. She wanted to crawl inside his skin and be a part of his strength. Nothing was as consuming as her hunger for him, not pride, not self-respect. They were empty posturings when they rose in conflict with desire.

Jake's lips moved from her breast and trailed a burning path to her throat.

"I feel the beat of your heart," he whispered hotly against her skin. "It's pounding, Sarah, pounding. Saying the things you will not say."

He lifted his head until his mouth was a scant inch from hers. "Dance for me, Sarah. Dance with me, dance under me. Just for me and only me."

His voice was as hard as his body and as insistent as her passion.

"Only you," she whispered. "It was always only you."

He seemed not to have heard her confession as his

lips covered hers, and his tongue played against the flesh inside her mouth. He tasted the way he always did—of the salt spray from the ocean, of the thick sweet Turkish coffee that he drank, of the musky darkness of desire.

Sarah ran searching fingers across his shoulders, seeking the bare skin at his neck and the coarse curls of black hair at his nape. Her eyes fluttered open for a moment, and she saw the thick black wave of his lashes against his burnished cheek. His closed eyes made him look young and dear and as vulnerable as she felt.

But, oh, the knowing lips and tongue reminded her of Jake's expertise. Once again his hips pressed her to the wall. Every part of his body demanded acquiescence and more, the dance of responding rapture.

Anticipation caused Sarah to shiver.

She could give him the promised dance.

Arching her body against him, she brushed her tongue against his. A growl escaped from his throat, and she deepened her kiss. Unbidden, her hands roamed across his shoulders and back, edged down his powerful upper arms and once again pressed against his chest; only this time she moved her fingers across the taut sinews, worked frantically and much too slowly at the fastenings, and at last stroked his bared skin, the memory of which she could never erase from her mind.

Jake broke the kiss and pulled her to the carpeted floor, stretched beside her, and became a madman, kissing, stroking, demanding her body yield all that it could.

The jewelry at her abdomen and ankle jangled as she responded. She was like a wild animal beneath him, but his stroke did nothing to tame her rampant desires. With maddening slowness, he began to undress her, pulling the full silk trousers low on her abdomen, then down her thighs and long legs, his eyes following his hands as they bared her burning skin. The wool rug was rough beneath her, and the floor unyielding, but Jake's hands made her forget the unimportant discomfort.

She watched in fascination as he slipped the ankle bracelet into his shirt pocket. His eyes trailed slowly up her naked body. When at last his gaze locked with hers, he surprised her with a crooked smile. Her heart turned over, and she bit at her lower lip.

His own clothes were disposed of more quickly, and she met his return embrace with eager hands and lips. In a tangle of arms and legs and aching need, she discovered for a second time the natural force that drew her inexorably to him, her body moistening with both sweat and the liquid of desire that formed deep within. She parted her legs and he eased inside. She ceased to exist except where Jake touched her; she became a part of him, an extension of his passion. The thrusts of his body became her thrusts. Together she and Jake set a dizzying pace.

When ecstasy came, it was for them both. It lasted for eternity and was over far too quickly, although Sarah had no idea how such opposites could both be true. She clung to him until the whirling world settled around her and both of them were still.

"Sarah," he whispered in her ear. He drew a ragged breath. "Sarah." The last was more a sigh.

He held her for a long time; she was afraid to move, knowing that the next words spoken were the most important that had ever passed between them. The first time with Jake—could it have been only the previous night?—he had been questioning and then heartbreakingly apologetic, when all she had wanted to hear were soft lies of love, of how wonderful she was, of how splendid had been their joining. She had not loved him any more than he loved her, but it could not hurt to pretend.

Tonight they had faced each other like warriors, but their battle had soon changed to something far more seductive and far more dangerous. A dance of love, she could call it. But the dance was done.

She suddenly became aware of where they were. The floor, for God's sake. She was filled with shame. She would have wondered what madness had taken possession of her, but she knew. Jake Price. She had no sense of decency or restraint where he was concerned.

And words of love would be a cruel jest. She had wanted to hear them, there was no denying the fact. Surely in such a situation, all women did. Somehow it justified the wanton abandonment of every emotion but lust.

Jake broke the embrace and brushed the damp tendrils from her face. "Sarah—"

"No," she said, afraid of what he would say. "Don't ask if I'm all right." She gave him one quick glance before cutting her eyes away.

His hand stilled.

"And don't," she added, "apologize."

"I had no intention of doing either," he said as he slowly eased away from her and sat, giving her a view of his lean, muscled back. One hand raked through his hair. "Any other instructions?" he asked.

She turned from him, her arms gripped protectively around her middle as though she might keep herself from harm, or hold within her the memory of what had gone before.

He had talked about the drugs for sale in the Grand Bazaar. For her, Jake was a drug. Twenty-four hours ago he had rescued her from the Grand Seraglio. Since that time she had opened herself to him twice. Given the opportunity, she would do so again.

He was an addiction far worse than opium. Around him she forgot the massacre aboard the *Leviathan* and the threatened assassination of Harun. She forgot her promises to herself and her father, and she forgot honor.

She must get away; she had no choice. But why did she feel as though her heart were breaking? Were all women such fools when they tasted rapture?

"I have no more instructions," she managed. "Just a realization of something you already know. It's time for me to leave. As soon as it's light." She tried to make her voice sound casual. "I should have gone to Ralph when we got back from the island. You were right. I've made a mess of things."

She felt his eyes on her.

"Is that what you call what happened just now? A mess of things?" asked Jake.

"I'm not calling it anything—you would know more about such matters than I—but so much has happened, and much of it because I've tried to postpone the inevitable." She forced herself to sit and look at him. "I'm sorry you didn't get your money tonight. Truly sorry. But for that I can't take the blame. Fatima was leaving by the time I arrived. She must have seen you and knew why you were there. If it's any consolation, she was terrified."

His glance was dark and enigmatic. "I'll try to be appeased."

Now that was the Jake she knew.

Exhaustion washed over her. She stood and, taking great care to keep her back to him, picked up the robe that he had thrown aside. Slipping it over her exposed body, she walked to the bed.

She heard him stir and knew he was getting dressed. The faint jingle of the ankle bracelet came to her. Let him keep it as a remembrance. Without anything to hold on to except the images in her mind, she had enough memories to last for a lifetime.

"You don't have to leave, Sarah," he said.

She turned to face him. "Why not? What else can I do? Surely you're not suggesting I stay with you."

"I've met Ralph Pettigrew, remember? You're right. He's not for you. I'll help you work something out."

Like what? she started to ask. *Like keeping me here for your pleasure?* She added honestly, *And for mine?*

Sarah was smart enough to know how convenient she was to have around. But for how long? And where was she to go when they were done?

Her father had barely tolerated her harmless escapades, as had his London friends. She would not want to test his parental affections, already tenuous, by living openly with an American adventurer. Almost of equal importance, those friends of his formed the backbone of the society to which she must, of necessity, return.

They thought she craved adventure, with no thought spared for the resultant notoriety. If ever she had been that young and foolish, such was no longer true.

"I've inconvenienced you far too much already," she said. "I'll go by rented carriage in the morning. You've already got your reward, so there's no reason for you to accompany me."

"My reward?" He glanced at the rug, then back at

her. He mocked her with his eyes. "I'd say I've been well paid."

The shock of his words silenced her, but before she could form an answer that was harsh enough and equally shocking, he had headed for the door and was gone.

Chapter Sixteen

When Sarah awoke early the next morning to merciless sunbeams streaming through the lone high window, she decided she was as tired as she had been the night before. How arduous were the activities of dancing and making love with Jake. She had spent much of the night tossing and turning alone in his bed, trying to forget some of the particulars of the two events.

After pulling on the layers of clothes she had selected at the Grand Bazaar—trousers, smock, waistcoat and caftan—she answered a knock at the door and found herself confronting a somber, pasty-faced gentleman wearing the uniform of a carriage driver in Hyde Park. On the street behind him loomed a carriage and a spirited gray gelding. A young boy in livery stood at the gray's head, reins gripped in his gloved hands.

"Hello," Sarah said in surprise.

As the driver opened his mouth to answer, a pair of excited Turks passed between him and the carriage, their voices raised in argument. At the same moment a wagon loaded with cloth-wrapped cheese lumbered along, casting sour smells and dust into the morning air.

The driver paid them no mind, instead devoting all his attention to the rough caftan and to the trousers visible just below the hem. His gaze moved on to the room behind her. His lips pursed.

"Miss Whitlock?" he asked in the disapproving way she so well remembered from her reckless London days. "Mr. Price thought you might be ready for your ride to the embassy."

"How thoughtful of Mr. Price," Sarah said in her own London don't-fool-with-me voice. She looked past him at the closed carriage. It sat high above the street, its satin-lined cab providing elegant room for two passengers behind the driver's perch.

"A brougham," she said. "However did he manage to find one here?"

"Through the embassy. Mr. Price insisted on the best."

Sarah felt a cold, sinking feeling in the pit of her stomach. Jake could not wait to send her on her way, and in style, as though if she went grandly enough she would be less likely to return.

Once he had said she would need an armed guard to travel safely through the streets of the city to the embassy. Unless the waiting driver and footman were far more fierce than they appeared, it would seem he had changed his mind. After dragging her from the coffee house to his apartment, he had tested her vulnerability and decided she could fend for herself.

She tried to tell herself she was being unreasonable. *She* was the one who insisted she leave. But he had not put up much of an argument last night, and in the light of morning she was certain he must have been relieved.

You're more trouble than you're worth.

His words came back to haunt her.

Shoving them aside, she rubbed her toes against

235

the rug. Her lone pair of slippers were somewhere in the back room of a Turkish coffee house. If she were really to go in style, Jake should have sent a cobbler along with the brougham. She brushed her fingers through the loose-flowing tresses that rested against the coarse brown robe. The inclusion of a hairdresser and tailor as well would not have been remiss.

"What is your name?" she asked the watchful driver.

"Matthews," he said with aplomb.

Sarah admired his control. She would do well to follow his example. "I'll be right with you," she said. "Please wait outside."

She closed the door and unwillingly put on the leather socks and overshoes purchased along with the clothes. They were stiff and uncomfortable after her days of wearing light slippers or, better, wearing nothing at all on her feet.

She turned for a last look at the apartment. Gathering up a bundle of clothes, including the harem costume in which she had disgraced herself last night, she took a deep breath. Jake had spent less time in the room than had she, inclined as he was to hurry away after taking what she had to give, and yet the aura of him was sharply present.

Jake with his dark, disturbing stare and heart-stopping smile. His long-legged swagger could carry him across a room in the blink of an eye. The lightest touch of his hands could melt her stiffest resolve.

Her gaze drifted past the table and the porcelain bowl she had admired, stopping for a moment at the bed before dropping to the rug. Her cheeks burned with the memories of what had taken place the past two nights. Whatever it had meant to her, it had not been enough to gentle Jake Price.

What foolish, sentimental notions, Sarah told

herself. She stiffened her spine.

A knock at the door interrupted her thoughts.

"I'll be with you in a moment, Matthews," she said sharply over her shoulder.

"It is I" came a singsong voice from out on the street.

She opened the door and let Bandit enter, ignoring the raised eyebrows of the man who waited to take her away.

Bandit extended a parcel. "Perhaps you will find these of some use."

She opened the bag. "My slippers." Something about the sight of them made her want to cry. She looked at Bandit with gratitude. "It is possible that I might, indeed, find them of use."

"They were at the coffee house."

"Jake gave me no chance to get them last night."

Bandit glanced over his shoulder toward the open door and the carriage outside. "Bossman is sometimes as impetuous as the lady."

Sarah bent to trade the heavier Turkish footwear for the slippers, careful to avoid Bandit's eye. "He is only doing what we both agree is best. How was the coffee house this morning? Still standing, I assume." She straightened and smoothed the folds of her skirt. "Jake would have me believe the men might have torn the place down after I left."

"The possibility did exist for a while, but all settled into calm. Faruk saw me as I was leaving and asked that I convey a message to the beautiful, fair-skinned foreigner who brought such glory to his humble business."

"I'm not sure I want to hear what he had to say. It doesn't involve revenge of any sort, does it?"

"Do not underestimate yourself. If ever you should find yourself in difficult circumstances, he expressed

237

an interest in offering employment. Fatima has never received such a wild response."

Sarah found the news enormously satisfying.

"If you should see Faruk again, tell him I will keep the offer in mind."

"Miss Whitlock—"

"Couldn't you call me Sarah?"

The expression on Bandit's dark, weathered face was unreadable. "It would not be fitting."

"How polite you are," she said, then thought of another kind face besides his that she would never see again. "Nadire is the same. Missy Sarah, she says. She even calls your Bossman Aga Jake."

"Nadire is wise," Bandit said, not bothering to hide a smile. "She knows the Bossman well."

As did Sarah. Far too well for peace of mind to visit her before a week or a year had passed. "We must leave," she said.

"Is it not possible for you to remain away from the other English?" asked Bandit. "You are not like most of your fellow countrymen. And please, I mean this as a compliment."

Sarah thought of her father and of her betrothed. "And how do you find my countrymen?"

He shrugged, and she caught a glint of amusement —or was it appreciation—in his black eyes. "They do not adapt so well to a change in their surroundings."

"Like a harem or a Turkish coffee house."

"If they should find themselves in such unlikely abodes."

"As I did. No," she said with a sad smile. "I don't suppose I am like most of them, which has been a source of great discomfort for my father."

A lump formed in her throat. Impulsively, she brushed her lips against Bandit's brown cheek. "Thank you for your help and understanding," she said. "But I really must leave. It is best for all concerned."

"You are like Nadire. As clever and brave as you are, you seek refuge in what you know." His answering smile carried the same sadness as hers.

She hurried past him, her bundle of clothes crushed to her breast, and allowed Matthews to assist her into the interior of the small carriage. The driver took his place on the high outside seat and gathered the reins from the young boy, who scampered around to his post at the rear.

Not once did Sarah look back, nor did she think about her destination. She did not feel clever or brave, just terribly tired. It had been weeks since she had gotten a good night's sleep—and last night had been the most unrestful of all—but she could not relax. Too many memories and too many regrets rode with her through the streets.

Once she tried to imagine what dancing for Faruk would be like. A sheer fantasy, of course, and one she would never bring to reality, but she hoped it would help to pass the time as the carriage pitched and swayed on its slow journey. All she could think of was Jake watching her performance from the dark.

Crossing the viaduct over the Golden Horn, she could not resist giving a glance at the forest of ships' masts along the wharfs. Somewhere in all that wood and rope and canvas was Jake's dhow. Small and unnamed, it beckoned to her still.

Pride, Sarah, pride.

Th silent lecture worked. By the time Matthews reined the gray to a halt in front of the British embassy, she was once again approaching her composed self.

With Matthews trailing behind her, the small bundle of clothes under his arms, she swept up the long steps, nodded to the uniformed guard stationed outside, and strode into the marble entryway. Its high, arched roof studded with ceramic tiles reminded her of the corridors of the Grand Bazaar.

But there the similarity ended. There were no exotic scents to entice her, no babble of voices, no charm. The room was bare and cold and reeked of boiled meats and soap. Very British. Very bland.

A fair-haired, fortyish gentleman in rigid white collar and black suit hurried through one of the doors opening onto the foyer.

"I say there," he said. "May I help you?" The tone of his voice belied the polite words.

"I am expected," she said coolly. "Miss Sarah Whitlock."

"Oh!" His eyes took in her plain Turkish garments and unbound hair. "Sir Edward's daughter."

"You know my father?"

"It was my pleasure to meet him several months ago at a dinner in London."

Sarah pictured the kind of evening it must have been: a long table with stiff-necked gentlemen and jeweled ladies picking at course after course of underseasoned food and overspiced gossip with nary a dancing girl in sight.

"You were expecting me, I believe."

"Of course. Please forgive my tardiness. Allow me to introduce myself. Phillip Somersby, assistant to the ambassador. You must be exhausted from your ordeal. Mr. Pettigrew told us what little he knew. We are all anticipating a thorough report once you are rested."

Sarah did not care much for the glint in his eye, as though her story would of course extend beyond what everyone expected—perhaps, if he were fortunate, it might be titillating. She took an instant dislike to the man, most likely, she admitted to herself, because he was right.

But she did have much to report, news that was long overdue, especially concerning the threat to the Sultan Harun. Before she could respond, Somersby snapped his fingers, and a clerk hurried through another closed door. Without uttering a word of protest or assent she was swept up once more in the regularity of British life. Escorted to a room in the far wing of the second floor, she was introduced to the woman who would serve as her personal servant.

"Mrs. Morgan," the kindly-faced woman said. "I've served many a lady in London. You'll be having no complaints about me. Have you eaten? Looks as though you've been starving yourself. Won't do at all."

"I haven't—" Sarah began.

"No back talk," Mrs. Morgan said, the gentleness in her voice taking the offense from her words. "You're exhausted and that's the truth of it. First we'll get you some food, and then it's out of those clothes and into a warm tub and a soft bed. There'll be time enough to talk later."

Sarah found herself being treated like a child who had gone without food or rest for a long time. She loved it. A cup of tea and a tray of cakes appeared from nowhere. Sarah emptied them both. Certain that she would be unable to relax, she could barely stay awake long enough to bathe. The miracle worker Mrs. Morgan produced a soft flannel gown. Donning it, Sarah was asleep by the time her head rested on the down pillow.

Still exhausted, she awoke in mid-afternoon, begged off from a meeting with Ralph Pettigrew, who Mrs. Morgan reported was waiting below in the embassy drawing room, and arranged to meet him in the morning after breakfast. She had a light supper in her room, gave a cursory glance to the clothes hanging neatly in the wardrobe—"Mr. Pettigrew arranged for their purchase," Mrs. Morgan explained—and continued her drugged-like sleep throughout the night.

She awoke early the next morning as tired as she had felt the evening before. She had not the faintest idea why.

Once again she submitted herself to the ministrations of the kindly Mrs. Morgan, who selected a rose-colored gown for the long-postponed meeting with her betrothed. High-necked and full-sleeved, the silk dress was tight at the waist and extended to the floor in three tiers of flounces which covered a horsehair petticoat supporting three additional petticoats of linen. Sarah thought to herself that the yardage included in the complete ensemble—more even than the Turkish garb from the bazaar—was enough to clothe a good portion of Harun's harem.

Sarah had to admit her hair style was a work of art—parted in the center with the sides puffed out and a chignon at the nape of her neck just above the lace trim on the dress. Golden wisps framed her face. Mrs. Morgan studied her in admiration.

"Like an English flower you are. Mr. Pettigrew is a lucky man."

Not really, Sarah could have told her. Not if he expected a bride who was pure of body and mind, and not if he hoped for a wife who could one day give him her love. At that moment Sarah did not think she could ever love any man.

As she left the room, her silk flounces rustling, she glanced around for the simple clothes she had worn yesterday. They were nowhere in sight. Probably burned, she thought. She would do well to do the same to her memories, with the exception, of course, of her long overdue report on Harun and the true fate of the *Leviathan*.

The living quarters of the embassy boasted a small dining room, where she found a sideboard loaded with English fare—kidneys and eggs and sausages, toast and muffins, tea and coffee, butter and jam. There was not a pomegranate in sight, nor a bowl of yoghurt, and she settled on tea and toast.

She had much to think about. Her betrothed would be here soon. Should she tell him the truth of what had happened on shipboard? Harun had been so much concerned that the tenuous friendship between England and Turkey would be harmed by news of the attack and her kidnapping, but she could not let such a tale of horror go unreported. If for no other reason, Captain Reynolds and Etheleen Murphy and the others on board deserved to have their true fate known.

But was Ralph Pettigrew really the person to whom she should report? Sarah wished she were wise enough to know.

Phillip Somersby found her gazing into a cup of cold tea.

"Good morning," he said from the doorway. "I trust you have been well cared for."

Startled, she glanced up. "Oh, yes. Mrs. Morgan is wonderful." She caught the approving look in his eye, but she did not know if it was for her or for Mrs. Morgan's handiwork.

He stepped into the room. His suit and stiff-collared shirt were replicas of yesterday's attire, as was the anticipatory glint in his eye. His fair, straight hair was slickly combed across a rising forehead, and his hands, slender for a man's, were gripped loosely

243

at his waist.

"Please let us know if there is anything the staff can do to make your stay more comfortable," he said. "After all you've been through, I'm certain it must be a great relief to know you are once more among your own kind."

Sarah bristled. Somersby sounded remarkably like her father, and the dislike she had felt on first meeting him intensified.

"Would it be possible for me to see the ambassador?" she asked. "I would like to tell him about . . . about several things."

"About your rescue, I imagine. You'll be wanting to describe that bit of excitement, I'm sure. Unfortunately, Lord Stratford is away from the city at the moment," Somersby said, "touring the provinces. I am his representative, however. Anything you would say to him you should feel free to say to me." Pouring himself a cup of tea from the sideboard, he sat at the table opposite her and waited for her to speak.

Vicarious thrills were what he sought, and if Sarah hadn't been ready to relate the salient details of the past days, she might have told him she remained too exhausted to talk. If only the ambassador were available. . . .

Sarah's timing on this too adventurous journey was definitely off.

Closing her eyes to the sight of Somersby's eagerness, she tried to think of where she could begin. With Scarface and the blood-soaked deck of the *Leviathan*? With her first trip into the Grand Seraglio? With her second? And of course there was Jake. How could she ever tell anyone about him?

The truth was, she could not, at least not everything. He was a memory she would have to clasp to herself. His bravery in her rescue from the wharf and later from Mustafa's harem certainly should not be kept secret; but the journey to the island and the nights in his arms—those were for her alone to know. As was her performance at Faruk's coffee house. There were some things respectable Englishmen would never understand.

She opened her eyes. The watchful look on the diplomat's face left her unable to begin.

"You said last night you knew my father," she said, stalling.

"A most distinguished and knowledgeable gentleman."

"But you and I have never met."

"I would most certainly remember even a brief acquaintance with such a lovely and"—he smiled superciliously—"remarkable young lady."

Warning signals went off in Sarah's head. "Remarkable? Whatever do you mean, Mr. Somersby?" She forged on without attending to discretion or tact. "Are you speaking of my reputation as somewhat of a madcap?"

Somersby did not so much as blink, and she got the feeling he was actually enjoying her outspoken ways.

"A hellion is what I heard, since you bring up the subject. A beauty who seeks out risks and does not mind who knows. Miss Whitlock," he said in a lowered voice, "you do not disappoint."

His gaze dropped to her lips and throat and the fullness of her breasts beneath the rose-colored silk— but only for an instant. If she had not been watching, she would have missed the perusal altogether.

Phillip Somersby considered himself too much the gentleman for one of Jake's lingering looks, but he was still an arrogant man. Worse, he was a boor.

Insulted as she was by the insinuations of words and glance, she was not at a loss for a response. It took great strength of will for her to put aside her mounting revulsion.

"Whatever you have heard about me," she said with great dignity, "please forget for the moment. We have things of far greater import to talk about than the gossip of the *ton*. Since Lord Stratford is not available, I am forced to tell you. Quite by accident I have stumbled upon information concerning the sultan." She took a deep breath. "His life may be endangered."

This time Somersby widened his eyes, not in amazement at her shocking revelation but in open disbelief.

"How excitable you are," he said, demonstrating by his calmness the way he seemed to think she should behave. "What on earth could have given you such an impression?"

Sarah was hit by her own disbelief. Of all the things she had imagined when her story was at last told, scorn was not among them.

"I am twenty-five years of age," she snapped, "not a child. I know what I know."

"Of course. There is some sort of threat upon the Sultan Harun's life, is that what you said? Might I ask the nature of this threat and how you came by it?"

Well, you see, Phillip, I was thrown into his harem, and when I tried to get away I overheard a conversation in Turkish which I managed to interpret. Harun's throat is to be cut.

Only the slimmest hold on her temper kept her from blurting out the scandalous truth, which would have been carried by half the passengers on the first ship leaving for London. For the first time in her life she regretted the reputation for seeking out challenges and a naughty name that she had acquired during the past few years. At the moment when she most wanted to be believed, it lent an air of absurdity to her farfetched but truthful tale.

"Perhaps," she said stiffly, "it would be better if I waited for the ambassador to return before relating the details."

"Lord Stratford de Redcliffe is a most intelligent man, and a very busy one. His time is much too valuable to waste upon the stories born of an active imagination. Surely what you witnessed can be given a less dramatic interpretation."

Sarah could be just as intransigent as the self-important clerk.

"As a citizen of England, I demand that you let me present my story in person. Let Lord Stratford decide how much of his time I have wasted."

Somersby frowned. "Does this mean you no longer wish to speak of your rescue today?"

"How clever you are to determine my meaning. Whatever I have to say, Mr. Somersby, you will have to learn from the ambassador."

At least, she thought with shallow satisfaction, the diplomat knew a rebuff when he heard it—even if he had to hear it several times.

She was pleased to see a flash of anger in his eyes. "When he returns," he said, "I will pass on your request."

Sarah let out a sigh of impatience. She knew exactly how her petition for an audience would be presented to the highly regarded and popular ambassador. She would be described as a fool—charming, of course, but one hardly to be believed. She must endeavor to overcome the prejudices that would be put in Lord Stratford's mind, but she was by no means confident of success.

Ralph Pettigrew loomed as the confessor who should next hear her warnings concerning Harun.

"Has my fiancé arrived yet?" she asked, bringing an end to the interview. "I was to meet him this morning."

Somersby stood and bowed briskly. "If you will excuse me, I will see if he awaits." Returning a moment later with the news that indeed Mr. Pettigrew had arrived at the embassy, he guided her to the small parlor where the long-dreaded meeting with her betrothed was to take place.

As she walked into the room, Sarah realized that she was not dreading the moment after all. She truly needed the support and sympathy her fiancé could provide.

Pettigrew rose from his chair and turned to face her at the same moment Somersby exited and closed the door. Her fiancé was much as she remembered him, tall, portly and distinguished, and a little grayer than he had been seven years before. His lips, unsuitably thin in his broad face, curved into a welcoming smile that was matched by the light in his pale eyes.

"Ah, Sarah," he said, striding to her and taking her hand. "You are even more lovely than the picture I carried in my mind."

"Mr. Pettigrew," Sarah said, lowering her eyes and praying that these first awkward moments would hurry past.

"Ralph, please." He squeezed her hand. "Let me hear you say it."

Sarah swallowed. Her fiancé sounded decidedly amorous, and his palms were ominously damp. She had been imagining a far more platonic meeting than he obviously had in mind.

"Ralph," she said to the floor.

He lifted her chin and placed a chaste kiss upon her cheek. She caught a strong whiff of bay rum.

"My dear," he said. "I have waited so long."

She pulled free.

"Ah, I have embarrassed you," he said. "I forget myself in the presence of your innocence."

Sarah blushed. This was going all wrong.

He directed her toward the sofa. "Please rest for a moment. You must still be weak from all that has happened to you."

His solicitous concern threw her deeper into confusion. *All that has happened to you.* If Ralph only knew.

She settled onto the center of the sofa and spread her full skirt to the right and to the left, effectively barring him from taking a seat beside her. But she could not keep him from drawing a chair close by.

She lifted her lashes. "I have something I need to tell you."

He leaned near. "You may trust me with your deepest confidences, my dear."

Sarah sifted through the details of the past weeks and settled on the one basic fact that must be told.

"Harun is in danger."

"I beg your pardon?"

Ignoring the Somersby look of incredulity on his face, she rushed on. "I heard a conversation in Stamboul. Between a man I could not see and a man with a scar."

Ralph's eyes narrowed. She had his full attention.

"A man with a scar?" he asked.

Sarah nodded. "Tall and thin and mean looking. He looked more like a skeleton than a living human being." Something in her fiancé's expression prompted her to ask, "Do you know him?"

"Of course not," he said.

It was a rather sharp reply, she thought.

"What exactly did you hear?" he went on.

Now came the tricky part. "I couldn't make out the

details, but I heard the sultan's name and Scarface—"

"Scarface?"

"That's what I named him for wont of anything more specific. He made a gesture across his throat—"

"A gesture, you say."

"A cutting move. As though he were holding a knife." Days later and in the sanctuary of the embassy, she still shuddered at the remembered scene.

"Can you repeat exactly what you did hear?"

"They were speaking in Turkish."

Ralph settled back in his chair. "I see."

"You don't believe me," said Sarah, fighting to keep the exasperation from her voice. She did not care to be called excitable twice in the span of an hour.

Maybe what she needed—as she had suggested to Jake—was Scarface waving a scimitar over Ralph's head. She did not doubt that under that terrible circumstance he, too, might feel a quickened pulse.

"You've been through a terrible ordeal, Sarah, what with the rescue at sea and the loss of memory. And, of course, your stay with the American family cannot have been comfortable. You must tell me about them later. This Jake Price who came to see me hardly looked like the sort of company Sir Edward would choose for you."

Even as he admonished her, he seemed distracted— as though he were saying one thing and thinking something else.

Sarah refused to be drawn into a conversation about Jake. "I am not suffering from delusions, regardless of what you choose to believe."

"Of course you're not," said Ralph hastily. "I believe you saw and heard what you did. What I find hard to accept is the interpretation you have given to it. Just when and where did this conversation take place?"

Sarah gripped her hands in her lap. "Scarface was standing in a doorway as I passed. I could not see the man to whom he spoke."

"The Americans allowed you on the streets?"

"Briefly."

His expression clearly indicated that this was exactly the sort of remiss guardianship he had been worried about. "Describe again the man with the scar."

Sarah recreated the image in her mind as accurately as she was able, her fiancé quiet and still while she talked. The fear of that night returned to her in full force, and she made no attempt to keep it from her voice. "The other man seemed to be giving the orders." She shuddered and leaned toward the edge of the sofa. "Orders to kill. You simply *must* believe me."

"I believe you saw such a man." Ralph's voice had taken on a hardness that had not been there before. "Did this Scarface see you?"

"I believe he did. At least for a second."

Ralph sat in silence, stone-faced, and for a moment she saw a glimpse of the strong-willed man who had single-handedly turned a small shipping company into one that was known around the world.

He took her hands in his and squeezed hard. "It would be best if you do not tell such a tale to anyone but me. I will do what I can to investigate, but I repeat: Do not speak of this man you call Scarface to anyone else."

The harshness of his hands and voice was supported by the grim look on his face, all signs of disbelief gone. Sarah looked at him in surprise. If she did not know better, she would think he looked afraid.

"Promise me you will do as I wish," he said.

"The story I have told you will be passed on to no one else," she said, knowing not what else she could say. She spoke the truth. The story she had told was far from a complete accounting of the past and would not be repeated. When Lord Stratford de Redcliffe returned from his tour of the country, she would not try to convince him with half truths.

Leaving out only a few personal details that were of no one's concern but her own, she would reveal all to the ambassador. In return, she would try to find out why such a danger to the sultan of Turkey should have thrown the stodgy shipowner Ralph Pettigrew into what she could describe only as a state of near panic. She would almost think it was his life that was at risk instead of Harun's.

Chapter Seventeen

The next two weeks were the longest of Sarah's life. Mrs. Morgan continued to be as kind and solicitous as she had been that first day at the embassy and Ralph as attentive a fiancé as any girl could wish— far more so, in Sarah's case—but she felt a decided chill on the part of the remaining British community.

In the beginning the wives and daughters of the diplomats and businessmen had sought her company, visiting her in the embassy parlor and inviting her to tea at their nearby Turkish homes.

Ralph had insisted she not stray from the embassy without his personal escort, and she finally decided to remain behind the solid walls.

"What do you think of Constantinople?" she asked her first visitor, the dour-faced Rowena Primm, who was the wife of a British importer. She and her husband had lived in the country two years, and she claimed herself an expert on all things Turkish.

After five minutes in the woman's company, Sarah decided her visitor bore an appropriate name.

"Hot. Dry. Uncivilized," Mrs. Primm had sniffed. "And barbarian. To think they call us infidels."

Sarah flew to the defense of the country she had

come to admire. "What about the kitchens open to the poor? They do not let their people starve."

Mrs. Primm was quick to answer. "Just encourages begging. We in London have the good sense to keep our unfortunates in their own sections of the city."

So much, Sarah decided, for appealing to Rowena's charitable nature, and she tried another approach.

"There's the Grand Bazaar—"

"Surely you haven't been to that smelly place!"

Sarah's answer was to offer a plate of heavily sugared cakes. She did not bring up the subject of Turkey again during any of the following visits of the English ladies.

The realization came soon enough that their kindness was bolstered by a natural curiosity concerning her rescue at sea and subsequent weeks in Stamboul. The memories were too painful for parlor talk. Afraid that once she mentioned the least detail the rest of her story would come out in a flood, she refused to speak at all of the recent past.

The women took her silence as a rebuff, and she found herself more and more alone.

Except for Ralph, of course. She could not fault him for his attentions, and he visited her as often as she would allow. More often than she would have liked, he showed a decided interest in the man who had informed him she was still alive.

"This Jake Price. Seemed a rough sort," he commented once.

"In some ways, he was. But in some ways he was quite concerned about my well-being." Sarah could think of no other way to describe the moments she had spent in Jake's arms.

"Still," Ralph continued, "he's not the kind of man I prefer taking care of my fiancée. Couldn't figure him out, truth to tell."

Ralph went on to give a few more opinions about Jake and a few facts as he saw them. Sarah knew he was watching for her reaction. She remained remarkably noncommittal, even while she hung on some of the more interesting things Ralph had to say.

Every time she raised the issue of Scarface, her fiancé drew behind his own wall of silence.

"I am investigating," he told her. "The source of information that I am forced to rely upon is not available at present."

"Are you speaking about the ambassador?" she asked.

"The man I refer to travels with Lord Stratford."

"A member of his staff, then."

He shrugged, refusing to tell her more, and she had to be content knowing that the Sultan Harun, seen occasionally on matters of state in the city, was still in good health. Phillip Somersby informed her as much. Not a word was said of Mustafa, and Sarah never asked for news of the sultan's son.

She spent her enforced hours of repose trying to assemble a pattern for what had happened to her. No matter where she started, she always ended up with the conviction that she had stumbled upon plans for the assassination of the sultan. She would have doubted her conclusions, if not her sanity, had it not been for her memory of Scarface on the bloodied deck of the *Leviathan* and her midnight dash through the town with him close in pursuit. Sometimes late at night she could still hear those scimitars swish through the air.

At the center of all her discomfort were the memories of Jake. Jake who had fought off those slashing blades. Jake who had rescued her more than once. Jake who had taken her into his arms and taught her what there could be between a man and a woman. Oh, how she tried to accept Ralph into her heart, but she failed.

Sarah chastised herself for an inability to care for someone who would never invade a harem on her behalf; it seemed a farfetched standard to place on any mortal man. But she was not thinking strictly with her mind. Her heart was decidedly involved.

Continuing to put him off in his insistence that she set a date for their nuptials, she knew she would have to make a very important decision soon . . . not whether to break the betrothal, but how and when.

She was not the wife for Ralph. She wondered if she were in truth the wife for anyone. What she needed to do was tell her story to someone who would listen and who would take appropriate action. Lord Stratford had gained quite a reputation for fairness and diplomatic dealings where sensitive issues were concerned. He was the man she must see. Then she could turn to her personal concerns.

At the end of the second week at the embassy, she was elated to learn the ambassador had returned from his tour of the countryside. A ball was slated in welcome four days hence. She would make every attempt to see Lord Stratford before then, but if a meeting proved impossible, she would accost him in the middle of the dance floor. She had waited long enough.

Lord Stratford had been accompanied on the long tour by several delegates in his own staff as well as by members of the Turkish court. Even Mustafa had joined him in the latter part of his journey, Somersby reported. Both sultan and son would be at the ball.

Sarah took the news calmly. While she had no wish to confront her one-time captors, she would not hesitate to do so should Lord Stratford prove as skeptical as his temporary replacement Somersby.

They would no doubt deny she had ever been inside the Grand Seraglio, but she could substantiate her claims with such details that even the critical Phillip Somersby would realize she spoke the truth.

With nothing much to occupy her time except speculation and worry, she turned her attention to the gown she would wear. Her father's business representative in London had forwarded funds, along with a letter saying news of her safety had been sent to Sir Edward at the country home he was visiting in Virginia. Part of the money had gone to repay a strongly protesting Ralph for the clothes he provided her.

She had yet to hear from her father, but she knew that when she did the correspondence would be brief and cool. Somehow he would figure she had been at fault in her misadventures.

At least she had Mrs. Morgan, who saw to it that Sarah's order for fabric from the Grand Bazaar was carried out exactly as she wished.

"A fine choice," Mrs. Morgan said when the parcel was delivered and she unfolded the yards of blue silk shot with silver threads. "It'll bring out the blue in your eyes and the warm tones of your skin. And I know of a dressmaker who can do whatever you wish in the manner of style."

Sarah pressed the silk to her face and was gratified to find it held the scents of the bazaar—the perfume and incense that reminded her of the brief, far different existence she had tasted so recently and yet so long ago.

"Yes," Sarah whispered, "it's perfect."

The finished gown, fully boned and lined, was scooped low across the bosom and narrowed to a tight waistline that was pointed in both front and back. Somehow Mrs. Morgan found a Turkish woman to embroider tiny pink and yellow flowers across the bodice and around the bottom of the full skirt. All was done according to Sarah's specifications.

The night of the ball her hair was piled high toward the back of her head and fell in a cascade of blond curls against her long, slender neck. An embroidered strip of blue silk was wound through the tresses and tied in a bow at the side. She decided that except for the pearl ring Ralph had given her, she would wear no jewelry—nothing that would jangle or lie with ticklish cold against her skin.

"What a lovely young lady you are," Mrs. Morgan purred as Sarah slipped her feet into the soft white leather shoes she would wear for the dancing. "Your father should see you now."

"He would find fault," said Sarah.

"Surely not."

Sarah picked up a white lace shawl that would serve as protection should the many windowed ballroom downstairs prove cool. "Perhaps you are right." She could not explain her father to Mrs. Morgan, and if she tried the woman would think she was feeling sorry for herself.

And that, she had never done. Whatever happened, happened. It was up to her to make life the best, and right now the best thing she could do was capture a private moment with the ambassador and unload on him the heavy baggage of her experiences since she had sailed into the Aegean on the ill-fated cargo ship.

A servant's soft knock at the door announced her betrothed awaited below to escort her into the ball. Despite all her worries, she did indeed feel pretty as she swept down the marble stairs. The heads of several waiting gentlemen turned to watch her progress, and she caught more than one side glance from the women as she greeted Ralph. Sarah had accepted their coolness without bitterness, but she was feminine enough to accept their envious looks as well.

"Sarah," Ralph said, pressing her gloved hands into his own. "What a beauty you are."

She smiled up at him. "You look handsome yourself." She meant it. He wore a black tail coat, matching trousers, and white ruffled shirt, and there was an ornate gold stickpin in his black tie. The formal wear was well tailored to disguise his normal portly look. "Quite distinguished, as a matter of fact."

He frowned. "I hope you do not mean quite old."

For the first time Sarah saw a vulnerability beneath his formal façade. Intent as she was upon considering the unsuitability of their union from her viewpoint, she had not considered it from his.

She squeezed his hand. "I mean distinguished, just as I said."

Her arm in his, Sarah walked beside her fiancé down the long, flower-lined corridor that led to the embassy ballroom. The sounds of music and excited talk and laughter guided them on their way, and she entered into a candlelit room of enchantment that seemed more appropriate to London than Constantinople. The English had somehow managed to recreate a scene from their homeland—groups of chattering men and women, the indispensable row of chairs for the matrons and the girls who awaited an offer to dance, the orchestra working away on a dais in one corner, and the side tables of punch and light refreshments.

The only discordant note was the line of Turkish guards down one side of the room. Clad in crimson coats and black trousers, scimitars sheathed against their sides, they made a formidable appearance. Sarah searched their number for Scarface or any other sentinel that might look familiar. As far as she could tell, she had never seen any of them before.

In deference to the unusual appearance of the sultan and his son, the normal receiving line had been dispensed with. She spotted Harun and Mustafa garbed in full red robes and seated at a long table with a dignified-looking gentleman she assumed was the ambassador. Pausing at the side of the room, she tried to picture what the imperial Turks would do when they spied her. The last time each had seen her, she had been dressed in far different clothes and had been very much under their control—or so they had supposed.

Purposefully she edged nearer to where they sat, Ralph in tow. She stopped a dozen yards away. Harun, studying the crowd of dark-suited men and their women, paused for a fraction of a second when his eyes lighted on her. His gaze moved on, but she was certain there had been a moment of recognition. As far as she could tell, Mustafa never looked her way, which was just as well with her. She was more than willing to take her cue from them both. They did not know her; she did not know them.

At that moment the music began and the dance floor soon filled. She caught the look on Harun's face as he watched the unveiled and bare-shouldered women whirling about the ballroom floor in the arms of men. He might have several hundred half-clad women ready for his gratification at any moment night or day, but in public those same women were expected to cover themselves from head to toe. It was obvious what he thought of the English ladies, the wives and daughters of the very proper

Englishmen with whom he dealt. They looked like odalisques.

She put the idea to Ralph.

"Wherever did you learn such a word?" he asked, shocked.

"It's part of the education I've picked up in my travels."

"Sultans live different sorts of lives. Not at all the sort of thing you should worry yourself with."

"But I do," she insisted, rankled by his all-too-protective response. "And I'll bet I'm not the only one."

She was sure her fiancé almost smiled. "As a matter of fact," he conceded, "I have heard the point discussed. The feeling was that the sultan would consider them rather immoral."

Remembering the faultfinding women who had visited her, especially Rowena Primm, Sarah decided Harun's judgment of them had an ironical touch that she liked.

"Is it possible for me to meet Lord Stratford?" she asked.

"Once he starts to circulate, of course. It would not be at all suitable for you to be introduced to Harun or his son."

"They might find me immoral."

Ralph's answer was a request for the upcoming waltz, to which Sarah readily agreed, and she tossed her shawl onto the nearest chair. She truly enjoyed dancing, and while she couldn't help but compare the stylish waltz to her exhibition in the coffee house, she found whirling around the room under the guidance of her fiancé an unexpected pleasure. Ralph was surprisingly light on his feet for a man of such size.

She went from his arms into the arms of Phillip Somersby.

"Are you enjoying the evening, Miss Whitlock?" he asked.

Sarah was surprised to detect a slur in his voice. He must have been imbibing more than just the bland embassy punch.

"Quite," she said.

"Don't suppose you've had the opportunity to meet Lord Stratford."

She looked him straight in the eye. "I fully intend to."

He stumbled, then caught himself and continued with the dance. "Do not," he said, carefully articulating every word, "embarrass 'im with those outlandish tales of threats against Harun. Or have you long since realized not to try such silly mischief here? I have been hoping so."

Sarah came to a halt at the edge of the floor and pulled free of Somersby's limp hold. Her position was strategically near the hall leading away from the dance, should she want to get away fast from the drunken, boorish diplomat.

"I assure you," she said, looking around to gain control of her anger, "that I—"

She stopped. The sight of the man coming into the ballroom left her unable to go on.

"Jake," she whispered.

The scattered throng at the edge of the dance floor parted enough to give her a full and unsettling view. He was wearing the formal tail coat, straight trousers and ruffled shirt that was the expected wear for all the men. But he did not look the same. Tall and lean, his broad shoulders enhanced by the cut of his coat, his legs seeming even longer by the fit of his trousers, he made all the other men look dowdy. A shock of black

262

hair rested across his forehead, and beneath thick black brows his eyes searched the room in careful perusal before settling on Sarah. From twenty feet away, Sarah felt a jolt.

"Are you all right?" Somersby asked. "Didn't mean to be too harsh."

Sarah ignored him.

Jake made his way through the crowd and stopped in front of her. "Do you mind?" he said to Somersby, not waiting for a reply.

It was as natural as breathing for Sarah to slip away from the diplomat and into Jake's waiting arms. She could not look away from his midnight-blue eyes.

He smiled.

Sarah's heart turned over.

"We're supposed to be dancing," he said softly.

His words brought her back to herself. When he began to glide around the dance floor, Sarah forced her gaze to his velvet lapel. His hand burned against her back as he guided her with expert skill.

"I didn't expect to see you again," she said.

"I've grown as impulsive as you. When I heard about tonight, I decided to see how things were going."

"How did you manage an invitation?"

"Need you ask?"

"Bandit."

"It seems he has a cousin working in the embassy."

"And how is he?" she asked and thought, *What ordinary talk when all the time my heart is pounding so hard that it hurts.*

"Bandit's the same," said Jake. "We've been doing a little work on the boat."

"I thought you might have left the country."

"Not with unfinished business to take care of."

Sarah's eyes darted upward. "And what would that be?"

He stared down at her for a long moment. "The gold. Surely you haven't forgotten."

"Ah, yes, Fatima." Sarah felt a whisper of cold air brush across her bare shoulders, and she could not hide a shiver. "Have you found her?"

"Not yet." He whirled her around the room in silence. At last, he asked, "And how is Ralph?"

"Insisting I set a date for the wedding."

She felt the pressure of his hand tighten against her spine.

"Still engaged, then. What did he say about your adventures? Or maybe I should ask just how much you revealed."

The blood rushed to her face. "You most certainly should not!"

"Temper, Sarah. I only wondered how I should greet him, since he's been staring at me with what can only be described as undisguised dislike."

"I've told him nothing about you," she said, her feelings masked as much as she could manage, which was miraculous considering the way her heart continued to pound. "I decided that whatever happens to our betrothal, there is no need for your name to arise." She raised her gaze to his. "What's past is past, Jake. You know that as well as I."

"Liar," he said, a glint in his eyes. "I saw the way you looked when I came into the room."

"You took me by surprise. I didn't know you owned a coat, much less such formal wear."

"An uncouth American, right?" He came to a halt in the midst of couples gliding around them. "What if I really showed your friends how uncouth I can be? What if I kissed you right here in the middle of the dance floor? They're all speculating about what's going on. We could give them something to really talk about.''

Sarah knew he was fully capable of doing what he threatened. The trouble was, she wanted him to—more than she wanted anything else in the world—but there must not be a scene tonight, not with the ambassador so close. If so much hadn't depended upon her maintaining a sense of decorum, she wondered just what she would have allowed Jake to do.

Her eyes fell to his parted lips. Memories of hot, sweet kisses rushed into her already reeling mind, crowding out all thoughts of time and place. A dancing couple whirling in time to the music jostled her, and she was forcibly returned to reality. How close she had come to making a fool of herself and proving to the world's critics that she was no better than they claimed.

But still, a nagging voice inside said, if it were not for her responsibilities. . . .

In self-defense, she stepped away from his touch. "Thank you for the dance, Mr. Price," she said over the music. "I find I'm rather tired this evening. If you will excuse me. . . ."

Turning, she found her way through the crowds around the dance floor, down the long hall, and into the room that had been set aside for the ladies seeking a place to rest. Claiming a chair in the corner, she closed her eyes and pretended she did not hear the rustling of dresses around her or the whispered speculations about the handsome man with whom she had danced.

But she could not stay there forever. Lord Stratford awaited. When her heart had settled into a normal rhythm and the flush was gone from her cheeks, she pushed a curl around, smoothed her skirt, and forced her feet to take her back to the ball. Jake was standing by the punch bowl; she headed for Ralph at the opposite side of the room.

It took her several minutes to wend her way through the crowd. She kept her eyes downward to avoid the curious stares. Trying as hard as she could to be unobtrusive, she seemed to be calling a great deal of attention to herself.

Welcoming her to his side, Ralph took her hands in his. "I was worried about you. That ruffian American—"

"Simply wanted to know I made it to the embassy all right," she finished, very much aware of the listeners surrounding them. "I was rude not to send him word, and he grew concerned. Now," she said firmly, "is there any chance I can meet Lord Stratford? He doesn't seem to be with the sultan any longer, and I would like very much to thank him for the hospitality of his staff."

From the opposite side of the room, Jake watched Sarah clutch at the hands of her betrothed. The musicians had taken a pause, and he got a good view across the empty dance floor. Did she know just how close she had come to getting kissed? But that would have been a disaster for her. She was every inch a lady this evening, not at all like the graceful wanton who had danced in the coffee house . . . not at all like the spitfire who had pulled down his hut . . . not at all like the woman of passion who had lain in his arms.

When he caught his first glimpse of her tonight, standing in conversation with another man, he had known she was the most beautiful woman in the room. More, she was the most beautiful creature he had ever seen. With blue silk caressing the curves of her body and with her honeyed hair accenting the lines of her face and her long, slender neck, she was the angel whose image never quite left his mind. He admitted with regret that she looked very much at home in the setting of the formal ball.

But then, by damn, she had looked just as much at home in the coffee house and in his room and on the island. She was the most amazing, exasperating, fascinating woman in the world, and he hadn't been able to stay away. The conclusion left him furious, and he set down his cup of fruit juice in disgust. What he needed was a shot of whiskey.

"Useless waste of a punch bowl, if you ask me."

Jake turned to face the speaker, the man Sarah had been talking to when he walked in.

"Somersby here," he said, extending his hand and swaying ever so slightly. "You a friend of the hellion's?"

Jake ignored the proffered handshake, at the same time wondering where the man had hidden the liquor he had obviously been drinking. "Are you referring to Miss Whitlock?"

Somersby glanced in her direction. "Damned fine-looking woman. Old Ralph's a lucky man—once he gets under her skirts." He smirked. "Probably has. From what I hear, she's lifted 'em a time or two back in London. Don't know what she's been doin' here, but you know what they say about a leopard changin' its spots."

Jake's hands clinched into fists. "You talk too much, Somersby." Only concern for Sarah kept him from giving the diplomat a fat lip.

"Only sayin' what everyone's thinkin'," Somersby said.

Jake looked past him to Sarah, who was being guided by her fiancé in the direction of a crowd around the British ambassador.

"Lord, hope she don't stir up any kind of trouble with her talk about the sultan."

"What talk is that?"

"Something about Harun being in danger. Tried to tell me some absurd story when she first got here. Told her I knew about her reputation back in London. A real little hellcat, she is. But we got enough troubles here wooing the Turks away from the Russians without her stirring things up more. I shut her up proper like, but she insisted she'd talk to the ambassador when he got back. Too smart to try her wild tales on me."

So Sarah had not been believed. Jake watched as she was led through the crowd to the side of Lord Stratford. The attention of the room seemed riveted on her. For her beauty or the proud way she carried herself or her reputation for getting into scrapes, Jake couldn't be sure.

After a few words passed between them, the ambassador pulled her aside. The indefatigable Ralph followed close behind.

A blur of red caught Jake's eye, and he turned to see Mustafa stand and head in their direction. Harun must have said something sharp, because Mustafa looked back over his shoulder at his father and scowled. Studying the dark expression on the Turk's face, Jake could well believe the stories that circulated about his prowlings through the dark streets of the city and his even darker deeds with the women he found.

The line of Turkish guards took a step into the room, more than one with a hand on his sword.

"She's gonna cause trouble," Somersby said, swearing under his breath. He made his lurching way across the empty floor. Jake hurried after, aware that the young man was even drunker than he had at first supposed. He should have flattened him when the thought first occurred. If he had, the diplomat would not be a threat to Sarah now.

The two arrived in time to hear Sarah say, "Lord Stratford, please let me talk to you alone."

"Not now," Ralph implored, his glance shifting between her and the fast approaching Mustafa.

The onlookers crowded around them might have been part of a painting, for all the sound they made. The voices of the speakers carried across the immediate vicinity loud and clear.

"Miss Whitlock," Lord Stratford said, "your request should go through the proper channels. I will be most pleased to grant you a meeting time. If you will check with my secretary in the morning, perhaps we can work out a time in a day or two."

"A day or two!" Sarah said.

"So much work has stacked up in my absence, that is the best I can do."

"I beg your pardon," Somersby said, interjecting his body between Sarah and the ambassador. "Tried to tell her not to bother you, sir. Likes to start up trouble."

"See here!" Ralph said, turning on the diplomat. "You'll take that back immediately."

"Needs to be said," Somersby threw back at him.

As the voices rose, Jake caught sight of Mustafa backing away. The Turk's hard stare never once left Sarah.

Sarah turned widened eyes on Jake, who moved in close.

"Gentlemen," Lord Stratford said, "perhaps we can settle this in private."

"Not necessary, sir," Somersby insisted. In his pale eyes was the light of inebriated righteousness. "I've already handled it for you. Stirs up trouble, she does. Own father complains. Pettigrew here's a good enough sort. He'd admit the truth, only he's blinded by what she's lettin' him have.''

His voice rose and cut clearly through the close, hushed air. "Nothing but a slut, that's what—"

Jake's fist against his mouth stopped any further discussion of Sarah's lightskirt ways. Somersby stumbled backward against Ralph Pettigrew, and the two fell in a tangle on the floor.

"Oh, no," Sarah cried, barely managing to pull her gown free of the fallen pair.

Behind her, a woman screamed.

"My dear," managed her betrothed, looking up at her, then of necessity turning his attention to the struggling Somersby, who seemed to have taken it into his head that Ralph was the one who had thrown the punch. The diplomat was intent on returning the favor.

Lord Stratford stared down at his battling assistant. "Phillip!" he said sharply, but Somersby was too far dedicated to avenging his honor to pay attention to his superior.

Scattered cries came from the surrounding crowd, and there was a flurry of movement as more onlookers attempted to get a closer view of the fight.

"Sarah—" Jake began.

"What a disgrace," a woman said. "All the hellion's fault!"

"How right you are, Rowena," another woman agreed. "You heard what the man called her. Can't even say the word."

It seemed to Jake the full-skirted wives and daughters were physically pulling away from the scene, leaving only the men to crowd in. Sarah's eyes darted across the throng and settled on him.

"Get me out of here," she ordered over the scuffling men.

Jake didn't question the wisdom of her request, nor the wisdom of his compliance. Taking her arm, he hurried her through the buzzing crowd, past the flowers in the hallway, and into the embassy's front entryway. A half dozen guests were milling about, and there was a servant by the door.

"There's quite a fight in there," he said, nodding in the direction of the ballroom. As if they were of one mind, the guests headed down the hall. The servant hesitated, eyeing Jake and Sarah suspiciously. One look from Jake, and he turned his attention to the door.

Sarah came to a halt at the base of the stairs. "They don't believe me," she whispered to her twisting hands.

Jake resisted an impulse to take her into his arms. "Perhaps they'll believe me. I witnessed a scene or two, remember?"

When she looked up at him, he thought he had never seen such despair. "They don't believe me," she repeated. "I don't belong."

He gripped her arms. "More than anyone else, you belong, Sarah. You just have more to say than most. You're more alive."

"You heard what the women said. They wouldn't look at me . . . wouldn't put into words what they thought."

"To hell with them, then," said Jake. "You're worth the lot of 'em."

She shook her head. "I'm too different. Papa was right. Even Harun did not acknowledge my presence, and you can wager the money you have left that he recognized me right away."

He expected her to burst into tears. But not Sarah.

271

The despair that had gripped her gave way to a stubborn light in her eyes. "A hellion, am I? I'll show them what being a hellion means. Ralph will be here any minute. I must get away. Take me with you."

"You want to leave with me? Are you sure?"

"I'm sure." Her chin tilted. "Unless you have other plans, in which case I'll find some place to stay and arrange for my passage home."

Jake hesitated for only a second. He hadn't come to the embassy to carry her off, only to satisfy a need to know she was all right. Looking into her wide, proud eyes, he knew that he had no choice except to do as she asked.

He grinned crookedly. "I have no other plans. You know my wastrel ways." The grin faded. "But you need to know how things will be between us, Sarah. If you leave with me, it will be to return to my bed. And I've slept my last sleep on the deck of the dhow."

"I wouldn't have it any other way."

He felt a tightness in his loins. God, but he wanted her. Yet he wasn't sure she completely understood what he was saying.

"I'm not offering what Ralph does. No ring, Sarah. No ceremony."

Blue fire flashed in her eyes—pride mixed with passion. He felt a momentary regret for his last words, but she hurried on.

"I wouldn't accept you if you were, Jake. I know full well how things are between us. I won't outstay my welcome, and you won't hold me back when it's time to go. There's a back door to the embassy. It opens onto a garden with a gate. Do you think you can find it?"

Jake nodded.

"I have something I need to do first. Meet me there in fifteen minutes," she said.

In a whirl of blue silk, she hurried away from him up the stairs. Loud talk from the direction of the ballroom told him the about-to-be-deserted bridegroom was on the way.

Jake decided upon the wisdom of retreat. Wanting Sarah as he did, he knew there was an equally compelling reason to take her away. She was in danger. He had known it when he saw the way Mustafa stared at her. The bastard wanted her under his control once again.

Jake had never crossed wills with the son of a ruler before, but then Sarah had led him to several new experiences. With a vision of an upturned, ardent face and a heaving bosom burned into his mind, he strode past the servant who was studiously perusing the ornate door and hurried into the night.

continued to wear were the blue silk with drawn
cousin Jane had worn last night. Mrs. Morgan's
elegant two dresses... and one large
general items.

Chapter Eighteen

Alone in her room, Sarah scribbled a hasty note to
Ralph, tore it up, tried again, and settled for a cryptic
*I'm sorry things haven't worked out. I'm not the one
for you. Please understand.*

He would be hurt, more from embarrassment than
from a broken heart. But the embarrassment would
ease, and he would agree she was right. She placed
the note inside an envelope, along with the pearl
ring, and addressing it to him, placed it in the center
of her table.

One of the embassy servants knocked at the door
and informed her that Mr. Pettigrew was awaiting
her downstairs.

"Right worried he is, miss," the girl said.

"Assure him," Sarah said through the door, "that
I'm all right. I've retired for the night." She listened
as the servant made her way back toward the stairs.

Declining to disturb Mrs. Morgan from her rest in
the adjoining room, she changed quickly from the
blue silk into the coarse caftan and trousers she had
found hanging in the back of her wardrobe. Like her
memories of Jake, they had not been destroyed after
all. She took grim satisfaction in leaving the embassy

in much the same condition as she had arrived.

The only parts of her evening's ensemble she continued to wear were the knee-length drawers, cotton chemise, and white leather shoes. Hastily selecting two of the simpler gowns and one limp petticoat, she threw them and a few personal items into a valise.

As a final gesture of denial to all that her world considered respectable, she shook out the curls that Mrs. Morgan had so carefully constructed, brushed at them savagely, and added the brush to the small collection she was taking with her. Slipping a cloak over her shoulders, she gave no backward look to the small room as she stepped into the deserted hall.

Her destination was the servants' stairs, which she reached and descended without detection. Actually leaving the embassy, however, took more careful planning. The route to the back door took her through the kitchen, which was filled with activity in preparation for the late night supper ordered by Lord Stratford. She stood in the shadows of a doorway leading into the hot, smoky room and waited for the moment when she could slip unnoticed past the ordered bustle. The valise was tucked out of sight beneath her cloak.

"Typical English meal he wanted," one harried cook complained as she hefted a heavy tray of roast fowl onto a table near the door. Slapping at a wisp of sweat-dampened hair against her cheek, she added, "Nothing but foolishness, if you ask me. It's all the same to these heathens. Don't know sweet cream from cow's piss, they don't."

"Hush, now," intoned a man behind her. "We'll have none of your vulgarities tonight. Too much to do."

Sarah recognized him as the butler who directed

the serving of the embassy meals. She watched in admiration as he supervised the comings and goings of a dozen members of his staff, much as the conductor must at this very moment be leading the musicians in the ballroom.

The removal of a slab of beef from the brick oven beside the open fire, and the near disaster when it slid dangerously close to the edge of the roasting pan, gave Sarah the minute she was waiting for. In a flash she was through the room, past the door leading to the wine cellar, and into the cool night air of the back garden, where vegetables for the embassy were grown.

For an instant she thought of the stuffy ballroom and the scene she had so quickly abandoned: Ralph and Phillip Somersby scuffling on the floor, Lord Stratford casting a baleful eye at the flying arms and legs, Mustafa striding toward her hell-bent for she knew not what, and behind them all a wall of shocked and titillated onlookers taking their pleasure at her expense.

And of course there had been Jake. She turned her attention to finding him.

Moonlight flooded the garden with silvery light, and she kept close to the thick hedge surrounding the small plot. An arched break in the shrubbery revealed the bolted gate that opened onto the street. Noisily slipping the lock from its moorings, she stepped through the opening and into Jake's arms.

"Oh," she said in a muffled voice against his coat. For the first time since leaving her room, she took a deep breath. She felt safe and secure.

"Did I startle you?" he asked against the hood of her cloak.

She breathed in his scent. "No. I knew right away who you were."

He lifted her chin. "Having second thoughts? This isn't any kidnapping you can explain away, Sarah, as being out of your control."

"I haven't been able to explain anything away, as you observed. So why not do what I want?"

He brushed his lips against hers. "Then let's get out of here."

Behind him on the back street was a small open carriage pulled by a lone dray horse. "Not very elegant, I'm afraid," he explained as he lifted her onto the seat and tucked the valise at her feet. "When I rented it earlier, I hadn't planned on company."

Sarah found the news comforting. She had been picturing him with a different woman every night.

She took his hands in hers and held on tightly for a moment. "I'm not after elegance. Surely you know that about me now."

Freeing his hands, he kissed her palm and hurried around the carriage to spring onto the seat beside her. Sarah held the tingling hand against her breast.

He cracked the whip over the rump of the horse, and the carriage jerked into motion. At first Sarah concentrated on remaining upright as they bounced along the hilly streets. When she felt passably at ease, she stole a look at him. The moonlight fell on his black, tousled hair and lean face, accenting its sharp planes. His mouth was held tight, and she wondered if he were regretting the hasty decision to carry her away.

Everything that happened between them seemed hastily done, born of necessity or impulse, prompted by too much emotion and too little thought.

He glanced at her once, and the grim set of his lips relaxed. A sense of rightness flooded Sarah. There was no reason for the sudden feeling—certainly nothing rational—but she welcomed it nevertheless.

They made a curious pair, Jake in his formal tail coat and ruffled shirt, his white gloved hands gripping the reins with unstudied expertise, and Sarah in her coarse cloak and hood pulled about her person. They were, in truth, a curious pair on several fronts.

Neither spoke. Crossing the Horn, Sarah was surprised to see the wagon turn away from the center of town and begin a winding route through the dark streets leading to the wharf.

It took him ten minutes to reach the dhow amidst the taller ships. "My apartment is too easily traced," he explained as he helped her from the carriage. "I don't want you found."

Sarah bit at her lip. Despite her own confidence in her decision, she could not shake the speculation that he might have changed his mind about keeping her with him. She was too brazen by far, something that half of London and all of the British community in Constantinople would readily attest to—not to mention a growing number of Turks. But none of their opinions mattered to her nearly so much as Jake's.

"I'm glad to hear you say it," she said, drawing free of his helping hand and scrambling onto the wonderfully familiar boat.

He stepped after her, set down the valise, and swept her into his arms. His lips covered hers, forcefully, completely, but all too soon he broke the kiss.

Sarah could barely breathe.

"Get in there," he said, indicating the low sleeping quarters on the back deck. "I'll get rid of the carriage and be right back." One light kiss more. "You'll be all right now, Sarah. I'd not leave if I thought otherwise."

Before she could protest, he was gone, horse,

carriage and man swallowed up in the shadows surrounding the moonlit wharf. She looked down the way. In the ghostly light the shapes of goods stored against the buildings took on ominous meanings. Even the naked masts of the ships anchored fore and aft of Jake's small craft seemed to threaten.

Nonsense, she told herself. Jake said she would be all right, and she was. She took one last glance at the warehouses lining the dock. Inside were stores of ivory and silk, of pearls and spices from the Eastern world. All told, they were treasures beyond comprehension. She would not take the lot of them for the dhow.

She tucked herself into the low-ceilinged chamber as Jake had ordered, snuggling her cloak around her as though it could provide protection, and waited for the sounds of his return.

She didn't hear him until he was on board. The creak of the mast and ropes and the grating of the lateen sail told her he was about to cast off.

Without questioning their destination, she scurried out to help him. He'd thrown his tail coat and cravat aside. The full, cuffed sleeves and ruffled front of his white linen shirt captured the light of the moon. Sarah took a luxurious moment to admire the look of him, with his long legs encased in the tight black trousers, his tousled hair catching on the night breeze.

As he shifted about the narrow deck, his movements were sure and smooth and graceful, even more so than they had been on the ballroom floor. She felt at home with him; Jake was at home on his beloved boat. Their eyes locked once, briefly, and she was struck with longing as powerful as if he had reached out to fondle her breasts.

The skills she had learned from watching and helping him before came back readily. Discarding her cloak, she donned the gloves she had thrown into her valise and bound the ropes as he instructed, coiling their extra length out of the way. Mostly she stayed clear as he navigated the dhow into the slow movement of the Horn and at last into the swifter currents of Bosporus Bay.

Theirs was not to be a long journey, she realized as he guided the craft into the seclusion of an inlet off the widening body of water. Curve of land and growth of trees and shrubbery close to the bank protected them from view. He did not speak until they were anchored for the night. He stood beside her on the deck, light from the low-hanging moon filtering through the stand of trees a dozen yards away. Desire flowed like wine in Sarah's blood. Each time they had come together, it was in passion fired by anger.

Not tonight.

"Welcome aboard, mate," he said.

Her breath slowed. She could almost believe he meant more by the last word than he did. *No ring. No ceremony.* She had to keep his warning always in the back of her mind.

"Aye, Captain, it's a pleasure to serve."

Jake laughed. "Serve? Since when?"

Her body pulsed with a primal urge. "Since right now."

Glancing quickly around to make certain they were unseen, Sarah saw only the thick branches of trees growing close to the water and the slivers of moonlight drifting onto the deck. Away from land, the bay was still and serene, unlike her pounding heart.

She slipped off her shoes, unfastened her caftan, and dropped it to the deck at her feet. As she worked, the smile on Jake's face burned into a different kind of pleasure. She could read approval in his dark eyes and in the twitch of his lips.

Next came the chemise. As he stared at her bared breasts, the catch of his breath was unmistakable. Her knees weakened at the sound, but she could not stop now. Dropping her head until her hair curtained her burning cheeks, she unfastened the full trousers, let them fall, and untied the tapes of the linen drawers that were the last barrier to her nakedness. The underclothing joined the other apparel on the deck, and she nudged them aside with her foot.

Under them the boat rocked gently. The night air was chill against her bare skin, but she felt no discomfort. Jake watched without movement or speech. She might have believed he'd had second thoughts about the wisdom of her boldness, except for the sharpening glint in his eyes and the swell in his wonderfully fitted trousers.

She stepped close, the tips of her breasts brushing against his shirt as her only point of contact with him.

"Sarah," he whispered huskily and opened his arms.

She threw herself against him, crushing against her bosom the folds of linen and the sharp studs that served as fastenings. Her hands cradled his face, and she met his lips hungrily with hers, needing to erase the memories of her humiliation in the ballroom, desperate for complete acceptance.

At that moment she cared not what the rest of the world thought of her—only Jake, with his magic hands massaging her shoulders and back, trailing firm fingers down her spine and cupping her buttocks against him. The swell of his manhood rubbed against her abdomen. She stood on tiptoe, desperate to feel the pressure against her responding core. She thrust her tongue deep inside his mouth while her body pulsed against his. She was consumed by desire.

Sarah tasted the erotic freedom of nakedness in the arms of a man who was still fully clothed. She rubbed her nipples, taut and hard, against the ruffled shirt, rubbed her thighs against the rough cloth of his trousers, and felt the buttons of the trouser fly stroke through her pubic hair.

Jake broke the kiss and bent his head to her breasts, laving first one peak and then the other with the rough tip of his tongue. The thrills he elicited were so intense that they came close to pain.

She cried out.

"Sarah," he said, lifting his head.

"Don't stop," she whispered, caught in helpless hunger, wanting him to taste her, to touch every part of her body, to take the same pleasures from her that he gave in such incredible abundance.

The heels of his hands moved in firm strokes up her sides and rotated against the swell of her breasts. At the same time he outlined the fullness of her mouth with his tongue and with his own lips. Sarah struggled for breath, arcs of fire leaping out wherever his hands touched.

His lips moved to her neck, to her throat, and once again to the fullness of her breasts. "I've missed you," he rasped against the valley between them.

Through the heat of rapture, she realized what he was confessing. While she had lain sleepless remembering what had gone between them, he had been doing close to the same thing. Perhaps not with the same urgency as she, nor with the same constancy, but he had missed her. Free-living wanderer Jake. Man of the world. Man of experience. He had missed her. The awareness inflamed her as much as his touch.

His hands moved back down her sides. One palm edged between their bodies until it stroked between her thighs. She quivered against its rough demands, her hot throbbing response strengthening until she had to grip his shirt to remain upright. When his fingers penetrated her, she opened her eyes in wide surprise. Never had he done such a thing. She found him looking at her with a dark stare that burned into her soul.

She could not look away, not as the insistent massage of his palm quickened, not as her body milked against his fingers, not even as her body collapsed against him and he had to use one strong arm to keep her from falling.

The pulsing increased, and she closed her eyes at last to the velvet darkness of passion. She climaxed against his hand, clinging to his shoulders, crying into his ruffled shirt, a thousand shooting stars exploding in the vision of her mind.

He held her tightly against him until the trembling abated, his hand still pressed to the moistness that no longer gave her embarrassment. When at last her erratic heart slowed to a heavy, steady beat and her breath gave her opportunity to speak, she whispered against his chest.

"I didn't know it could happen that way."

His lips brushed against her hair. "The education of Sarah Whitlock has barely begun."

His deep voice and the promise of his words sent new thrills skittering through her.

"What about you?" she asked, lifting her head to press eager lips against his sweaty throat. "Could I do the same to you?"

He moaned. "Oh, yes, Angel. You'll get the chance. But not just yet."

Slowly he lowered her to the deck and helped her inside the sleeping quarters. Stripping the clothes from his body, he joined her in the narrow space, nestling beside her on the blanket and pulling her back in his embrace. She felt his hardness against her thigh.

"Are you sore?" he whispered. "Sometimes a woman's body is sensitive for a while."

His fingers stroked the valley between her legs and brought a return of desire.

She shook her head, rubbing her cheek against the matted hair covering his chest. The wiry curls felt manly against her skin.

"Then it's time to show you that once is not necessarily enough."

Before she could respond, he settled his body on top of hers, one knee urging her legs apart.

"You're still aroused," she said, wishing she could see his face in the dark.

"There's every possibility," he said with a low chuckle, "that I'll be this way for several days."

"And there's every possibility," she answered, kissing the hollow of his throat, "that I won't mind in the least." His pulse quickened under her lips.

His penetration was quick, and Sarah discovered that despite her disclaimer, her body was at first sore from its own taking of pleasure. His thrusts, each one deeper than the last, soon put the discomfort far from her mind. Incredibly, Jake was right, she decided when she could think clearly again—after they had shuddered against one another in mutual repletion. Once had not been enough.

He held her for a long time. She listened to the gradual steadying of his breath.

"I thought about this a long time ago," she said in a small voice when she feared he was about to fall asleep. "Being here like this with you on the boat."

"When was that?" he asked, his fingers stroking silkily down her arm.

She should have realized Jake would be wide awake.

"The first time I ever saw you."

"Surely you don't mean when Scarface was in hot pursuit."

"Before that. From the deck of the *Leviathan*. When you seemed to rise out of the sea, you looked like a god coming to claim another nymph for your watery harem, although I didn't make the connection between you and Harun until just now."

"You're not my slave, Sarah."

"I said I was here to serve." She tickled her fingers against his chest. "I'll play at it for a little while, if you don't mind."

He caught her hand and took it to his lips. "I don't mind."

He was quiet for a while, and then she heard a low laugh.

"What's funny?" she asked, trying to pull away.

He held her imprisoned. "Your thinking such lusty thoughts when you saw me."

"Believe me, Jake, I didn't know what lust was at the moment. It was just idle speculation. You did look rather incredibly wonderful." She teased at his nipple with her thumb. "Bare chested. Legs apart. You seemed to control the sea."

"Want to know what I was thinking at the same moment?"

"I'm not sure I do."

"I came up out of that deep swell to find the cargo ship hovering a little too close for comfort. Took some manipulating to navigate down the length of her. And there was the distraction of this angel standing at the rail. Your hair was blowing free and caught the sunlight from behind. Your cloak billowed out like wings. I thought you'd come down from the clouds."

Sarah smiled to herself. "I didn't know you were a poet."

"Until that moment, neither did I."

She hesitated a moment. "I have changed my mind about one thing, however, since that day."

"What's that?"

"Your name. Neptune doesn't suit you. Jake is so much better. Direct. To the point. Like you."

He slanted a soft kiss across her lips. "I rather like Angel," he said. "And Sarah. They show two sides to you, one down to earth—that's the Sarah—and the other. . . ." He kissed her again. "You have a way about you, Angel, that makes a man think fanciful thoughts that never before occurred to him."

Sarah took pleasure from his words and told herself that wrong or not, he already saw more in her than anyone else had ever done.

A silence descended between them, a comfortable pause after all that had gone before during the long, painful, glorious night. Sarah listened to the water slap against the sides of the boat and the wind play against the taut ropes in the mast.

She knew there was something more that must be said, tonight, while it was fresh on her mind. "Thanks for everything, Jake. I was going through a pretty bad time back there."

He did not ask what she meant, for which she was grateful.

"Probably shouldn't have hit Somersby," said Jake. "He was too drunk to know what he was saying."

"He knew, all right, and so did I. So did everyone else within hearing distance. But it's not true, you know. Ralph and I never—"

"You don't have to tell me that, Sarah. I already know."

"And then there was Mustafa moving in fast, as if he wanted to know what was going on."

"I wasn't sure you saw him."

"Oh, I saw him, all right. That was one reason I was trying to get Lord Stratford alone. During the past few weeks I've been doing a lot of thinking—"

"I'm sure you have. It's one of your faults."

"Do you want to hear what I have to say or not?"

He began once again to stroke her arm. "As a matter of fact, I do not. Tomorrow, Sarah. You've got to learn to postpone what doesn't actually have to be faced."

"It goes against my teachings."

"Much of what you do goes against them, I imagine."

"Jake," she said, hurt.

He kissed her forehead. "I'm just not sure you've been taught the right things."

Sarah settled against him. "All right," she conceded, "tomorrow. What happens then?"

"There's this island I know about. Needs a little work done on it. A little reconstruction, as a matter of fact. Been meaning to get back there, but I didn't have the right help."

"And you do now?"

His hand caressed her breast. "I do now. You're quite a woman, Sarah. A true angel. Tomorrow we'll find out how you work out in the building trade."

Sarah settled her body against his. With sleep stealing over her, she barely managed to mumble, "I'll try not to disappoint."

Chapter Nineteen

The next day a brisk breeze blew them on their way to the island. It seemed to the high-spirited Sarah that nature, agreeing she had been right to leave the embassy, was determined to speed the dhow along the surface of the Aegean's dark waves. The first doubts about her decision came in late afternoon as they neared the crescent strip of greenery that Jake claimed unofficially as his.

"Land ho!" he shouted, his face breaking into a grin.

His eyes drifted to her, and Sarah returned the smile. He didn't seem to notice it was forced.

She stood on the deck, hands twisting in the folds of the gown she had selected for the arrival—a simple green chambray that she thought brought out the golden tones of her skin—and watched the approaching land. Her untamed hair caught in the salty spray blowing off the water and whirled about her head like a cloud in a storm. Her breath was shallow, and she felt a knot in the pit of her stomach.

The last time she had seen the island had been through a haze of anger and humiliation. Too well she remembered each moment she'd spent there—her happy arrival and her ignominious retreat. In the protection of the hut Jake had built, he had rejected her first feeble attempts at lovemaking; later, she had rejected him. Her rejection had come in a somewhat more dramatic fashion, pulling down the hut along with her pride. Was she right to return?

When Jake began to take in the dhow's sail with his usual balletic grace, Sarah focused her attention on helping him. She would find out soon enough the answer to her question, even if she could never put it into spoken words.

Wearing only a pair of coarse-woven brown trousers tucked into a pair of black boots, he pulled at the ropes and sails with masculine efficiency. Sarah worked as he directed, but she could not keep her eyes from straying to the smooth swell of muscles along his upper arms and across his back. The corded skin at the back of his neck was the color of mahogany from his years spent on the sun-kissed seas.

The undulations of the waves beneath the dhow were as pronounced as the undulations of her heart. Since she walked into his arms behind the embassy—and even before, since she saw him stride into the ballroom—she had felt bound to him in ways that had nothing to do with the sexual pleasure they shared. Or at least, she admitted, only a part.

She did not yet know how or why or when he had become such a vital part of her existence. She knew only that what was happening to her now held far more significance than any of Jake's previous rescues. He could remove her from an embassy ball, a Constantinople coffee house, a horde of fanatical Turks—even from the depths of Mustafa's seraglio— but he could not rescue her from herself, or from the dictates of her heart.

Whatever drew her to him went beyond the bounds of physical attraction. The realization frightened her and at the same time filled her with an inexpressible joy.

When they were anchored, he disappeared for a moment below deck into the shallow galley where he stored supplies, returning shortly with a bundle of tins and extra blankets.

"I'd been planning on returning here," he explained in answer to her questioning look. "Laid in goods for several weeks. Good thing, wouldn't you say?"

Several weeks. "It's a very good thing," she breathed.

"You've got two choices. Either undress or hitch up your skirt. We're going to shore, and I'll be carrying this," he said, indicating the bundle. "I can't manage to carry you, too."

Sarah chose to bind her gown into a tight wad of cloth at her waist.

Jake stared at her full white drawers that bloused just above her knees.

"Those are the ugliest things I have ever seen," he said.

"No one's knees are handsome," she protested.

"I didn't mean you. I rather like your knees." His voice warmed. "Especially the backs of them. As I recall, I've kissed them a time or two."

The portion of Sarah's anatomy under discussion almost buckled under her. She recalled very well indeed just where his lips had strayed.

"If you mean my drawers, they're the latest thing. And highly essential for the proper dress of a lady."

Then, Sarah could almost hear him ask, *what are you doing with them on?*

Her honesty told her he would be right. She wasn't

291

a lady, not in the sense accepted by her father or Ralph or Phillip Somersby. The conclusion brought her little regret.

"Let's get on shore," she said, turning from him. "I'm starved."

"Good. It will take a hearty appetite to down some of the tinned meat I've got here. Tomorrow we'll worry about fresh fish."

They waded through the waist-high water, each with hands overhead and bearing food and supplies. A cursory examination of the pile of rubble that had once been the hut told them their work was cut out for them in the morning. They would need a great deal of sustenance tonight.

Their dining table was a blanket on the warm, sandy beach; their food, the bland meat Jake had warned her about, served on a chunk of crusty bread; their wine, the fresh water from the hidden pool. Coffee, black and unsweetened, completed the feast. As Sarah stretched out under the canopy of stars, she thought it far better than the repast she had seen in the embassy kitchen, seasoned as it was with freedom and open air.

And, of course, with the company of Jake Price. During the meal he regaled her with stories of his adventures at sea, of drunken captains and courageous mates, of storms and ports from Australia to Zanzibar. He talked always of others, the men with whom he worked aboard the sailing vessels, the natives and strange places he saw ashore. He never mentioned the women she knew he must have attracted; he never mentioned himself.

Soon a picture emerged, one she had seen the first time they had sailed. He was a part of the sea, as much as the winds and the waves, as much as the strange creatures that swam in its depths or the gulls that lew overhead. Salt water flowed in his veins. He would never be tamed to settle down—not with one woman in one port. The temptresses calling to Jake with their irresistible siren's song had no resemblance to voluptuous Turkish dancers or Russian princesses or even hapless English women in need of his help.

Jake's mistresses were the oceans of the world.

No ring. No ceremony. Those were terms she had accepted, but with the growing realization of her ties to Jake, she was finding the pronouncement hard to endure.

An uncomfortable silence stole over them as they cleared away the few supper things. Sarah knew it was her fault for thinking foolish thoughts. He sensed her discomfort. She watched as he built up the fire with the driftwood they had both gathered earlier. He did not look her way.

As she stretched out on the blanket and let the night wind waft over her, she did not fight the wandering of her attention back to Constantinople.

"I've been thinking about the attack of the pirates," she said to Jake, who lay supine beside her. For all the horrors it brought back, it was a safer topic than the festering new worries that had beset her.

"Do you think that's wise?" he asked, his head turned at last to her.

She directed her words to the stars. "I think it's necessary. You said last night to postpone everything that I could—the pondering, the talking, the trying to reason things out. That's easier for you than for me. The memories linger. When I least expect, an image of the ship's deck flashes across my mind. Too much of what has happened is a puzzle to me. I'd like to talk now."

"I'd like to listen."

She took him at his word.

"Before the other ship began its attack, Captain Reynolds said there were no pirates in this part of the world, not for the past year or so. And yet the men who jumped aboard gave all the appearance of being just that."

"So the captain was wrong."

"I don't think so. Have you heard any talk of such a band of cutthroats sailing the sea? Have they attacked another ship?"

Jake conceded she had a point.

"I got the strangest feeling at the end . . . when everyone but the pirates lay dead or dying . . . that they never intended to kill me. That their purpose was far different. Maybe rape—" The word caught on her lips and she shuddered.

Jake took her hand in his and rested it on the blanket between them.

"But they didn't," he reminded her.

"And why not?"

"You were perhaps more valuable on the slave market as a virgin."

"I never made it to any slave market. Drugged or not, I would remember something of such an experience. I know that to be true, even if my certainty is without rational explanation. Besides, such markets are rare enough these days, or so Nadire informed me once. I haven't yet discovered any of her information about this country to be wrong."

"Are you saying the pirates—or whoever they were—took you to the palace hoping Harun would look on you with favor?"

Sarah shook her head. "The sultan is not even interested in that kind of thing anymore. At least he wasn't interested in me."

"Then," Jake said, his voice low and dry, "he's not

interested in any woman. Take my word for that. What about Mustafa? I don't believe he's above taking what he wants from any source."

"Apparently I was destined for his part of the Grand Seraglio from the beginning. Mustafa said so when he called me to his room. He was only repeating what Nadire had already told me, that the Kizlar Agasi saw me when I was brought to the palace and appropriated me for Harun. According to Nadire, he thought I would tempt his master once again into bed. At the time I wasn't sure whether she was just repeating gossip. I've grown to believe she spoke the truth."

Jake squeezed her hand. "For a eunuch, this Kizlar Agasi has good taste."

Sarah took a moment to enjoy his words, then went on spinning out her puzzlement.

"So that leaves me with the conclusion I was kidnapped on purpose, that someone knew I was aboard the *Leviathan* and sent Scarface after me."

"Any idea who that might be?"

"As far as I know, my fiancé was the only one to whom my father had written. In the little time I spent with Ralph, I gathered he has no confidants. I could, of course, be wrong. Perhaps he mentioned my journey to someone with whom he is doing business. That would almost have to be someone from the serai if I was really taken to serve Mustafa. And that I refuse to believe. Even you can't claim my charms could cause such slaughter. That's for women like Helen of Troy."

"You have your resemblances to the fair Helen."

Sarah could imagine Jake's twisted smile.

"I've launched one small dhow. That's hardly a thousand ships."

"We'll discuss your charms later," said Jake, his

fingers stroking her palm, "along with their power."

Sarah filed the promise in the back of her mind. Slipping her hand from his, she folded her arms beneath her head and stared up at the black sky with its points of crystalline light. But her thoughts could not be pulled from the past.

"Scarface's appearance at the palace really complicates matters," she said. "I definitely overheard something that was highly secret and dangerous. If only I knew to whom he had been talking."

"Mustafa? We can feel fairly sure he's involved in all of this in some way."

"It's possible he wants the death of his father. But what's the point? Harun has already settled on him everything he intends. At Harun's death, Mustafa's older brother becomes head of the country. Nadire says they do not get along. He could easily be evicted from his imperial home. No," she concluded, "Mustafa, unpleasant though he may be, has several reasons to want his father alive, and none to wish him dead."

"None that we know of. You have given this a great deal of thought, haven't you?"

"I had a little time on my hands in the embassy."

"And while you were there, so did I. We think alike, Sarah. I've been drawing the same conclusions and arriving at the same dead ends. You know, of course, there's one person we need to approach."

"Ralph."

"Right. Find out who he talked to about your arrival."

Sarah sighed. "I need to see him again, anyway. The note I left was rather brief, but I couldn't think of anything to say. And don't," she warned, "make a comment about the rarity of such a situation."

Laughing, Jake turned on his side toward her, his

head propped on his hand. "It was the farthest thing from my mind."

Sarah twisted to face him and found herself looking into his eyes. She and Jake were remarkably close for two people who did not touch. The power of his glance ensnared her as it always did. Light from the moon and stars and from the glowing coals of the nearby fire was doing wondrous things with the angles of his face, and the breeze off the water played with his already tousled hair.

Sarah dropped her gaze. For dinner he had donned his shirt, but she could see the wisps of hair curling at his throat. She could not look away. Was his heart pounding as hers was? One touch of her lips to his pulse would tell her for sure.

He shifted closer until his breath stirred her hair and warmed her cheek.

"Anything else on your mind?" he asked.

"You didn't take any money from Ralph." The words slipped out. She had not planned to mention the subject tonight. She did not know when she planned to tell him that she knew.

"He told you."

"I didn't introduce the subject. Ralph did. He couldn't understand why you had refused. Neither can I." She reached out to touch his chest, her wise fingers seeking and finding the sinewed muscles concealed by his shirt. Her eyes locked with his. "Unless it's possible you're not the avaricious rascal you like to pretend."

He seemed to draw within himself, the warmth of his expression turning cool along with the deepening night. "Impossible," he said. "You know what a bastard I can be."

Sarah was not put off by his withdrawal. She was certain she had discovered a new side to Jake, a tender side that had nothing to do with sex. He had not wanted to gain a profit from her near tragedy, nor from his brave rescue when he fended off Scarface's blade. Perhaps he thought such a resistance was a sign of weakness; Sarah knew it was a sign of strength.

What it most certainly was not, however, was a sign of commitment. Jake was simply more of a hero than he knew.

Let him be enigmatic. There was one area in which she could get him to reveal his thoughts and his wishes. He might know that their time on the island was only a brief respite, but they both knew that while they were there, they would not be able to resist making love. He had denied her once, as she had him. Never again.

"The wind is picking up," she said.

"Would you like me to cover you with the extra blanket? I could stoke up the fire."

"What I'd like," she said, her fingers exploring the knolls of his chest, "is for you to cover me with you."

A low growl sounded in his throat. "Right now?"

"Right now."

"I thought you were the servant and I the master."

"I plan to serve, all right."

Jake shifted his weight until he was stretched out on top of her, his legs extended on either side of hers, his elbows supporting his weight by her shoulders. Sarah could feel the sand move beneath the blanket.

His fingers combed the wild tresses that were spread against the blanket. With the sources of light behind him, his face was in the dark, and Sarah had to imagine the expression in his eyes. It would not be enigmatic, she was sure.

"You're a beautiful woman, Sarah Whitlock," he said. "A passionate woman. Do you realize how much? Or how rare that combination is?"

Sarah let his words warm her. "Is this another of my lessons?"

"Most definitely. Beautiful women are often consumed with themselves, but you give as much pleasure as you take. And," he said, bending his head to brush his lips against the corner of her mouth, "you are insatiable."

"You make me sound wanton," she managed.

The memory of Somersby's *slut* cut into her mind, and she squeezed her eyes closed to hide the pain.

Jake seemed to read her thoughts. "Sarah . . ." he said softly. Untying the bow that held her gown together at her throat, he pulled aside the restrictive soft cloth and pressed his lips to the exposed flesh of her rounded breast.

"There's nothing wrong with what we do. I want to make you feel wanton. That's all that matters now." His kisses burned their way to her aroused nipple. His teeth and tongue played with the erect tip. "Do you feel wanton, Sarah?" he asked against her skin. "Tell me how you feel."

Sarah could hardly think, much less speak. She moaned.

"Not good enough." He laved the nipple once again. "Tell me how you feel. You asked me once if it was all right to talk. I assure you it is."

Sarah took a shallow breath. Jake had a way of getting what he wanted by simply making her want the same things. Her hands stole around his waist, and she lifted her hips to the demanding tumescence that pressed against the juncture of her thighs. "I feel hot and hungry. I want you inside me, Jake. Here. Now."

Incredibly, he shifted his weight off her and stood to look down on her. "Undress me, then."

She took his extended hand and stood beside him. Dizzy, she had to lean against him a minute to regain her equilibrium. She studied his face, which was once more visible in the shadowy light. Unsmiling, he seemed molded from copper.

"You really mean it, don't you?" she asked.

"I really mean it."

Sarah welcomed the idea. She worked at the fastenings of his shirt and tossed the garment to the sand, pausing to admire the expanse of his muscled chest. When she moved her questing hands to the waistband of his trousers, she expected him to come to her assistance, to speed the process that they both wanted to be brief. He did not, instead watching as she fumbled at the unfamiliar opening.

"Are you enjoying this?" she asked, not looking up.

"I am."

So he was teasing her, was he? Two could play at that game. She let her fingers drop until they cradled the fullness of his manhood. His gasp was all the reward she could have wanted.

She began to stroke against his trousers.

"Sarah," he said in a warning voice, and then when she didn't stop, "Sarah" came out in a whisper.

Jake was the one who completed his undressing. She considered it a victory of sorts, one which multiplied as she stepped back and gazed on the length of his naked frame. He was a magnificent man, his body long and lean and yet finely sculpted. The grace with which he performed his tasks aboard the dhow was the result of muscles he had developed through years of physical labor, sinewed power of legs and arms and back.

"You're beautiful, too," she managed.

"Lift your skirt, Sarah."

Her eyes flew upward. "What?" It seemed somehow a curiously coarse request.

"The only thing I want off your body, Angel, are those damned drawers."

Sarah grinned. "I'll take care of them soon enough."

Her hands groped beneath her skirt for the appropriate tapes. She slid the drawers to her ankles and kicked them beside Jake's shirt and pants.

"Good enough?"

With a low growl, Jake scooped her in his arms and laid her once again on the blanket, her skirt tucked about her waist. He placed his body over hers, warming her with more than just his natural heat. Passion fired her, too.

With Jake lying between her naked thighs, Sarah was struck with a longing that overwhelmed her. Her hips lifted and writhed against him.

Deftly Jake shifted her from underneath him, and she suddenly found herself lying atop him, her legs straddling his hungry body.

"If you want me inside you, Angel, you'll have to put me there."

It seemed the most sensible thing in the world to do as he suggested. She had only to rotate her hips, and he was where she wanted him to be. It was the movements that she controlled, the thrust and shift of her body that elicited the thrills she had learned to crave. Pressing her mouth against the side of his neck, she gave her thoughts to the quickening throbs.

Exactly when Jake took charge, she did not know, but suddenly she realized his hips were lifting to meet hers, his thrusts matching all that she could give. The inescapable tentacles of ecstasy tightened and drove her to madness.

She climaxed first. Clinging to her, Jake soon

followed. He wrapped her in his embrace, her half-clothed body covering his nakedness, the night pressing them together in their private world.

Stroking her back, Jake pulled down her skirt to cover her bare buttocks. Sarah kissed his neck, his ear, the strong curve of his jaw. At last she covered his mouth with hers. He held her tightly for the length of the lingering kiss.

With a sigh, she broke away. "That was . . . nice."

"Nice, eh? I hope that was an understatement."

She smiled down at him. "And how would you describe it?"

"The earth took an extra spin or two."

"You go too far."

"Would you believe the ground shifted under me?"

"That's just because we're lying on a bed of sand. I'd lift the blanket over us, but we'd be covered with the stuff," she said with a rueful laugh.

"I'm not cold. Quite the contrary."

"I wouldn't want you to get sick."

"I'm disgustingly healthy."

"There's nothing disgusting about your health," she said, kissing him once again. "I liked tonight's lesson. Me dressed and on top." She snuggled against his chest and let her hair serve as the blanket he eschewed.

"There was only one thing missing," he said.

"And what was that?" she asked.

"Your knees." He stroked her hair and settled his hand across her back. "I wanted to kiss the backs of your knees."

Chapter Twenty

Sometime around the hour of midnight Sarah and Jake moved away from the water and into the protection of the thick growth of brush at the outer edge of the beach, Jake's shirt and trousers and her drawers donned once again as protection against the brisk night air.

Jake had carefully shaken out the blanket before taking her into his arms and settling down for much-needed sleep. By the time Sarah awoke the next morning to a bright Aegean sun, she had learned one inescapable fact about island life. She did not like sand.

She had not paid particular attention to it on her previous visit, concentrating instead on her newly acquired safety and freedom. She paid attention to it now.

The ground not only moved under them, as Jake had claimed so romantically the night before, it moved over and around them, too.

Borne on the damp breeze wafting over the blanket and stirred from underneath by a couple of restless sleepers, sand had worked its way into her hair, her mouth, her clothes. It gritted between her teeth; it scratched her skin. For the first time she understood Jake's proud attitude toward the once protective hut. With its dirt floor and windproof walls, it kept out the hated sand. If she had to work from now until the moon disappeared, that hut would be completed before she settled down for another night's rest. Despite her propensity for adventure, Sarah had a very practical side to her nature, and a strong stubborn streak.

She sat up and gazed at the sleeping Jake, who was curled into a ball on his side. He had shaved yesterday morning, but his face was heavily bristled once again. The whiskers, along with his disheveled hair, gave him the look of a hibernating bear. She wondered if he was grumpy in the morning. He had not been yesterday on the boat, but then he had been the one to wake up first and get to work.

She glanced across the white beach and at the water, where the dhow was anchored. With the shifting of the tide, it rested in the choppy water with its stern to the island. Sarah saw immediately the work Jake had been doing on the boat.

"Jake," she cried out.

Leaning down, she brushed her lips to his bushy cheek, and he turned his head. She kissed him full on the mouth. When she stopped, he cracked his eyes open.

"Don't quit," he said, rolling to his back and running his hands up her arms.

She kissed him again, her tangled hair tickling his face.

Pulling her down on top of him, he returned the favor, his mouth covering hers for a long, sweet time. At last he said, "Woman, you know how to wake up a man."

Her eyes sparkled down into his. "You named the

dhow *Angel*."

"I wondered when you would notice."

"Why did you do it?" Sarah asked boldly.

Jake grinned. "She needed a name. And," he said, stroking her cheek, "you were the first woman to sail on her."

But not the last. Sarah was certain of that.

Pulling free of his embrace, she sat with her face to the water. "I've never had a boat named after me," she said brightly, determined to keep her happy mood. She sprang to her feet and without thinking shook the hated sand from her skirt. The fine grit caught in the breeze and blew back onto Jake.

"Woman," he growled.

"I'm sorry." She kneeled to kiss him, then stood. "We need that hut, Jake. I'll look for driftwood."

When he was up and stirring, she headed down the beach on her search for fuel for the fire. Coffee satisfied them both, and within half an hour they were shuffling through the debris of dead fronds and wooden frames of the former shelter. Much was reusable, but not all, and Sarah helped Jake search for the strong, thick-leaved branches that he insisted they needed to build a sturdy structure.

"In case you decide to leave again," he explained.

"Which is unlikely," she answered with a smile, "since I know now exactly what it is I would be running from."

Unshaven, Jake worked wearing trousers and boots. Sarah plaited her hair into one thick braid that bounced against her back as she moved. She used her chemise as a blouse, tucking it into the waistband of the Turkish trousers. Designed to be worn beneath the caftan, the trousers did little to disguise the outline of her hips and legs.

"Very nice," Jake assessed.

She regarded his bare chest, her eyes roaming over the expanse of corded muscle. "I agree."

She caught the glint in his eye. "The hut, Jake," she reminded him.

Once he had elicited a promise or two about how they would celebrate its completion, Jake settled down to work. After brief consideration, he announced the best place for the reconstruction was adjacent to the former site, in the clearing between the island jungle and the beach.

Their labors soon fell into a pattern—Sarah seeking out the necessary strong branches and Jake wielding a small hatchet to fell them. By midmorning, declaring they had enough raw materials, he set to work rebuilding the frame.

Listening to the sailor's song that sprang to his lips, Sarah felt contentment settle into her heart. No matter what the rest of the world thought, her being here with Jake was not wrong.

Unless she let him do all the work. She turned her attention to a string and hook he had gifted her with shortly after their Spartan breakfast. For bait she used a leftover piece of meat from the previous evening. It was with great pride that she announced beneath the high noon sky that lunch was served. She had caught, cleaned, and cooked her first fish.

As they sat cross-legged in the shade near the freshwater pond, Sarah took a bite of moist white meat and laughed.

"What's so funny?" asked Jake.

"I was thinking about the expression on my father's face if he could see me now. He thinks I'm rather useless." She glanced down at her broken nails and work-reddened hands, then back to Jake. "I've proven him wrong, would you not agree?"

Jake shook his head. "I can't imagine why he

would ever say such a thing. Tell me about him."

His request took her aback. Sarah had never told anyone about the tenuous, sometimes broken peace that lay between her and Sir Edward. She toyed with the remaining food on her plate and, without willing the words, heard herself telling Jake about the death of her mother and about the long line of nannies and governesses that had served in her stead.

"In the past few years I've been pretty much left to my own devices. Within the strictures of society, of course. Papa always hoped the censure of his peers would make me a prudent daughter."

"Were Papa's hopes always realized?"

Her answer was a recounting of an adventure or two. "Somersby knew of my reputation as the hellion of London," she said. "He accused me of wanting to call attention to myself, of being excitable and looking for drama. That's why he didn't believe what I said about the danger to Harun."

She shrugged, no longer hurt or angered by his attitude. "I guess I can hardly blame him. You know the story of the little boy who cried wolf once too often? When danger really came, no one believed him. I didn't cry wolf, just got myself into scrapes."

She watched for Jake's grin, listened for a sarcastic retort, but his response was to regard her with a disconcerting look of interest and sympathy.

Staring into space, she paused in her discourse and listened to the song of an unseen bird in one of the branches overhead. The rustle of leaves provided musical accompaniment.

"I really wasn't totally useless, you know, even in London," she went on at last. "Through the years I learned about Papa's business, usually when he was off on a buying trip. I grew to love the objects of art that he sold. I even offered to keep the books." She

307

shuddered at the memory of his response. "I only asked once. Papa said no daughter of his should concern herself with matters more properly left to men. I knew that he really thought I would make a hodgepodge of his records."

"And would you?"

"Of course not," said Sarah. "I'd been doing some work he never knew about—helping out with time and money at the Deaf and Dumb Asylum. Young children who needed love and attention as well as instruction. I knew I could be relied upon, even if he did not." Sarah caught herself and looked at Jake. "Until this moment, I've never spoken of my connection to the asylum."

"Surely that wasn't work more properly left to men."

She shrugged.

"I knew you were an angel," he said warmly.

Embarrassed, Sarah leaped to her feet. "I was restless, that's all. Bored. Don't make me sound noble, for heaven's sake. And quit postponing the work we've still got to finish. I am determined to sleep in that hut tonight."

Jake groaned. "What a slavemaster you are."

"And don't forget it."

Within an hour after lunch, Jake announced the framework, with its center pole firmly anchored in the ground, was in place. Hard labor throughout the afternoon brought about the completion of their tasks.

As the sun neared the edge of the horizon, its purple and orange rays reflected across the mirror surface of the dark sea, Sarah stood at the edge of the sand and eyed the structure critically.

"Not St. Paul's, of course, nor Buckingham. But it will do."

"Glad you approve," said Jake drily. "Only one thing left and it's finished."

He left for the dhow, returning with her valise and a large blanket-wrapped bundle held high over his head and away from the lapping water. The damp trousers clung to his muscled thighs. Sarah could hardly wait for the celebration he had planned.

"The pond is yours, Angel," he said, handing her the valise. "I've a few last minute things to take care of here."

Sarah welcomed the cool water of the secluded pond and the moment of privacy her bath allowed to consider her deepening feelings for Jake. He made her feel good about herself as no one ever had. He listened to what she had to say.

She had talked too much, of course. He must have thought she was championing herself with all those details about the asylum. She had not planned for anyone else to know. Those hours when she worked with the children were precious to her—and private. Yet she could not really regret telling Jake.

She didn't regret doing anything with him. No matter what happened between her and Jake—and she could not yet allow herself to consider the future—he was a part of her life. Whether she was a part of his, she would not speculate.

At last she forced herself from the water, brushed her clean hair until it began to dry, and selected from her valise a blue dimity gown with rounded neck and short puffed sleeves. Its fitted waist gave way to a full skirt that brushed against the sparse grass at the edge of the pond. Pulling on a clean pair of white linen drawers, she decided that if Jake didn't like them, he could remove them at the appropriate time.

The thought warmed her as she rinsed the sand from the clothes she had worn all day and hung them from the branches where they would catch the breeze.

Jake met her when she arrived at the door of the hut. Clean-shaven and dressed in ruffled shirt and formal black trousers, he presented her with a glass of wine and moved aside to allow her to enter.

She stepped into candlelight. Its soft glow reflected against the deep green fronds and brown branches that were the hut's four walls. He had somehow managed to resurrect the table that had been under all the debris; on it rested a half-filled bottle of wine and the porcelain vase she had admired in his apartment.

Entranced, she took another step forward and realized she was standing on the apartment's deep-piled rug. She rubbed her toes against the fibers. She had special memories of that rug.

Her eyes raised to Jake's.

"It's beautiful, but how—"

He stopped her with a smile. Her heart turned over.

"I told you I'd been planning to return here. Thought I would fancy up the place."

"Bandit's tastes must be rubbing off on you."

"Bandit's," Jake said, "or more probably yours."

Sarah's knees began to demonstrate their usual propensity for weakness when she was under the scrutiny of a pair of dark, glinting eyes. "Better be careful, Jake. You're becoming civilized."

He touched the soft flesh of her upper arm just below the band of her sleeve. His fingers moved slowly back and forth. He might just as well have touched her with a jolt of electricity.

"Is that what I'm becoming? I've wondered."

The silence grew heavy between them. *Why don't you speak?* her mind screamed. *Why don't you tell me how you feel?*

There came the dread suspicion that she was better off not to know. She lifted her glass. "Shall we toast the fruits of our labors?"

They sipped at the wine.

"Afraid it's tinned beef again," he announced. "And bread that's not so fresh."

"It sounds wonderful."

Dinner was a quiet affair, both of them exhausted from the day's work. But Sarah knew that Jake also had weighty matters on his mind. Things she had been considering . . . questions she was not ready to ask. If at that moment he had reminded her of the fragility of their relationship, she would have burst into tears.

Sitting beside him on the rug, her back against the table and her bare feet tucked under her, she studied the last of the wine in her glass. "I talked rather too much about myself this afternoon. What about you?" She looked up at him and caught a frown on his face.

The frown gave way to an enigmatic smile. "Boring. I've no secret charities to reveal."

Sarah took offense. "I wasn't trying to impress you or to entertain you this afternoon."

"Of course you weren't, Sarah, and I didn't mean to imply that you were. But I couldn't help comparing my life with yours. You've been searching for something. I haven't. I was meant for the sea. I knew it the moment I crawled across a Boston dock and tried to make my way up the nearest gangplank."

"I can't picture you that drunk."

"I was nine months old at the time. My mother, of course, was the source of my information, she being the one who had brought me there, but I'm convinced I knew in my heart that I was where I belonged. She disagreed. She'd already given my father to the sea. His ship went down somewhere in the Orient. She never knew exactly where. Later my brother was lost in a storm off the cape."

"I'm sorry."

"My only regret is I had run away by that time to take what I thought was a grand adventure as a cabin boy. It was damned hard work. I returned to Boston to learn about my brother. And," he said in a low, hard voice, "about her. She had died of influenza, they said, but I always figured grief had a great deal to do with it. Women who link themselves with sailors lead a hard life."

Sarah knew too well what he was saying. "They do it by choice, don't they?"

"Maybe," he said. "Anyway, I shouldn't be rambling. It was a long time ago." He finished off the wine.

Sarah made her voice light. "So why aren't you captain of a ship by now? Or at least chief mate?"

"I was a mate for a while. My problem, Angel," he said with a smile, "is that I don't like taking orders. The only solution is to have my own frigate. That way there's not even an owner back on land to dictate what I do."

Sarah could not keep from comparing him with Ralph Pettigrew. Jake had the same ambitions—to have his own shipping company, even if it consisted of one vessel—but there the resemblance ended. He did not care to stay ashore, and he did not care to be encumbered by a wife.

Sarah set her glass aside. In that moment she knew beyond all doubt that she loved him and would do so for the rest of her life. The acceptance of that love that should have thrilled her and given a reason for

312

her very existence came close to filling her with despair.

But she had come with him knowing the way things were. She had accepted disappointment much of her life. Never had she wallowed in self-pity. She would not now.

Carpe diem, she recalled from a lesson that a Latin-loving governess had taught her. *Make the most of the day.* It seemed like good advice.

Kneeling in front of his seated figure, she wondered if he could hear the thundering of her heart. "So you don't want to take orders, do you? Wouldn't that depend upon what those orders were?"

Jake, too, knelt and rested his hands on her shoulders, his thumbs stroking the rise of her breasts above the blue dimity. "So tell me what to do. You'll find out soon enough whether I agree."

His voice was full of such suggestive power that it made her dizzy. She cradled his face, and he bent to kiss her wrist. His lips lingered against her skin. "Your heart is throbbing," he said.

"Everything about me is throbbing. I order you to do something about it."

Jake announced he needed to hear no more. They undressed one another, and he made not one comment about the drawers, intent as he obviously was at revealing what they covered. When they stretched out on the rug, Sarah's back was close to the center post.

"I've anchored it more firmly," he said in answer to her questioning look. "It would take quite a pounding to bring it down."

She started to say that it could very well receive that pounding; but his lips stopped her, and she gave herself up to the man she loved.

313

Sarah held nothing back. Their tongues met in an erotic dance, and she let her hands rove over his incredible body, hungry to touch every plane and contour of its powerful length. He matched her with probings of his own.

She was caught in the wonder of emotion. Jake had taught her the mysteries of sensual experience, had taken her to the heights of ecstasy, had held her during the slow descent that was the inevitable conclusion to rapture. She would show him what it was like to lie with a woman in love.

With lips and hands she told him what her words could not. With their bodies entwined, she became as much a part of him as his own heart. If he would only accept her forever. . . .

She pushed the thought aside. Tonight he was hers. She would ask nothing more.

She was by turns tender and passionate, gentle lips brushing against his eyes, his cheeks, his throat, and demanding lips covering his and drawing nourishment from his manly taste. Stroking hands became insistent, seeking the secrets of his hard body. Gradually the tenderness slipped away as the demands of her own body drove her to the sweet madness of release.

He seemed to sense her urgency and matched her with an urgency of his own. They knew each other completely; their flesh was one. Their physical joining was a natural continuation of the joining of their minds and desires. If Jake's heart was not enjoined with hers, she knew that she had every other part of him.

Their shared culmination was the single most exhilarating moment of Sarah's life. Wanting it to last forever, she clasped herself to him in quiet desperation. Jake held her tightly. At last he moved away to extinguish the candle. In the darkness she felt his arms wrap around her once again. She was grateful he did not speak. There was nothing that either he or she could say that would add to the beauty of what they had shared. And nothing would ease the heaviness that was settling in her heart.

In time Jake's breathing became regular and marked with a soft, soothing snore, but it was a long while before she joined him in sleep.

Over the next several days their lovemaking was repeated, but never did Sarah again experience the poignancy of that first night in the resurrected hut. Jake was a masterful teacher, showing her that any time of day or night was right if the two people involved were of the same mind. For his classroom, he chose the hut, the bank beside the pond, and one wondrous morning the shallow waters of a small bay on the far side of their little strip of land.

Passion was there; each time the flames seemed to grow hotter. She was as insatiable as Jake.

But she knew there was an edge of desperation about the pleasure they took from one another, at least on her part if not on his. Both knew they would soon have to leave, but the question of exactly when was never raised.

Sarah was riding the crest of a wave. She tried not to think of the inevitable downturn, but the unwelcome thoughts hit her when she least expected them.

She would catch a glance of him as he strode naked from a swim in the sea, once again her Neptune come to claim his nymph, and she would wish his claims were of a different kind.

Or she would serve him a plate of fish caught and prepared entirely by her hand and think that she could serve him thus forever.

Even when he waited on her, cleaning up after a meal he had prepared or hanging out her wash on the high branches she could not reach, she saw how well they could serve one another.

She was certain she covered her private thoughts well. Jake saw only a happy side, a passionate side, and on occasion a thoughtful side when in answer to his questions she talked more about her past. He took such a dislike to her father that she had to assure him Sir Edward was not a monster. She had never been abused, only ignored. She could have told him he was certain to do the same.

The end of their idyll came at the beginning of their second week in exile. Jake caught sight of the approaching sails shortly after noon. Together they stood on the warm sand of the beach, watching and wondering who the intruders could be.

The boat, not much larger than the dhow, dropped anchor farther out in the bay. Both Sarah and Jake smiled in recognition of the small, dark man who rowed the dinghy into shore.

"Bandit," shouted Jake, waving.

Bandit answered his wave as the small craft swept through the shallow waters.

Their smiles died when their visitor turned from the banked rowboat and they caught the expression on his face.

"Bossman," he said, "Miss Whitlock."

"What's wrong?" she asked, instinctively taking Jake's hand.

"There is much trouble in the city," he answered, his dark eyes darting from one to the other as he walked toward them across the sand. "An attempt

316

has been made on the sultan's life."

"Oh, no," Sarah cried.

"The attempt failed. It is an added complication that the English have been blamed. I did not want to disturb you, Bossman," he said, "but I thought it best that you knew."

Chapter Twenty-One

Jake listened to Bandit's unfortunate report, but his eyes were on Sarah, who paled visibly beneath the golden tan she had acquired during the past few days. She had been happy on the island, a different woman from the one who had faced him in the embassy and asked him for his help. He didn't know how or when it had happened, but somehow she had become his responsibility. He did not want to see that happiness end, but there seemed little he could do to hold off the outside world.

"What happened?" she asked, wind stirring the wisps of fine, honeyed hair that had pulled free from the thick braid at her back.

He took her hand in his, and she held on tight. Bandit's sharp eyes darted between them.

"Shots were fired into the sultan's carriage as he left the British embassy. It all happened very fast. Even so late at night, crowds had lined the street to watch the procession. When Harun takes such a journey, even a short one, there are many in his entourage. The British, I am told, like spectacle. It was from the crowd that the bullets came."

"But no one was injured," said Sarah.

Bandit looked apologetic, as though he were the one responsible for the assault. "A guard, I regret to say, gave his life in defense of his sultan."

Her grip on Jake's hand tightened.

"And the assailants?" he asked. "Anyone spot a man with a scar on his face?"

"Some of the guards reported seeing an Englishman rapidly depart the area from which the sounds of gunfire came, but there was much confusion. His identity has been the cause of much speculation."

"And how," Sarah asked, "could they know he was English?"

Bandit shrugged. "He wore the clothes of the English."

"I wore the clothes of a Turkish dancer. That doesn't make me one."

"You gave a damned good imitation," Jake put in as he thought of that night in the coffee house. The memory of Sarah's performance, as angry as it had made him, could still bring heat to his loins. He was pleased to see a slight blush return to her cheeks.

"Bossman—" Bandit hesitated.

"Spit it out," said Jake. "I was afraid we hadn't heard the worst." Sarah leaned toward him. He liked her dependence on him. He liked it a great deal.

"There is much talk—"

"About me," said Sarah.

"Now what makes you say that?" asked Jake.

"Because there always is. I don't even have to be in the same country as the talk."

"In truth," Bandit said in a worried voice, "Miss Whitlock is correct. She predicted there would be such an attempt. And then she disappeared. The two events, so close in time, have not gone unnoticed."

"As I recall, you once mentioned a cousin who worked on the embassy staff," said Jake.

"It is an English friend of my cousin who provides the information. A woman who works in the kitchen reports of midnight sessions in the office of the ambassador. There is much talk and speculation about how Miss Whitlock came by her information. They wonder if the shooting and her warning were a coincidence or if she in truth possesses knowledge that could be of help in these difficult days."

"They are wondering rather tardily, aren't they?" Sarah said. "Phillip Somersby, especially."

"Mr. Somersby is no longer on the premises of the embassy. It is my understanding that he has returned to England. At the request of the ambassador."

Sarah sighed. "There will be someone like him to take his place."

Jake wasn't used to hearing such gloomy prognostications from her. As she went on to question Bandit about the staff, about the talks, about the speculations concerning her, Jake only half listened. He had nothing to ask that touched on political gossip and wished that Sarah was of a similar mind. Right now anything she found out could only add to her worries. They were worries she did not deserve.

Sarah was impetuous, inquisitive, daring to the point of foolhardiness, and altogether the most exciting, passionate woman he had ever known. And she had managed to be all these things with a background that included an unloving, critical father she insisted on defending and a host of countrymen who judged her harshly even while they enjoyed the antics in which she was engaged.

She had unnerved him, pleasured him, destroyed his sleep and peace of mind, and at the same time made his last few days the most contented of his life. Both of them had always known their retreat to the island had to come to an end. He had to keep re-

320

minding himself of that fact.

His determination was not helped by the way her dress, blown by the damp wind, clung to her gentle curves—her high breasts and narrow waist and the long sweep of her hips and legs. The sun had kissed her face and throat, her arms and ankles, and left them the color of dark gold.

A sprinkling of white sand, borne on the wind, covered her cheeks and neck and the skin of her arms below where she'd rolled the sleeves of her gown. Oh, how she hated that sand. Which had led to many baths. Which had led to other things.

"Jake."

He pulled his mind away from the thought that even now in the midst of their new worries, he was fully capable of carrying her back to their hut and making love to her for the rest of the day.

"Jake," she repeated.

He said what he figured was on her mind. "You want to return."

"Lord Stratford has never been told about the *Leviathan* or what I overheard in the seraglio. Not unless Ralph told him what he knew after we left."

Jake's anger flared. "Do you really think you owe those English bastards anything?"

"The ambassador never heard a word of my story, at least not from me. Maybe he won't reject it out of hand. And even if he does," she added solemnly, her eyes dark with remembered pain, "I owe it to Captain Reynolds and the others to report the truth."

Jake had to be blunt. "But what if he doesn't believe you? What then?"

"I will know I have done all I could. And there's the danger to the sultan. If Harun dies because I have not done everything possible to report what I saw and heard, I will never forgive myself."

Jake pulled his eyes away from her and stared toward the dark, rolling waves of the sea, past the dhow and the larger craft anchored in deeper water behind it, and on to the horizon. The afternoon sun hung like a red ball in the cloudless sky, its heat dissipated in the breeze. Overhead a gull soared, swooped toward them in hopes of food, and with a cry of displeasure when he was ignored, banked toward the sun and was gone.

It was another perfect day in a series of perfect days. Almost.

Sarah was right. They had to leave.

Jake asked Bandit to come with them to the hut for a look at the resurrected structure and for a meal of fish and island berries.

"Where did you get the boat?" he asked him when they were settled in the cool shelter and the simple meal was finished.

The two men talked across the table while Sarah sat in silence, her back to the center pole, legs bent into the folds of her skirt, fingers stroking the nap of the rug. Since leaving the beach, she had spoken little, and her eyes had avoided those of both men.

"It is borrowed," Bandit replied. "A friend of my cousin owns several such vessels which are used in the trade between the small merchants of Constantinople and the people of the islands. The crew I pay myself. From the money I have made while we are in Turkey."

He went on to explain the nature of his new business, trading in the fine porcelains and textiles he found in the many bazaars scattered throughout the city. He'd been doing such trading ever since they first arrived, and he proclaimed with evident pride that there was nothing illegal about the enterprise.

"I have uncovered treasures that even a sultan can

value—especially one with the knowing eye of Harun. More than once, against the custom of all the sultans who have come before him, he has allowed me inside the Grand Seraglio to display my wares. Such visits are a great honor and more, they have allowed me to see the slave girl Nadire, who has returned to the safety of the sultan's harem. Never was she comfortable with the women of his son, wondering when he would return. She instructs me to inform the Missy Sarah that she is well. I can verify that such is the truth."

Sarah stirred. "Nadire," she said softly. "I would like to see her again."

"It will be arranged," said Bandit.

Insisting she rest, he took Bandit for a walk about the island. Neither spoke until they were well along a narrow path that wound through the growth of brush near the pond.

"Bossman," Bandit said as he trailed along behind Jake, "there is one thing I did not say in front of Miss Whitlock. Given her inclination for activity, I felt it best to tell you when we were alone."

"Good thinking," Jake said over his shoulder.

"I have seen the man she calls Scarface."

Jake came to a halt and turned. "Where?"

"In the shadowed corner of a coffee house. Not," he hastened to assure Jake, "the one belonging to Faruk, but another such establishment. I came upon him by accident. He spoke with a man I recognized. A man from the palace."

"Mustafa!"

Bandit shook his head. "Not one so prominent. You, too, know this man. He is the vizier with whom you spoke concerning the sale of the death mask to Harun. His name, I believe, is Pinar."

The news took Jake by surprise, and he did some

fast reflecting. Here was possibly the identification of the man Sarah had heard speaking to Scarface the night she escaped from the harem. He knew of only one way to find out for sure.

"We'll have to confront this Pinar."

"The Bossman has taken on Miss Whitlock's battle as his own."

Jake stared at his friend for a moment and at last grinned. "I seem to, haven't I? If I don't, she'll probably start a full scale war between England and Turkey, with Russia thrown in for good measure."

"It is also possible that another reason exists. One more delicate. If I may be forgiven for speaking so boldly."

Jake waved aside the words which too closely echoed his own recent and unsettling thoughts.

"Whatever ideas you've got, maybe it's best you keep them to yourself. Things are complicated enough. Sarah will be going back to England, I imagine, as soon as she tells her story."

"It will not be so simple for the Bossman and Miss Whitlock to part."

"I'm a sailor, Bandit, first, last, and always. Grief killed my mother after the sea took her husband and her first born. I was as good as lost to her, too. Do you really think I would wish such a fate on Sarah? No," he hurried on as much to himself as to his friend, "she must return to England. It's the sensible thing for her to do."

"Has Miss Whitlock grown sensible during the past days?"

Jake had to think that one over. "Not by English standards," he said, remembering a time or two when she had startled him by her unguarded pleasure in what they were doing. Hiking, swimming, making love. She entered everything with open enthusiasm and a kind of innocence that had nothing to do with the skills she had quickly learned in his bed.

"I'll just have to convince her," he continued, "that after all she's gone through, unless she's ready to marry Ralph Pettigrew, a return home is her only choice."

And, he thought, *convince myself at the same time.*

They continued their walk for a while, each lost to private musings. Jake was a sailor, all right; his home had always been the sea. But each time he tried to picture the expanses of water that had called to him through the years, he saw Sarah staring up at him from their blanket bed, her lips full, her eyes a fathomless blue. Sunlight on the waves became the spill of her golden hair, the salty air forgotten in the assault of the flowery sweet scent that she carried on her skin.

She had turned him inside out. Him, Jake Price, who until now had let no man or woman dictate the course of his life. She was by turns settling and unsettling, and the strange part was that he did not in the least mind.

But they had been living on an island, and their isolation was finished. By the time he returned to the hut, he was sure he was doing the right thing in seeing that she returned to civilization. For Sarah's sake. For his own.

Bandit insisted on returning to the boat. He would, he promised, send one of the sailors ashore with a dinner of fresh vegetables and cheese and a bottle of wine. Both vessels could set sail on the morning tide. Jake did not argue.

The evening meal, eaten late by Sarah and Jake, was as quiet as lunch had been. Sarah's uncharacteristic solemnity worked against his patience. He could read her mind.

"You didn't cause the death of the guard," he said at last.

"I could have gone to see Harun."

"You tried to talk to him once—when you were in the harem—and he would not listen. Remember, Sarah, Turks aren't inclined to credit women with any sense. Especially ones bearing bad and farfetched news. A ship's crew and passengers murdered? He and his viziers would have demanded to know why no one else had heard. This Pinar would have planted suspicion in his mind."

"As a matter of fact, I did tell him about the *Leviathan*."

"And his reaction?"

She shrugged. "Much as you described. But that was before I saw Scarface again." Her voice turned bitter. "At the very least I should have stayed at the embassy and tried again to speak to Lord Stratford."

She seemed might damned quick to push aside the past few days as though they had meant nothing special. As though they had interfered. Jake knew they were over, but he didn't wish they had never been.

"Maybe," he snapped, "you should."

A silence descended between them that had not been his intent. When at last he lowered the light, slowly extinguishing it until the hut was kept from blackness by only a soft mist of moonlight, the uneasiness grew. Now was the time he wrapped his arms around her—or she wrapped hers around him—and they fell onto the blanket in their own special celebration of another glorious day.

Tonight they had nothing to celebrate.

Undressing one another had become a nightly ritual with them. This evening he stepped outside and gave her a few minutes to prepare for bed. She did not call him back. Not a smoking man, he would have given a great deal for a cigar as he paced back and forth across the dark beach.

There was still half a bottle of wine remaining, but Jake decided against going back for it. The alcohol would only loosen his tongue, not make him drunk, and he didn't want to argue with her.

He ran impatient fingers through his hair. Hell, he didn't know what he *did* want.

At last he returned to the hut. In the semi-dark he could make out her clothed figure on the far side of the blanket. Stripping his body of shirt and trousers, he threw them in a corner. He'd be damned if he would sleep in clothes just because Sarah had other things weighing on her mind.

When he stared at her slender, vulnerable figure, his anger evaporated. He sympathized with her worry. If anything, he was looking at the situation more realistically than she. No one could have tried harder at the embassy ball to get her story told, but too many things had worked against her: a small-minded, drunken subordinate trying to further his career through her humiliation, a delicate situation between the countries involved, Sarah's London reputation. Instead of trying to talk to Somersby and Pettigrew, she would have been better off writing the ambassador a long letter and catching the first clipper ship home.

He stretched out on the blanket. Never had the floor of the hut felt harder. Sarah stirred, her back still to him. He opened his mouth to offer some kind of comfort, some words to ease her troubled thoughts. She apparently wasn't in the mood to accept the kind of comfort that he really wanted to give.

"Hold me, Jake," she said.

Sarah had a habit of taking him by surprise.

He did as she asked, one arm under her shoulders and the other resting naturally around her waist. She nestled against him, her thick hair spilling across the arm and shoulder protecting her from the hard ground. He realized that instead of being fully clothed, she was dressed in a chemise and petticoat.

He listened to her shallow breathing.

"I'm sorry for tonight," she said.

"You've nothing to apologize for."

"Tell the truth, Jake."

"Well, maybe a little. Not apologize, exactly. How about explain? If you want to talk, that is."

"Maybe I do. But not right now. Later."

Her fingers began to stroke the arm at her waist.

He pressed his hand against her abdomen and silently cursed the linen that kept him from feeling her bare skin. She would be warm and silken, and the pale curls of hair between her thighs would tickle the tips of his fingers.

The longer he touched her, the warmer her skin would get, until he could feel the heat rise from her like a beckoning hearth fire welcoming the weary traveler home.

He buried his face in her hair. It smelled of sunshine and sea.

She took his hand and cradled it against her breast. Through the chemise he could feel the distended tip.

"Sarah—"

"No words," she whispered. "Not yet."

He took the nipple between thumb and forefinger and rubbed gently, back and forth, back and forth, felt the bead harden, and listened to her quickened breathing. Her body tensed, then melted backward against him as though the two of them could physically become one. He used his chin to brush aside her hair and pressed his lips against her neck.

She was moist with perspiration.

His lips trailed upward, and he circled her ear with his tongue. A cry escaped from her throat. She twisted in his arms until she was facing him, her face inches from his, the petticoat tangled thickly against his legs.

"It's our last night here," she said against his mouth. "Make love to me."

Against all the reasoning of the night, he wanted to tell her that it need not be the end for them, but her kiss stopped him. She had learned her lessons well. With teeth and tongue she assaulted him; with hungry hands she searched the planes of his chest, fingers stroking downward past his waist and through the thickening hair of his abdomen and at last grasping him, her thumb playing at the tip as he had played at her breast.

He eased his hands down her spine, lifting the petticoat and caressing her rounded buttocks and the backs of her thighs. Scrambling about the island and swimming through the surf had left her muscles tight and sleek. She was even more desirable than the night she had danced in the smoky Turkish coffee house. He thought he would explode with wanting her. Her own hand did not cease its torturous probing, but he felt her hips move closer to him, as if she wanted to feel him against her moist heat.

He stroked the sweat-slick outside of her thigh and slipped his hand between their bodies, his palm against her leg. She shifted to give him access, and his palm worked against her pulsing nub. Her breath was hot and heavy now and came in gasps as she thrust herself against his massage.

Afraid he would not be able to contain the sexual demands that were building in him, he grasped her wrist and pulled her stroking fingers away. It was the single most difficult thing he had ever done.

She broke the kiss and pulled him on top of her. Their bodies joined. Completion for them both was almost instantaneous, over as soon as it was begun. Too soon, his mind cried, but his body was in control. He should have loved her long and leisurely; instead, their shared passion had come frenzied and fast. He had not even had a chance to take off her clothes.

Shifting to lie beside her, he held her against him and listened as her breathing slowed. He could hear her heart pounding, then decided it was his own. He stroked the matted damp hair away from her neck and buried his fingers in the thick tresses, his lips pressed to her forehead, and waited for her to speak.

When she moved away from him, it was without a word. She undressed, tossing the underclothes into the corner beside his shirt and trousers, smoothed the wrinkled blanket, and lay down again, this time on her back. Jake could see enough to tell she was staring at the leafy ceiling. Their bodies did not touch.

She curved one arm beneath her head as a pillow, and he ran his eyes down her long, slender body silhouetted in the moonlight.

Our last night. She had said it herself.

"I have to go to the embassy," she said at last. Her voice was cool and strong, and he tried to believe she was convincing herself not to stay on the island. But Jake was honest enough to realize that such was not the case. She was trying to convince him.

If he detected an underlying tension in her words, it was probably only his imagination—or his own confused feelings projected onto her. Sarah knew the way things were between them. He had made them clear from the start. If he wondered now about the

330

wisdom of the strictures he himself had set, he had only himself to blame.

He took his cue from her.

"Bandit didn't tell you everything," he said, matching her coolness. She turned her head sharply to stare at him, and he went on to tell her of the scene in the coffee house.

"Pinar," she said. "I don't know the name, but then I was never considered important enough to learn much concerning Harun's advisors. Few of the harem women were. As I found out, Turks don't regard women as having sense."

"Harun will have to be confronted." Jake hesitated a moment. "You won't like my next statement, Sarah."

"I know already what you're planning. You want to confront him without me."

"At least let me make the first approach. If he agrees to see you—and remember we're talking about a sultan who is used to absolute obedience from his women, the same one you ran from—then I will take you to him."

"You make his acceptance sound unlikely."

"All I ask is that you let me and Bandit talk first. Your presence might complicate matters."

He could feel her anger rise, then dissipate. "My presence has complicated matters often enough. Harun didn't believe anything I had to say before. I can't imagine he would now."

"Don't tell me you are going to wait meekly while Bandit and I go to the palace."

"I'll wait impatiently. That's the best I can offer."

She twisted away from him and lay on her side. "It's late," she said. "We need to get some sleep if we're to leave on the early tide."

Jake touched her arm.

"Good night," she said.

Somehow, he thought as he stared at the dark outline that was Sarah, she had acknowledged his control and at the same time kept it for herself. She was an enigma and an exasperation, fragile and strong at the same time. She had told him good night, but he got the unpleasant feeling she was really telling him good-bye—which was what he, too, wanted to say, he reminded himself.

How in hell had he ever gotten himself into such a mess? When had he turned into such a fool? He shifted uncomfortably. Never, he thought again, had the ground seemed so hard.

Chapter Twenty-Two

The recently christened *Angel* was nearing the Golden Horn mid-morning of the second day away from the island when Sarah startled Jake with an announcement.

"I'm going to America."

Jake finished tightening the rope he had been working over and glanced to the post she had taken by the starboard waist. She was wearing one of her embassy gowns, the blue one that matched her eyes, and her hair was twisted into a demure bun at the nape of her neck. Stubborn tendrils blew in the wind, softening the edges of what seemed to Jake her determined respectability. Her gaze was directed toward the prow, and her chin was raised.

"I don't believe," he said, "that the dhow will manage the Atlantic."

She looked sharply at him.

"A jest, Sarah," he said quickly. "I'm sure you have other transportation in mind."

He turned his attention to the wind in the sail and waited for her to speak. Up until this moment their conversation aboard the craft had been about the business of getting back to the Horn, but he had known there were other thoughts weighing on her mind. He was in the same state.

Last night as they lay side by side in the sleeping quarters, Sarah giving no sign she wanted his lovemaking, he had been tempted at least to draw her into conversation; but he could think of little to say except to offer platitudes about being brave, and she was already that. He wasn't ready to begin talk about what would happen after the problems with Harun were settled, and in the end all they had told each other was *good night*.

Now he learned that while he was thinking about their immediate past and present, she was looking to her future. Sarah was truly an amazing woman, he thought as he turned to study her proud profile. She deserved more from this life than she had ever received. And that included a wandering sailor for a lover. She had made that decision herself.

The idea rankled. And America. Jake did not like her plans at all, and worse, he did not know why.

Sarah ran her fingers along the low rail, but her gaze remained straight ahead. "I can't, of course," she said, "return to England permanently. Oh, I could, but what would be the point? It's a small world, at least as far as the *ton* is concerned. After a few stories make their way back to London—if they haven't already—the dozen or so who shared in my exploits won't be rushing to include me in their circle of friends. One can, after all, go only so far."

"And you've overstepped the bounds."

She nodded. "For one thing, I ran away from the embassy with the man who had just struck down one of Her Majesty's diplomatic representatives. Such things are just not done."

"Somersby was sent away," Jake reminded her.

"Yes, he was." She hesitated. "For another thing, I

don't regret running away, and I can never say otherwise."

Jake saw a hint of a smile soften her lips. He wanted nothing so much as to kiss her, but as he had done last night, he kept his longing in check.

"So what will you do in America? Do you know anyone there?"

"My father does. Especially among those who trade in works of art. I know his business. I have only to prove it to him, but I imagine he will be willing to listen. With the betrothal a thing of the past—and Ralph won't have me now even if I would consider having him—Papa will have little choice."

She turned to look at him, and he was jolted by the stately loveliness of her face. "I know few Americans. Maybe you can give me a hint or two about how I might get along."

She was damned eager to make plans about getting away, Jake thought, even while he told himself he ought to be glad. "If you're talking about the wealthy," he said, more sharply than he intended, "I can give you little advice."

"That's not what I meant," she shot back, hurt in her eyes. "For all I know Americans exist as one happy family. Money no discriminator. Social classes unheard of. That's what you Yanks would have us believe."

"I don't imagine it's that way any place on the face of the earth. Money is *always* a discriminator. Think of the wealthy in Constantinople. Did you see them in the bazaar? In the coffee house? On the streets? They were in the fine carriages that stirred up dust for the less fortunate pedestrians. They ride in carriages in Boston, too, and they stir up the same kind of dust."

"The lowest class of all, Jake, are the women. In

Turkey I realized it as I never have before. We're not veiled in England, of course, but I'm well aware of our place. We put finer trappings around our lower order. We are expected to keep hearth and home for the masters who are chosen for us, to bear and raise their children, and to entertain. For this we are clothed and fed, quite nicely as a matter of fact, at least among my acquaintances. Except for the deaf and dumb children, but then few women or men know they even exist."

Sarah's cheeks were flushed by the fervor of her words. More than ever, Jake felt trapped by the necessity of letting her go.

"Why are we arguing?" he asked.

The speech she had been ready to continue died on her lips.

"Is that what we were doing?"

"It had most of the signs."

Their eyes met. She was the first to look away.

"I supposed you were telling me I wouldn't fit in with Americans any more than I have with my own countrymen."

"It might have sounded like that, but for all its pretenses to society much like yours, there's still an openness to the States that you will like. You'll be fine. I can see you taking those sharp Yankee traders for a bargain or two."

She smiled. "Bandit could probably give me a few pointers."

"I wouldn't take seriously everything he said."

Her smile died. "I don't take seriously anything a man tells me, Jake. Surely you know that by now. Except, of course, when he warns me not to be serious. I always listen to that."

The gentle friendliness that had hovered briefly between them died as quickly as it had been born. A sudden and powerful shift in the wind coming across the water drew his attention back to the dhow, and by the time he had adjusted the sail to take advantage of the breeze, Sarah was so lost in her private thoughts that he could not bring himself to intrude.

He had laid down the rules, and she had followed them. She had harbored no expectations and made no demands, but as far as he was concerned, she had picked a damned poor time to do what he said.

They did not speak again of anything other than sailing until they were safely docked on the Horn. Bandit, having arrived hours earlier in his larger, faster craft, was waiting for them on the wharf.

The noon sun beat down on them with relentless concentration, and the line of warehouses effectively held off any breeze that might have alleviated the heat. More than ever he missed the cool, verdant island.

"We have time, Bossman," said Bandit as they stepped ashore beside him, "to visit the imperial palace. If such is your wish."

"The sooner the better," he said.

"Do you still have the apartment?" asked Sarah. "I can wait there."

Jake wondered what thoughts were sifting through Bandit's mind behind his darting eyes.

"The apartment awaits your return" was all he said.

A hired carriage bore them to the single room.

"I'll be comfortable here," she said, glancing around at the four solid walls. Her eyes settled on the carpet replacing the one Jake had taken for the hut. He knew she must be thinking of the openness of her recent home.

"Until you get back," she added with underlying impatience. "Please don't be long."

"We'll return with a full report," said Jake. "With any luck we should not be long."

"Remember, Jake, if you need my corroboration, I will brave the palace once again," she said.

"I hope that will not be necessary."

Getting to see the sultan proved more difficult than Jake had planned. Since the attack in the English sector, security had tightened. They chose to go on foot, but they had no sooner neared the entrance to the serai on one of the city's broad main streets than they were surrounded by guards.

Bandit had possessed the foresight to bring along with him a fine porcelain vase he had bought from a peddler weeks ago. "The sultan would not take kindly to those who keep him from such beauty," he told them in English and then in Turkish, knowing that many of the sultan's trusted men spoke both languages.

One of the guards at last recognized him as the merchant who had indeed brought other such treasures to his ruler. Much consultation took place among the men, all of the talk in Turkish, and at last one of them was dispatched inside. He returned with Kizlar Agasi, Harun's chief eunuch who had served him as advisor for so many years.

Beside the tall and powerfully built black man, Bandit looked small and pale. But he did not cringe, instead launching into a rapid dissertation about the wonders of the vase and the joy it would bring to the sultan in these troubled times. His mention of the latter was the closest he came to the subject that was on everyone's mind.

The eunuch studied the fragile porcelain, twisting it around in his broad hands, and at last gestured with it toward Jake.

"And what of this man?" he asked. "Why does he

need to see the sultan?"

"Mr. Price is the one who brought the golden mask to the wise Harun. It is he who owns this vase."

At last the eunuch seemed satisfied and with a bark of orders to the nearby guards turned toward the closed gate that led into the palace. The gate opened for him, and with the guards circling Jake and Bandit, they were escorted inside.

The Kizlar Agasi disappeared through another gate, and they were led down a long corridor and into a small room. The furniture, a small sofa and two chairs, came from the West, but whoever had been responsible for the decoration could not resist adding a scattering of pillows across the thick-piled rug that covered much of the floor.

There they waited for an hour. When at last Harun entered, he was in the midst of a half dozen guards whose hands were held close to their sheathed swords. The guards wore the traditional red robes, but their sultan was dressed in the clothes of the English, a dark suit, high-collared shirt, and bow tie. The suit was well tailored to disguise his rotund figure.

He had been dressed similarly when Jake sold him the Egyptian mask. The clothes were a reminder of the attempts he had been making to bring his country in closer alignment with England and away from the threats of the openly voracious Russia which lay across the Black Sea.

He stood before the two visitors, his height falling halfway between Jake's six feet and Bandit's shorter stature. His olive skin looked drawn, and his hair, thick and black despite his sixty years, hung lank. But there was no doubting he was a ruler. It was in the lift of his head, the demanding look in his black eyes, and the regal set of his mouth.

"You have brought me another treasure, I am told," he said.

Bandit produced the cloth-wrapped bundle and unveiled it for Harun.

The sultan's expression told little about his opinion of the offering, but when he took it into his hands, Jake thought he turned it toward the light with an almost reverent caution.

"We bring this as a gift," Bandit said.

"And why," Harun said with narrowed eyes, "would a merchant do such a thing?"

Jake saw right away what Bandit was about, and he answered. "Because of the news we bring. It is hoped that the vase will ease the sultan's distress."

Harun lowered the precious work of art. "Questions," he said with infinite sadness. "So many of them crowd into my mind. Why should I listen to words that bring pain? Have I not suffered enough to know that those who have been welcomed into my country wish me harm?"

"It is widely known that Harun welcomes the truth." Jake knew no other way to approach his difficult task other than straight on. "An Englishman did not fire the bullets into the imperial carriage. The gunman was most likely hired by one of your own people."

Years of training enabled the Turkish caliph to maintain his composure, but Jake was certain he saw a tightening about the royal mouth.

"You are an American, are you not? An impulsive breed, I am told."

"And you are a Turk," said Jake. "A descendant of the courageous Ottomans who conquered much of the world. Now you try to live in peace. I want only the same thing. And so do the British."

A wily look settled in Harun's eyes. "Lord

Stratford knows that you are here?"

"He does not. I come with knowledge that he does not possess. Knowledge that only my servant and I hold. And one other. The English woman Sarah Whitlock. It is her story that I come to relate."

For once Harun looked surprised. "I remember Miss Whitlock well. She found it necessary to seek a life away from my protection."

"Like the Americans," said Jake, "the English can be an impulsive breed."

He glanced around at the guards, who had placed themselves at intervals at the edges of the small room, a pair of them standing squarely in front of the door.

"It is possible you will not want her story to be overheard."

"Do you dare question the loyalty of the imperial guards?"

"I question the loyalty of one much higher than they."

Again Jake caught the flicker of surprise on the sultan's face. It lasted only a moment, then Harun motioned for one of the guards to relieve him of the vase. When he sat on the sofa and gestured for the visitors to occupy the chairs, his enigmatic mask of ruler was settled back in place.

"These men are loyal beyond question. And they also speak little English. Please proceed."

Jake reminded him of Sarah's story about the attack on the *Leviathan*.

"There was no proof that she told the truth," Harun said.

"She had no reason to lie."

"Except, perhaps, to gain her freedom."

A warning glance from Bandit was all that kept Jake from launching into criticism of the way Harun had kept Sarah a prisoner against her will. Bandit was right. Now was not the time to bring up such ethics as variously viewed by East and West.

Instead, he spoke of the night Sarah escaped and of the terrible moment when she overheard the planned assassination. Harun sat very still.

"I know this man you call Scarface," he said when Jake paused. "Once he was an officer of the guards. I removed him at the suggestion of the Kizlar Agasi, who said only that he was not reliable. It would seem that he was far worse."

Jake went on without comment. "I rescued Sarah at the dock where she was chased. That was when we first met, but later when I tried to take her to the embassy, Miss Whitlock decided she preferred talking to you directly."

"As I recall," Harun said, "the English woman had a mind of her own."

"Unfortunately, Sarah's singlemindedness sometimes lands her in trouble." From that bit of understatement, Jake launched into a description of her second visit to the Grand Seraglio, glossing over the rescue he and Bandit had brought about. But he knew Harun was not interested in how she escaped once again from the well-guarded palace; his concern was how and, more important, why she found herself in the harem of his son.

"At the embassy Sarah tried to tell her story to the ambassador but was unfortunately kept from doing so."

"Ah, the strange evening," Harun said, "when the women paraded themselves before strangers in states of undress. Well I recall the incident. Of course I had no way of knowing the details of the disturbance, and afterward other events pushed the early part of the evening from my mind, although I did have concern that she was trying to tell stories about her time in the

342

Grand Seraglio."

"She was trying," Jake said, holding his temper, "to save your life."

Harun conceded the point with a nod. "For which I must thank Miss Whitlock. Earlier, Mr. Price, you gave hints of someone high in authority as a possible traitor."

"By chance Bandit saw this conspirator guard in private conversation with one of your advisors. The vizier Pinar."

If he had expected an explosion of anger or disbelief, he was to be disappointed. Harun gave no indication, by even the flick of an eye, that he was surprised or distressed.

"Describe this conversation," he said to Bandit, who did as the sultan ordered, but he was able to tell him little more than had already been said.

Harun turned to the guards by the door, snapped an order in Turkish, and fell silent as the two robed figures departed. He did not speak again until they returned with the vizier Jake remembered from their earlier negotiations over the mask. Like the sultan, Pinar was dressed in the style of the West. His face was ashen, and beads of sweat formed on his upper lip. His hands twisted nervously at his waist.

He greeted his ruler in their native language. Harun spoke quickly. The vizier, blinking rapidly as he listened, shook his head in denial of his ruler's words. The guards stepped closer, narrowing the space of the room, and Jake wondered if Pinar had been checked for a hidden gun.

Bandit sat in silence and listened, his dark eyes shifting back and forth between the men. Able to pick out only isolated words and phrases, Jake heeded the inflections of the sultan's voice that might give him a clue as to his state of mind. Harun seemed sad and at the same time intransigent. At last Pinar, with a longing glance at the closed and guarded door, sobbed out what could only be a confession.

Jake picked out the name of Mustafa and then another that rang with the clarion of familiarity. He could not believe he heard right. Even the normally enigmatic Bandit started.

Harun waved his once trusted vizier away from the room in the company of two guards and looked at Jake. In the span of half an hour he seemed to have aged a dozen years, the lines of his round face deepened, the expression in his eyes deep and dark. Even the suit hung limp on his body. He bore the sadness of the world.

But his voice held strong. "I know not how much you understood, Mr. Price, but you have earned the right to know all. It would seem the evil of the opium that grows in my country's fields has entered the palace and spread its poison. I speak not of addiction to the poppy but an older addiction. The desire for profit. The worldly goods that I have bestowed upon my son Mustafa have not been sufficient to satisfy this desire. He has entered into a conspiracy against his father, along with my trusted vizier."

Jake wasn't surprised, but when he tried to offer sympathy, Harun waved his words away. "His commerce is with the Chinese. It is a highly profitable trade, but it is also one I have forbidden. And thus the need for my replacement. Mustafa feels that when his brother takes his foreordained place as sultan, he will be able to gain approval for his ventures, which can then be pursued openly. I know not if he is right. I pray to Allah that such is not the case."

"Is this trade the reason he is so often gone from the city?" asked Jake.

Harun nodded. "He began by sending the drug overland by caravan from the eastern end of my country where the poppies flourish. Such travel was long and costly, and there were many losses along the way. My son is a clever man. He has sought a more efficient method for the execution of his schemes. He has found such a way."

"By sea," said Jake.

"So you were not completely ignorant of my conversation with Pinar. You are correct. By sea. Cargo ships could easily call upon the port of Samsun, close to these poppy fields. A return trip through the Bosporus and the Dardanelles would lead the ships to the oceans of the world—except that Mustafa fears using any of his own country's vessels. My people are loyal to my wishes, even if my son and my advisor are not. He could possibly find a captain and crew who would place greed above that loyalty, but he would be taking a chance."

"He would not have such difficulties with the ships of another country," said Jake. "As far as I know, the ships of England are not forbidden to such enterprise."

"The ships of Eastern Ports of Call, to be precise. My son deals with the Englishman Ralph Pettigrew. Soon they plan to begin the forbidden trade."

Chapter Twenty-Three

It was Harun's decision to have Pettigrew brought to the palace. Jake agreed that was the best way to face him. If he caught the bastard alone, he might have broken his neck.

By the time the sultan's messenger and guards returned with a white-lipped Ralph, Jake had reasoned out answers to most of the puzzling things about Sarah's troubles. Each step in the process fed the rage that burned within him. It took all of his self-control to sound reasonable and calm as he convinced Harun to let him begin the questioning.

They were gathered in the same room where Pinar had broken down—Jake, Bandit, the sultan, and of course the guards.

Pettigrew stepped inside in front of his armed escorts. "Your Highness," he said with a shallow bow. He glanced around the room. His eyes widened.

"Price!" he said.

"Hello, Ralph," said Jake, rising from his chair. His fists flexed at his side. "We've been waiting for you."

The Englishman cleared his throat, his pale stare shifting between Jake and Harun.

He settled on Harun. "Your Highness, I do not understand your summons."

"You soon will, Mr. Pettigrew," said the sultan. His voice was icy and did not encourage response.

Pettigrew turned back to Jake. "Where is Sarah? Is she here?"

Jake stared in contempt at the tall, gray-haired Englishman who had been Sir Edward Whitlock's choice as husband for his only child. Pettigrew did not look so pompous now with his skin pasty across the flat bones of his cheeks, and his eyes watery and unfocused.

The fiery rage that had been building within Jake turned cold. "Strange that you should be concerned about the welfare of your fiancée," he said, "considering the danger in which you have placed her."

"What—" Pettigrew cleared his throat and continued. "What are you talking about?"

Jake gestured toward the chair. "Please sit and I will explain it to you."

Pettigrew turned to the sultan, who stared at him blankly. He edged into the chair as though he were afraid Jake would strike him. Jake thought it was the first smart thing he had done since his arrival.

"I'm talking about your arrangements with Mustafa for the use of your ships, Ralph. I'm talking about Sarah's kidnapping from the cargo vessel that was carrying her to her wedding. You do remember the wedding, don't you?"

Pettigrew shrank against the back of the chair, and Jake went on to outline the recent past as he now understood it—how Mustafa had arranged for Sarah's kidnapping and the sinking of the ship that bore her, determined there could be no evidence behind to give clues as to her whereabouts. Let his English partner think she was dead, and then oh so carefully let him

347

know that she was still alive and in his power.

If Pettigrew wanted to see his beloved safe, he would have to do whatever his Turkish partner demanded.

"At least that's the way I see it," said Jake, his voice hard. "Correct me if I've made a wrong assumption."

But Pettigrew was in no condition to do any correcting. "She was here?" he asked hoarsely. "In the seraglio?"

"Mustafa did not harm her. She escaped before he could. Your betrothed, or should I say the woman who was once your betrothed, proved more daring than her captors."

Jake left out any mention of his own part in her adventures. Neither did he see any purpose in revealing that she had been in the Grand Seraglio twice, once under the power of Harun. The sultan had not robbed her of her virginity. Jake had been the one to do that.

"When she tried to tell her story," he went on, "she was met with scorn at the embassy. Even you, I believe, scoffed at her tale of a conspiracy against the sultan."

"She did not tell of the kidnapping, only that she had overheard of the danger to Harun and had herself been seen." Pettigrew's face was flushed with indignation. "I did not scoff. I wanted to keep her safe."

"How?" asked Jake. "By keeping her close to the embassy where she could be ridiculed daily? Did you once defend her to that little bastard Somersby?"

"I—" Pettigrew swallowed. "I could not be certain of the source of danger to her. And there were those I needed to question before I spoke."

"Mustafa, you mean. Only he was out of the city arranging for the start of your business together."

Pettigrew's eyes darted to the sultan and back to Jake. "I have told you all I intend to, Mr. Price, until you tell me where Sarah is."

"You're not exactly in a bargaining position, Pettigrew. Sarah is where no one can harm her. That's all you need to know. There's one thing I'm curious about. Why did you enter into a secret agreement with Mustafa against the wishes of the sultan? Was it pure greed?"

Pettigrew did not meet Jake's scorching glare. "I have been a fool. That much I will admit to you, but no more. I wish to talk to Harun. Alone."

"For a man in trouble, you make a lot of demands."

"What I have to say is for the sultan alone to hear. An assault has been made against his life. I assume the gunshots outside the embassy are associated with—" he stumbled over the words—"with the matter at hand."

Harun spoke. "Mr. Price, I ask that you and your friend wait in the garden. It is quite lovely in the late afternoon."

The sultan spoke as he always had, with calm authority, but around his eyes and mouth there was a strain that had not been there before the news of his son's betrayal.

Jake started to argue, then realized he had little choice but to accept the sultan's hospitality. As he and Bandit walked from the small room, they left behind them a pair of solemn, graying men surrounded by a cadre of armed guards.

The garden was an open space lined with tall cypress trees, cloistered walkways, and low buildings. Paths wound among beds of flowering shrubs, and the whole was meticulously trimmed. For all the skullduggery that took place behind those surrounding walls, it was an island of serenity.

At one end lay the Gate of Felicity, through which was the walkway into the harem. Two additional gardens existed for the women—one for those belonging to Harun and one for the women who were slaves to Mustafa. It was the latter that Jake had seen. No men other than eunuchs and the sultan were allowed behind that gate—except for the day when he and Bandit had come for Sarah. It seemed security even in a sultan's harem could be breached.

So many voluptuous, half-clad women had thrown themselves at him that day, all claiming to want the scented oil he rubbed onto his hands. The only one Jake could think of was Sarah and the way she had, through stubborn audacity, insinuated herself under his massage. Just as his hands had done, his thoughts lingered on her silken skin.

He breathed deeply of the flowery scent that hung on the warm evening air and thought of the way her skin held that same scent, as though she herself were some precious blossom, the fruit of an exotic plant.

Everywhere he looked he thought of her; everywhere in the city, on the island, and across the open waters which linked the two, he thought of those impudent, flashing eyes and that golden hair that had trapped the sunlight.

Jake had no experience in dealing with such singlemindedness except where the sea was concerned. It made no difference whether he liked it or not; he couldn't get her out of his mind.

Did other men remember women with the same detail? He glanced at Bandit, who walked beside him among the lengthening shadows of the garden, his eyes downcast.

Jake took a swallow of the thick, sweet coffee that

one of the guards had brought. "Are you thinking of Nadire?"

"The memory of her lingers."

Jake understood.

"Psst." The hiss came from behind them and to one side.

They halted.

Again, "Psst."

Jake turned toward the sound and saw only a moving shadow in the dimly lit cloister beside the garden.

"If the Bossman would excuse me for a moment . . ."

Jake nodded, but Bandit had already taken his leave. Cousin or Nadire, he wondered. He decided on the woman.

Bandit disappeared into the dimness, and Jake turned his attention once again to his pacing. He didn't understand why his friend's rendezvous with the beautiful slave should upset him, but it did.

It was a day for being upset, and for reasons beyond his haunted recollections. Part of the anger he had felt when he talked to Pettigrew had been directed toward himself, he readily admitted. Sir Edward had foisted his daughter off on an unscrupulous man, but Jake had gone along with the plans when he arranged for her journey to the embassy. Worse, he had made the decision to do so after visiting Pettigrew and deciding the shipowner was a pompous fool. The one act that left him with self-respect was his refusal to accept the bastard's reward.

Sarah had been, despite her impatience, so damned cool and reasonable when they'd left her in the safety of the apartment a few hours ago. Not at all like the woman he had come to—

He stopped. He had come to what?

Here he was back to her again. Hell's fire! He wasn't given to pondering his emotions. He liked a good time, was reasonably considerate in seeing that the woman he was with had a good time, too, and made sure he didn't hang around too long. He had been satisfied with the roving days no woman could ever accept. He had wanted those days above all else. So what was happening to him that he couldn't forget a blue-eyed hellion who had more courage than good sense?

He wondered what the hellion was doing now. How would she react when she learned of Pettigrew's dealings with Mustafa and of the indirect way he had been involved in the massacre aboard the ship? Jake didn't welcome the idea of telling her. Somehow or other she'd twist things around until she blamed herself for the loss of life.

Darling Sarah. She worked for the unfortunate children of London in secret, took on the worries of the world, and yet she could openly run away with an American sailor and live with him for a short while in wantonness. Never once had she blamed Jake for making her what those in her class would label a fallen woman. And they would do so loudly and often. Too well did he remember the embassy ball.

America was the refuge that she chose. From London, from Ralph, and from him.

He was the one who usually did the leaving. Sarah had turned his life completely upside down.

"Bossman," said Bandit from the shadows. "The sultan joins us."

In an instant, the area of the garden where Jake stood was surrounded by robed guards. Harun stepped through them. "Let us walk."

Hands behind him, he began to pace slowly, Jake

at his side. Bandit remained behind.

It was a full two minutes before the sultan spoke.

"Mr. Pettigrew has returned to his home, a penitent man. He is also one I can understand."

"The sultan shows much forbearance," said Jake. "I figured you would throw him in the nearest Turkish jail."

"He has broken no law. Not of Turkey nor of his own land. I am not a barbarian, Mr. Price. I will not go down in history as such."

"No," said Jake, "I don't imagine that you will."

"Mr. Pettigrew is a man ten years younger than my sixty years, yet we are of the same generation. We both feel life slipping away. We both want something to give us purpose . . . to give us, how do the French say it? A *raison d'etre*. A reason for living. I have chosen my country as my cause. I wish to see it take its place in the world beside the other powers. To be an equal with England and France. To face the Russian bear with courage and strength."

He paused in their walk, lost in thought, then looked at Jake. "Mr. Pettigrew has chosen the lovely Miss Whitlock."

"Are you saying he loves her?"

"With all of his heart. Any man, Mr. Price, be he sultan or beggar, can hold a great passion in his heart. Age can slow the body, but it cannot completely quench the fires."

"If Pettigrew had a burning passion for his betrothed, then why get himself involved in something that he knew was dangerous? Especially when she was on her way to their wedding."

"It was precisely because of that passion that he did so. His business suffered. Losses of ships and cargo, which he conjectures now were not the result of storms but of an ugly plan. He feared his only hold on the young woman was his wealth. He feared that he alone was not enough to satisfy her wants. Just as I have not been able to satisfy the wants of my son.''

Jake did not know how to respond, and he chose silence. Again they began to walk.

"I owe you much," Harun said as they turned direction back toward where their walk had begun. The sun had dropped behind the horizon, and as if on command, the lanterns along the surrounding walkways brightened.

"You owe me nothing.''

"Mr. Price, you are a man of much pride. Listen to what I say. There are those who fear telling the sultan what he does not wish to hear. In centuries past my noble ancestors would have taken your head. You brought me news of much sadness. You did not try to soften its harshness. You accused Pinar, but I think you also suspected the perfidy of my son.''

"The idea had crossed my mind," confessed Jake.

"I repeat, I owe you much. I insist you let me make amends for keeping Miss Whitlock here against her wishes. Please understand. I wish my country to be friends with the West—to be a part of this wonderful nineteenth century—but I cannot forsake the old ways completely. I do not use the women of my harem as I once did; but they are still my women, and for a while so was she.''

He halted. "So name what it is you want. I cannot let you leave without something. I have a palace of treasures. All is yours." A smile briefly crossed his lips. "Except, of course, the golden mask.''

Jake didn't know what to say. He looked at Bandit, who stood a dozen yards away. And then he knew.

"I want one of your women.''

Harun's eyes widened. "This is not usually done, you understand. But since I am no use to them, one night perhaps would do no harm. I fear, however, it will make the chosen one grow discontented after you leave."

"I don't mean for me. I want freedom for one of your women. The slave girl Nadire. She was a friend to Sarah. I ask that she be allowed to leave with me and my servant."

Bandit heard him. Jake could see it in his eyes.

"To grant freedom to a slave?" asked Harun. "Never have I done such a thing."

The authority was back in Harun's voice. Jake wondered if he had gone too far.

"In the past few weeks I've done a lot of things I never did before, Your Highness. It's practically become a way of living, this breaking from the old ways. How do the French say it? It's my *raison d'etre*."

A brief silence followed, and Jake knew he had won his point when the sultan smiled. "Consider your request granted. I will send for her."

Bandit coughed. "That won't be necessary, Your Highness. I believe she is nearby."

From out of the shadows Nadire, veiled and robed, stepped beside him. Her eyes were downcast.

Harun walked closer. He lifted her chin and gently lowered her veil. His whispered words were in Turkish and indecipherable to Jake. Nadire made no response. The veil was returned to its proper place, and he said, "I have given her the freedom you have requested."

He turned to face Jake. "The hour grows late, and there is much that weighs heavily on my mind. Let us hope, Mr. Price, that when we meet again, it will be on a happier occasion."

There was such sadness in his eyes that Jake wondered if the powerful and wealthy ruler of millions would ever be happy again.

Outside the gates they found one of the sultan's carriages waiting to bear them back to the apartment.

Back to Sarah. Jake found he could not face her, not until he had decided what to say to her. How cool she was with her decision to go to America. He wasn't cool about it at all.

As they rode through the twisting streets, pedestrians and vehicles alike moving quickly out of the path of the recognizable equipage of their exalted ruler, Nadire sat in wide-eyed silence, and Jake gave brief instructions to Bandit. Sarah should be told that the sultan, needing no corroboration from her, had taken the news of the conspiracy well, that Pinar had confessed to arranging the shooting, and that in compensation for Sarah's earlier imprisonment, Harun had given Nadire her freedom.

There was no reason tonight for her to learn of Ralph Pettigrew's involvement in the scheme. Tomorrow was soon enough for the delivery of that particular bit of news.

Jake would remain in the carriage while Sarah greeted her friend from the seraglio. He would give them the night to talk. Bandit could stay or go as he saw fit, but then he always did.

And Jake would keep busy elsewhere. It was time he checked back at the coffee house of Faruk. Fatima perhaps had returned to take her place on the small stage. If not, he might be able to pick up a clue as to exactly where she had gone.

Sarah paced the length of the room, pivoted, and retraced her steps with the conclusion that somehow it had shrunk during the days she had spent on the island. Never had she felt so hemmed in. Even in the depths of the Grand Seraglio, she'd not had this urge to gasp for breath, this need to see the open sky.

The source of her discontent was easy to settle on— her relationship with Jake. Too long had she been strong around him. Too long had she pretended that her heart wasn't torn in two at the thought of leaving Turkey without him.

Too long had she risked losing all.

The journey from the island to the city had been the most difficult time of her life, and she had gone the entire way without breaking down once. Jake probably thought she slept the night they had lain in the small sleeping quarters. He had probably been relieved that she was taking their imminent good-bye with such nonchalance.

But maybe not. She had caught him looking at her when he thought she didn't know it. She had liked the pensive look on his face, especially the lines of worry that appeared for the first time between his thick black brows. She liked them very much. She was suffering. Let him do a little of the same.

What if—the thought had struck her during the long hours while he was with the sultan—he had begun to care for her in the same way she cared for him and was too stubborn to admit it? What if, like her, he was too proud to put his feelings into words? Pride had always been her source of strength, but it could just possibly be her downfall, too.

Her pace increased. She seemed to be running after the elusive answers to the all-important questions. The only possible thing to do was tell him how she felt. She would know right away whether she had made a mistake.

At last came a knock at the door. She came to a halt and wondered why he did not just unfasten the lock and enter as he usually did. Perhaps he was showing concern. A gentled Jake. She smiled at the thought.

Or perhaps it wasn't Jake asking entry. Perhaps the sultan had taken great offense that one of his trusted viziers could be accused of seeking his death. Perhaps—

She flung open the door and stared at the veiled woman on the threshold. She took a moment to respond.

"Nadire!"

"Missy Sarah, hello."

So ready had Sarah been to fling her arms around Jake, she did not know what to say. Behind Nadire stood Bandit. Never had she seen such a smile on his face.

And Jake—

She saw the high, gilded carriage that occupied much of the street behind the pair. She saw the shadowed figure inside. She saw the driver stir on his perch, heard the crack of the whip over the broad black rumps of the horses, and watched as the carriage got under way, taking the shadowed figure with it.

No more than a few seconds had passed, but in that brief span she had felt the death of hope. Incredible and hurtful as it was to her, Jake was riding away. It would seem that despite her deepest wishes, last night had been a portent of all the nights to come.

Her eyes burned with unexpected tears. She blinked them away. And, oh, how proud she was of her smile.

Her show of pleasure was not insincere.

"Nadire," she said, stepping aside, "please forgive me for keeping you outside. It's only the shock of seeing you here, not the degree of my delight."

In the privacy of the room, Bandit delivered the messages Jake had discussed concerning the evening's events. "Bossman gives the women time to talk. I will do the same."

"How thoughtful of him."

Bandit looked curiously at her. She met his stare straight on. He excused himself and left, and Sarah locked the door behind him.

At her back, Nadire said, "It was Aga Jake who arranged for me to leave the Grand Seraglio." Her voice softened. "Perhaps the missy wishes he were here in my place."

Sarah turned. "I would be a fool to wish such a thing, would I not?" She managed a smile. "Men can be such an encumbrance."

She gestured for her visitor to sit beside her at the table. With veil lowered and hood thrown back, Nadire was as lovely as Sarah remembered her—wide velvet-brown eyes set in a slender face, and her skin the color of creamed tea.

"You're free, Nadire," she said. "Do you have any idea what that means?"

"It means," Nadire said with a shrug, "that I am poor and alone with no one to care for me. It means I must find another man, one far poorer than the sultan, one who will very likely not have my respect."

The answer took Sarah aback.

"Did you not tell the sultan you had no wish to leave the Grand Seraglio?"

"Missy Sarah, one does not tell the sultan what one wishes to do. Not even an English woman, or do you not remember?"

Sarah remembered.

"What about Bandit? He seemed inordinately proud to escort you here tonight."

"He showed much interest in me," Nadire responded flatly, "when I was not available. I fear the condition of my slavery was much of my charm."

"You judge him too harshly. He is a good man."

Nadire's features softened. "My worries drive me to harshness. He is what you say. Yet his talk in the carriage was not of the care he would provide me, but of the freedom that I now possess. He did not ask, nor did he seem to wonder, whether I might know what to do with such a condition."

"Perhaps he wanted you to enjoy a time in which you owed allegiance to no man."

"Then he truly does not know me very well. As I have said, Missy Sarah, the condition of my slavery could have been what drew his interest to me. I must consider at least the possibility I will be left alone and make my plans in accordance."

"Left alone. . . ." Sarah thought of Jake. For her, it was more than just a possibility.

"Well," she said briskly, "we will just have to work out some solution that will keep you from being any kind of slave."

Nadire shook her head. "In my country all women are slaves, whether they be wives or concubines or odalisques." The hint of a smile tugged at her lips and lightened her delicate features. "I must confess, Missy Sarah, that I am nevertheless pleased to taste for a moment this sweet fruit of freedom."

At the moment Sarah felt a great kinship with this young woman who, though the same age, had lived a vastly different life from her own. Nothing must spoil this time for her. Keeping busy was the solution for avoiding worry, or so it had been for Sarah through the years.

"Have you ever been to the Grand Bazaar?" she asked impulsively.

Nadire shook her head. "Some of the more favored women have gone by carriage with their eunuch guards. I have never been so trusted."

"It's a place of wonder," Sarah said. "Beautiful objects from all over the world. Tomorrow we will go there and buy you some clothes and whatever personal items you might need."

"I have no money—"

"We will borrow from one of the men. I'm running up quite a bill with them, but before long I expect to be earning a salary of my own and repay my debts. Now," she said, a determined light settling in her eyes, "let us put our minds together and see if we can't come up with a solution that will solve the problems that we share."

Chapter Twenty-Four

As they prepared to retire for the night, Sarah tried to force upon Nadire the loan of a chemise and petticoat, but the girl could see no use for such excesses on a warm night. After much pondering on whether to choose the floor as her resting place instead of the feather bed, which she claimed "smothers one who is not used to its strangeness," she slept naked beneath the light covers beside Sarah, who took for herself the underclothing as night wear.

Nadire muttered often in her sleep, offering Sarah hints that her newly acquired freedom was not yet accompanied by peace of mind, but the words were in Turkish and gave no clue as to their meaning except through the harsh tone of their deliverance.

The next morning they dressed in the traditional caftans of Turkish women, their veils close at hand, and waited for the return of one of the men.

Bandit was the one who arrived. Sarah's feeling of having been deserted by Jake, unfair though it might be, grew sharper, but it was not mingled with surprise.

Nadire kept her eyes downcast as Bandit took her hands in his and greeted her good morning. They spoke in Turkish, and Sarah felt like an intruder.

Lifting her veil and hood in place, she stepped into the doorway, her back to the whispering pair, but she really did not care to walk boldly into the street and leave them completely alone. With the way her luck ran, a galloping horse would trample her the moment she stepped out of doors or, worse, its rider would scoop her into his arms and carry her away for ransom.

Thus kidnapped, she would be on her own to make her escape, Jake having obviously done all the rescuing he planned—and, in truth, far more than she had any right to expect, no matter how much her heart told her different.

Sarah was hard at work convincing herself she no longer needed his help. During her discussions with Nadire the previous evening, she had come up with an idea. If, as Nadire feared, Bandit proved inconstant and she found herself truly on her own, then the two women would simply join forces and take their leave together.

Sarah wanted to go to America. She would need a traveling companion. Nadire needed a place where she could move, too.

Forged in the heat of unhappiness and hammered by necessity, her plan took care of them both. Nadire worried about putting further distance between her and the only security she had ever known, but in the end she reluctantly agreed.

Sarah turned and caught the dusky-skinned beauty staring soulfully into another pair of warm dark eyes.

Don't depend too heavily on Nadire.

Sarah's self-directed warning was one that years of independence had left her able to heed.

When Bandit and Nadire showed no signs of breaking the silent communication, she coughed delicately.

"Missy Sarah," Nadire said, her olive cheeks blushing innocently. No one in the world, Sarah thought, would ever believe where the girl had spent most of her life.

Sarah felt a pang of jealousy. "To the bazaar," she announced and headed out. Galloping horses be damned.

Bandit and the veiled Nadire caught up with her, and they made the short walk to the bazaar in silence through the noisy, crowded streets, the women playing their meek parts with eyes directed to their shuffling feet. The sky was a fathomless blue, marked only by the orange disk rising over the minarets of a mosque to the east. Heat waves hovered in the air like hummingbirds. A hot wind blew from the south, and the dust that it stirred settled in Sarah's throat, its arid grit tasting of the deserts from Algiers to Damascus. The caftan scratched against her skin.

As trickles of sweat pooled between her breasts, she remembered with longing the cool breeze of the island. It had blown off the water like a gift. With surprising fondness she recalled the sand borne by that breeze, which told her more than any of her discomforts what a sad state she was in.

As they paused near the entrance, she glanced at Bandit and heard herself ask, "Will Jake be joining us later?"

She could have bitten off her tongue.

"This I do not know," said Bandit.

"I assumed you spent the night with him on the boat," Sarah said, for all her chagrin unable to keep quiet.

Bandit did not have to tell her that the assumption had been wrong.

So where was he? The question would not leave her mind.

Grabbing Nadire's arm, she guided her toward the corridor down which worked the peddler who had sold her the peasant garb an eternity ago. Before she'd seen Ralph. Before the embassy ball. Before the second journey to the island.

The high, arched ceilings and labyrinthine passageways, the colors and babble and aromas that had once overwhelmed her and filled her with awe, had little effect on her now. There might be spices and incense hanging on the close air, there might be the indecipherable chattering and arguing and laughter of men who spoke a different language from her, there might be the treasures of porcelain and rugs and tiles in every stall they passed, but she was cognizant of none of them.

They came to the peddler, whose wares were just as Sarah had remembered them. They held no fascination for her now. As Nadire made her selections, urged on by Bandit, Sarah stood in the background and reflected. Such musings were becoming her besetting sin.

Perhaps Jake had not deserted her; it seemed incredible that he should do so with such cruel suddenness after the past few days of perfect bliss. Bandit had said the sultan took the news of his vizier's betrayal well—no other details, just that— but what if, to save her worry, he had lied? What if Jake had been detained for further questioning, and Nadire, ignorant of the true circumstances, freed in his stead?

Things could have gone that way. Sarah had assumed it was Jake in the carriage last night. She had felt it. Whenever he was anywhere near, he seemed to put out invisible waves which curled about her senses and held her in thrall.

But what if for once her feelings had been wrong?

Nadire had never said outright that it was Jake riding away, and neither had Bandit.

She grew impatient to get outside and question the two of them more thoroughly. Silently she cursed herself. Here she had been thinking Jake was already putting her out of his mind—or at the very least helping her to forget him—and all the while he could very easily be incarcerated in the sultan's dungeon.

She tried to think where such a dungeon might be.

Practically dragging Nadire down the dim, crowded corridors, Bandit scurrying to keep up, she hurried into the sunlight. It seemed a thousand people, peddlers and pedestrians alike, had congregated in front of the bazaar, and every one of them was speaking at the top of his voice. She dragged Nadire away from the crowd into a quieter side street where they might talk without having to shout. Stone buildings gray with dust lined what was little more than a narrow lane, and she was grateful for the relative calm.

Perhaps in the quieter surroundings her own agitation could abate. She felt rather like the first fish she had landed on the island, flopping back and forth with no direction, guided only by fear.

"Miss Whitlock," Bandit called as he hurried to keep close behind.

Sarah did not respond except to nod with her head that he should follow. During their short stay in the bazaar, ribbons of clouds had made latticework of the sky. Despite their presence, the heat of the day seemed to have doubled, and the caftan cut off any cooling air that might possibly make its way to her itching, damp skin. Beneath the hood her hair lay thickly against her neck, and the veil came close to suffocating her; but the worst of her afflictions abided in her heavy heart.

Blinking at the brightness of the sun, she let go of Nadire's arm.

"Bandit—" she began, unmindful that as a woman she was not expected to speak in public.

The hoofbeats of an approaching horse and the rattle of the carriage warned her to step close to the near stone wall.

A woman's shrill cackle cut through the noise of horse and buggy. It was followed by the deep roll of a man's echoing laugh. Familiar invisible waves enfolded her. The clatter of the carriage became a roar as the blood rushed to her head. She could no longer hear the sounds of hilarity, but she did not need to in order to know the identity of the man.

Hooves pounded against the street directly behind her, and the carriage wheels flirted with the hem of her robe. She whirled in time to get a clear view of the passengers, their backs to the driver, their bodies leaning close. The woman was gossamer veiled, and her head was thrown back in gaiety. Beside her on the open seat, his lean face broken by a matching smile, was Jake.

For a searing moment their eyes met—and then with a clatter and a cloud of dust the carriage was gone. The woman was not Fatima, Sarah thought with the last vestiges of rationality, but her heavily decorated eyes which flashed up at Jake and her fine features faintly discernible through the veil gave evidence she was just as beautiful as the Turkish dancer.

Jake had not wasted any time in finding a replacement for his soon-to-leave English woman. Sarah could not recall that he had ever made her laugh in just such a way, and she gave in to a blinding hurt.

A supporting hand slipped under her arm, but she did not know or care whose. Leaning against the rough stone wall, she fought for breath. Who would have thought mere emotion could bring such pain? No one had ever told her a heart truly could break.

"Missy Sarah."

"Miss Whitlock."

The last thing Sarah wanted right now was pity. All she really needed was a minute—or a year—of solitude. It seemed typical of her life's experience that in this most desperate of moments she would find the former given to her in unwanted abundance and the latter impossible to attain.

She did not know how she managed to shake off the supportive hand and the concerned questions as to her well-being, words being impossible for her, and gestures weak. Somehow she let Nadire and Bandit know she was all right—or if not all right, at least capable of walking back to the apartment without the use of their support or the carriage Bandit offered to hire.

She had known she would have to leave . . . had made no demands . . . had expected nothing in the way of commitment from him. But a woman caught in the snares of unrequited love was vulnerable to an anguish that had no connection with reason. It was one thing to know the man she loved did not love her in return. It was quite another to see him wooing someone else.

Jake might at least have waited until she was on a departing ship.

When Bandit offered to see her to the room and then escort Nadire to the *Angel*, where she could change into her newly purchased clothes, Sarah gave no argument. He took time to buy a basket of fruit from a passing vendor and placed it on the table with a suggestion that she sort amongst the figs and pomegranates and grapes for her breakfast.

Sarah removed the hood and veil. "I'm not—"

Bandit left again before she was finished.

Nadire, standing beside her in the warm apartment, said, "He wishes only to help."

Sarah avoided her eyes. "There's no need to coddle me. I was merely overcome with heat."

"Perhaps. Nevertheless, it is best to let him complete the tasks he has set for himself. Like the dervishes who whirl themselves into a fever in worship of Allah, he becomes caught in his purpose."

Bandit returned within minutes, a swarthy Turk behind him bearing a water barrel. The wooden container was deposited in the corner of the room, and the Turk departed.

"For drinking and for a bath," Bandit said.

She thanked him, assured Nadire once again that it had been the heat which overcame her, and ignored the searching looks in the two pairs of dark eyes that refused to leave her face.

As the door closed behind them, she came close to giving in to her grief.

But Sarah had behind her a lifetime of accepting rejection that she could call upon. It had made her strong. Whatever suffering she was going through was no one's fault but her own. She had dropped her defensive shell of certainty that she and Jake must part . . . had allowed the tantalizing dreams of *what if* to soothe her troubled soul. For those few sweet moments of possibility, she must now pay the price.

If she could only remove the robe that rubbed against her skin like sandpaper, then she could begin to have some physical relief. If she concentrated long and hard enough on matters of such inconsequence, she might find herself able to blunt the razor-edged thoughts that scraped across her mind.

Stripping away her clothes as she might have taken the peeling from the fruit, she poured a pitcher of water into the bowl on the corner table. Unmindful of the puddles she was leaving on the floor, she splashed the cooling liquid against her reddened body, but the inadequate bath left her feeling itchier than ever.

Grabbing up a brush, she attacked her damp and tangled hair with the vengeance she could turn on nothing else. What a sight she must be, pacing back and forth on the Persian rug, wearing nothing more than a rash from the heat and raking through her long pale hair as though, like Lady Godiva, she were preparing for a ride through the streets.

Except that Sarah was restricted to this damnable room with its memories and confining walls. If only she could confine her contemplations as well.

A course of action was what she needed—a carefully deliberated series of steps through which she could get from this one-room prison in the heart of Constantinople to the shores of the United States. With or without Nadire, although she rather thought she would be going alone. Her emotional state would just have to take care of itself. She had other things to plan.

Even with the aid of the inimitable Bandit, she would find the leaving difficult—there were so many things she needed to do. First must come a visit to the embassy. Lord Stratford de Redcliffe could not turn her away. The same story that had been given to the sultan, she would give to the ambassador. She would tell him about the bravery of the English crew of the *Leviathan* and the truth about the deaths of all aboard.

She would, of course, gloss over her first kidnapping. She had, after all, been destined for Mustafa's harem, and that was where she had finally gone.

Ralph, too, had to be seen. She must have humiliated him at the embassy ball, even more than she herself had been humiliated. He deserved to hear firsthand what had happened to her and why she had run away. If he would see her, she would give him the opportunity to tell her directly that they would no longer suit.

It was true she had promised Jake not to leave the room, but that was before he had gone to the Grand Seraglio and had made promises of his own, at least by implication, that he would return. Somehow other things had supplanted her in his mind.

Fumbling through the valise she had brought back from the island, she pulled out her best gown, the blue dimity which was wrinkled beyond acceptability. It would have to do. Smoothing it across the bed, she searched further for her underclothing. First came the chemise and drawers, and with the latter came the memory of Jake's critical eyes when he studied them for the first time. She hadn't worn them often around him.

Turkish dancers never wore them at all.

Sarah shivered. She hadn't thought it possible to remember sounds with any clarity, but she could very well recall the clatter of the approaching carriage and, worse, the exact pitch of the unknown woman's laugh and, of course, the answering deep-throated chuckle from Jake.

A heaviness pulled at her heart.

What were they doing now?

Shaking hands reached for her petticoats.

Had they gone to the woman's quarters? Or had he taken her to the *Angel*, thus causing an embarrassing encounter with Bandit and Nadire? Which, of course, might not have been all that embarrassing. She was the one who objected to the company he kept.

The dress whispered over her head, and the skirt billowed gently over the petticoats. She had to work at the back buttons, but through sheer determination completed the task. Stockings and white slippers, hair in a knot at her neck—she looked quite proper, except for the thousand wrinkles in her gown.

She debated whether or not to wear the robe. The debate lasted no more than a few seconds. She was English, not Turkish. She would get more attention on the streets—and a hired carriage that much faster—if she went out as she was. Scarface could not possibly be after her, the schemes against the sultan having been exposed. Besides, she wasn't thinking about her safety; she was concentrating on getting away.

With her reticule and locked valise in one hand, she reached for the door, took a deep breath, and flung it open.

Her progress was halted by a looming body in dark shirt and fitted trousers.

"Jake!"

He stood on the threshold no more than a foot away. Ebony hair fell across his forehead; his lips were tight, his eyes blue-black stones.

"It would seem, Angel," he said with icy calm, "that I have arrived just in time."

Sarah found she could better concentrate if she did not look directly at him, and she shifted her gaze to the heat waves that rippled in the air behind him and on to the increasingly cloudy sky.

"It makes no difference whether you're here or not. I have decided to leave."

He glanced at the valise. "So I see." But he made no move to let her by.

Sarah forced her eyes to his. "I should think you would be glad to bid me good-bye."

"And so I should."

The hard lines of his face softened briefly, and Sarah wished with all her heart she could for that moment read his mind.

"I figured you were going to do something foolish again," he said. "That's why I hurried back."

Sarah stared at him. Getting out of the sultan's carriage last night would have been hurrying back. Shedding himself of a Turkish whore with whom he had spent the night was not.

She whirled away from him to hide the welling tears. Fury was her best weapon against the more vulnerable emotions assailing her, and she had no trouble mustering it from its place just below the layers of her anguish.

"Then summon me a carriage and I'll go in safety to the embassy."

"You're angry, Sarah—"

Her spine stiffened. "How clever of you to notice. I thought you would have the courtesy of at least reporting what happened with Harun. Instead—" She could not force herself to go on.

He slammed the door closed, and she heard the lock fall into place. "You've got last night all figured out, haven't you? I'm a genuine bastard."

She pivoted to face him. "You said it, not I."

The look of pain on his face struck her with all the

power of a physical blow and threw her into confusion.

"And you, of course, are the English lady who is hurrying along toward the inevitable end to her foreign adventures," he said.

She must have been mistaken. What she had taken for hurt was in truth anger that she dared be upset with him.

"You were the one who insisted the end was inevitable, Jake, not I. I simply agreed."

Jake laughed sharply. "There's nothing simple about anything you do. For a while there you had me so confused that I almost changed my mind."

Sarah could hardly believe his words. What did he expect her to do, pant like a happy puppy because he had *almost* decided she could hang around for a while?

"Get out of my way, Jake," she ordered with all the hauteur she could command.

He jerked the valise and reticule from her hand and tossed them aside. Sarah stepped backward and felt the frissons of fear ripple up and down her spine.

"At least, Miss Whitlock," he said, narrowing the distance between them, "you have convinced me beyond any doubt that I was right."

She watched his mouth while he talked, felt the warm breath stroke her cheek, and recognized the tingling in her spine as a sensation far more dangerous than simple fear. Inhaling, she caught the sickly sweet scent of a woman's cheap perfume.

She drew back her hand to slap him, but he caught her wrist and twisted it against his chest.

"You'd make a damned poor fighter, Sarah. Don't you know by now that your talents to subdue me lie in a far different direction?"

She struck out with her free hand, but it, too, became imprisoned with its mate.

"It seems I have one more lesson to teach you," he whispered huskily, pulling her hard against him, his eyes burning into hers. "The right way for a man and woman to say good-bye."

Chapter Twenty-Five

Sarah rebelled against his arrogance and fought her rising desire.

"I know what's got you upset," she said, twisting her bound wrists to no avail. "You never thought I would be the one to walk away."

Jake continued to hold her against his rigid body. "Who leaves first has nothing to do with how I feel."

"Quit lying to yourself. And to me. You want to make love to me one last time, and then, as you have a habit of doing, you can be the one to leave."

"Give any reason you want to it, Sarah, but we will make love." His eyes glittered darkly. "One last time."

Sarah wanted to pound against his chest, to cry out her denial of what he said, but the rush of warmth that spread through her trembling body spoke louder than any words that he was right. *One last time.*

She was filled with self-loathing that she could be so vulnerable to him. He carried another woman's scent and the memories of another woman's body enfolding him and giving him pleasure. She wanted to hurt him as much as he was hurting her, but how could she when he did not love her?

Jake's feelings—including his sense of responsibility for her—sprang from carnal lust. She knew that as well as she knew anything.

She stared at the sharp lines of his face, at his bristle-shadowed cheeks, at his lips waiting hungrily only inches from hers. Where was the anger; where was the pride that would help her fight him and her own weak will?

She could not look away from his mouth. How sensual it was, tight and slightly parted, ready to do its will. It was a mouth capable of giving and claiming pleasure. But it was also a mouth that told lies.

Anger and disgust flared anew, and again she tried to twist away; but her wrists were bound tightly by one of his hands, and the other was pressed against her back. She was his captive. Or so he thought.

Drawing still, she forced her eyes to his. "Let me go."

"Not so easily," he said. "Not just yet."

"Let me go," she repeated, this time in a suggestive whisper.

Miraculously, the steel fingers eased their hold, but the mark of them lingered on her skin, reminding her of the tattoo of entwining lovers she had seen on the forearm of the *Leviathan*'s chief mate. She hated the redness, wanting no visible evidence of Jake's power over her.

She spread her hands against his chest and felt beneath her palm the beating of his heart. Knowing he expected a caress, she shoved with all her strength and jumped away from him.

"Go back to your Turkish whore," she hissed. "I am not yours to be taken whenever you wish."

But Jake was not so easily deterred, and he stood tall and unmovable between her and the door. "I don't intend to take you against your will. That won't be necessary." His eyes glittered darkly. "You know it as well as I."

She whirled away from his knowing gaze. Shame washed over her. God help her, she wanted him and he knew it. Wanted him for that one last time. He had read it in her eyes. What was wrong with her that she could abandon everything she had ever believed about herself whenever he was near?

Blood pulsed thick and hot through her veins at the thought of what he demanded of her, and her own unbidden demands brought her breathing to the irregular rhythm that marked the beginnings of passion. If she fought him, he would take her, despite his denial. If she gave herself willingly, the result would be the same.

Suddenly his hands were on her shoulders.

"No!" she cried out.

As he turned her to him, she twisted her face, but she was not quick enough to escape the mouth descending on hers. She was truly trapped by him. Her lips were pliant under his, parting, tasting, and something inside of her exploded. Behind her closed eyes, unwelcome realizations skittered across her mind. Jake had removed her options of pride and self-respect. Lonely years stretched in front of her in endless, ugly progression. She thrust them from her mind.

She knew no shame. She must have today.

This time when her hands touched his chest it was to work at the buttons of his shirt and to feel the tightening of his muscles beneath her probing fingers.

Jake broke the kiss, and his hands, unemployed for only the briefest of moments, cradled her face, his thumbs tracing the outline of her mouth, then dipping inside to circle in the moisture he had once called *nymph's nectar* in one of his more lyrical moments on their private isle.

Sarah bit at the stroking thumbs, and Jake's fingers spread across her cheeks and tickled the outlines of her ears. She wanted to nestle herself against him at every fiery place he touched. As a sweet substitute, she suckled his thumbs.

"My God," he said.

His mouth descended to hers once again, and his tongue invaded. Sarah became a creature of passion, letting need wipe out all thoughts of regret or doubt or humiliation that she should be so completely his slave.

They worked at one another's clothes in hungry desperation as they had done so often before. His hands made quick work of the buttons that had taken her agonizing minutes to fasten, and the dimity slipped from her shoulders, drifting to the carpet like a blue descending cloud.

Jake paused only once, to stare at the unfeminine drawers.

"I never thought to see those again," he said huskily at he pulled them from her body.

Sarah kicked them aside and stood before him naked, then finished, with his help, undressing him.

She leaned forward and covered one of his nipples with her lips. Her reward was twofold—the salty taste of his body and the sharp intake of his breath. No longer could she detect the scent of another woman's perfume; Sarah inhaled only the male aroma she associated solely with Jake.

He worked at her carefully pinned-up hair, and in seconds she felt the weight of the bun lighten and the tresses tumble against her back.

Lifting her in his arms, he carried her to the bed

and covered her body with his. Sarah writhed under him, willing his flesh into hers, covering his lips, his face, his throat with her kisses. She gave herself no chance for thought or doubt.

He answered her passion with his own, hands and lips seeking and arousing her to new hungers, new desires. He lifted his head once. Smoldering-coal eyes burned a trail from the honeyed hair spread across the pillow, to her swollen lips, and to the slope of her throat and the rise of her aching, hard-tipped breasts.

His eyes branded her in the searing tour of her flesh. With a low cry she pulled him back to her, and then he was inside, filling her with his manhood as completely as thoughts of him filled her heart and mind.

"Jake!" she cried out at the moment of climax.

At his own moment of completion, he answered by whispering her name. She held tightly to him and to the dying waves of ecstasy that he had brought her. For this instant in time Jake was hers and she was his. Her rapture was like a brilliant light that burned across her mind, blinding her to everything but the oneness that was the product of their shared pleasure.

Cleaving herself to him, their sweat mingling, their pulses still pounding with a matched, erratic beat, she remembered that this was the last time.

Her throat ached with the tears she longed to shed. She could not face him, for then she would have to face the terrible truth that she did not regret what had just happened. She had taken everything he could offer her, and if it was not enough, that was only because she expected too much, expected things he had never promised.

When he first came into the room, he had indicated that perhaps he wanted her to stay; but it had only been a hint, and she knew that whatever he considered saying would be for just a little while.

More than anything else at the moment, Sarah feared clinging to him while he tried to extricate himself from her embrace. The ignominy of that act would be almost as unthinkable as was the projected lifetime she would somehow have to get through without him around to torment her.

But he made no attempt to draw away.

"Sarah—" The name was whispered into her tangled hair.

Here it came, that moment she dreaded. He would either say good-bye before she had a chance, or he would make the intimated offer to keep her for a while. Neither posture was endurable. And yet he might do worse and show her kindness and gentle regret—and worst of all, gratitude. She had, after all, shown him a very good time.

It was another unthinkable notion in a morning of mental agony. She could not abide his kindness nor any other attitude of its ilk. Rather scorn than charity. She had her memories. She would have to sift through them and keep the ones that carried the least pain.

Summoning the last store of her courage, she shifted her head so that she could look up at him. "You were right," she said. "You did not have to take anything from me."

She might as well have slapped him. He drew away from her fingers brushing the matted damp hair from his forehead. She was proud of that last, dangerous touch.

For one horrible moment she could not stand the expression on his face—so searching, so wary, as though he had not shared with her a time of supreme bliss.

She lifted her head and brushed her lips against

his. For truly the last time.

The look on his face softened, and his eyes met hers in warm affection. Of course they would. He had often gazed down at her in such a way after they had mated, and she took it for a masculine trait.

She wished that just once she had caught the same expression on his face after they fought. *That* would have been a test.

She managed a smile—admittedly not much of one, but at least it was an improvement over her swallowed tears.

"I'm glad you got back before I left, Jake."

The warmth died.

"And why is that?"

She could not hold the smile. Withdrawing from his embrace, she directed her gaze to the swirling plaster that patterned the ceiling. She could feel his eyes resting on her profile. At least she no longer had to mask the feelings that the direct sight of him aroused.

"Because, as you said, there was a better way of saying good-bye."

"Sarah—"

She gave him no chance to respond. "I was angry when I saw you in the carriage this morning. There's no use denying it." She tried to sound analytical of her feelings. She rather thought she managed very well to toss out a mild description of what had been the depths of despair.

She hurried on. "I can imagine what happened. You left me alone to visit with Nadire and got involved." Here she almost stumbled. "Bandit described the meeting with the sultan. The vizier confessed to conspiring in the assassination attempt, although there was no mention of a motive. Surely there was more to the plot than I've been told."

Jake didn't respond right away, and Sarah was forced to look at him. His head was propped on one hand, and he studied her with unblinking concentration. He reminded her of the Great Sphinx of Egypt. There was no reading what was behind those eyes.

"Is this really what you want to talk about?" he asked. "Sultans and viziers and shootings?"

She allowed herself one show of emotion. "Of course not, Jake." She sat up and bent her knees into her chest, her arms wrapped around them to keep from reaching out for him. Or to keep from striking him. She didn't know which she wanted to do more.

"I would prefer," she added, "to talk about how you taught me things I could have learned from no other man. That these past weeks have meant more to me than you can ever know. But what good would that do?"

The cursed lump in her throat returned. She swallowed hard. "We each have separate lives to get on with. I don't suppose there's anything more tiresome on the face of the earth than a love affair that has outlived the needs that gave it life. I wouldn't know for sure, of course, and you can correct me if I'm wrong."

Whatever he muttered, she could not with precision decipher, but she rather thought it had something to do with having almost made a terrible mistake.

He shifted from the bed and sat for a minute with his back to her. She stole a last glance at his beautiful body, then jerked her eyes away, deciding the glance had been a mistake. Just when she had been building her strength to leave, she *had* to look at him. As Papa said, she never knew when enough was enough.

Although, she reflected, the lofty Sir Edward would be very much chagrined to find that his daughter, hellion though he thought her, would apply his pronouncements to such a time.

"As a matter of fact," Jake said, directing his words to the floor, "Pinar did implicate someone else. Harun's son Mustafa."

"We were right."

"Yeah," said Jake. "We were right." He ran the fingers of one hand through his hair. "Get dressed, Sarah. I can't think with you sitting like that behind me."

She took wry pleasure from his words.

They each donned their clothes, backs to one another as though they were strangers in one of the Turkish baths. Without her asking, Jake fastened the buttons of her gown. He did so without once touching her.

It was a peaceful, domestic scene, she thought, at least to a casual observer if there could be such a one viewing a man and woman dressing after making love. The observer would have to look inside the hearts and minds of the two in order to realize there was nothing domestic about Jake and nothing peaceful about her.

As she bound her hair once again into a tight bun and splashed water on her face, she moved as if in a trance, forcing herself to perform the common acts of a woman who had not a care in the world. The worst part was ignoring the lingering feel of his skin that lay upon her body and the masculine scent that mingled with her own.

She turned to face him. "Did Pinar give any reason for the conspiracy?" As painful as the memories of her adventures were to her, they seemed the blandest subject for her to mention now.

For some reason Jake looked uncomfortable. "Greed. They wanted to trade in opium with the

Chinese. The problem was the sultan said no. It was part of his reform program for Turkey."

Harun was, indeed, an unusual man for his place and time, she thought, and was relieved to find that as time—even these heartbreaking, brittle minutes—separated her from the last giving of her physical love, she was able to think of someone other than Jake.

"That explains every point but one," she said. "My kidnapping. Or were they after something else aboard the ship?"

She thought for one frightening minute that he was going to take her hand in his, and she recoiled.

Jake made no attempt to persist. "He implicated Ralph, too."

"Ralph Pettigrew?" she asked in amazement, as though she had the acquaintance of a dozen Englishmen in Turkey with that given name. The picture of her righteous one-time fiancé plotting with a sultan's son to smuggle opium to the Orient was too ludicrous. "I don't believe it."

Jake shrugged. "Harun summoned him to the palace. He confessed to being part of the conspiracy. He was to supply the ships that would carry the drugs. Mustafa wanted you as insurance against Pettigrew's being struck by an English conscience and backing out. Of course, you got away before he could use you as such, but I don't think your capture was ever necessary. Your fiancé never threatened to withdraw."

"You heard this from Ralph's own lips?"

"Harun questioned him in private."

Sarah shook her head in disbelief. What a fool she was about men.

Papa . . . Ralph . . . Jake.

She glanced at the crumpled bedcovers, then stared

at the door.

"Forget Ralph for a minute, Sarah, and listen to me."

The urgency of his voice brought her attention back to him. Indeed, it never strayed from him for very long.

She met his gaze. "I'm listening."

"The woman this morning—"

"I understand." Sarah spoke quickly before Jake could apologize or, horror of all horrors, tell her she was better in bed. "I already told you that. I'm a woman of the world now," she said, grim but with her chin tilted against any argument he might make. "And we don't owe each other anything except maybe a thanks or two."

Jake stared at her for such a long time and with such an unreadable intensity that she thought she would break down.

"Maybe we don't, Sarah, maybe we don't. It looks like you're the one who's teaching me how to say good-bye."

"It's time you admitted I could teach you something."

"Oh, you have, Sarah Whitlock, lady of England. You have."

He spoke with a bitter regret that surprised her. For the life of her, she could think of nothing to say. A silence descended between them that held all of the anguish of their relationship and none of the joy. She wanted above all else to leave him with dignity. Picking up her valise and reticule from the floor where he had tossed them an hour ago, she managed a calm glance in his direction.

"Would it be possible for you to summon me a carriage?"

"You're not doing anything foolish like calling on

Pettigrew, are you?''

He still thought her a reckless fool.

"Don't be absurd," she said, although she had been considering just such a journey. "I'm going to the embassy. I rather think the ambassador will find time for me in his busy schedule, don't you?"

"Sarah—"

The teachings of a dozen governesses and nannies helped her to stiffen her spine. "Don't you dare touch me, Jake Price, or offer any thanks or apologies, or anything other than a simple 'Yes, Sarah, I'll get you the carriage.' "

She turned from him and faced the closed door.

"Yes, Sarah, I'll get you the carriage." Somehow the words sounded more sarcastic on his lips than they had on hers.

He brushed past her and went into the street.

Sarah kept her body rigid and concentrated on what she could say at the embassy. If she could think far enough ahead, she might forget that when Jake returned she truly would have to bid him farewell.

Chapter Twenty-Six

A half hour later Sarah answered a discreet knock at the apartment door and found a uniformed driver standing on the threshold.

"Matthews," she said in surprise.

"Miss Whitlock," he said with a bow.

The driver was just as she remembered him from the time before when he had taken her to the embassy—somber, pasty-faced, and straight-backed. If he harbored any surprise at repeating the journey, he kept it to himself.

As much as Sarah had been expecting Jake, she should have known he would send Matthews, or someone like him, in his stead. After all, she had asked him to get a carriage, and he had done no more than she wanted. He was also sparing them the embarrassment of a final confrontation. She should have been swept with relief, but there was nothing about this moment that was not filled with anguish. She knew the feeling would dwell in her heart forever.

For Sarah, prepared as she had tried to be to face the inevitable, the time of leaving came too abruptly.

"Give me a moment," she said and closed the door.

She drank in each detail of the room, the small carved table and chairs, the porcelain pitcher and bowl, the carpet.

Nadire had once told her that flaws, tiny and hard to find, were worked into the fibers of the finest Oriental rugs.

"So that the Evil Eye should not gaze upon perfection and grow jealous," she had explained. "Great suffering would be brought down upon those at fault."

Like the fine carpets, Sarah's affair with Jake was woven with imperfections. The Evil Eye need not worry her.

Last, she looked at the bed. Her gaze lingered on the rumpled covers. If she crushed them to her, she would still be able to detect the scent of their final lovemaking.

"Oh, Jake," she whispered and closed her eyes, letting a feeling of *déjà vu* wash over her. She had left him once before thinking never to return. Only this time was different. They had said their final farewells.

Sarah had been looking for patterns in her life; she saw them all too clearly now. Everything was happening in pairs: two trips to the Grand Seraglio, two to the island, and, thanks to Jake's careful arrangements, two by brougham to the British embassy.

The only occurrence that came with greater repetition was the times she and Jake made love. If she allowed herself to remember even one second of those times, she would break into the tears she had been holding inside.

And that, she must not do. Not now. Not yet.

Grabbing up her valise and cloak, she turned toward the door, but the hem of her dimity gown caught on one of the chairs and held her in place like a restraining hand. She yearned to take it as a sign that she was not meant to leave, but she knew that if it held any significance, it meant that she would never be completely free of that room.

Outside she noticed that black clouds had darkened the sky, and the air, still oppressively warm, held the humid threat of a coming storm. Bring on the rain, she thought, and let the heavens weep for her. She would not weep for herself.

Handing her belongings to Matthews, she glanced into the high carriage. An indistinct figure sat against the far side of the dark interior. Sarah caught her breath.

Could it be—

The figure shifted. "Missy Sarah," a soft voice said, "I hope it pleases you that I am here."

Sarah felt like a fool. She must not start looking for Jake in every shadow. He would never be there.

Allowing Matthews to help her inside, she smiled at the heavily robed and veiled woman who had once been her slave.

"Of course I am pleased," she said and on impulse hugged Nadire. "I am very happy to have you with me."

"Bandit said you would not wish to be alone."

An edge of distress in the girl's voice killed Sarah's already tenuous smile. Had Nadire been sent away by the man she loved? The question could not be put to her so bluntly, but Sarah's mind would not let the idea go. At least that same active mind held a plan that would accommodate them both. America. If circumstances allowed them to join their fates, they would have to concentrate on where they were going and not the people they would leave.

The carriage jerked into motion. They rode in

silence, each given to her private thoughts.

Arriving at the embassy, Sarah searched her feelings for signs of apprehension, but she searched in vain. She was dispassionately clear-headed and calm concerning her return, and she swept into the foyer as though she had not left it with disgrace almost two weeks before. The guard at the door was the same one who had witnessed her conversation with Jake. There were few people outside of the kitchen help who had *not* been witness to one or more scenes of that evening. With all that had happened to her, she found that she truly did not care.

The realization was liberating.

A dark-suited man in a stiff-collared shirt came through one of the doors that led off the entryway. Younger than the fortyish Phillip Somersby, he had a more businesslike look about him, not the personal, gossipy interest Somersby had shown in her plight.

It was another liberating thought.

"Good morning," he said. "May I help you?"

"You most certainly can." In her best no-nonsense voice, she introduced herself, asked that her maid be allowed to rest in a private room, and announced that she must see the ambassador right away. She stopped just short of making the latter a demand.

"Of course," said the junior diplomat without so much as a twitch of an eye. Instructing the guard to see that Nadire was escorted to a room upstairs, he turned to Sarah. "Lord Stratford has been hoping you would return, Miss Whitlock."

She took the news as a compliment. It seemed that the ambassador did not think her too cowardly to show her face again. If anything disturbed her calm, it was hostility—to everything and everyone in the

British sector of Constantinople outside of Lord Stratford himself.

In the ambassador's large private office, where portraits of Queen Victoria and Prince Albert covered much of one wall, she was met with a friendliness that she recognized as genuine.

Tall, slender, and gray-haired, Lord Stratford de Redcliffe saw that she was seated and provided with a welcome cup of tea, then proceeded to apologize for the events at the embassy ball.

"There has been much concern among our countrymen, and women, too, I should add, for your safety. We are not all as rude and unfeeling as you must have been thinking."

Sarah decided that the distinguished ambassador deserved his reputation as an able representative of the crown.

"Thank you," she said sincerely, "for not trying to pretend that the awful evening did not take place. But I've quite gotten over it. All I want is your attention for an hour. I'm afraid it will take that long to tell my story."

"There is nothing I would rather do than spend the afternoon with such a charming lady."

Yes, Sarah thought, he certainly was a diplomat. Her dress was wrinkled and her hair roughly pinned into a chignon, and if she didn't have dark circles under her eyes from exhaustion, it wasn't her fault or Jake's.

"What I have to say, Lord Stratford, is not charming, nor is it the sort of story you usually hear from a British lady. But I promise you, every word is the truth. I am not," she added, thinking of the sultan and his view of women, "without a degree of sense."

Sitting on the edge of her chair across from the ambassador's desk, she began slowly with a retelling of her journey aboard the *Leviathan*. Lord Stratford looked appropriately attentive. By the time she got to the first scimitar waving over the rail, she had her listener in thrall.

Sarah did not spare herself or make any attempt to sound like a heroine in the tale of her kidnappings and her two escapes from the Grand Seraglio. If she omitted any details, they were the ones concerning Jake's lost treasure and her affair with him, including the night she had danced for him at Faruk's coffee house.

But she told about the apartment in Stamboul and the island. Lord Stratford could draw his own conclusions about how she spent her time.

"Jake and Bandit have already told most of this to the sultan," she said in conclusion. "One of his viziers has confessed to plotting his assassination, implicating Mustafa as the instigator of all the trouble."

She hesitated. "He also implicated Ralph Pettigrew."

The ambassador's eyes widened. "Ralph?"

"Not in the assassination, Lord Stratford, and not in my kidnappings. In a scheme to smuggle opium from Turkey to China against Harun's wishes. Ralph was to provide the ships."

"I see." Lord Stratford paused. "It's not against British law, of course. Opium may not be used in England, but thus far Parliament has not seen fit to ban its sale or transport to other shores. Commerce with foreigners, it would seem, calls for different standards of ethics from those applied to our own citizens."

"Ralph needed money."

The ambassador's eyes rested on her face. "I can see where he would believe so."

"If you think I demanded it—"

"Not at all. Let us say, Miss Whitlock, that a fortune might make your betrothed feel more secure. You are a beautiful woman. And very young."

At that moment, Sarah felt as old as the Constantinople hills. "It's all such a mess, isn't it?"

"Even situations as complicated as this one can be sorted out." Again his intelligent eyes studied her. "You must be exhausted, my dear. Let me send for a fresh pot of tea."

How British, Sarah thought fondly, and declined.

His face softened. "Perhaps, then, a glass of sherry. You've been through more than any half dozen men I could name. And," he added with open admiration, "except for needing rest, have emerged unscarred."

Sarah had scars, all right, but they were ones that did not show.

"I'll take the sherry," she said.

Lord Stratford served them both a small glass. The liquid warmed her throat.

"What you have told me, Miss Whitlock, clears up a mystery or two. I've received overnight reports of activity within the walls of the serai," the ambassador said as he returned to the high-backed leather chair behind his desk. "Guards entering and leaving in greater numbers than usual. One report said Mustafa had disappeared. Word has gone out he is to be found and returned."

"You have spies in the palace?" Sarah asked in amazement. She half expected him to answer that he had a cousin or two within the walls. It was what Bandit would have said.

"Not spies. We prefer to call them informants. But they have told me little in comparison with your news. I must speak with them about their efficiency."

Sarah set the sherry aside and stood. "I'd like to see Ralph. Would it be possible for a carriage to be summoned?"

"Is that wise? You must not push yourself too much. Besides, I feel responsible for your safety—a little tardy, I'll admit, but I cannot allow any harm to come to you now."

"Ralph offers no danger to me. As you said, he has broken no law. And I will not go alone." Sarah saw no purpose in revealing her traveling companion would be a freed slave, one day out of the seraglio.

"And as for resting," she continued, "I have a lifetime for that after I leave Turkey. I owe Ralph an apology for running away. And he owes me one, also. Neither of us has handled our betrothal very well."

Reluctantly, the ambassador agreed to her request. "Your fiancé spends long hours at his place of business. It is there, I am sure, you will find him."

"In addition to the carriage," she said, "I will need information about booking passage back to England. For two, I believe, although I will have to let you know for sure whether my companion has decided to travel with me."

The ambassador tried once again to dissuade her from leaving the embassy, but she assured him she felt perfectly safe. She was not looking forward to seeing Ralph, but if she had learned anything in the past weeks, it was to accept the inevitability of difficult times.

By the time she and Nadire were in the ambassador's private carriage and traveling over the cobbled streets toward Eastern Ports of Call, the first splats of rain were falling. Rolls of thunder heralded the carriage's approach.

Requesting that the driver return within an hour, Sarah entered the shabby building with Nadire close behind. The two women were met by a stillness that was chilling. The small outer office was empty save for a cluttered desk and an overturned chair.

"Missy Sarah," Nadire said, her voice muffled by the thick veil, "should we not leave?"

"In a moment."

Sarah's eyes fastened on the partially open door behind the desk.

"Ralph?" she called.

There was no answer.

Refusing to cower, Sarah forced her feet to march around the desk. Nadire followed.

When she attempted to open the door wider, she found it blocked. She was already shoving her way into the inner office by the time she realized what was barring easy entry—the body of a man lying in a twisted heap just inside the room. Blood pooled on the wooden floor beside an outslung arm.

Sarah gasped in horror.

"Missy!" Nadire cried behind her.

Sarah willed her heart to slow, and she fought a rising nausea. She could not shift her gaze from the still, suit-clad body. The man was too small for Ralph; she had never seen him before. All she knew for certain was that he was dead.

Taking a deep breath, she forced her eyes to circle the room. No other door offered access. No one could enter or leave except where she stood.

"Ralph," she called out foolishly to the empty space. The answer, which came from behind the massive desk at the far end of the room, was a low moan.

396

Sarah threw herself past the body and toward the sound. Ralph was lying supine in the narrow space between the desk chair and the wall. His eyes were closed, and his white shirt was stained with crimson; but she saw with great relief the timid rise and fall of his chest.

Thrusting the chair out of her way, she knelt beside him. "It's Sarah," she said. She prayed he could hear and understand.

Again he moaned.

She stroked the wisps of gray hair away from his face and gently loosened the tightly bound cravat at his throat. His eyes fluttered open, and the hint of a smile passed across his lips.

"Sarah," he whispered.

"Hush," she said gently. "I'll get help."

"Too late." His eyes closed once again. "Stay." His breathing was shallow. "Listen."

She fought back panic. Ralph spoke with the urgency of a man who knows he is dying, and she gave in to his request, cradling his head and shoulders in her lap as his blood spread with alarming speed across the blue dimity.

"You came back," he said.

"Yes, Ralph, I came back."

Again came the forced, shallow breaths.

"Wanted you." His voice was a raspy whisper, and Sarah had to bend close to hear what he said. "Old fool."

"Please," she said in anguish, "don't say such things."

"Mustafa—" A cough stopped his words.

"Did Mustafa do this to you?" asked Sarah, helpless to do more than keep his forced words to a minimum.

"Met with him . . . had it out . . . got poor Samuel, too."

"Then he will pay."

Ralph's eyes opened once again, and Sarah watched as he struggled for the strength to continue. When he finally spoke, his voice was stronger than it had been.

"Told him deal was off. No ships. Not after I learned what he had done to you. Kidnapping. Not part of it."

"I know," she said in hasty assurance. Tears scalded her eyes.

"Sarah." He reached up and she took his hand in hers. He squeezed hard. "All yours now . . . everything . . . yours. Love—"

His body stiffened, then fell lax, his head dropping to one side, the grip of his hand giving way to a limpness that announced with dreadful certainty he had breathed his last.

Insanely, Sarah imagined herself once again on the blood-soaked deck of the *Leviathan*, cradling the dead Captain Reynolds' body against her breast. The image was so strong, she could hear the wind in the rigging and the moans of the dying sailors. She sat rigid, unable to clear her mind, unable to ease her hold on the body in her arms.

"Missy Sarah." Nadire knelt beside her. "We must let someone know what has happened."

Sarah slowly focused on the girl, who had removed her hood and veil and now stared out with wide brown eyes.

"We are not safe from harm," Nadire said. "We must leave."

"I killed him," said Sarah.

"Mustafa killed him," said Nadire. "And he will

398

kill Missy Sarah if we do not leave."

But Sarah could not bring herself to let go of the man who had wanted nothing more from the remaining years of his life than to have her as his wife. If she had remained at the embassy and not run away from disgrace, Ralph might very well be alive.

The tears that she had not shed for Jake now spilled freely for the man she could not love.

"It is not enough to cry," said Nadire.

No, Sarah thought, it was not enough to cry, but there was little she could do until the tears were spent. At last she brushed them aside and, with great tenderness, edged the lifeless body from her lap and stood.

"The carriage should be returning before long," she said, as much to reassure Nadire as herself that they were all right. "We will report to Lord Stratford—"

She hesitated. Something was wrong. It took her no more than a second to realize what that something was—the sound of the outer office door opening and easing closed.

Nadire's frightened stare gave evidence that she had heard it, too.

The two women glanced at each other in mutual fear. They were not alone in the Ports of Call. And with only one way to get in and out of the office, they were trapped.

"Perhaps," Sarah said with bravado, "it is the carriage driver returned early."

"Yes." Nadire trembled.

Sarah took her hand. "We'll just go out there—"

The door separating the two rooms began to edge open, and the lifeless body that had been blocking it was shoved aside.

Sarah stared open-mouthed at the tall, skeletal figure who came into sight. Recognition turned to horror. She knew the man only as Scarface. He held an unsheathed scimitar in his hand.

"Miss Whitlock," he hissed in a heavily accented voice, an ugly grin breaking his harsh, maimed face, "at last we meet again."

Chapter Twenty-Seven

After Jake made arrangements for the carriage to take Sarah away from him forever, he found himself with time hanging heavily on his hands.

Time, hell. What he had was the rest of his life. It stretched before him in endless, unpromising days and nights. He would have to fill the hours somehow, but without Sarah there would be no joy.

Never in his life had he experienced such emptiness. It was as though someone had carved out his heart.

Walking the crowded streets of the city through the oppressive heat, he called himself a fool for letting her get to him the way no other woman ever had. But something inside him far wiser than his muddled mind told him the truly foolish thing he had done was letting her go. At least he should have told her how he felt.

For the first time in his life Jake was in love. Until Sarah, he'd had no idea such feelings really existed. He knew now. There was no deed he would not perform, no mountain he would not climb, no ocean he would not swim if only Sarah could be his prize.

She had him thinking poetic thoughts, comparing

her hair to the morning sun and her eyes to the blue tidewater that caught in the rocks of the shore. He saw beauty where he had never seen it before—in the sough of the wind, the soaring path of a wide-winged bird, the finely wrought porcelains that she so admired.

With Sarah he was more alive than he had ever been.

How gloriously brave and beautiful she was, how maddeningly impetuous and obstinate, how delicately vulnerable. She brought out a tender side of his nature and a generosity of spirit that he had never known he possessed, and a willingness to walk into hell to keep her from harm.

Before Sarah, he had considered himself a lusty man, but he hadn't known what hunger for a woman really was until he hungered for her. The more she fed that hunger, the more he longed for her. All other women paled beside her golden enchantment.

Sarah was everything.

Except, of course, she was not his.

In the distance a roll of thunder sounded, and Jake glanced up at the dark clouds moving in fast over the city. Even the elements shared his torment. He welcomed the sudden chill breeze that stirred the dust and trash of the city as he made his way along the street. It matched the chill he carried inside.

One dreadful point in time would stay with him forever—the instant when he had looked down from that damned carriage and seen her stricken eyes looking back at him. With a woman at his side, she had assumed the worst, which was a good indicator as to the kind of man she thought he really was.

He would spend the rest of his life wondering if he had done the right thing in letting Sarah believe he was seeking pleasure with that laughing creature.

She fancied herself beginning to care for him; she would not want him looking at someone else.

Jake caught himself. Sarah had been more than just upset. She had been enraged. Jake suspected the real injury was to her pride, which, he had observed often enough, she possessed in ample supply.

Sarah's true feelings for him were a mixture of awakened passion and gratitude—not love. He had saved her life, and he had unveiled a side of her nature she had not known existed. Even when she had been caught by the spell that had wrapped about them, she was planning a future alone—in America, representing the business interests of her father. Once she and Sir Edward made their inevitable peace, she just might do all right there.

So he had been right not to tell her what was in his heart. It wasn't much consolation, but he would hold on to it. Let her continue with her belief that she had been betrayed. She would get over her infatuation faster.

Jake would not get over his love.

He had one last task to perform, and then he would get the hell out of Turkey. The decision came after a couple of hours of wandering through the streets under the threat of a storm. This morning when he had taken that ride with one of Faruk's dancers, he learned where Fatima lived. The information was all he had wanted from the woman, and all he had taken, although she had offered more.

Like many of the dancers, including Fatima, the woman spoke English and a few other languages as well, all of them learned from the sailors who came into the Horn.

When Fatima wasn't with a man during the day, the smirking woman had reported, she slept in her apartment as part of her ritual in preparing for the night's performance.

"Fatima is getting on in years," her so-called friend had said. "She needs more rest than I."

Jake was feeling a few years himself. Retrieving his gold was, at least, something specific to concentrate on beside the passage of empty time.

He found Fatima's lodging with little trouble, an ancient building that was part of a row of dingy stone structures less than a mile from the Grand Bazaar. The room he sought was on the second floor.

As he stood on the narrow road that ran in front of it, fat splats of rain hit the ground around him. He hurried inside.

Stale body odors hit him as he made his way up the back stairway and into the dark hall. The heat that had been driven from outside by the approaching storm had gathered up here in full force—as if it were hiding until the weather cleared and it could once more descend to the streets.

Fatima's locked door was the last one down the hallway, but his knock brought no response.

He knocked again, louder, and called her name through the crack between door and frame. He was certain she would not recognize his voice, since they had done damned little talking the night when he took her to his boat. Right now he was only a man seeking an afternoon's entertainment. If she did not respond, he would sit outside her door and wait for her to leave.

Or, maybe, kick his way in. Once the idea occurred to him, he found it growing in appeal.

Before he could carry through, however, a throaty whisper came back at him. In Turkish.

"English, please," he said. "I was with a friend of yours earlier. She bored me. I longed for Fatima."

"You know Fatima?" was the response.

"I know only what is said, but it is enough. Fatima is beautiful above all others. I have grown eager for just one glance."

Jake paused, decided he preferred a well-placed boot to his muttered lies in order to gain access to the room, and was preparing to deliver just that when the door opened a crack.

He shouldered his way in.

Fatima stumbled backward, and her wide dark eyes became saucers. *"Amerikahyim!"* she cried.

Thick black hair tumbled to her shoulders, and the flesh-toned gauze gown that she wore did little to hide her dark-tipped, heavy breasts and the triangle of black hair between her fleshy thighs.

Jake closed the door behind him and took a quick glance around the room before settling his eyes on her. He spied one door and one high window, through which he could see the quickening rain. She had no way to escape.

"Hello, Fatima," he said in a low voice. "It's been a long time."

Her eyes did not leave his face. Wily eyes they were, trying to find some weakness in him that would enable her to get free. But they were fearful eyes, too. She thought he had come to kill her. He would let her hold on to that belief for a while.

"Do we know each other, *Amerikahyim?*"

"Not as well as I had once planned. But I know you, all right, and you know me—enough to know I'm American. Do you always run away from Americans? You've done it to me twice—once on the dock and again at Faruk's."

Fatima's full lips curved into a smile. The brightness of it in her dusky face had been what attracted him to her when she unveiled herself for him on the street the night they met. That and her

405

rounded hips. He had been looking for a voluptuous, willing woman, and she had promised to fill his needs.

She took a step closer, and then another. With each movement the diaphanous gown clung suggestively to the curves of her body.

"You are the sailor, are you not?" she said as though she had just realized who had forced his way into her room. "The night of the wild blades flashing. Ooh, I was so frightened. Later, when I returned to the waterfront, you were not there."

"You returned?"

Her tongue moistened her lower lip. "As you have said, sailor man, we did not know each other as we planned. I wanted so to see you once again." She cupped her hands under her breasts, her thumbs stroking the dark round tips. "I have thought of you often."

"I imagine you have."

Her fingers moved to the fastening at her throat. It took only one pull at the drawstring to loosen the gown and send it floating to the floor at her bare feet. She stepped over the gauze and slowly closed the remaining space between them, giving him ample opportunity to view everything that she offered.

She was shorter than Sarah, the top of her head coming only to his shoulders, and her body was thickly curved. Jake viewed her coldly. Gone was the appeal she had once held for him.

"I know many ways to please," she whispered huskily, her breasts brushing against his shirt. She dropped one hand and stroked his thigh with her nails. "A little pain, if that is what you choose. For me or for you."

"It won't work, Fatima. All I want is the gold."

The nails dug in. Through the thickness of his

trousers, he could feel their sharp points. He caught her wrist. "The gold."

She twisted free of him and screamed. The rain pounded against the lone window, and thunder crashed over the city.

"No one can hear you," he said. "And if they do . . . You mentioned pain. Surely screams have come from your room before."

She dropped to the floor on top of the filmy gown and pulled the gauze around her like a shield. The sideways glance she shot him held the hunted look of a cornered wild animal.

"If necessary, Fatima," he said, leaning back against the door and crossing one ankle over the other, "I can bind you and make you talk."

"Never!"

"You claim to know many ways to please, but I know the ways of torture. My travels to the Orient have been most instructive. I will, of course, begin with your face."

"Hayir!"

"Do not tell me no, Fatima. That is not what I want to hear."

She crouched as still and as silent as a stone. Upright, she had carried herself with erotic grace; bent as she was now, Jake could see the lax muscles of her abdomen and thighs and the sagging of her breasts.

He wasn't very proud of himself, and he was about to call a halt to the entire mental anguish he was putting Fatima through when suddenly she scrambled to her feet.

Hands on hips, she faced him and said flatly, "As long as you do not kill me."

The change from temptress to barterer had come so unexpectedly that Jake almost laughed. "You are a practical woman," he said. "And a fine actress. I must remember that you are a performer."

"I have learned to get by." Shrugging, she grabbed her gown from the floor and slipped it over her head. "So the fortune is not mine after all," she said, her voice resigned more than resentful. "This comes as no surprise. I was stupid to stay in Constantinople. How certain I was at first that you had been killed that night and your body tossed into the water."

"You saw me at the coffee house. At Faruk's."

She nodded. "I said I was stupid. There is a man I did not choose to leave, but I did not quite trust him enough to reveal to him the gold."

"You surprise me," said Jake.

"Because of this man or because I offered myself to you? Perhaps it is both. I must somehow survive. He has a wife and ten children. And he still wants me, but not enough to run with me to the far corners of the world. Love," she hissed. "Bah!"

Turning from him, she swept aside a mound of pillows in the corner of the room, lifted a section of the wooden floor, and pulled out a familiar pouch. It jangled as she tossed it to Jake.

"Take it and go, sailor man. It will not buy me what I want."

Jake did as he was bid; downstairs as he stared out at the rain through the open door, he remembered Fatima's last words. He tucked the pouch inside his shirt, where it formed an awkward lump. He tried to summon a sense of satisfaction in the retrieval of the gold, but his victory did not fill the emptiness inside him. The gold would not buy him what he wanted, either.

Stepping into the rain, he turned up his collar and headed toward the apartment. By the time he had gone two blocks, his shirt and trousers were plastered to his skin. The once crowded streets were deserted except for a few poor souls who, like him, scurried to their destinations. He had halved the distance to his lonely, waiting room when he came up against a familiar figure.

"Bandit," he yelled over the unrelenting rain. "For God's sake, man, get to some shelter."

"Bossman, there is trouble. Always I bring bad news."

Jerking him into an open doorway, Jake held tightly to his shirt. "It's Sarah, isn't it?"

"The man to whom Miss Whitlock was betrothed has been killed. Today. In the office where he conducts his business."

The news hit Jake harder than he would have expected. He knew Sarah would be affected by his death—probably blame herself. She had done too damned much of that already.

"Does Sarah know?"

"She and Nadire left the embassy of the English more than an hour ago to visit Mr. Pettigrew."

"Don't tell me she found the body," Jake said. Ugly images formed in his mind.

"No one knows what the two women discovered. When the embassy driver returned to the building, they were not where he had left them."

Cold fear took hold of Jake. "What in the hell are you getting at?"

The same fear shaded Bandit's eyes as he spoke. "Bossman, the women have disappeared."

Chapter Twenty-Eight

During the next few hours Jake put Bandit's vast network of relatives and friends to work looking for Sarah, figuring they were more effective than the informants that Lord Stratford was relying upon. Distributing a portion of the coins from the leather pouch he had retrieved from Fatima didn't hurt his investigation, either.

He worked with grim concentration, gathering messages from the palace, questioning sailors along the waterfront, sending out inquisitive emissaries to the city's coffee houses and bazaars to pick up what gossip they could. He sifted through the information with no more frenzy than that of a banker at his books. But he would have killed anyone who held back information.

By midnight, in consultation with Bandit at the apartment, he put together the facts he had been after and charted his plans. A single piece of information stood out from all others. One of Ralph Pettigrew's ships, the clipper ship *Sea Witch*, had left its anchorage in the Bosporus Strait shortly after dusk and was headed for the Black Sea.

Ralph Pettigrew had given no orders for the unscheduled sailing. By dusk he had been dead three hours.

Neither had the ship's captain been responsible. His body was found bobbing in an inlet off the strait by a seven-year-old boy who had stolen to the waterfront to skim for dead fish after the afternoon storm.

It wouldn't take much guesswork to name who was aboard the Eastern Ports of Call ship—Mustafa scrambling in desperation for safety from his wrathful father and, equally important, for the long-coveted riches promised by the forbidden opium trade. He would be surrounded by the faithful guards who had slipped away from the seraglio during the previous night. The crew would have been hand-picked already in preparation for the long-planned journey to China.

But Mustafa would not be satisfied with ordinary precautions. Sarah and Nadire most likely were aboard as insurance he would succeed. Jake would bet his life on the conclusions. The only trouble was, his was not the life at stake.

Jake did not doubt for a moment that he could stop Mustafa and free Sarah—he couldn't afford to think anything else—and together with his thoughts and a solemn-faced Bandit he hurried from the apartment, which had served as headquarters during the nighttime search, and headed for the dhow anchored in the Golden Horn.

A chill wind blew down the steep street, all that was left of the day's turbulent weather. The stars had faded into the midnight sky, and all the world seemed watchful behind the closed doors of the dark buildings they passed. Even the few pedestrians that were still about made way for their procession, sensing somehow that these men were on no ordinary mission.

"I have studied the maps, Bossman," Bandit said as he ran to keep up with Jake's longer stride. "They go to the port of Samsun in the eastern portion of Turkey. There, I believe, they load the opium which awaits. At least this is what I have guessed from what we have learned."

"Don't be wrong," snapped Jake, not breaking the pace of his walk.

"It matters to me, too, that we succeed," returned Bandit in a voice harsher than any Jake had heard him use.

Jake glanced at his friend. In the dim light he could imagine in Bandit's normally calm, watchful eyes the same desperation that he struggled to control, and he regretted his hasty words.

"The embassy will want to send ships after them," he said. "With many men. If, that is, the embassy finds out what we know."

"We do not wish for these ships to fire upon the *Witch*."

"No, Bandit, that we most definitely do not wish. This rescue takes a subtler approach."

"The Bossman will tell me what to do."

"Help me get the *Angel* under sail. We'll chase down the bastard ourselves."

Jake knew he was asking a great deal of Bandit. They could call upon the vast forces of Harun and the sanction and advice of Lord Stratford, a man who knew well the people and land of Turkey. But accompanying that assistance would be armed men with their own ideas about how to stop Mustafa. They would not understand the true purpose of the undertaking—freeing Sarah and Nadire.

On board the *Angel*, the two men worked silently

beneath the dark, cloudless sky. Jake would allow himself to think of nothing more than the sail and rigging, the countless vessels crowding the harbor, and the wind that propelled them across the quiet waters of the Horn into the choppy Bosporus, and at last into the deeper, rolling swells of the Black Sea.

In the lonely dark, Jake imagined the sea to be vast and deserted, as though it had swallowed all vessels that dared to sail upon it. Somewhere in that vastness Sarah was held prisoner. He could accept no other belief.

Charting a course toward the unseen eastern horizon, Jake threw himself into his work. As the hours crawled by, there came a time when he could not ignore the cold, angry fear that lay like a heavy weight in the pit of his stomach. He tried to judge Sarah—tried to condemn her for going to Pettigrew's office—tried to tell himself she had brought trouble down on herself by acting in her usually incautious way.

Jake knew where the fault lay. Whether Sarah admitted the truth or not, she was his responsibility . . . certainly until she was free of the country that had charmed and at the same time endangered her since she first arrived. She was in his care, simply because he loved her.

If Jake had not been close to breaking down for the first time since he learned to walk, he would have laughed aloud at that thought. There was not anything simple about love. It altered a man.

"The wind shifts, Bossman," said Bandit as they skimmed eastward across the sea. It was the first time either had spoken since they left the Horn.

To starboard lay the dark hills of the Turkish coast. The horizon directly ahead met the water with a thin-edged rim of black light that promised the approaching dawn.

"Right," answered Jake, welcoming the interruption of his musings. Thinking was a danger. It could weaken him . . . make him forget the final purpose of his mission . . . open up the possibilities of what could go wrong.

Bandit worked in silence beside Jake, trimming the sail to take advantage of the wind. "Nadire will be my wife," he said at last.

"She has agreed?"

"She has not been asked. I will tell her."

Jake opened his mouth to give a word of advice, but the words died unuttered. Who the hell was he to tell a man how to woo a woman?

The wooden hull of the dhow slapped at the surface of the waves as if in applause at his decision.

The hour of dawn came and went, and with the early morning wind at their backs they shot forward through the rosy light like an arrow. Jake knew the boat as well as he knew Sarah's body, and he was able to perform the necessary tasks without benefit of concentration. With Bandit staring into the distance in the company of his private thoughts, Jake found himself once again at the mercy of his memory. Mostly he remembered his mistakes.

They arrived at the port of Samsun at noon. The harbor area was far smaller than the Horn, and amongst the dozen anchored vessels Jake picked out the tall, naked masts of the clipper ship *Sea Witch* right away. It took the last ounce of his will to keep from maneuvering through the small crowd and ramming the *Angel* into its stern. Anchoring a quarter mile west, he set Bandit ashore in the dinghy, paced restlessly for an hour, and practically lifted him bodily from the small rowboat when at last he

414

returned from his fact-gathering visit along the wharf.

"Much activity aboard the *Witch*," he reported. "They arrived early in the morning and have loaded much cargo. Hard men, they say, unlike most sailors that arrive in Samsun. And there are armed men of Turkey also aboard. Such is most unusual."

"Mustafa's guards," said Jake. "Any talk about what their cargo might be?"

"No one will say, but I read the eyes. It is the evil freight of *Sheytan*, the devil. It is the harvest of the fields of poppy. Heavy guards have kept it in the warehouses along the wharf for the past week. Mostly the people here farm in the countryside. Food is what is shipped. These crates contain no figs, Bossman."

"I don't suppose there have been any women sighted on board."

"It is curious that you should ask."

Jake took a hard look at his friend. "Damn it, Bandit, if you know something, spit it out."

"It was only the story of one ancient sailor I stopped on the street near the water. A Christian. The old man swears he saw someone strange in appearance floating amongst the barrels that had been loaded on the *Witch*'s aft deck. Hair like the morning sun, he said. Not a woman, though. An angel in a blue gown come down from the sky. At least that is the image he remembers seeing before shadows crossed over her and she disappeared."

Jake's pulse hammered in his throat. "What kind of shadows?"

"The sailor could be no more specific. A befuddled mind, he had, Bossman, but he seemed certain of his tale."

Jake did not know whether to shout for joy that his

Angel had been seen, or rage at the heavens because of the shadows that dimmed her radiance. He chose neither.

"All right, Bandit, we'll have to assume they're both on board and safe for the time being. Mustafa's probably planning on setting sail before long. He can't wait in port here without the risk of a pursuit vessel eventually finding him."

"Such as the dhow."

"He's thinking of something more easily spotted and better armed—and not arriving for a day or two. The man's wily. With the Black Sea having no other egress, he'll have to retrace his route through the Bosporus. The best time to sail past Constantinople is during the middle of the night."

"Such is what he must want all to believe," said Bandit.

"Is there some reason we shouldn't?"

"A word dropped here and there would lead the listener to decide as you have done. I heard such words. But I am a suspicious creature, Bossman. I ask myself why such secrecy about the cargo and incaution where the sailing plans are concerned."

"A valid question, Bandit."

"And I remember the words of Harun. They have made me think."

Jake leaned against the low rail of the dhow and stared at the *Witch*'s main mast. Sarah was close—so close he would be able to see her if she wandered on deck. He could not allow himself to speculate any further than that or he would go mad.

"Tell me more," he said. "Tell me what grows in that fertile mind of yours. Then we'll pray to God and Allah that we come up with the right plan."

*   *   *

Aboard the *Sea Witch* Sarah twisted uncomfortably in the damp, sour corner of the hold where she and Nadire had been thrown. Arms bound behind her and ankles firmly roped together beneath her full-skirted gown, she thought bitterly of her near escape. By feigning sharp pains in her stomach, she had distracted the guard who watched them in the deck cabin where they were first held. Nadire had felled him with a small stool artfully applied to the base of his skull.

Sarah had taken to the open air like a shot, her companion close behind. She had almost reached the rail; from there it was only a short swim to the dock of the unknown port where the ship was anchored. And then all those sailors had seemed to come from nowhere. Rude hands had bound them and pitched them ingloriously into this dark, fetid hold.

She had seen Mustafa only once—right after Scarface had brought them on board. Harun's wayward son had made no assault upon their persons, but Sarah caught the way he looked at her. Cruel lust. It was the same look she had seen in his black eyes the night she was brought to his room at the Grand Seraglio. Then he had taken his strange satisfactions from an odalisque.

But now. . . .

She must not dwell on frightful speculations. She would face Mustafa when she had to, but there was no purpose served in imagining the torture that lay ahead.

Jake had brought comfort to her time and again. She would think of him. Never mind the abyss of misery into which she had been thrown when he walked out the door. When she had been with him, heaven was hers.

A heartfelt sigh broke from her lips.

"Missy Sarah must not despair." In the dark, Nadire's voice was strong and encouraging.

"I've really done it this time," said Sarah. "Jake warned me not to see Ralph right away. I let him think that such a visit was the farthest thing from my mind."

"The two of you were saying good-bye," Nadire said softly. "A woman does not think clearly at such times."

"As bad as things are, there's one thought I can't forget. Jake will grieve for my disappearance, of that I'm sure; but the grief will pass, and he'll be left with the knowledge that I wasn't really able to take care of myself. That I was no more than a foolish woman who could not stay out of trouble without him."

"And this gives you pain?"

"More than I can say, Nadire. More than I can say."

The two women lapsed into silence, and a curious image flashed across Sarah's mind—that of an infant crawling up the wooden gangplank of a tall sailing ship. His behind was thickly swaddled, but the rest of his small, strong body was bare. Tiny hands gripped the splintered wood, and fat knees scraped along in heedless hurry toward the high deck. The baby's head was finely shaped and covered with thick, black hair.

The intrepid voyager was the infant Jake as he had once described himself to her. Jake the sailor before he could walk. Jake the independent adventurer. Jake the marvelous.

Cast in a floating dungeon, she felt a wondrous tenderness fill her heart. That imagined child could well be the one they would never have—unless she carried within her Jake's seed. Oh, if only she did. Scandal be damned. She was past caring what others thought. What a splendid child he could give her. She knew the possibility of her increasing existed, though it might be slim, her monthly flow having come and gone during her previous stay at the embassy.

There had been those glorious days and nights on the island. Just maybe she could take a part of Jake with her to the United States. For the sake of the child, she could pose as a widow. No one need be the wiser. . . .

She caught herself and stifled a sob. What madness had overtaken her? If she really carried within her womb Jake's child, the infant would suffer whatever fate awaited her. The reasons for freeing herself multiplied, and she threw herself into dreaming up ways she might escape.

If somewhere in her prison she could find a sharp edge against which she might cut her bonds . . . if she could surprise the guard who brought the next meal . . . if she could make her way into the water . . .

An ominous scurrying and scratching amidst the barrels at her back brought a quick end to her schemes. She shivered at the image of fat, hairy bodies with long tails that flashed across her mind.

"Missy Sarah," hissed Nadire.

"I heard. Filthy little beasts, aren't they, but I suppose we will have to get used to them."

"I do not mean the rats. Outside in the corridor. Someone comes."

Before Sarah could respond, the door was thrown open, and a shaft of light cut cruelly into the dark. Blinded, she could make out only the short, squat figure of a man standing in the doorway. Rough hands jerked her upward, and like a sack of meal she was thrown over the sailor's shoulder. With a blanket tossed over her, she was carried from the room. The door to the hold slammed closed with Nadire still inside.

The hard shoulder cut into her abdomen and cut off her air as she bounced in awkward progress up the narrow hatchway that led to the deck. She caught no more than a whiff of fresh air through the stale blanket before being carried into another cabin and tossed unceremoniously onto a narrow bunk. All this she could detect by no more than sound and the use of her imagination, but when she heard the door slam closed, she wiggled from the smothering blanket and saw that she was correct.

Her arms ached from their confinement at her back, and she twisted her wrists against the rope that bound them. The raw skin burned, and she ceased the useless fight, turning her energies instead to studying the small cabin. A desk and a chair were the lone furniture, and there was a leather-bound trunk against the wall opposite the door. Halfway up the wall, a small porthole opened onto a clear sky.

Even if she could free herself, Sarah knew she would never be able to squeeze through the narrow opening, and she contented herself with taking a quick look at the patch of blue that for her constituted the outside world.

Beneath her the bunk shifted, and she was aware of the shouts of men on deck, of the whine of rigging and the slap of canvas as the sails were unfurled. They were leaving port—wherever it was they had stopped—and with no other choice left to her, she lay back and tried to imagine the scene outside. Try as she might, she could not picture Jake striding up the gangplank to her rescue.

A half hour later the regular, rocking motion of the ship told her the *Sea Witch* was under way. Body held tense, she waited for the door of the cabin to open and for her troubles to increase; but the minutes crawled by, and no one arrived. Sarah allowed herself to relax, as much as she could with arms bound behind her and ankles tied so tightly that she feared they had begun to bleed. At last, her weary body gave in to the worried, restless hours of the night, and she fell into a troubled sleep.

The creak of the door awakened her sometime later. Through the porthole, she could see that the light had faded, and she drew her attention back to the only world that mattered right now—the cabin where she was imprisoned. Mustafa, tall and lean in full-sleeved shirt and fitted trousers, stood in the open doorway. His cheeks were sunken beneath eyes that burned like coals down at her helpless figure. She caught for an instant the sense that he was a hunted man. Driven to desperate means, he sought release from his troubled thoughts.

Sarah knew with cold certainty she was to provide that release.

He slammed the door closed behind him. "You will not get away from me this time, English whore," he said, his deep voice silky in contrast to the cruel words.

Sarah pressed herself against the wall of the bunk. Her throat constricted, and she found herself unable to say a word as she remembered the bruises discoloring the buttocks and thighs of the odalisque Tezer—bruises inflicted upon her by Mustafa's hand.

"Frightened?" he asked. "Good." His thin lips twisted into a leer, and she wondered how she could ever have thought him handsome.

She tried with her eyes to tell him how she felt.

Mustafa's boots hit the wooden floor of the cabin with sharp precision as he closed the distance between them. Standing beside the bunk, he trailed a thin, long-fingered hand down her cheek.

"Don't touch me," she hissed, twisting to get away.

He gripped her chin with a fierceness that killed her moment of defiance.

"I want you to fight me, Sarah Whitlock." His free hand grabbed a hunk of her yellow hair and pulled hard.

Her eyes blurred from the pain.

"Weep for me. You make the heat build in my loins."

Sarah's tears dried instantly. Burning into her mind was an image of Jake fighting off the slashing blades of Mustafa's men. Whatever horrors awaited her, she would face them with equal courage.

"You have seen the last of my tears, Mustafa. No matter what you do to me now or tomorrow or next week, I will welcome death before I cry."

Mustafa threw back his head and laughed—a deep-throated baritone that was the clarion of evil.

"Death before tears? That may well be, Sarah Whitlock," he said, his fingers edging like a knife down her throat. "I believe the next hour may prove to be a most interesting one indeed."

Chapter Twenty-Nine

If Mustafa meant to terrorize Sarah into hysterics, he had made a terrible misjudgment of her character and determination. She was frightened, all right— only a fool would not be—but her condition was for her and her alone to know. She lay still as a board, eyes closed, refusing to continue with her defiant talk since all she accomplished was the arousal of his twisted humor and lust.

His hand squeezed her breasts until she thought she would retch from the pain. She concentrated on remaining absolutely still. Never had she been so proud of an accomplishment.

Mustafa was not put off. "There is sweat on your brow, pretty one. I will yet make you beg with your cries."

He left her for a moment to rummage in the desk; when he returned, cold metal rubbed across her throat. An involuntary shudder rippled through her body as she realized he was holding a knife.

"Better, whore, but not quite good enough."

The point of the knife touched the bosom of her gown. "Shall I cut your clothes from you? How easy it would be to pierce your delicate skin."

Sarah hated the frailty within her that allowed another tremor. Perhaps if she lunged upward, the knife would penetrate her heart, and the torture would end.

She could not make the necessary move. Within her was more than frailty or fear; she seethed with the will to survive.

"Perhaps the bindings keep you from struggling. For struggle you must."

Sarah's eyes flew open. "Why must I, Mustafa? Is a helplessly struggling woman the only kind that can stiffen your limp body? I remember well how you treated the slave from your harem. Perhaps you have no choice but to treat all of us thus."

She gazed contemptuously at the juncture of his legs, which came to the level of her eyes. With all his talk of heated loins, he should have been bursting against the confining trousers. He was not.

She looked away. "I see that I am right."

The back of his hand struck her cheek, and for a moment she thought her jaw might be broken. She bit at her lip to keep from crying out. In helplessness she tugged at the wrists bound behind her back.

"I see you do not care for such manly deeds," he said. "Good."

"What manly deeds? Striking a woman? Or," she said, glancing at the dried bloodstains on her gown, "perhaps you refer to the murder of Ralph Pettigrew."

"No one deceives Mustafa! He would have denied me the use of his ships."

A hard knock sounded at the door, and a gruff voice muttered, "Land ho."

Mustafa shifted impatiently. "I hear you. Do what is necessary."

"You're the cap'n now," the voice returned. "Figured you'd want to know."

"I am not a common sailor like you English, but the son of a sultan. Let me know when it is time to go ashore."

Sarah watched contempt harden Mustafa's face as he spoke. With her tormentor momentarily distracted, she twisted away from the bunk's thin mattress, trying in vain to sit, and screamed with the full force of her lungs. Mustafa slapped her back against the bed and once more placed the point of the knife at her throat.

Fighting tears, her head reeling from the blow, she listened to the sound of shuffling footsteps growing softer. She closed her eyes to the triumphant look on Mustafa's face.

"They know to obey me, these infidels of the sea. Your cries could be taken as cries of pleasure. Or not. It is no one's concern but ours."

Sarah spat at him, but the spittle went no higher than the upper sleeve of his shirt.

Mustafa's only reaction was an ugly leer. "Our destination is near," he said. "We will go by camel across the deserts for many weeks. In all those days and nights, no one will help you, whore. You will be mine to do with as I choose. But I want you now."

At that moment the cabin rocked as the ship took a sudden lurch, but Mustafa seemed not to notice.

He used the knife to lift her skirts and with a downward slash cut the ropes that bound her ankles. Roughly he turned her over and freed her hands. Her arms ached at the sudden release. She knew her wrists, like her ankles, were bleeding where the hemp had cut. Struck by the injustice of what was happening to her, she twisted around and lunged upward, her open hands thrust outward to shove him aside, but Mustafa was too quick for her as his steely fingers gripped her wounded wrists.

"Now the body stiffens," he gloated, lifting her until her terrified face was close to his. She knew beyond doubt from the wild light in his eyes that he was insane.

Half mad herself, Sarah brought a knee hard against the loins that filled him with such pride. His yelp of pain was sweet in her ears. He threw her hard against the wall, then turned from her. Sarah's head struck the unyielding surface, stunning her for a moment—a precious moment when perhaps she might have darted from the bunk.

By the time she had her wits about her, he had turned. Whatever wildness she had seen before was nothing compared to the madness burning now in his eyes.

"For that you will pay."

Another pounding at the door enraged Mustafa.

"Away!" he yelled. Only the most foolhardy or the bravest of men would have answered that sound.

One word stilled Mustafa's orders.

"Fire!"

Mustafa strode across the room and flung open the door. A barrel-chested sailor with a patch across one eye stared up at him. "Fire," he repeated. "Stern's been struck by a boat. Thought Your Highness should know."

Sarah caught the sarcasm in the sailor's voice.

"Fools! How could such a thing happen?" demanded Mustafa.

The sailor did not flinch. "Damned thing burst into flames just as she came up on us. We'd trimmed back for the harbor. Made an easy target, we did."

The bluster died in Mustafa's widening eyes. "Another ship ran us down? One of my father's?"

"Nothing so grand as a sultan would use. A dhow, that's all, but the trouble is the fire's spreading to the

426

barrels on deck."

A dhow! Sarah came off the bunk, her legs buckling beneath her, and she caught herself on the back of the chair to keep from falling.

"My treasure!" snapped Mustafa. "It must above all else be saved."

The men forgot her as they hurried from the room. For her part, Sarah forgot her weariness and her aching limbs. Her spirit soared. Jake was here. Thinking only to find him, she hurled herself through the open door.

She collided with the skeletal form of Scarface, who grinned wickedly down at her.

"Not so easily done this time," he said as he shoved her back into the cabin and slammed the door closed. She stumbled and fell to the floor, then listened in horror as a key turned in the lock and his footsteps receded down the way.

The panic that she had controlled so well earlier took hold, and she cried out one word—"Jake!"— before flinging herself forward and pounding against the door.

Jake crouched between the barrels and prayed he had not made a fatal mistake in sacrificing the *Angel.* What if the fire spread before he could find Sarah? He had counted on the ship's crew putting out the flames. With such a dramatic distraction, he and Bandit would be free to roam the *Witch*'s corridors and rescue the women they knew were aboard. But what if he had figured wrong?

He did not rely solely upon prayers for the success of his quest. In his right hand was a pistol loaded and ready to fire; in his left was an unsheathed knife.

Bandit was already in the hold doing his part in the

search. With dusk moving in fast and casting shadows across the ship's deck, Jake moved stealthily away from the shouting men who had formed a bucket brigade to put out the fast spreading flames. His face and hands darkened with ashes, Jake prayed he would be invisible amongst the turmoil and smoke.

He did not wait to look for Mustafa or the man Sarah called Scarface among the dozens of men crowding the deck, although he was certain both were aboard. Scurrying feet came in his direction, and he threw himself into the open doorway of a cabin. He recognized the man hurrying past as one of the palace guards.

The sickly sweet smell of burning opium choked the sea air. "More water!" someone barked. "Faster, you lazy bastards, or we'll lose the lot."

With the crew of the *Sea Witch* thrown into the battle against the fire, Jake moved in the opposite direction, darting down the narrow corridors and hatchways, flinging open the doors of cabins without heed of who or what might be inside, pounding at the locked doors and calling Sarah's name.

The sound of footsteps caught his ear, and he turned in time to see a dark, thin figure looming directly behind him in the corridor, a wicked curved blade hovering in the air above his head. Jake fired the single-shot pistol, the roar reverberating in the narrow corridor, the skeletal face of the guard Scarface staring down at him in disbelief.

The guard's blood spattered on Jake's shirt as the body toppled toward him like a felled tree. Jumping out of the way of the sword's sharp blade, he stared at the sprawled, lifeless figure of the man who had brought such fear to Sarah's heart.

"Drop the gun, mate," growled a voice behind

him. "And the knife as well. I've a knife here of me own, and I'd as soon fillet your ribs as look at you."

Cursing his luck, Jake could do nothing except comply. Ahead he could see a pair of sailors scurrying down the passageway toward the sound of the shot. As they neared, he stepped over the dead body and with sudden fierceness threw himself against the first man, who stumbled backward, bringing down his companion with him. Jake attempted to jump over them, but flailing hands and arms held him trapped.

Fists flying, he fought to get away, but he was outnumbered. A blow to the base of his skull ended the fight almost as soon as it was begun, and with his arm twisted painfully behind his back, he was shoved to the open, smoky deck.

Shaking away the dizziness of the blow, he was met by the rest of the ship's crew, grim-faced and dirty from their struggle to put out the burning barrels of opium. Flares struck against the dark gave them a devilish look.

"Look what I ran across," said the man who had him by the arm. "Come to rob us or murder us, one o' the two. Someone get a rope."

Jake stared around at the crew, most of whom he determined to be English. Ralph Pettigrew's men. When he had returned from the shore, Bandit reported the *Witch*'s sailors as being hard men, but how much did they know about the killings they had left behind and the assault on Harun? How far did their allegiance to Mustafa extend?

Behind them ranged a dozen guards from the Grand Seraglio. They seemed content to let the sailors fight their battles. Mustafa was not in sight.

"I'm a sailor," Jake shouted over their growls, "like yourselves. Have you turned pirates and killers under Mustafa's hand?''

"Sounds like a cursed Yank," one of the sailors yelled. "Get the rope for sure."

"I'll answer to whoever is in charge," Jake threw back, "but not a pack of cutthroats."

"That'll be the Turk," said a peg-legged old tar who stood close by. "Captain ain't aboard. Disappeared back in the strait."

"Then you haven't heard," said Jake, giving the grizzled sailor all of his attention. "Your captain's body washed ashore right after you heaved anchor."

The muttering around him ceased; he had their attention now. One of the seraglio guards barked something in Turkish, but the sailors paid him no mind.

Jake let his eyes wander closely across the watchful faces of the crew. Grim faces they were, weathered by wind and time, but he could see questions begin to edge into their minds. He took the peg-legged sailor as a leader and turned his attention to him.

"The ship's owner is dead, too. Shot down behind his desk. Unarmed. He was not a fighting man. Like you, Pettigrew was a man of the sea."

The old sailor's rheumy eyes locked on Jake for a full minute, then shifted to the other men. Around them the half-trimmed canvas sails whipped in the wind.

"I came only to free the women," said Jake. "The two who were captured by the guards of Mustafa. Has this son of a sultan promised you much money for your loyalty?"

"Damned right he has!" came an answer from the dark.

"And for this money does he expect you to follow him across the deserts all the way to China or Afghanistan or Persia or wherever he plans to complete his business? He won't get his gold until then."

"We're sailing back to Constantinople," the old tar said.

"If you do, it will be without Mustafa and his men and the opium. Armed ships await you near the Horn to blow you out of the water. This Turk who leads you tried to kill his father. Harun has taken unkindly to the attempt."

Jake waited for the sailors to demand proof of what he said, but the guards provided it for him. Swords drawn, they moved in on the crew.

Jake was the forgotten man on deck as the sailors, outnumbering the guards two to one, fell to defending their lives. Sailors' knives, more ordinarily given to whittling and mending, became weapons in their angry hands. He had no doubt the Englishmen would rout their Turkish foes.

Ignoring the melee, Jake headed once again for the nearest hatchway, but before he could leave the deck, he was met by Bandit and Nadire. Her face wan and her eyes wide with fear, she clung to her rescuer as though she had no strength to stand alone.

"Bossman—" Bandit stopped and peered past him to the brawling sailors and guards. "I see that your presence has been noticed."

"You might say that."

"Do they fight over who is to be the American's executioner?"

A flying body landed on the deck beside Bandit and lay still.

Ignoring the fallen guard, Jake brought Bandit up to date, then turned to Nadire. "Where is she?"

Nadire tore her gaze from the sprawled figure at Bandit's feet. "Missy Sarah was taken from our dark prison hours ago," she said in a trembling voice. "I do not know of her fate."

"Get her to the dinghy," he ordered Bandit, gesturing toward the small boat they had anchored at the starboard side of the *Witch*. Without waiting for a reply, he plunged once again toward the hatchway. The roar of a gun behind him brought him to a sudden halt.

Whirling, he looked past Bandit and the slowly dying battle scene to the man standing on the aft deck a dozen yards away. Mustafa's legs were spread wide, and his right hand held a smoking pistol high in the air; his left gripped the wrist of Sarah.

The sounds of fighting ceased, and an eerie hush settled on the ship. Already the sailors had routed the seraglio guards.

A growl sounded in Jake's throat. He stared at Sarah for a minute, and through the smoke and flickering torch light, he saw that she had spied him. Her gown was torn and stained, and her hair hung in matted strands against her shoulders. Despite the weariness that rounded her usually straight stance, she managed to smile. She was his angel standing there, and a wildness to finish her deliverance swept over him.

"Bossman!" Bandit hissed from somewhere behind him.

Jake held back, standing stiff and letting the cold certainty of success take hold. But he could not look at her again.

"At long last we meet, Mr. Price," Mustafa called out in a hard, proud voice that carried over the night wind. The sailors edged away from the corridor of masts and rope and smoke-filled night air that separated the two men.

"Let her go, Mustafa," Jake returned. He took a step forward.

"I have one shot left in this gun," his opponent warned, waving the weapon in the air. He stood tall and sure of himself on the higher deck and stared contemptuously down at Jake. "I save it for the woman."

Jake stepped again. "Your men are defeated, and so are you. Let her go."

"That, I cannot do. Always I have known she is my assurance of safety. As you can see, I am right. If you do not do what I want—if all these men do not do what I want—the woman is dead."

"And so are you, bastard."

"An inaccuracy. I am the legitimate son of Harun. A second son. The post has little value for me."

"Harun did not give you all that your greed demands?" Another, broader step.

"My father does not extend my rightful inheritance."

And still another. Jake was close to the ladder leading up to Mustafa and to Sarah, who stood still and white-faced next to her captor.

"Your father knows you have little value," said Jake.

Rage distorted Mustafa's sharp face. He lowered the gun until the barrel was pointed at Jake, all his concentration on his American foe. "Cease this—"

Sarah flew into action, bending and sinking her teeth into Mustafa's wrist. Yelping in pain, he dropped the weapon. Jake bolted for the stairs.

Blue clouds of skirt whirled away from the once proud Mustafa, and Sarah came to a halt against the aft rail just as Jake reached the first rung. The sight of the scimitar in Mustafa's hand brought him to a sudden halt. Jake could only guess he had somehow strapped the weapon at his back.

"I will kill her before you can kill me," Mustafa

said. "This is the weapon of the Ottomans. I know it well."

"Why not take me first? Then you can do what you will with her." Jake took the second rung of the ladder.

"No!" Sarah screamed.

Behind him, all was still, and Jake took the third step. He was halfway to the deck. "Do not listen to the woman, Mustafa. You are the son of a sultan. Women do what you say. Kill me and you can have her for your own. To do the things you like to do." Jake's voice softened. "I know about these things, Mustafa. It would be a shame if she escaped you through her death."

"She dies, one way or the other," said Mustafa, but Jake caught the hesitation in his voice.

"It is the way of death that matters to a man, is it not? Let her die from your ecstasy." Another rung, and Jake was almost there. Two more—

Without warning Mustafa hoisted the scimitar over his head, its handle gripped in two hands, and charged for the ladder. Instinctively Jake lifted his left arm in useless defense against the descending sword. It caught him in the forearm, cutting through cloth and skin and laying the flesh open to the bone.

At the same time his right hand grappled for an instant in his boot. The long, pointed blade of his knife shone in the light for only an instant before plunging into Mustafa's heart.

The Imperial's grunt of death was no more noble than the death cry of his lowest subject, and he collapsed against Jake. The two men fell heavily onto the lower deck.

Spread-eagled against Jake's twisted body, Mustafa did not move, and with his blood pumping from an almost severed arm, Jake found himself too weak to lift him.

Unseen hands pulled the dead weight from him, and he opened his eyes to the tear-streaked face of Sarah, who knelt at his side and attempted to bind his wound with her petticoat.

"Jake," she sobbed.

"Hello, Sarah," he said weakly and awaited her kisses.

She brushed aside tear-dampened strands of hair with the back of her hand. "Jake, you fool," she said, concentrating on her task, her eyes avoiding his. "You could have been killed!"

Darling, unpredictable Sarah.

He managed a smile. "All in a day's work, Angel. All in a day's—"

Dizziness overcame him. He closed his eyes for a minute to regain his senses; but behind his closed lids a dark velvet void beckoned him, and he slipped into unconsciousness.

Chapter Thirty

Sarah paced outside the small tent that had served as Jake's hospital ever since they brought him ashore and found only vast stretches of deserted land and distant mountains awaiting them. A cool wind whispered across the Turkish plain which met the Black Sea, and dust whipped around her skirt.

"It's time he was awake, Bandit. He's been out for almost twenty-four hours."

"Miss Whitlock," said Bandit, standing in the late afternoon shadows and observing her ritual walk, "Bossman's body demands that he rest. The blood must replenish itself. Already his color grows better and the fever has gone."

Sarah knew he was right. She had given Jake the best care that she could—washing out the wound with a bottle of rum donated by one of the ship's crew, sewing the skin with her own hands as she ignored the tears which would not go away, bathing his body with the rain water that had been stored on the *Witch*'s deck.

Mostly, she had sat beside him through the night and held his hand, willing her strength to go into him. He would not die, but, oh, dreadful thought, what if he lost his arm? Jake was a sailor, meant for the sea. A one-armed man would have a hard time plying his trade when that trade called for skills he no longer possessed.

Around her on the vast stretch of open land, she could see a half dozen campfires where the crew, refusing to leave, had bedded down for the night. To a man, they had refused to depart until Jake was well enough to travel with them.

"We owe 'im a mite of thanks," said the sailor with the peg leg. "No tellin' what that Mustafa rascal would have tried to pull on us. Mr. Pettigrew always treated us fair enough. Wages not much, but he never held 'em back, even when the times got hard. Wouldn't want to do much dealin' with the murderin' son of a— Beg your pardon, ma'am."

"No pardon to beg," she had assured him. "You've got Mustafa described exactly right."

She had learned from the sailor that like Ralph, Mustafa had lost a ship at sea. As best she could gather, it was the pirate vessel that had attacked the *Leviathan*, and she took grim pleasure from the news.

It occurred to Sarah that as Ralph's heir—or so he had indicated with his last breath—she owned the *Sea Witch*; the crew worked for her. The possession meant little to her, and she decided that as long as the men did everything she wanted them to do in helping Jake, she would not bother telling them they had no choice. Not if they expected to receive their pay.

Jake had sacrificed the dhow in the rescue. She would give him the *Witch*. Surely he could not refuse. It seemed a fair trade. She wanted to give him the world. In one sense, by giving him a ship in which to sail away, she was giving him just that.

But, oh, her heart would break. She had said good-bye to him more than once already. How strong was a woman supposed to be?

"Why did he do it, Bandit?" she asked, her voice tremulous as she came to a halt and stared at the man she called friend. Her loose hair caught in the breeze and blew wild. "Why did he come after me and risk his life? Never in all my life will I forget that blade—" Her voice broke, and she could not go on.

"You will have to ask the Bossman why he does what he does."

"I almost caused Nadire to lose her life, too," she said, glancing toward the tent. Inside Nadire watched over the sleeping Jake while Sarah got a breath of the cool night air.

"Nadire has led a life of danger. Never do I think was she afraid, not for herself, only of my request that she be my wife. This has brought the worry to her eyes."

"She turned you down?"

Bandit's eyes twinkled and matched the early stars in the twilight sky. "At first when I made my demands. A wise uncle once told me a woman is a difficult creature to control with the whip or with commands, but with a gentle stroke she becomes docile. I think my uncle overstated the situation. Docile, no. But I stroked Nadire with kinder words, and she has agreed to be mine."

Sarah hugged Bandit. "I am happy for you both."

"And what of Miss Whitlock and the Bossman? Do you not think he will awaken with kind strokes of his own?"

"I have no idea. He fancies himself my protector, Bandit. In his weakened state he will remember the good times we have shared and perhaps—"

She swallowed the lump in her throat. "If he wants

me, I am his—for however long he says. If I have learned nothing else from my troubles, it is that pride can be a greatly overrated trait."

She turned to stare at the distant mountains. "But he told me once that I was more trouble than I am worth. He could very well remember those words. He would have every right."

"You are very hard on yourself, Miss Whitlock."

"Not nearly hard enough."

A rustle from the opening to the tent caught her attention, and Sarah turned to see Nadire beckoning her. "Aga Jake awakens, Missy Sarah."

"Oh," Sarah whispered, and hurried past her into the tent. A single lantern sat in the corner near the pile of blankets that served as Jake's bed.

She knelt beside him and stared down at his bristled face. Thick black hair lay limp across his forehead, and dark shadows formed circles under his eyes.

His lids lifted slowly, and he stared up at her.

"Guess I passed out," he said. His lips twisted into a smile, and Sarah's heart thrummed.

"Yes you did. I was worried."

I was out of my mind with fear, she could have said. She took his good hand in hers, and her eyes fell for a moment to the bandaged arm which lay across the covering blanket.

"You ought to know a mere scimitar can't bring me down," he said.

"I forgot that. Jake—" Her voice broke.

"Do me a favor."

"Anything."

"Kiss me."

He did not have to tell her twice. Bending her head, she brushed her lips against his, then reluctantly pulled away.

"Not like a sister. Like a woman who wants to be in my bed."

With her head close to his, her hair curtained out the light, and she was aware only of his warm breath against her cheek. "Is that what I am, Jake? A woman who wants in your bed?"

"Maybe not right now—"

She covered his lips with her finger. "Oh, yes I do, Jake Price. Right this very minute. If I didn't think I would have to sew in those awful stitches again, I'd have both of us stripped before you could say my name."

"Forget the stitches."

"You haven't gotten a look at them yet. They're beautiful, if I do say so myself."

"Did them yourself, you say?"

Sarah leaned close and kissed him again, this time with a whisper more of strength. "That I did."

His hand snaked free from hers and worked its way to the back of her neck. He held her close. "Again."

Sarah complied for a long, long time.

When he broke the kiss, he said, "Yes, you want in my bed, all right. Gives a man incentive for gaining his strength. There's only one thing worrying me— whether I can wait until after we're married to make love to you again. Somehow seems wrong—"

"Married!"

"Don't you want me as a husband, Sarah? I'm no bargain, that's for sure. It'll be a while before I can hold you with two good arms—"

Sarah broke in with a resounding "Yes!"

Jake grinned at her. "I like a woman who can make up her mind."

Flushed with joy, Sarah said, "I had to answer quickly before you changed yours."

Jake stroked her face, and his fingers brushed

against her lips.

Sarah kissed the tips, then grew solemn. "Maybe I answered too soon. You're a sailor," she said. "The sea has been both your mistress and your wife, and if you were healthy and clear-headed, you would realize it. It's an awesome responsibility to try to take her place."

"Running after you gave me a chance to do some thinking. Some men are content with the wind in the sails and an endless stretch of water in front of them. Not me. Not any longer. The sea is an adventure, Sarah, but it's a tame one beside you."

She stared at his wounded arm. "I'm more than an adventure. A catastrophe is closer to the truth."

"I was wrong, Sarah." The hardness in Jake's voice took her aback.

"What are you talking about?"

"When I said you're more trouble than you're worth. As a matter of fact, you're the only woman on the face of the earth who could make me see all that life has to offer. If that means an excess or two, I welcome them."

Sarah's face burned. "You heard me talking outside."

"Voices carry on the night air. I've been awake for a while, trying to remember what happened on the *Witch*. I knew you had an incredibly versatile body, Angel, but I didn't know about your bite."

"I really am a hellion, Jake."

"You're my hellion."

It wasn't exactly a declaration of love, but Sarah allowed her heart to soar.

Lifting her head, she stared down at his tired, lean, bristled, wonderful face. An overwhelming devotion washed over her, a need to be with him forever, to care for him, to share whatever life he chose. Most of all, she would have to protect him from herself.

"I could reform," she said in a rush. "Be a good, dutiful wife who would cause you no worry."

"Like hell you will."

Sarah did not know what to say.

"I love you just the way you are, Angel. Beautiful, brace, impetuous, passionate, kind, generous, smart—"

She laughed in delight. "You make me sound like a saint. Except for the passionate, of course."

"I refuse to leave that part out."

Sarah caressed his hand against her cheek. "I love you, Jake Price. I have no idea what the days and weeks and years ahead of us hold, but I cannot bear to think of living them without you."

"Good."

His pronouncement called for one more lingering kiss.

"Jake," she said, gathering her composure, "do you think you could swallow some broth and a cup of tea? You've got to build up your strength. I most certainly do want in that bed of yours, but such a kind, generous woman as I am—you did say kind, didn't you?—would not want to take advantage of a weakened man."

Epilogue

Sarah knocked at the door of her father's study and entered without waiting for him to respond.

"Our guests are here," she announced.

Sir Edward looked up from his desk and scowled. "Your guests, Sarah," he corrected. "I do hope they are all that you claim."

"They are much more," Sarah said blandly.

Her father's brusqueness did not bother her—not any more. When she had returned to London three days ago, she found that during their separation she had become toughened against his slights.

Which didn't mean she no longer cared for her father. If anything, she had a greater affection for him and, more important, a greater understanding than she had before Constantinople.

She stepped aside.

"Mr. Fevzi Gozaydin and his wife, the Princess Nadire," she said.

A turbaned man in a finely tailored swallow-tail coat and trousers strode into the room. On his arm was an olive-skinned beauty in a flowing gown of iridescent pink, a matching scarf draped over her head.

"Mr. Gozaydin," Sir Edward said, rising from his desk and coming around to shake the man's hand. "And Princess Nadire."

Sarah noted the admiration on her father's face as he addressed the former slave. She did indeed look regal.

Nadire had fought against the title, but Sarah had insisted. After all, she could not swear that royal blood did not flow in her veins. As an Eastern princess, she would find herself the darling of London, and she had been closely associated with an imperial palace for most of her life. Surely she had earned the right to stretch the truth.

"Princess," Sir Edward continued, "I believe you are Russian, is that not so?"

Nadire lowered her eyes. "Your daughter has been speaking of me."

What a charming picture she made. But then, so did her husband Bandit, who had at last admitted to his name. Persian he was, or at least on his mother's side. On his father's, he was not quite sure. He knew little except that his mother claimed the man had been of a wealthy class and had been fascinated with beautiful things.

Bandit's sharp eyes took in the details of the room, and he settled on a Venetian vase resting on a pedestal where it could catch the morning light. "You are a connoisseur of fine porcelains, Sir Edward."

The Englishman smiled. "My daughter tells me you share my interest."

"Did she also tell you I wish to expand my trade in the art works of the Orient?"

"She said something to that effect."

Nadire looked at Sarah with twinkling eyes. Sarah winked in return. She could tell by the alertness in her father's eyes that he was impressed.

444

Who had he expected her to escort into his study, a sharp-eyed thief and an odalisque?

Bandit and Sir Edward fell to talking particulars concerning the field that interested them both. Sarah listened for a moment, then said, "I will leave you two. Princess, would you care to join me with my fiancé?"

Nadire nudged her toward the door. "I will remain with Fevzi. Since we have married, I feel responsible for him. Your father may need some protection if the two enter into a business arrangement."

Sarah glanced at the rapidly talking Bandit—she would always think of him by that name no matter how respectable he became—and agreed, although she rather thought her father could hold his own.

With a promise that she would soon return, she hurried from the room. How wonderful it was to be in her father's house and feel no resentments or hurt or, best of all, the need to defend herself.

Some day, when time had distanced her from the sad memories of Turkey, she would tell more than the barest details about what had occurred—of Harun and the Grand Seraglio; of her visits to the Grand Bazaar—but no matter how long she waited, she knew he would call her the hellion of Constantinople.

Papa would never change. He had loved one woman in his life, and that woman had died. His was an affection that could not be transferred, especially not to anything so fragile as another human being who might also go away. He had sought comfort among those objects that would endure.

Even though she was not increasing, Sarah knew she would love the children she and Jake some day brought into the world. With a lightness of step, she went to where he awaited, in the rose garden behind

445

the town house. She found him pacing on one of the back paths. Dark-suited, his black hair uncharacter- istically in place, he looked decidedly respectable.

He caught sight of her, and a welcoming gleam lightened his eyes. "About time you got here," he said.

Sarah's heart skipped a beat. "You should have come in with Bandit and Nadire."

"A little of your father goes a long way, Sarah. We're friends now. Especially since he agreed to our marriage. The best way to keep things peaceful is to maintain our distance."

Sarah stepped close. "I agree. He keeps giving you terrible advice."

"Like using a firm hand with you?"

She shrugged. "He did say that once or twice."

He pulled her into his arms.

"Is this your idea of doing what he says?" she asked.

"I'm only trying to keep the peace with him, remember."

"And what about with me?"

Jake kissed her.

"That's not an answer."

He kissed her again.

This time she kissed him back. "I suppose in a way it is." Her hands played at the lapels of his coat. "I'm wondering if perhaps you haven't decided I was right about settling down to being a dutiful wife. Since you've agreed to take the ships—"

"One ship, Sarah."

"I've only got two. After Ralph's debts were paid and the men were paid their wages, the *Witch* and a small frigate were all that I had left. I still can't see why you don't take them both."

"One's all I need. Whatever profits are made from

the second, we will designate as the property of our children."

She and Jake thought alike often, but there was one thing they had not adequately discussed.

"What do you plan to do with the ship?"

"As a matter of fact, I have an idea. Something that will get me out of coats and ties and the two of us away from respectability."

Intrigued, Sarah smiled up at him. "Tell me more."

"First of all, comes the wedding. Keep it simple, won't you?"

"Oh, I promise you that."

"And speaking of simple, I have something I want you to wear on our wedding night."

Sarah tingled at the words.

Jake reached into his pocket and pulled out a shiny, jangling object and placed it in her hand. Sarah looked down at the ankle bracelet he had taken from her the night she danced for him in the Turkish coffee house.

"You kept it," she whispered. "And you want me to wear it on our wedding night?"

"What I meant to say was, I don't expect you to wear anything else."

"Oh," Sarah managed. She and Jake had not made love since leaving Turkey a month ago, their chaste behavior being his idea, and she assured him with a few additional kisses that she would be able to comply with his request. Would he, perhaps, like a demonstration tonight?

"Soon, Sarah, soon. Now to the major part of my plan. I've got a ship and most of the gold from Harun, and you've got the expertise to stock it with valuable objects of beauty. There's a place I know where money is flowing like the ocean in a storm.

447

Endless supplies of it in the hands of big spenders who need someone to give them a little taste. A touch of English class."

"Where on earth is this?"

"You once thought about going to America. So have I. California. Gold was discovered there a couple of years ago. They're paving the streets of San Francisco with it. Don't see why we shouldn't export a few foodstuffs and supplies and perhaps a vase or two. Should turn a tidy profit."

His lips twisted into a grin. "It could provide one last escapade before we settle down."

"California." Sarah matched his smile. "Darling, it sounds wonderful. I could keep the books and help with the buying, and I promise, oh, I promise, to be very, very good."

"The books and the buying, I'll go along with," he said, tightening his embrace. "As for the good, Angel, we'll have to see."